ADVANCE PRAISE FOR *CAZZAROLA!*

"In Romani culture, when enjoying music we don't say, 'Did you hear that?' We say, 'Did you feel that?' I didn't just read *Cazzarola!*, I felt it. As a Romani woman who has lived in Italy, this very relatable novel often echoed the pages of my own life. Bravo, *Ta Aves Baxtalo!*"
—Julia Lovell, Romani activist and filmmaker

"*Cazzarola!* is a powerful, blunt, epic scream against social injustice."
—David Lester, author of *The Listener* and guitarist of Mecca Normal

"A brilliant title for a brilliant story of love and rage, which the author shares with his characters in every page. *Cazzarola!* reads like a film, a sort of Bertolucci's *Novecento* recast in contemporary Italy. Nawrocki skillfully manages to interweave scenes of everyday Italian life and fine psychological analysis in a grandiose historical fresco."
—Davide Turcato, historian of Italian anarchism and editor of *The Complete Works of Errico Malatesta*

"A stunning achievement! I am usually leery of politically engaged novels that attempt to conveniently intertwine radical history with the 'ins and outs' of a tempestuous love affair, because history usually ends up as a mere backdrop to the lovers or else the lovers are used as cardboard cutouts to illustrate a political point. Yet, as *Cazzarola!* clearly demonstrates, history has a romance of its own and can be more than mere exotic context for character development or fodder for heavy-handed agit-prop in search of an engaging protagonist. Antonio and Cinka are not simply better understandable as characters because of this context, they are unimaginable without it."
—Ron Sakolsky, author of *Swift Winds*

CAZZAROLA!
Anarchy, Romani, Love, Italy

a novel
by Norman Nawrocki

CAZZAROLA! Anarchy, Romani, Love, Italy
© 2013 Norman Nawrocki
This edition © 2013 PM Press

ISBN: 978-1-60486-315-4
Library of Congress Control Number: 2013911519

Cover: John Yates / www.stealworks.com
Interior design by briandesign

10 9 8 7 6 5 4 3 2 1

PM Press
PO Box 23912
Oakland, CA 94623
www.pmpress.org

Printed in the USA, by the Employee Owners of Thomson-Shore in Dexter, Michigan.
www.thomsonshore.com

CONTENTS

CAZZAROLA! FAMILY TREE

The Discordia Family:
— Great-grandfather Discordia (1880-1980 . . . but his spirit lives on)

Great-uncles, the triplets:
— Ricardo Discordia (1900-2000) Antonio's grandfather
— Rafaele Discordia (1900-1990)
— Massimo Discordia (1900-1946)

— Alphonso Discordia, triplets' cousin, Livorno (1901-1922) AdP & Partisan
— Antoniolo Discordia, triplets' half-brother (1916-1994) AdP & Partisan
— Enrico Discordia, triplets' cousin (1910-1988) a Partisan
— Elisabetta "Rose Bud" Discordia (1924-1946) married Enrico, a *stafetta* Partisan

— Grandmother Discordia, Gracia (1915-2012) married Ricardo
— Grandfather Discordia, Ricardo (1900-2000) an anarchist
— Grandmother Apaluto, Consuessa (1907-1995) descended from Great-grandfather Discordia's second marriage, sister to Antoniolo, mother of Isabella
— Grandfather Apaluto, Fabio (1914-1996) a monarchist, married Consuessa

— Loretta Discordia (b.1944), daughter of Enrico, married Augusto Apaluto
— Isabella Discordia (b.1947) Rafaele's aunt, sister of Augusto, married a Discordia (unknown)
— Augusto Apaluto (b.1945) Rafaele's father
— Gino Lucetti, very, very distant Discordia (1900–1943)

— Antonio Discordia (b.1979)
— Rafaele Apaluto (b.1977) cousin to Antonio
— Simona Apaluto (b.1985) sister to Rafaele
— Massimaxo Matcha (b.1978) best friend of Antonio & Rafaele

The Dinicu Family:
— Cinka Dinicu (b.1986) twenty-two years old
— Luminitsa Dinicu (b.1963) mother, forty-five years old
— Corvu Dinicu (b.1996) brother, twelve years old
— Celina Dinicu (b.1998) sister, eleven years old

PRELUDE

GREAT-GRANDFATHER: THE NIGHT OF THE GREAT ROCKSLIDE, 1880

I was born the night of the great rockslide. There was a deafening roar that echoed across the valley and not a moment's notice when part of the mountain slid into a ravine carrying with it several houses. Then the earthquake struck.

Everyone in our village ran outside with lighted candles and crossed themselves, falling to their knees praying it was not the end of the world. Dogs howled. Goats and sheep brayed. Terrified children and parents screeched and looked to the starlit sky for answers. My father, a poor sheepherder, grabbed a pitchfork and was prepared to engage whatever monster appeared demanding flesh and blood. My mother couldn't leave the bed since she was in the middle of childbirth, screaming like a demon.

But I didn't cry when I arrived. Or so my mother said. The midwife said it was a mixed omen. A sign from above.

"He will be a contented baby and grow into a man who never complains."

She was wrong.

Generations later, over many bottles of wine at the dinner table, my entire family—the Discordias—still debate the midwife's controversial prediction. It disappoints me that they find nothing better to talk about.

But without the wrinkled old women to tell their tales,

who will pass along the peasant wisdoms we love to repeat? Wrinkled old men who own newspapers and TV stations and cavort with nubile teenage girls? Unlikely.

Our ancestral house in Abruzzo, like the twenty others in our village, was built into the side of a mountain. It was cold in the winter, cool in the summer, and always dark. My bed was carved out of the back rock wall. There was one door and a tiny window. When we were very young and times were good, we ate bread seasoned with salt, olive oil, marjoram, and cheese. When times were not good, we went to bed with growling stomachs after only a bowl of thin onion soup. As a child I learned with my brothers and sisters never to complain. I heard my father grumble to my mother about the landowners who lived in the next village, who could feed their families meat.

"Their children grow plump and strong. Ours grow lean. Off with their heads!"

My mother would nod silently as she mended our clothes or swept out the house. We said nothing, biting our tongues, crossing and uncrossing our bare feet on the dirt floor as we sat on a bench hoping for the day more food would magically appear on the table. Later, our grandfather taught us how to trap birds, small rodents, and hares so that we could help feed our parents and ourselves. These times were better.

When we were old enough, our mother sent us up and down the slopes in search of wild mushrooms and berries. Like the boars, we roamed widely through the beech forests. It was not easy. Too often we were tempted to steal a chicken, eggs, or fruit from the landowner's magnificent, lush, terraced garden, but we held back knowing "another day will come," as our father said, that distant look in his eye.

At fifteen, while I was tending the landlord's sheep in an alpine meadow, I met my wife-to-be. I was sitting on a rock playing my wooden flute, watching white clouds race one another across distant mountaintops. Then I heard a sweet unexpected female voice echo the melody I was playing. I looked around, saw no one, and assumed it was just the wind. I kept playing, and again the voice echoed it note for note. I yelled out, "Who are you?"

No one replied. I played and again the voice followed. Then the most beautiful girl I had ever seen stepped out of the forest, laughing. Her brown bare legs showed under a red skirt. She wore a kerchief and carried a basket overflowing with flowers and wild herbs. I was smitten. Two years later we married.

Of our ten children—and my six others with my second wife—I had the highest hopes for the triplets: Rafaele, Massimo, and Ricardo. They were the brightest (at least two out of the three) and seemed destined to leave our village and make their mark on the world.

I, who had never travelled further than two villages beyond ours, never dreamed that these boys would accomplish what others only spoke about. But for the sake of our family, our village, and our ancestors—poor sheepherders all—I am proud of them. From rock and hunger, blood and sorrow, my triplets gave the world their precious lives. They lived their dreams so that others could dream, too.

And me? I am still a great-grandfather. Soon, I shall become a great-great-grandfather. But will anyone remember me? Unlikely. Like all mortals, I died. But unlike most of them (don't ask me how this happened!) I now inhabit the spirit world of the old, the very old, and the older-than-that-by-countless-generations.

A thin puff of smoke? That's me. The ticking of a clock? Could be me, too. The floating bubble from dish soap? The raindrops that hit you? A cherry blossom borne by the wind, or even an annoying fruit fly? Guess who! I am, for reasons unknown, ever-present. Perhaps to tell stories like this one . . .

THE TRIPLETS, 1900

The three boys were tall and strong and hard to tell apart. Except for their hair. Rafaele combed his straight back and treated it with olive oil. Massimo kept his short. Ricardo let his choose its own wild fate. Too poor to attend school, they worked in the landowner's garden from the age of five, tilling and watering the soil, trimming the vines, pulling weeds on their hands and knees. With the assistance of a local priest, they taught themselves to read.

Growing up, they became inseparable. They would egg one another on with riddles and conjectures about nature, astronomy, and the world at their feet. One night, lying on their backs on the rocks outside their house, they debated the lives of the stars above.

Rafaele: "By day, the stars must travel inside the fastest clouds to move quickly from one side of the sky to the other."

Massimo: "This is why the clouds are whiter than the blue sky—all the stars illuminate them."

Ricardo: "But if the clouds hide the stars by day and the mountains hide the sun at night, what hides the moon?"

"That's easy. The moon rides on the back of a large owl who hides it by day in the tallest tree deep in the forest."

"This is why we hear the owl hooting at night. It reminds the moon when it is time to shine."

"Therefore, the owl is the smartest bird of all. It knows where to return the moon each night to its proper place in the heavens."

"Exactly!"

PART I

SHE'S NOT THERE

SAN LORENZO, ROME, ANTONIO'S STORY

As the warm night wind blows through the open window I can still smell the scent of her hair and the scent of her body. I feel her breath all around me and hear her laughter. I think that any minute she'll call me for tea. So I turn around, see the curtains ruffling in the wind, and feel her breath on my face.

Sitting here at my desk, sipping my beer in the glow of my lamp, I remember her relaxing over there in that wicker chair, a smile on her face, a book in her hands. So much I took for granted!

She was right here with me. I could see her, walk over and caress her, kiss her on the cheek, taste her lips, feel her warmth and the curve of her breasts under her blouse.

I see her eating an apple. I watch her smiling at me as I smile at her, loving the moment. I want her to come and stand beside me so that I can wrap my arm around her waist and pull her closer and tell her how much she means to me, how much I love her. I want to kiss her. But I can't.

She's not here. She's disappeared. I don't know where. Not a word, not a note, no phone call, no message. Nothing. And I don't know how to find her.

I choke on the tears. I want to cry. I don't want to cry. I want to call out her name. But I can't. I'm afraid of the silence I know will follow.

I try to stay sane, calm, and rational. She's just off somewhere. She'll return soon. She forgot to call me, to tell me where she is. She'll be back. But it's been two weeks. She's carrying our baby. The wind has stopped blowing.

GREAT-GRANDFATHER: MY FAMILY

Like most families, ours forgets. Almost everything. Will they remember me generations from now? Of course not. Do they have any idea of the pain in our backs from working the fields? From carrying rocks? From hauling firewood? The hunger in our bellies? The babies crying? The sleepless nights of worrying how to keep our families fed? No. But this is normal. Time erases memories of hardship.

And who, then, had the luxury of paper, pencils, typewriters, or even the time to write books? Not I, certainly. I can tell a few entertaining family legends. Mostly scandals. And someone out there still treasures a few family photos. Later, they had home movies, but so what? All gone. Forgotten.

Ah, but these modern times, you say, all these wondrous inventions! Now the young have millions of photographic images—talking ones, too—but good for what? "Look! Look at me!" No one can tell the old stories the young will never know. Of course, there are a few good new ones.

"SHE'S A GYPSY?"

A sliver of a limoncello moon hangs low above Rome's rooftops. Sewer rats tear the shadows of the night. Most of the city sleeps. Not Antonio Discordia.

He paces the room, alternately staring out the open window at the charcoal sky, and at a photo of his girlfriend on his desk. He fights back the growing lump in his throat. Holds a shirt close to his cheek, the one that she left at his apartment. He asks the same questions over and over:

Where could she be? This isn't like her. Something's wrong. Something has happened. I know it. I've looked everywhere and she's nowhere. What can I do? I can't report her missing. What will the police say:

"She's a Gypsy? Good riddance!" Cazzo!

He studies the framed photo beside his computer and remembers:

When I first saw her playing violin, five months ago in the *Piazza Navona*, I swear I thought she was a dark-haired angel.

Her smile, her eyes, were so full of life. She was beautiful. A woman like this you don't meet every day. I fell for her hard and kept coming back. I'd bring friends to see her play.

"You've got to hear her. She's incredible. No one in Rome plays like this . . ."

She was shy. I was patient. I bought her coffee and sandwiches and hung around. We talked music, philosophy, history. She's smart, a real thinker with opinions about everything.

"You also play jazz and Frank Zappa? And your own compositions?"

She told me she loved to read and study history—when she could find books. We got along effortlessly. And talented? Man, she makes her violin sob, laugh, and sing. She's a virtuoso.

Cinka is a Gypsy and proud of it. Not your stereotypical fortune-telling Gypsy. Not at all. She's a "Romni"—the correct term for her and her people.

She comes from Bucovina in northern Romania. Her dad was the village violinist. After he died, Cinka came to Rome with her family hoping to make a living. But it's not easy for Roma people, especially today. And now she's gone? Her mother, brother, and sister too? Just like that?

He slumps into a chair. As the tears stop falling, he nods off to sleep. A pale finger of moonlight caresses his cheek and runs through his hair. He dreams of Cinka flying above the rooftops of the city. He calls out to her. She turns to look down at him.

WHO ARE YOU, ANTONIO?

My name is Discordia, Antonio Discordia. I have red hair and blue eyes. I am finishing my degree in philosophy and I play the guitar. I live with three roommates on Via dei Reti in the

San Lorenzo district of Rome. I have no criminal record. No STIs. No neurotic tendencies, at least none that I am aware of.

I love red wine, beer, and gelato. I'm always online. I designed a web site for my noise band. Every day I upload our songs and videos, like *"Campana suona per la prima volta,"* our newest. I surf the net daily for new music. Call me a net addict. I call it research.

I love to travel and dream of visiting North America. For now, I have a boring job in a call centre. It pays the bills. If my father could handle his crappy job in a supermarket, and my grandfather his shit job in a factory, and my great-grandfather who, they say, was a poor mountain shepherd . . . what can I complain about? The price of guitar strings?

This is why I study philosophy. To perfect the under-standing and the art of living. And to read the books that keep me awake at night. An indulgence my great-grandfather couldn't afford.

He had no schooling, couldn't read or write, but he raised a dozen kids—with my great-grandmother of course. He also took on the village idiots, the self-important ones who bossed everyone else and, according to him, ran the village like they owned it. He would take me out for a gelato and tell me stories I still remember to this day. I could listen to him for hours. He lived to be one hundred.

Great-grandfather was ingenious. He didn't want to pay the village tax that always ended up in some guy's pocket, he said, so he hid money in his garden. He also scoffed at the priests and their lies. Great-grandmother attended church, but he didn't. My great-uncles followed in his footsteps.

"They were original thinkers," Grandfather used to say with pride. "Educated themselves, read a lot, and were the first to leave the village and explore the world."

I, too, am proud of them. One day maybe they will be proud of me. As long as I don't fuck up.

This is another reason I study philosophy. To avoid turning into someone who didn't take the time to try to under-stand the things that really matter. I think I'm slowly getting it.

THE DIVISIONISTS, 1890

Two young Italian painters sit in a café drinking wine and talking shop. The curly-haired redhead smokes a pipe. The other has a full beard and wears a black smock.

"So this Frenchman, Seurat, uses little dots of colour on his white surfaces, like this."

Jab jab jab, finger onto tabletop.

"Red and yellow dots, they come together here, and now it's orange. See? Brilliant, yes? Everybody's talking about it now. But I'd rather use threads of colour, you know, little dashes, divide it up like this. Similar but different. We are Italians. We have our own way."

"Hmm . . . intriguing. I'll give it a try, too."

"But no pretty landscapes for me. I want to paint the new Italy, all the tension. I am not mistaken, am I?"

"No. The poor are learning to read, forming trade unions, demanding land redistribution in the countryside."

"Better wages for peasants and workers."

"I feel for them. Those poor peasants come all the way to Milan looking for work. They want construction jobs, to be maids for the rich, and what do they find? Bad housing, underpaid work. They demonstrate, go on strike, and the cops and the army smash their skulls. This is the Italy I want to paint. And I'll use that new technique."

"New form, new content! I love it! Maybe we'll start a movement!"

"Yesterday from my window, I saw this guy. He must have been a mason. He was hanging off scaffolding with one arm. He was urging the other guys below, 'Keep striking! Keep fighting for better wages!' And behind the huge crowd, I could see the cops and the army coming, their bayonets fixed, ready to charge."

"The king and the government outlaw these protests and strikes. What do they expect?"

"So we paint this Italy. Agreed?"

"While we can. Before the police start coming for us artists as well."

GREAT-GRANDFATHER: MY UNCLE

One of my uncles lived alone in a dark one-room stone house nestled in the mountainside. Inside a small, blackened fireplace was one iron pot. In it he boiled everything he ate: eggs, mushrooms, pasta. He had one table, one chair, one spoon, one sagging narrow bed. A few worn clothes were folded on a shelf. One extraordinary painting hung on the wall above my uncle's bed. He was so proud of that painting that his younger brother gave to him.

"He is a great artist," my uncle would say, "the greatest artist in all of Italy." And so he was.

THE LIVING TORRENT, 1895

This heavily bearded, short, stocky man, my uncle, on strike with his thousands of workmates, didn't expect to see his wife and newborn baby here. She walks beside him at the head of a march. Tears streaming down both cheeks, baby in one arm wrapped in a shawl, she pleads with him:

"The cupboard is empty. We have no more food. How will we feed our children? I need food to make milk to feed her."

"Now is not the time to talk. Get out of here. Go home."

Her husband stares straight ahead, watching the police and army form a solid black line ahead of the demonstration to block their path. She tugs on his sleeve, pleading.

"I said go home. Now! Do you hear me? This is no place for a woman and a baby."

He shakes his arm away, tearing his shirt.

"This *is* our place!" she cries.

This heavily bearded man on strike for several weeks, penniless, his eyes hollow, burning with rage at the landowners, and now at his fellow countrymen in uniform preparing to shoot him and his fellow strikers down in cold blood like a pack of wild dogs to be destroyed.

This nuisance of a strike that the bosses cannot tolerate.

"Crush it now, damn it!"

This defiance of authority. This affront to private property and the prerogatives of the elite.

"How dare they!"

As the march approaches the line of cops bristling with rifles, this woman with her broken shoes, her sagging, empty breasts almost exposed through her thin clothes, their newborn baby squealing in her arms, hungry, walks beside her husband begging him to do something to keep their baby alive.

This man on strike, carrying his jacket slung over one shoulder, staring straight ahead, doesn't know how to answer her—other than to keep walking into the sights of the soldiers and police, their guns trained on him, his workmates, his wife and baby.

NAPOLI: TWO GIRLS

It's a gorgeous hot sunny Napoli afternoon at the beach. Kids frolic in the water. Bodybuilders strut their stuff in front of giggling young women. Sunbathers sizzle and bake. Unperturbed, they stretch out on the sand near the corpses of two Romani girls. The girls drowned a few feet offshore. Their rescued bodies lie motionless under towels, ignored by hundreds of sun-worshippers. They could be two rocks, or two small boats. But they are two dead young Roma, not worthy of anyone's attention.

"They're not Italian, are they?"

"No, they're Gypsies. Pass me the sunscreen."

FROM BUCHAREST WITH FEAR

"Don't tell anyone you are Romanian. They will kill you."

The kids look wide-eyed, and the mother regrets her choice of words.

Tall and thin, with her blond hair in a ponytail, the young mother adjusts a cap, a scarf and a knapsack as she warns her three children before they leave for school:

"I don't want to scare you, but things are different now. Italy has changed. It is dangerous for people like us. Once they welcomed us, but no more. They blame us for all their problems."

"But why, Mama?" asks the eldest. "We didn't do anything wrong! Did we?"

"No, we didn't. But it doesn't matter. Italians are upset and angry. We must be careful. Keep to yourselves and watch out for the little ones. If anyone talks to you, don't answer. You hear me? Walk away. And come home immediately. Don't stop to play with anyone in the park. Understand?"

"Yes, Mama."

She kisses each child and watches them leave the apartment. Then she sits with her coffee and scans the newspaper headlines on the kitchen table:

> Prime Minister acts to expel foreign nationals if deemed a threat to public health or security . . . 50 Romanians deported. Opposition demands 20,000 expulsions . . .
>
> Human Rights groups condemn emergency decree . . . European Union officials decry witch hunt of Romanians . . . Romanians, especially Gypsies, head for the border as Italy gets tough on immigration . . .

What happened? How? Only a month ago she and her husband welcomed the arrival of her sister's family here in Monterotondo. She and her sister had degrees from the university in Bucharest, each looking for work. Their apartment is crowded, ten people living in two rooms, but at least they are together, safe and happy.

Then the terrifying news. An Italian woman—a naval commander's wife—raped and beaten outside a train station and left to die. The police arrest and charge a Romani man with the murder. The backlash is immediate. The government acts swiftly, approving an emergency law. They send police and bulldozers into refugee camps where Roma and some Romanians live, and raze them to the ground.

Italian vigilantes wearing masks and carrying clubs and knives attack and beat Romanians in the street. A local grocery store is firebombed. Now all Romanians, all Roma, live in fear.

She looks at the cracks in the walls, the leaking pipe above the sink, the hole in the window—everything the landlord should fix but won't.

My husband fights to get a decent wage, she thinks. They

pay him less than the Italians for similar work. We take the dangerous jobs no one else wants. We can't afford a better apartment. No one wants to rent to us. I hear the Italian neighbours talking behind our backs. They blame us for every crime. And now this! Is it time to go?

WE DON'T SERVE GYPSIES

Antonio has just put up posters looking for Cinka at a Romani refugee camp north of *Tor di Quinto*. He is walking past a hole-in-the-wall café on a busy street—a typical Rome coffee joint—when he notices the large sign in the window: *We don't serve Gypsies.*

Fuck them, he thinks, and walks in. Standing with his arms on the counter, he orders an espresso. The young barman serves it. Antonio points to the window.

"Your sign says you don't serve Gypsies."

The barman, puzzled, sneers.

"No, we don't. So what?"

"I'm a Gypsy," Antonio says.

"Oh, yeah?"

"Can't you tell?"

"Not really."

"So how do you know when you're serving Gypsies?"

WHEN ANTONIO FIRST MET CINKA

It was a summer-perfect, sun-steeped afternoon when Antonio first met Cinka.

Rome's *Piazza Navona* was abuzz with hordes of tourists and tour groups wearing their uniform shorts, fanny packs, and safari hats. He heard the music! Amazing music, he thought. Nobody plays like that around here.

Antonio wanted to see the talent, but a huge circle had formed around the lone violinist, blocking his view. He edged his way to the front. Then stood slack-jawed.

Cinka wore a white cotton blouse and a long multihued skirt. She was petite and moved like a dancer, lightly, around the circle, brown eyes flashing, long jet-black hair framing her olive-skinned face and pearly white smile. She looked into everyone's face, including his.

Fucking hell! She's incredible, he thought. *Where did she come from? My God. She plays so passionately. She dances like a gazelle. She doesn't miss a note. The woman I've been looking for all my life. And she's in front of me, right here . . .*

He waited until the last tourist shook her hand before making his move. He flashed what he hoped was an irresistibly charming smile as he approached.

"You're awesome!"

The young Romni smiled back, then lowered her eyes.

He extended his hand. "I'm Antonio. And you're . . . ?"

She crossed one foot behind the other and bit her lower lip. She wasn't used to Italian boys coming on to her like this. Who was this skinny guy with a guitar case slung over his shoulder, in his tight T-shirt, torn jeans, red sneakers, and sunglasses sitting high on top of his carrot-top head?

"My name is Cinka." She shook his hand.

"It's beautiful. Does it mean anything in your language?"

"My father named me after a famous woman violinist. A Romni. She lived in the eighteenth century. They called her the *Gypsy Sappho*."

"So, uh, are you like Gypsy or Roma? What's the difference?"

Cinka smiled again at the already-smitten Italian.

"My people are Roma. We don't use the word *Gypsy* anymore. And the correct term for me, a woman, is Romni."

"Amazing! You're the first Roma—I mean Romni—woman violinist I've ever met. Are there others?"

She laughed, thinking, who is this funny boy?

"Not so many. In our culture, women aren't supposed to play an instrument, only to sing and dance. But when I was a child, I picked up my father's violin and tried to play it. He made me a tiny violin from an old cigar box."

"Get out! You serious?"

"That's how I started. No one said anything because it was my father's decision. He wanted me to play. I haven't met any other Romni violinists either."

"But you're brilliant! Did your dad teach you?"

Cinka was amused. This inquisitive, cute guy with the warm smile seemed genuinely interested in her, but she had to wonder why. She pulled her hair back into a ponytail as she packed her violin.

"Of course. He taught violin and had a band. They were very popular. Played weddings, parties, baptisms, banquets, and funerals. The band broke up when he died."

Antonio noticed a wistful look in her eye.

"Before he died he gave me his violin—this violin—saying, 'Don't ever stop. Make sure your children—boys or girls—continue playing too.'"

Her violin was intricately decorated around the edges with pieces of abalone shell.

"And you?" She nodded toward Antonio's guitar case. "You've played guitar for a long time?"

"Since I was a teenager. I fell in love with punk music. You know, that whole sex, drugs, rock and roll thing."

The moment she frowned, he realized too late—*Idiot! Faux pas!*

"But, uh, punked up, I mean." He reached out to touch her arm. "You know. I don't do drugs. No, never. Who needs it with punk music, right?"

Her frown faded. "Hmm, I like punk music, too."

She growled out an imitation of a standard punk riff and they both laughed.

"But not all of it. In Romania, I heard punk bands playing in the local cultural centre. My girlfriends and I would sit on the stairs outside to listen. We were never allowed in."

"Why not?"

"Because most Romanians, like most Italians, don't like to see my people in the same room as themselves. They prefer to keep us at a distance."

"How could anyone say that about a girl as beautiful as you?"

Cinka blushed and turned away. Such compliments from a *gadjo*, a white boy from outside Romani culture, were unexpected. And mostly unwelcome. But not entirely . . .

And he *was* kind of cute. As he politely changed the subject—

"So in your culture, like, is it rare for women to have a musical career?"

"Oh, yes. By now, at my age, I'm supposed to be a mother and a wife, not a professional violinist. But I'm too busy making music to do anything else. I have my husband and my family right here." She lifted her violin case and patted it.

"I know the feeling! I work a day job to pay for my music. One day I hope to survive full-time with just my guitar." Antonio patted his guitar case.

"You will, I'm sure," she smiled.

He blushed. She's so gorgeous, her eyes, her smile, her laugh. She makes me nervous. What the fuck? Gotta keep her talking!

"I know so little about your music, only what I hear in the street. Do Gypsies—I mean Roma—play the same music all the time? For yourselves, too? Or is it different for Roma and non-Romas? You know, like the street music?"

Cinka was beginning to like this kind of shy, but not so shy, curious redheaded boy.

"We have an old proverb: 'For the non-Roma, play for the ear. For us, play for the heart.' I could tell you more, but now I must go. See you another time! *Ciao!*"

He watched her run off, violin case in hand, her long skirt and hair trailing behind.

KITCHEN TALK ONE

Rafaele Apaluto. A skinny, tall Roman with broad shoulders, blue eyes, long straight blond hair, ever-present blue jeans, and a rebellious beard. Clear thinking, usually focused, and always with a big smile regardless of how desperate the moment. Loves reggae. Makes good tomato sauce. Lives in his great-uncle's grapefruit-yellow Monterotondo two-story house surrounded by a flourishing vegetable and fruit tree garden.

Always cool, even through the crisis at work yesterday; the car accident that involved his good friend last week; the painful appendicitis operation his brother went through today, or his sister's newest tattoo drama. Breathe deeply, slowly.

"Focus, *ragazzo*, focus." Tag him chill-meister.

Massimaxo Matcha. Slight build. A shaved head, red horn-rim glasses, and always a red shirt and red sneakers with his jeans. Engineer by profession, musician at heart, fingers full of talent, alt-journalist in his spare time.

His noise band with Antonio described as the twenty-first-century offshoot of Einstürzende, The Boredoms, and the most obscure but renowned of Norwegian hardcore bands—but even more brilliant, post-punk, post-rock, 100 percent Ital-Ital-Italian with a huge following. Massimaxo is an atypical rock star, passionate about politics and chocolate. Tag him incorrigible dreamer, incessant blogger.

Antonio Discordia. About the same build as Massimaxo. Red curly hair, freckles and an always-trimmed red beard. A philosophy student, sometime teacher of English, dedicated musician, and hopeless romantic with a soft spot for everyone. Women, complete strangers, profess their love to him regularly. Whatever he has, women want it. Other guys can only guess. Tag him babe-magnet.

That night, Rafaele was tending the whitewashed fireplace in his bright blue kitchen, crouched in front of it. Massimaxo, his best friend, and Antonio, his cousin, had spent the afternoon at another anti-Fascist rally in Rome, the second in two weeks. The city was stirring. The boys, as always, stirred with it.

Rafael blew through a long thin iron pipe to feed the flames. The other two smoked at the table, exchanging now-obvious truths, nodding back and forth, finishing each other's thoughts. It was post-dinner and a few burps, the wine all gone, but the fridge still held nine cans of beer.

"We know now for a fact what people could only suspect back in 1969. This 'Strategy of Tension' was deliberately planned by the State." Antonio quotation-marked with his fingers in the air.

"In collusion with paramilitary right-wing groups and neo-Fascists." Massimaxo pointed his finger at unseen adversaries.

"Bomb and kill innocent people. Blame the Left—specifically the anarchists—because unlike the Communist Party, they have no resources to defend themselves."

"And thereby create a climate of fear and distrust. Turn people against the Left, against anyone promoting radical social change."

"Against the students and the workers' movements. Frame the anarchists."

"Use them to cover up the actions of their own state-sponsored murderers—the guys who bombed the Milano bank."

Rafaele spoke between long breaths into the pipe.

"Then allow the Right to step in, restore Law and Order, and return to the good old days of Fascism."

"I hate those fuckers."

GREAT-GRANDFATHER: OUR KING, 1878

Love our king? Are you kidding? The King of Italy, Umberto I, could never claim to be loved by most Italians. What did he ever do for us? Show contempt? Flaunt his wealth? Hold lavish parties while we starved? He had fans among the wealthy, but none elsewhere.

It came as no surprise in 1878, my father told me, when Giovanni Passanante, a poor cook, tried to assassinate Umberto during a parade in Naples. Passanante failed. He was buried alive, poor soul, imprisoned in a cell 1.4 metres high, wrapped in 18 kilograms of chains, in isolation, never allowed to speak to anyone, living in his own excrement and tortured until he went insane.

My father also told me that in 1897, Pietro Umberto Acciarito, an ironsmith living near Rome, tried to stab Umberto I on his way to the racetrack. When asked why, Pietro answered, "The king has money to spend on the horses but none for the poor."

While Italy's elite entertained their colonial dreams of conquest in Africa, the economic situation in Italy worsened. The price of bread rose, so people demonstrated. What would you expect?

On May 7, 1898, in Milan, an Italian general, Fiorenzo Bava-Beccaris, gave the order to his soldiers to fire cannons on the demonstrators. Hundreds were killed, a thousand more wounded. For what? For trying to feed their families? King Umberto was pleased, a happy man was he. He congratulated the general on restoring order to Milan and decorated him with a medal.

It came as no surprise in 1900, when the newspaper headlines shrieked:

UMBERTO I ASSASSINATED IN MONZA! FOUR REVOLVER SHOTS! ITALIAN FROM PATERSON, USA, GAETANO BRESCI, ARRESTED.

The Italian-American anarchist said he came to Italy to avenge those massacred by Bava-Beccaris. Such is our Italian justice.

MOTHER KNOWS BEST, 1899

The teenager is hunched over his soup, slurping and reading a newspaper at the same time. His mother hovers over his shoulder.

"Where did you get this? What is it?"

"I got it from my friend at school. It's just a newspaper, Mama, from Pisa."

"What does this mean?" she asks, pointing her finger as she reads the title slowly: "*Il Pensiero Libertario.*"

"It means Anarchist Thoughts."

She crosses herself.

"Oh, Mother of God! Please! Save my son!" She slaps him hard across the back of the head. "What are you thinking? Do you know what the authorities can do to you if they find you reading something like this? You want to go to jail? All of us will go to jail! Is that what you want? Stay away from these people and their crazy ideas. Mind your own business. Don't get involved. It's trouble. Get rid of this paper now!"

CRASHING LAPTOP

Dawn sighs as it looks through Antonio's open bedroom window. It's a pale, peaceful, sunlit morning. No one is yelling in the courtyard below nor in the other apartments. No one is banging on pots or pans, blaring the radio, or crying for attention.

A bleary-eyed and slightly hung-over Antonio smashes his ringing alarm clock off and pads barefoot to his desk. He automatically turns on his laptop, then heads for the kitchen to down cup after cup of black coffee.

He isn't shaving. He isn't hungry. He hits ON, hits RETURN, still trying to track down Cinka. This has been his morning routine for weeks.

The old laptop is stressed out, unhappy, uncooperative, overheating. But it boots up and it's time to check out all the sites again: hospitals, morgues, police stations, prisons, courthouses, immigrant aid groups, child protection. The daily rounds.

And then it crashes. Try again later. Too early for phone calls and the cell phone's battery is dead anyway.

Antonio slumps into a chair and stares vacantly out the window.

The church bell chimes seven high tones, one low. It's already 7:30 AM and he has to leave for a tutoring session with a young student.

He dresses, grabs his bag, throws in a few books and runs out the door.

On the street, the heat of the day smacks him in the face. A few puffball white clouds float in the sky. One looks like an angel. Or is it a unicorn? Antonio can't tell.

A man is picking through the garbage outside the supermarket, talking to no one.

A Sri Lankan selling jewellery drops an armful of bracelets on the sidewalk. Antonio stops to help him pick them up and they exchange weak smiles.

He walks quickly through the old market of San Lorenzo and remembers that he needs to buy a birthday gift for one of his roommates.

He scans the stall of used kitchenware, looking for a set of drinking glasses or a glass salad bowl. Nothing. Then out of the corner of his eye, he sees a woman with long black hair hurrying by, carrying a violin case.

"Cinka!"

She stops and looks back. An older woman with a scowl.

"You yelling at me?"

"Sorry. Thought you were someone else."

It's been this way for weeks. His desperate, tired eyes working double-time. A hundred times each day his heart has jumped, only to be disappointed another hundred times.

Antonio wipes a few renegade tears on his sleeve. "Fuck! Fuck! Fuck!" And hurries off to his tutoring session.

THEY CALLED US NAMES

The young Romanian mom sits at her kitchen table turning the pages of the daily *La Repubblica*, and spots an article about immigrant French youth rioting in the suburbs of Paris:

> Officials say this rioting is worse than anything before. The youth, reportedly angry about the suspicious deaths of two of their own at the hands of police, are now using shotguns to shoot at them. They want revenge, and have now injured 80 officers.
>
> The French president, who once said that the disenfranchised, mostly immigrant youth, needed a good hosing down, is pelted with rocks and bottles when he visits the community where the rioting broke out.

She shakes her head. All we want is to live in peace. To have the same rights as anyone else. But they won't let us. The doorbell rings. She answers. A neighbour holds the hands of her three children who sob uncontrollably. The eldest, nine years old, speaks:

"Mama, they called us names. Said we were dirty and evil

and we should go back to Romania. That we don't belong here, they don't want us here.

"They were going to beat us if we didn't leave. We couldn't go into the school. They chased us away, Mama. Why? What did we do? Mama, I'm so afraid."

SCANNING THE SKY

It's way past midnight, past the hour when everyone else in the building is sleeping, past the hour when the last TV set has been turned off, the arguments put aside, and all the goodnight kisses and apologies have been given and accepted.

Night has covered Rome with its dome of black. Dream time is in full swing. For some.

Antonio opens one shutter in his bedroom. Bleary-eyed, he stares out at the star-speckled sky, looking for any kind of clue, any hint that someone or something out there can hear his desperate plea.

If ever I needed a miracle, now, please, God, now. Is anyone listening? I've never been religious, I'm no fucking Catholic, but please, just listen to me.

My love for Cinka is crazy, mad, ball-busting, all-consuming. She's all I can think of, day and night. She lights up my entire world, sets me on fire. I can't believe she's just disappeared. Tell me please, where is she?

Again he feels the knot in his stomach grow, twist, and chew on him from within. The tears start. He wails softly into the crook of his arm. And remembers . . .

A violin track on a rock album? Why not?

"It would be so cool if you could come. You've already met the bassist and the singer. The sound engineer is a great guy. And we'll pay you for your time, of course. It would be a big favour for us."

Cinka came and blew everyone away. Then again. Every week, another session, another chance to get to know her better. She was grateful for the work and I always provided lunch and gave her extra food to take home.

"It's just a bit of pasta I cooked up this morning. They're tasty tomatoes, and the cheese is pretty awesome. No, no, please, I insist. Take it."

She was so proud, but I sensed she needed help. At the time, I didn't realize how desperate her situation really was. Now I hang my head in shame.

I remember the day I surprised her with a set of new violin strings.

She was so happy she jumped up and kissed me on the cheek. Right here. I kissed her back on the lips. After that, we, well . . . I was hooked. So was she.

I knew she took a big risk getting involved with me, an Italian *gadjo*. It was frowned upon.

"Antonio, I cannot spend the night with you. It is not possible. Please understand. And no one can ever know about us, about our relationship—for now. It's all right that I play music with your band, but please, we must be careful. You must do this for me, OK?"

She had no phone and refused to tell me where she lived. When I found out, I hung my head in shame.

Who could imagine me, Antonio Discordia, a philosopher/musician, in a political demonstration? My grandfather of course, some of my uncles, yes; but me? I even carried a sign. It was Cinka who convinced me to go.

"Antonio, we must go, both of us. It's important that they see *gadjos* in the street with Roma. We must show them we are not alone.

"My people are scared. I don't know how many will come. They don't want to be arrested. The more Italians they see, the better. If more Italians march in the streets, maybe then the government will listen."

She was right. Speak out together to show the Roma they weren't alone. To show the government we disagreed with their abuse of human rights.

We marched to demand housing and social services for Romani refugees. We were a few hundred only, Italians, Roma, and other immigrants. An equal number of police in riot gear surrounded us. What were they expecting? There were families with children in baby strollers. Nobody wanted to fight.

As Cinka and I listened to a speech by a Romani lawyer, I overheard one cop behind us say to another,

"Nice piece of ass. Too bad she's a Gypsy."

I turned and swore at him:

"STRONZO! FIGLIO DI PUTTANA! CAZZO!"

The two cops laughed and patted their clubs in their hands. What did I have in mine?

A cardboard sign.

One week later, when trees stood naked without their leaves and frost lay on the ground, there was a sensational murder. A Romanian man allegedly killed an Italian housewife during a mugging.

The politicians and the media went crazy. They demanded mass deportations, inciting a wave of anti-Romanian, anti-Roma hysteria.

Gangs of hooligans beat Gypsies and Romanians in the streets. Romanian shops were firebombed. Children were spat on and harassed, even in schools.

I told Cinka I was worried about her and her family. I said I didn't know what to do. I wanted to protect her somehow, but how?

"Antonio, don't worry about me or my family. You have no idea how many times every day we have to deal with this kind of attitude, this ignorance. In Romania we grew up with it. Here we can't escape it either. We're used to it. We know how to survive . . ."

The last time I saw her, Cinka told me that before she was only angry. Now she was afraid.

NEWS, 1913, New York: *All Italy faces a General Strike . . . Workmen's organizations in Milan vow to end the "Capitalistic Oligarchy" . . . Syndicalist and Socialist organizations urge unions to take immediate action and to carry on the strike to the bitter end.*

PICKET LINE CHAT, 1913

Walking toward the picket-line outside the factory, one mill worker, a cousin of Antoniolo Discordia, says to another: "Complain about wages or working conditions, you get black-listed. Get blacklisted and the company evicts you from the housing they own. You have to move from one stink hole to the next. You can't find work or lodging. And they wonder why we strike?" He spat on the road. "*Cazzo!*"

His friend nods and sighs.

"I know, I know. But think: what kind of strike is it this time? I don't want to be like those Americans who go on strike for eighteen months because the union gives them a bit of money to survive on. Then what? Nothing? Not me. This strike has to be like a national earthquake. Overthrow the whole damn system that lets a few get rich while the rest of us work for peanuts."

"You heard, just outside Milan, in Chiaravalle? This striker, one of our guys, he lay down on the railway tracks as the passenger train was approaching. The engineer slams on the brake and stops the train just before it hits the guy. The guy jumps up and yells at the train crew to join the strike. The station manager grabs the guy, blowing his whistle for help. The guy's friends try to free him. The *carabinieri* come running, beat and arrest all the strikers."

"I say next time they try that, we teach them a lesson. Raise your stick—we'll raise ours. You want to beat people? Taste your own medicine."

NEWS, June 1914, Rome: Popular uprisings in the Marches and Romagna ... Rebellious landless labourers confront strike breakers hired by landowners ... Police fire on anti-draft demonstrations in Ancona ... Strikers in Bologna take over city ... Romagna declares self a republic ... Rebels control Ferrara and Ravenna ... "Red Week" affects all of Italy ...

AN OLD FAMILY PHOTO ALBUM, 1985

Antonio once found an ancient, tattered family photo album at his grandparents' house. Faded shots of sombre-looking men and women in working clothes, fists and tools raised in the air.

"Grandfather," he asked, "are these people family?"

"Ho! Some of them. See, there's me with a few of your great-uncles where we worked. It was 1919 and 1920, the *biennio rosso*, the two red years of Italy. The country was on the verge of revolution."

"What's that?"

"That's when workers like us take things into our own hands, defy the bosses, the government, occupy the factories. Like in this photo. Then kick out the bosses. Change the way the factories are run. Run them ourselves. Big changes."

"Wow! The owners didn't mind?"

"Of course they did! All the big bosses were nervous, scared. *'Workers taking over our factories? No way!'*"

"So they called the police?"

"Worse. They called in Benito Mussolini. A strongman. A Fascist. With his own thugs! It was the only way they could control unruly, disrespectful working people like us. Mussolini's goons put an end to the uprisings, the strikes, the factory occupations. Violently. They spilled blood everywhere."

KITCHEN TALK TWO

"In 1969, my friends, maybe," Massimaxo said rubbing his head, "they didn't have all the facts. But the anarchists knew someone was setting them up. They couldn't finger the culprits, though. Who was actually behind the bombings?"

Rafaele and the boys were smoking hot that night in his kitchen, piecing together this controversial and complicated historical Italian puzzle.

"It wasn't clear immediately," Massimaxo continued. "They knew it was the Fascists, but which group? Anarchists don't carry out actions like that. They are more principled. Despite the fucking government and media portraying them otherwise."

Rafaele agreed with a nod. Massimaxo pressed on: "The press claimed that Fascist goons were the same as leftist goons.

To confuse the public. Make them think we were talking about the same thing: Fascist right-wing violence and leftists trying to defend themselves. Who else would bomb without respect for human lives? Who else would conduct pure terrorism targeting the public at large, workers, with no concern for basic human values?"

"How I love thinking out loud with you guys." Antonio stuck out his chin at the other two with a thumbs-up. Massimaxo wouldn't be interrupted.

"They were the real monsters. Black-shirted, black-hearted Fascist spawn from Mussolini and his followers. But they weren't alone. Now we know what no one suspected back then. That NATO and the Americans with their fucking CIA were involved in the massacres!"

Massimaxo's passion was deep and personal. His uncle, a trade unionist from Livorno, was one of the sixteen victims who perished in the bombing of the Agricultural Bank in Milano in 1969. His mother, a leftist journalist, made it her life's goal to help find the perpetrators and bring them to justice.

Some thirty years later, after many wrongful arrests, including the imprisonment of framed anarchist suspects, the murders of a few others, and a massive cover-up, the Italian judiciary finally located the real culprits. But the full story was still unravelling in the news.

Cazzo! Rafaele thinks. There are still pieces of the puzzle missing, involving high-ranking members of the Italian State. But now everyone knows: many bombings blamed on anarchists were carried out by the ultra-right. A conspiracy? Yes. American complicity? Yes. Italian judiciary? Probably. Are we fucked or what?

COMMON MYTHS ABOUT THE ROMA

Two unemployed, hungry labourers from the south of Italy, dark-skinned, stocky, each wearing an identical denim cap, saunter through the farmer's market in San Lorenzo, eyeing the food and chatting about the news.

"You know what they say about those damn Gypsies? They kidnap children!"

"Don't be stupid! They only say that to scare the little ones. To make them afraid of the Gypsies and not stay outside too late playing. Gypsies have their own families. They don't need our brats, too."

"They say they are dirty people!"

"The ones I have seen are cleaner than you! You know they wash their children not once but a few times each day?"

"No kidding?"

"And they don't let animals into their homes. Listen. In my village, during the festival of Saints Cosimo and Damiano, when we carry the statues of the saints in the procession to the sanctuary, the local Gypsies walk in the front and dance the *tarantella*. They are good people, understand?"

"Well, they say they are all criminals."

"Only because the government outlawed them. Blames them for everything. If everyone thinks you're a criminal because the government says so, then no one wants to work with you. If nobody wants to hire you, how do you feed yourself? Sometimes, you have no choice. Steal or starve. Like our people. Not all of us are crooks, right, but some of us have to eat, too. My brother once stole some food and was arrested. He had no money. Hmm . . . look at that chicken!"

RAFAELE IN HIS KITCHEN

Rafaele loved to cook. His photographer girlfriend, Bianca, was at work all day but he was off; his friend DJ Flashlight was coming over for dinner, so this day would be something extra special.

One bottle of homemade tomato sauce, from all the left-over tomatoes from last year; a dozen halved black olives; two big onions, halved, all into the pot to cook. Then, into boiling water, "bronze" pasta, not "steel" from Napoli—only the best pasta, of course. A salad of garden greens with hot red peppers and fennel. And the *pièce de la résistance*: fresh fish baked under a layer of rock salt. One bottle of *Frascati* was chilling in the fridge.

Rafaele congratulated himself on his dinner menu.

It was time for his smoke break by the open window. Rafaele surveyed the yard below: fat lemons ripening on the tree, peppers changing colours into brilliant reds, the cats patiently hunting unwary birds. It was a good life here in the country, peaceful, and far from the madness of Rome. Did he miss the nightlife, the vibrancy? No. In and out for work every other day was enough of Rome for him. Friends who mattered always visited, like DJ.

Rafaele and DJ Flashlight met years ago in engineering school in the southern USA, on a one-year exchange program before 9/11. On Halloween, immediately post 9/11, the two went to a costume party dressed as Osama bin Laden and associate. Rafaele's beard was long enough. They barely escaped the party alive. How did they know that all the American students chanting *"Death to Arabs!"* on campus in the weeks before were serious?

KITCHEN TALK THREE

Claps of thunder shook the open window as a fierce rain blew into the kitchen, dampening everyone present. Rafaele opened three more beers.

"Ah," said Antonio, squinting his eyes, exhaling perfect smoke rings, "today we think we know so much. We think we have surpassed that 1960s confusion of rampant class war, that 'Hot Autumn' as they called it. We think we live now in much better times. What crap! We're no longer as uninformed, sure, but now there is zippo excuse for ignoring injustice. We can't plead ignorance anymore. Fuck that! It's all out there, online, accessible. Anyone—even Americans, if they want to—can get all the critical opinions, theories, and history never reported in the sanitized media."

"Exactly," said Rafaele, banging his fireplace pipe on the floor. "Back then, they couldn't have known that 'Fortress

Europe' is part of an international mega-new-world-order strategy. Expand the military. Control the population. Establish new military bases to help launch attacks. Train for outbreaks of mass civil unrest. Make Italy part of the plan."

Massimaxo had just written an article tracing the recent history of exactly that strategy. Elbows on the table, his hands rocked back and forth in sync as he spoke:

"NATO was never stupid. Oh no! Postwar, they set up secret combat units here and across Europe. We're just as strategic as the rest. With access to the Mediterranean, the Middle East, North Africa—we're key to those NATO shits and the fucking Yanks.

"And damned if the CIA and that whole American military-industrial-oil machine isn't still behind it. Terrorize and destabilize the population! Fill them with fear! Target international 'terrorists,' immigrants—your choice, Arabs, Romanians, Roma, Asians, Africans, whoever. Make the public believe they are the villains. Then introduce new laws that give the advantage and the power to the Right, to the demagogues and the Fascists.

"Trash civil liberties! Censor the news! Present lies as facts! Pretend War is Peace. Call aggression 'pacification,' or 'reconstruction.' Then Italy is all yours! Eh! *Funculo!*"

"You mean, they dance their little pirouettes in their boardrooms and cackle, '*The people are immobilized. They can't think or act for themselves. We win! We win! Ha, ha, ha!*'" Antonio spun around on his feet and crashed into the table. Everyone laughed.

"Yes, but we live here, for Christ sake!" Rafaele helped Antonio to his feet. "Where are the largest anti-war demonstrations? The biggest labour strikes in Europe? Here! In Italy!"

"There must be cracks in their global Empire. I'm positive. Or else they wouldn't be resorting to such desperate measures. Right?" Antonio was wagging his finger.

"Yeah, afraid of getting their balls chopped off."

"It's obvious, boys. They're trying to find new ways to control unstable, unpredictable populations. The people are fighting for freedom, for scarce resources, for a better life.

They fear the instability from new migrating immigrants looking for work. Look out!"

"A potentially volatile mass of future discontent. Hey! *Cazzo*! Where's all the beer?" Rafaele stares into the beer-empty fridge.

NEWS, May 1915: *Italy declares war . . . Joins England, France and Russia against Germany, Austria-Hungary and Ottoman Empire . . . Launches massive attacks . . . bitter trench warfare . . .*
December 1915: *Italy calls off attacks . . . over 300,000 casualties . . .*

GREAT-UNCLE RICARDO'S WORLD WAR I INTERVIEW, 1973

A chubby, young, longhaired writer from the anarchist magazine *A/Rivista* walks up a steep flight of worn marble stairs into the anarchist library in Carrara. In his head he hums the *Canzone del Maggio*, the Month of May Song, from the newest Fabrizio De André album, *Storia di un impiegato*, Story of a White-Collar Worker.

He wipes the perspiration from his face and scans the sun-filled reading room through his thick horn-rimmed glasses. A group of card-playing elderly men sit in a corner joking loudly with one another.

"Excuse me, please," he asks, approaching them and passing out copies of *A/Rivista*. "I'm writing an article about anarchist war veterans. I heard some of you might be able to help. I'd like to record interviews with you, please?"

The four men laugh. They know the magazine, widely available at newsstands. The eldest, with a neatly trimmed white beard framing his jovial face, jabs a finger at the youth.

"Sure! I'll go first. Then the others can talk your ear off."

Ricardo Discordia, one of the Discordia triplets from Abruzzo, clears his throat, tips back his chair, crosses his arms, and in a booming voice accustomed to public speaking, begins.

"It's like this . . ."

"Wait! Please! I'm not ready."

Microphone in hand, the writer scrambles to turn on his tape recorder and pull a chair closer to Ricardo.

"I will never support war—any war. It is really stupid.

When Italy entered the First World War in 1915, I was only fifteen, and I lied about my age to join the army. Can you believe it? I lied to take part in their lie. They had no hesitation, no, about taking me, a young boy, to kill and be killed. I was unwitting and willing, just a gullible youth offering myself as cannon fodder. All the boys from the village signed up, except for my two brothers. They tried to talk me out of this foolishness, but I wouldn't listen. The rest of us thought it would be an adventure, a way to impress the girls. A nice uniform, a paycheque, good food, how could we lose? Why didn't I listen to my brothers?

"At the front I dug trenches and burial pits. I lost track of the number of stinking corpses we lowered into those pits. I had never seen so many dead, rotting, mangled men. When I started to recognize the guys from my own village without arms, legs, their faces half blown away, I cried.

"'Why, God, have you done this? What is the meaning?' No God ever answered me or anyone else."

"Where were you stationed?"

"I was transferred to a regiment of *Alpini* to fight the Austrians. What was an Austrian? I had never met one, but there I was, behind a machine gun, firing like crazy at these other young, mostly working-class men who, like me, had no idea why we were trying to kill one another. I was shooting at men who were fathers, brothers, men like me. So they had a different coloured piece of cloth flying above them. So what? We each shed the same red blood. Screamed when in pain. Ate the same hard bread. Pissed our pants yellow out of fear. Would rather be home drinking beer. Why should I kill them? What had these poor souls ever done to me? What had I ever done to them?"

"One day, shouting over the trenches, we realized that we even spoke the same language. So, after a bit of talking, we agreed to stop shooting for three weeks. We traded bread for tobacco and took pictures posing like old friends. We showed photos of our families, talked about our jobs, our villages, the girls we liked. We all agreed, Italians and Austrians, that we were brothers and saw no reason to shoot at one another. We shook hands. None of us really wanted to fight and die. For what? For a general to pin medals on his chest?

"We wondered if other groups of soldiers were also talking like us, not fighting. If enough of us did this, we could end the bloody war right there. No more killing or dying. Just men talking, sharing the little they had. Why should we do what some big-shot officer ordered? Why should we obey him? He in his shiny high boots. He who came from a rich family with no worries, ordering us to kill while he stayed hidden safely in a bunker.

"Austrians or Italians, on one side or the other, we thought as one man. As sensible men. No more war. So some of us dropped our weapons and walked away into the mountains. Call us deserters. We called ourselves sane."

THE YOUNGER MUSSOLINI, 1915

The dingy bar near the Milano train station was filled with pipe smoke and loud railway union workmen in dirty coveralls, sharing drinks shoulder to shoulder, talking politics and the war.

"You know this Benito Mussolini character, the socialist?"

"The bigmouth? Of course, who doesn't? Always talking up violence as the only way to have a socialist revolution."

"But he wasn't always like that. Remember, he started out against the war."

"Sure, I remember all that 'Down with war, up with humanity' stuff."

"Then he switched and called the war 'this great drama' and said that Italy should be part of it, the rat."

"I knew him when he was living in Switzerland, before he was a big shot. He used to beg and steal food. He bullied people even back then. Not a nice character. Always wanted attention. His ideas didn't make much sense. He wrote a bit for the socialist newspaper. Gave a few speeches, got himself a reputation."

"Later, he got elected as a socialist city councillor here in Milan, right?"

"He was a good speaker. Very theatrical."

"Sounded like a machine when he spoke, *rEck, rEck, rEck*!"

"Effective, though. Attracted all the socialists who believed in violence."

"I have a friend who worked with him on *Avanti* a few years ago before the war. Mussolini edited that paper, you know. Then he got fired because of all his talk about violence."

"And kicked out of the Socialist Party."

"I remember. Good riddance! Who needs socialists like him?"

"That's when he set up his own newspaper, *Il Popolo d'Italia*, right?"

"What a rag!"

"All that crap: '*Gather, warlike youth of Italy! . . . The flash of your knives and the roar of your grenades! . . . Kill the wretches who stand in Italy's way! . . . Let steel meet steel . . .*' blah, blah, blah."

"The shit that came from his mouth!"

"Now look at us, killing and dying for nothing."

"The arms manufacturers aren't complaining. They get richer, we fill the coffins."

"Where's Mussolini now?"

"In the trenches with the rest of the patriots."

"Killing the Philistines."

GOODBYE VILLAGE, HELLO FACTORY, 1916

In 1916, the Discordia triplets turned sixteen. Unlike Ricardo, Massimo and Rafaele refused to go to war and left their Abruzzo village to search for work. They travelled north to Perugia, then to Siena, Pisa, and Genoa. An uncle helped them find jobs in Turin as apprentice metalworkers in the Fiat factory.

They lived in a tiny dark room overlooking the factory and shared a sagging bed, sleeping head to toe, side by side. Their work was gruelling, but they found time each night to attend meetings and classes in a local community centre run by the Italian anarcho-syndicalist trade union federation. They were fast learners and loved to read and listen to lectures about history, economy, philosophy, and radical politics. Not shy, they debated others and sharpened their oratorical skills.

Massimo apprenticed with an older millwright, Giorgio, who had already lost two fingers to Fiat. The first day on the job he cautioned the young man: "Be careful. Pay attention. See this? No one will bring you a new finger—not the boss, not God, not a pretty nurse. I can still play the accordion, but sometimes now, my left hand goes numb and turns white. It's the vibrations from working on this damn machine. Five years, ten hours a day. Now it's your turn. Welcome to the machine. Your new mistress and master."

Rafaele apprenticed with a grizzled old anarcho-syndicalist, Giovanni, who repaired the machinery.

"When you stick your head inside these dark holes, pray to your own mother that no idiot will push the button to start up the machine. I've seen heads crushed, limbs mangled and shoulders ripped out of their sockets. Think before you start a job. And warn the others. Or you'll end up as dog food."

Each day, the brothers and the other workers watched the owner drive through the factory gate. He didn't ride a two-wheeled cart pulled by a mule. His ride was a long, shiny, chauffeured burgundy limousine.

At weekly union meetings, the twins learned that this flagship factory, the pride of the Agnelli family, was no different from any other auto factory in the city.

"Complain," Giovanni said, "and you lose your job and get blacklisted as 'undesirable.' You won't find any work in the industry. They play rough. *'You don't like it here? Then leave. Ten others will take your place.'* This is what the bosses will tell you. We say, don't leave. Work with us to change this hellhole."

Inhuman speed-ups on the assembly line, daily reprimands from prowling foremen—and always the noise and danger of the machines. Steel death traps. Iron maimers. Flesh eaters. Men lost fingers, hands, and eyes.

"*Cazzo!*" Blood gushed: a right hand ripped to shreds, another man down.

"Jesus Maria!" Two workers held a screaming man by the shoulders as two more tried to free his crushed arm trapped in a press.

"Mother of God!" A flywheel gone mad, spinning through the air, slicing off half the face of the closest man and lodging itself in the head of another.

Crushed limbs. Severed arms. Buckets of spilled blood. Weeping, broken, mutilated men. The Discordia brothers saw it daily. Heard the screams. Watched the shop floor run red. Carried out the maimed, the wounded, and the dead.

Don't blame the machines. Don't blame the operators. Blame the greed from above. Accidents resulted from direct commands to squeeze more money out of every minute every man spent on the factory floor. And always the same order:

"Faster, damn it! Faster! You're not being paid to drag your asses!"

Men were forced to pay with their lives to keep the shareholders happy. The happy ones never worked a machine or lost a drop of blood. Just raked in the *lira*.

Eager apprentices, the Discordia brothers learned quickly and soon joined in efforts to transform the nightmarish factory into something else. Massimo spoke up frequently at union meetings.

"Their minions yell at us daily. They follow us around with clipboards. They make notes about our every move; even how long we take to go to the toilet. Then the next day they return with a warning that we work too slowly and spend too much time eating and shitting. Enough is enough. I say we occupy the factory!"

Massimo wasn't alone. By the hundreds, up and down the line, fed-up men echoed the refrain. "Occupy! Occupy! Occupy the factory!"

NEWS, 1918, Rome: *First World War ends . . . After 3 years, 600,000 Italians dead, 1 million wounded, 250,000 crippled for life . . . Unemployment, inflation rise . . . Italy humiliated by Big Three Allies . . .*

PRELUDE TO FACTORY OCCUPATIONS, 1920

This day, August 31, 1920, in the intense heat of the giant Fiat-Central factory, amid the screech of steel on steel, over the rumble of the assembly lines, two words ring out, two words the Discordia brothers and others had been waiting to hear for years:

"Occupation! Tomorrow!"

Like a tidal wave engulfing the whole factory, line after line, shop after shop, the words spread quickly. From mouth to mouth, the phrase is repeated like a sacred vow, binding messenger to recipient, each new devotee granted the right to induct another, until all fifteen thousand workers know:

Occupation! Tomorrow!

These two words stamp themselves like a hot iron onto minds dulled and weary from hours and years of repetitive, dangerous work. Now the entire workforce is ready and willing to flex its collective muscle. Four long months of futile negotiations have gone nowhere. The employers have dug in their heels and refused to budge. The *Unione Sindacale Italiana* (Italian Syndicalist Union, USI) has called for an immediate expropriation of the metalworks factories before the owners' lockout shuts all the workers out.

It's game on.

"The landlords raise the rent, but our pay stays the same."

"We can't feed our families."

"And we have jobs!"

"You think Mr. Agnelli has to worry about choosing to pay rent or buy food each month?"

"No, he has tougher choices: red caviar tonight, or black?"

"What about the shorter lunch break?"

"The boss thinks we should eat while we work."

"Then we'd shit out nuts and bolts."

"Who'd want to buy the cars then?"

"Better than what happened to those two working the blast furnace last week. Burned to death because the damn foreman refused to get it fixed."

"And the guy who lost his arm on the belt last night?"

"Yeah, the foreman sped it up. No warning."

"Give me an axe and I'll chop his arm off, the insolent bastard. We'll see how he can write in his notebook without it."

In a loud voice between mouthfuls of bread and hard cheese, Massimo speaks to the small circle of workers from his metal stamping station. They sit on the worktables during their lunch break.

"It's a dialogue with the deaf. The bosses say one thing, we say another. There's no common ground."

The others nod. The oldest, a Sicilian anarcho-syndicalist with broad shoulders and a bushy salt and pepper beard, burps loudly, and wipes his mouth with the back of his hand.

"We have different interests," he says, open palms up, weighing the balance. "They want more money because they are never satisfied. We need more money to live on. The cost of living rises. Our wages don't. Fiat and friends got fat on wartime profits. Now they cry that they have no money. Idiots! They think we can't understand this?"

Massimo leaps to his feet.

"And they want us to pay for their conversion to peacetime production. So they reject our demands! Their investment first. Our needs last. Screw them! We'll show them!"

He pounds the table.

"But . . . but . . . occupy the factory?" asks one of the workers nearest him, a soft-spoken, stuttering bear of a man. The Sicilian answers.

"If the bosses can't give us what we need because they don't know how to run production properly, we'll run the factories. We know how. We do it every day despite their interference. We'll show them how to rationalize production according to our principles, not theirs."

The back-to-work whistle screeches. Massimo and his colleagues pat one another on the back and smile. "*Occupation tomorrow!*" How it will work in practice, no one knows. But they are ready.

Massimo surveys his workmates in their coveralls stained with factory grease and grime. He sees their faces furrowed deep as they concentrate at their posts. He notices their worn boots and shoes. Feeding the family comes first. Paying the landlord comes second. New boots last.

He sees the ever-prowling foreman breathing down everyone's back. He looks up at the filthy windows high above that tease each worker with a hint of the bright world outside. Inside, in here, there is only the humming, rumbling, rocking machinery that dictates his every move, every minute, and every hour on the job. Machines that follow him home and, uninvited, invade even his dreams. Machines that steal the best years of his life and in return give him only grief and monotony, aches, scars, injuries, and a ringing in his ears.

Because this is the exchange: a man's life for someone else's profit. This is the job. This is why you crawl out of bed before sunrise, get dressed, gulp a coffee, and walk out of your home dreading another shift.

You give your one and only life to the bosses, hoping to put a bit of food on the table, to keep a roof over your head, to have a few precious hours of freedom on Sunday with your loved ones. This is the trade-off of your life.

DAY ONE, FACTORY OCCUPATIONS
The morning of Sept 1, 1920, under a blistering, red-hot sun, four hundred thousand metal workers, heads held high, walk through the gates of their factories across Italy and occupy them. Peacefully.

In Turin alone, one hundred thousand workers occupy 185 factories. Everywhere the order is the same: "Continue with production. Work to union rules. Slow down. Make the factories ours."

Massimo climbs a ladder onto the roof of his section of

the Fiat factory. With two other colleagues, he secures a red and black flag on a pole to the highest smokestack. The wind blows and it snaps to attention. He paints in large white letters below the flag:

"Chains and fetters we break."

Lower down, on a high wall, a colleague paints:

"We want not wealth, but freedom."

Below them at the entrance to the factory, an improvised band with three mandolins, an accordion and a percussionist banging on pieces of metal, plays a rousing version of "The Internationale." Hundreds of voices join in. The old Sicilian, Giorgio, staggers out of a side shop door bent over with laughter, holding his sides.

"Hey everyone! We locked up one of the directors in his office! He refused to leave, so we handed him a blue slip! Reprimanded him for insolence! You should have seen his face! Like a squealing pig! Oink, oink, oink! We'll send him home for lunch."

DAY TWO

The union of railway workers sends in a railcar full of velour cushions "so the metalworker brothers can have a more comfortable sleep at night." Upstairs, groups of metalworkers take turns getting their photos taken as they sit at the boss's huge mahogany desk.

"My wife will never believe it!"

"I want to send a copy to my cousin in Canada!"

"Show him you're now the big cheese—still in your coveralls!"

Across Italy, a hundred thousand other workers occupy their own places of work in solidarity with the metalworkers.

DAY THREE

The occupiers' families crowd the gates bringing in food for husbands, fathers, sons, and boyfriends who now spend not eight or ten hours at their jobs but twenty-four hours every day, working and sleeping. They might be voluntary prisoners of the factory, but these strikers are now masters of this moment.

This night, the sky is thick with stars. Massimo sits on a bench at one of the gates on guard duty, his revolver in hand. His knees are folded under his chin. He turns to the Sicilian, Giorgio, beside him and in a voice full of pride says:

"Can you believe it? Turin is ours! A workers' Turin! Who could ever imagine?"

Giorgio nods. "And now that we are half a million strikers, Italy is almost ours."

"Even in Palermo, I hear, the factories are occupied."

"Not just factories, but the steelworks, foundries, forges, blast furnaces, the dockyards—everywhere we *metalos* work. And so far, no incidents."

"Thank goodness. The newspapers say we're armed to the teeth. Look at this huge weapon I hold in my hand. So big I can't hold it in my mouth."

Massimo toys with his gun. Then grows serious: "We'll defend the factory with whatever it takes, but I worry about the army."

Giorgio scoffs. "You think the factory owners will allow the army to blast us out of here with their artillery? They don't want their precious factories damaged."

"True," says Massimo. "As long as we stay inside these walls, we can defend this place. It's a natural fortress. But if we go out there, they'll slaughter us.

"You didn't see those tanks under wraps in the far storage room?" The Sicilian winks. "Leftovers from war production. And according to some of the ex-soldiers in our union, easy to drive."

"But if the army does break in?"

"Sabotage. And don't forget it."

Behind them through an open window, they hear a gramophone playing a popular romantic song by a mandolin orchestra.

"Ah, to be in love," Massimo sighs. "That's what I need. A union woman. To make this night perfect. To sit here beside me. Where are you, my beloved? Out there cooking supper for me?"

"Don't you know how to cook yourself?" laughs Giorgio, lighting a cigarette.

"Of course, but it doesn't hurt to fantasize."

"Keep dreaming, and your rebel woman will wake you up with a frying pan to your head and order you to fix the sink."

"Order," Massimo sighs. "The Factory Committee has issued orders for us to maintain hygiene and not steal from the factory. And also to prohibit card-playing and alcohol."

"A good thing, I say. Better that men spend their time reading books. Have you read anything by Malatesta?"

"No, but now that he's back in Italy the authorities are worried again."

"One man with subversive ideas, and they worry. Now we are five hundred thousand strong. They must be pissing in their pants."

DAY FOUR

Like most of his colleagues, Massimo is still giddy with euphoria.

"Come on, guys, no slacking the pace now! We're showing everyone that we can run the factory without the employers. We coordinate the production. We control the movement of material. We make sure we have supplies. Keep going, comrades! This is the future!"

At the General Assembly of strikers in the large, high-ceilinged hall, he and other workers from his department take turns speaking. Workers clamber on top of silenced machines for a better view, or sit with legs dangling from overhead steel beams. Their laughter and voices echo off the walls—voices silenced by the foremen for too long.

"Hey, it's not your turn to speak!"

"Up yours, you already spoke!"

"Order, brothers! Order please! One at a time. Everyone gets their turn."

"We need to clean the windows!"

"Yes! Get more light in here! Agreed!"

"How about safety goggles for every man in 'D' section? Agreed!"

"Replace the old belts on Line 10! Agreed!"

From everyday practicalities, the discussion turns to bigger concerns.

"We should expand our movement to other industries. Occupy them. Occupy the mines, the fields, the banks, and even the mansions. Agreed!"

"We're showing how workers' management can succeed here. Production is up. It's time to try it elsewhere! Agreed!"

"But if we send delegates out to the other factories, won't the police arrest them? No!"

As the debate intensifies about broadening the occupation, the room erupts into cheers or jeers. Men stomp their feet and bang tools in support or disagreement.

Scanning the faces around the room, Massimo observes that these are no longer the same men who were once enslaved to their machines. They have new sense of self-worth and dignity, on and off the shop floor. No one cowers before anyone else. Men no longer stand at their posts bleary-eyed, fearful, resentful, angry, tormented, or bored, unwilling to speak their minds. Now their work has a new meaning.

With no more bosses above them, they are working not to earn money for someone else, but to prove a point: that they, we, the occupiers/strikers, can run this factory as well if not better than the owners themselves. Run it differently, respectful of each man's role, each man's contribution to the process. Without foremen, without inhuman speedups or dangerous practices. But humanized, in our own way, in our hands.

During the General Assemblies, each man has a chance to participate. Decisions are reached not as orders from above but after discussion.

The Factory Council that now runs the factory consists of delegates from each section on the floor. Everyone has a say. This is something entirely new for each worker—to see the factory and themselves as working together, toward a common goal: the good of all.

Let the bosses moan and groan, Massimo thinks, at the prospect of losing this factory to a new historic reality. If workers control actually works, why not allow it? And why not expand the movement?

Massimo stomps his feet, whistles and bangs his wrench with the several hundred other workers around him. This is the new on-the-job reality. Fiat and Turin will never be the same.

DAY TEN

Nerves start to fray on and off the shop floor.

"Who is negotiating for us anyway? How can we trust them?"

"Have you heard? The army is preparing to attack."

"Nonsense. They just want to scare us."

"Well, I'm scared."

"When will we be paid for our work? It's already been a week with no paycheque."

"Be patient, friend. This kind of thing is still an experiment. We're still learning how to make it work. Once we start selling products like before, the money will come. You'll see."

"We must expand the occupation! The greater the movement, the greater our chances of success transforming all of Italy into a new society with no more bosses!"

In truth, the occupation was growing. Occupiers invaded other industries like the chemical and textile plants and convinced them to join. Michelin and Tedeschi rubber firms joined in; shoe factories, leather works, from city to province, too. Workers raised red flags or red and black flags above more and more workplace roofs.

"See today's news?" Massimo proudly announces to Giorgio over their morning coffee in the factory's now communal kitchen.

"It says here that now almost all the workers of Turin, about 150,000 people, are participating in the occupation! The chemical plant workers say they did it because they want to ensure that supplies keep flowing for us. Even dockworkers in Genoa took over three ships in port for the same reason. It's incredible!"

"Let's hope we can keep everyone happy and not slack off production. We need to keep the business healthy."

"Ha! You sound like one of the big shots, now."

"You think we're almost ready for a revolutionary popular uprising? Not yet. I say we keep focused on the current objective. As long as we show we are capable of working independently of the bosses, everyone will wait and see. We'll be safe. For now."

Later that morning, the whole factory is abuzz with the discovery of a confidential "blacklist" of known "subversives" in the company safe. Also found is a list marked "Our Ears" with names of company spies. The spies are rounded up, booted off the grounds, and warned never to show their faces again.

DAY ELEVEN

At a critical convention in Milano, to which the anarcho-syndicalist USI has not been invited, the Italian Socialist Party votes to reject the drive toward a revolution by a majority vote. No expanded occupation.

DAY TWELVE

The occupiers across Italy are stunned into disbelief by the Socialist Party vote.

"We were betrayed? How is this possible?" Massimo asks as a large group of occupiers gather to discuss the morning's news.

"Because there are cowards, reformists, snivelling party people who claim to want wide-reaching social change, but who walk away from the real thing. As it is happening under their noses!" answers Giorgio.

Others in the group voice their disapproval. Many refuse to work and walk away from their posts. Others commit acts of sabotage. Some weep openly. Their anger spills outside the factory gates.

One factory owner, outraged at the continued occupation, drives up and leaning out the window of his car, kills two workers with his pistol. He escapes the enraged mob that chases him.

DAY NINETEEN

It's the third "Red Sunday" of the occupation. Massimo, Giorgio and fifty other workers loll about the inner courtyard. Dejection reigns.

"I'm getting tired of these endless meetings, day and night," Massimo complains, hands in his pockets, fiddling with his revolver.

"You notice no one wants to work anymore? It's a real struggle to convince the comrades not to give up," replies Giorgio.

"Now there's talk about stealing tools."

"But didn't you hear? The guards caught two thieves last night trying to sneak out with tools. They were company spies trying to make us look bad."

"How could they impose a settlement on us from above? We control the city. We are running the factory better than before!"

"Exactly. Now they want us to help the bosses run the factory. Give them advice. Turn us into puppets. The government thinks this will keep everyone happy."

"They're asking for trouble."

"They don't learn the same lessons we do. We learned how to break the chains. They learned how to make them shorter."

"But will we be paid for our three weeks' work?"

"Who knows? For sure, we must hide our guns. Bury them in the hills and have them ready for next time."

DAY TWENTY-TWO

Gunshots ring out.

"Run! Run for cover! The police are shooting!" Massimo

is crouching at his post near the gate, eyes focused on a gun battle just outside the factory wall. Policemen on one side of the street are firing at scattered groups of armed workers, holed up behind trucks and cars on the other side. A scream.

"I'm shot!" Massimo sees one policeman drop to the ground. The gunfire continues for an hour until the police pull back. The workers half carry and drag several of their wounded back into the factory screaming for help. Massimo's hands are drenched in blood as he helps carry one man.

DAY THIRTY

The government decree allows more union control in the factories, but not factory councils. Every occupying worker has questions:

"Did we miss the great revolutionary moment? What happened? We were sold out, defeated, betrayed, but how? And by whom?"

"It's obvious that this new decree is a ruse. It means workers must collaborate with the bosses. It's a bourgeois manoeuvre, to save Italy from revolution."

"We came so close! We were destroying the old order. Building something new, something never seen before. And now, we go back to work because the government has passed a new law? What bullshit!"

All these weeks with no wages. Occupiers are tired, disillusioned and bitter. The initial euphoria and hope for revolution is now a memory.

The occupying workers evacuate the factories. The occupation ends peacefully.

At Fiat Central, a sentry on top of the roof whistles loudly and hundreds of men waiting in the courtyard form into a long double line. An official "welcome back" for the bosses.

A massive grey cloud suddenly lodges itself in front of the midday sun and threatens rain. From the main gate to the main doorway, at least two hundred men in dirty work clothes stand on each side, five deep. The bosses hesitate at the gate, then walk uneasily through the gauntlet. Their eyes focus straight ahead on the Factory Council sitting at a long table to await them as they return to take back control of the factory.

Massimo stands on a brick wall with Giorgio and their friends to watch. He lets out a low hiss as the bosses enter the gates.

"Look how they cower. They're afraid! Beneath their fine suits, they're just hairy, naked men like us."

"Yes, but unlike us, they have money stuffed in all their holes for safekeeping."

Who wants the workers to continue having decision-making power over their day-to-day working lives? It's too revolutionary and could lead to unpleasantries, like the total overthrow of the system.

THE NOISE BAND

Antonio, Massimaxo, and Agnesia are in a Roman electro-acoustic noise band called Hasta Nawzedrowia Siempre. The guitarist, bassist, and DJ self-produce albums and tour in a small car, playing to adoring fans across Italy.

One night, driving home from a gig in Napoli, Antonio turned his head to talk to Massimaxo in the passenger seat—at the exact moment that their car *thump-thumped* over a rolled-up carpet lying in the middle of the highway.

"What the fuck was that?"

"I dunno, but it didn't sound good."

Within moments, Antonio noticed it was getting harder to steer the car.

"Fucking Jesus! The alignment's gone! And I think I smell gas!"

Then the engine started to sputter and miss.

"*Cazzo!* We got a situation, *ragazzi!* Hang on."

Antonio manoeuvred the car to the side of the road and coasted to a stop in a gas station. One quick look under the hood confirmed it: broken fuel line.

It was 2 AM. The gas station was closed until 7 AM.

Massimaxo waxed philosophical.

"If anyone would have told me we'd be ending this amazing tour here, in the middle of nowhere, at a gas station near the gates of Caianello—one of the worst places on earth—I'd never have believed it. Good thing I scored some hash tonight. Old friend owed me."

The three smoked up and tried unsuccessfully to sleep in the broken-down car. A few miserable hours and ten euros later they were back on the road, only to be thwarted again by a truckers' strike blocking the highway. Antonio blared his horn.

"*Fanculo!* Is there no justice for a Roman noise band?"

Massimaxo held a microphone out the window to record the truckers' noisy demonstration.

"Inspiration, *ragazzo*, inspiration."

CICADAS

Like any Roman from today or centuries ago, Rafaele knows summer has arrived when the hot winds blow and the cicadas start to sing. As a young boy he was captivated by the sound and still is. In the city or country heat, cicadas rule Italian airwaves.

A non-Italian might comment on this weird, natural electronica—what is it, who didn't answer their super-loud telephone, and why is it so omnipresent? The cicada only sings when resting, but give it a sunny day, a hot spot, a few bushes or a single tree, with or without an audience, and it works its special muscles to fill the air with sweet music.

As Rafaele sips a beer with his friends outside *La Casetta Rossa* in Garbatella at a table under the shade of a magnificent towering pine, he listens to the cicadas' powerful song filling the air. The insect choir occupies the lush adjacent park.

A muscular and heavily tattooed young woman serves them bread, olives, and cheese. A slow, glorious sunset fills the Roman sky. Parents haul protesting children off the swings nearby and tuck them into strollers for the homeward walk.

Rafaele cups his chin in his hand, leans his elbow on the long wooden table, and studies his friends as they drink in silence. He's concerned that a particular anti-Fascist friend, a mole inside a Fascist cell, hasn't called yet.

NEWS: Italians clap and cheer as police move 300 African immigrants out after clashes with locals . . . Riots leave scores injured in Calabrian town . . . immigrant farm workers shot, beaten and run over . . . compare Italian south to 1920s Alabama . . .

NEWS: Far-right thugs menace Rome's tourist spots in wave of violence . . . Rise in race attacks is fuelled by drink and election of former neo-Fascist as mayor . . . gays, lesbians, immigrants and tourists targets of attacks . . .

NEWS: Gay disco burned down near Coliseum, neo-Fascists take credit . . .

NEWS: The United Nations High Commissioner for Human Rights asks Italy to stop driving Roma families out of their camps . . .

A ROMANI DOCTOR TELLS A STORY

The young Romani doctor, Selena, with the large dark eyes, crisp white lab coat, and sparkling smile shakes the hand of the Polish journalist, Marek. They met before during a formal media tour of the camp.

Once again, she invites the journalist to sit on a couch in her family's spotless house in one of the oldest and most established refugee camps in Rome. An Italian flag flutters above the front door.

This house is solidly built, with care, he notices. Rooms have been added onto the original structure. Compared to many refugee homes he's visited, it is well designed, airy, and spacious.

Selena's devoutly Catholic mother has decorated the walls with prints of saints, madonnas, and the pope. The tiled floors shine. It's one of the more comfortable homes in the camp. She serves him a cup of tea on a saucer.

"Lovely place."

"Thank you. We don't know how much longer we'll be able to stay here. Twenty years of peace, and now an impending eviction? It's unbelievable."

Selena sits on the couch beside the journalist, hands folded in her lap.

"So, Antonio suggested you talk to me? About Cinka and how I remember her?"

Marek nods.

She pulls out a handkerchief and dabs her eyes.

"I'll tell you. But let me first clear up one thing. I knew about Antonio but never met him. She was crazy about him."

"You're sure of that?" The journalist holds his recorder closer to the doctor.

"Of course! She was carrying Antonio's baby! They planned to marry! This other man people talk about—she never loved him! Whatever anyone says, it was never a serious arrangement. Cinka was no longer a young village girl. She was a woman who knew what she wanted. After her father's death, she grew up quickly."

"You came from the same village in Romania?"

"Yes, her family knew mine. A few weeks after she arrived in Rome with her family—a few weeks of hell—she found me. I live in Milan and come down when I can to visit my mother here."

"How would you describe Cinka?"

"She was twenty-two years old. Beautiful, talented, hard-working and hard-headed. She was a voracious reader. Very community minded. She had her own views about everything. She loved to talk about world affairs, music, nontraditional roles for Romani women. She was brilliant. I wanted her to attend a university, but she had no time. She had to earn money for her family. I understood. She was a very proud person."

"And her original family, back in the village?"

"She was born into a musical family. Her dad handed her a violin when she was five years old. While other children her age were playing with toys, she played her violin, imitating him. He was a highly respected violinist. Famous in our village.

"By the age of eight, she was accompanying him in his

band. She started to earn money. She was so talented, even at that age. By sixteen, I remember, she led her own band playing weddings and concerts. When her father died, Cinka became the sole breadwinner for her family.

"An uncle already living here suggested that they should join him. He was supposed to help them find housing and work. The day the family arrived, the uncle was deported. Poor Cinka and her mother had spent all their money on the move.

"They ended up in a refugee camp, like ours, behind a train station just outside Rome—one of thousands. They pieced together their first small hut.

"I remember Cinka's mother planted flowers around it. She said she wanted to make it look more like the little three room house they had in Romania.

"Cinka's mother tried to sell roasted chestnuts on the street. Her first day she was robbed and beaten by thugs who warned her never to come back. Thankfully, Cinka earned enough money busking to buy food for the family.

"But this city of love, you know? It's never kind to new Roma families. Cinka told me what happened when she asked about social assistance for her family. They brushed her off. It's a story I hear too often. 'We'll add your name to the waiting list. There are thousands of others. Don't worry, we'll call you. No phone? Check back with us next month. Sorry, that's the way it is. Next!'

"Cinka said she protested—loudly. But in vain. 'There are other people in line behind you. You have to leave. Don't raise your voice! Either you leave now peacefully, or we call Security.'

"She didn't leave. They called Security and threw her out the door. She showed me the bruises on her arms.

"The last time I heard from her, she called me to tell me she was pregnant. She was overjoyed. But afraid, too."

NEWS, Rome: Immigrants from Moldavia, Senegal, Bangladesh, Albania, China and Tunisia beaten up or stabbed . . . now arming selves to fight back . . .

NEWS: City of Rome plans series of fenced-in "Roma Ghetto-Camps" modelled on ghettos the Nazis set up in Poland in the 1940s . . . Internees, including children, to receive special permits to enter the camps . . .

NEWS: Vatican police clash with Roma seeking refuge in the grounds of St. Paul's after city destroys refugee camps . . . Local and foreign pilgrims cry "Shame! Shame!"

SITTING AROUND A CAMPFIRE

The night before the police raided their home in *Tor di Quinto*, Cinka sat around a campfire with her refugee neighbours. Three older men—a carpenter, a cook, and a barber—discussed the news.

"Did you hear? They passed a new law. The government says we are all thieves and murderers and wants to deport us. All of us."

"Ha! If one Spaniard commits a crime, will they deport all Spaniards? No. If one Italian commits a crime, will they deport all Italians? No. Any excuse to get rid of us."

"But how can they deport us? We're citizens of the European Union, yes?"

"So what, we're Gypsies."

"You worry too much."

"You drink too much."

"You talk too much."

"What if it's true? Where will we go?"

"I heard from a cousin it's better in Germany."

"Better than Italy? Ha! All those Nazis?"

"No, they say there are no more Nazis. It's against the law."

"You're dreaming. It's against the law here, too, and look at all the Fascists in government."

"Well don't you want to go somewhere safer?"

"Sure. See that nest of stars up in the sky?"

PART II

SHE IS

ANTONIO IN LOVE

Massimaxo, Agnesia, and Antonio are flopped on the big sagging couch in the recording studio, laughing, trying to sing an AC/DC love song. Three bottles of wine later, they still can't get the words right. It's an early start to Antonio's birthday celebration.

"I'm so fuckin' happy with everything—our band, the new album, the weather. And this beautiful new loopin' unit you gave me, it's so fuckin' cool! I'm happy too, 'cause you know what, guys? I think I'm in love." He burps.

"Come on! Who?"

He slides off the couch and tries to stand up.

"Whoops! I, Antonio Discordia, am, as of this birthday, officially in love. But it's kind of secret, you know. Taboo. Understand? Shhhhh!"

He points warningly at his two friends.

Massimaxo laughs and looks at Agnesia, who is also laughing.

"Lover boy, what do you mean?"

Massimaxo yanks Antonio back onto the couch. Now Antonio is laughing.

"'Cause I can't tell you who she is 'cause she'll get in trouble, and then it won't happen, that's what I mean!"

Agnesia raises his almost empty glass.

"A toast! To your new mysterious violin-playing lover—whoever she is!"

CINKA ASKS QUESTIONS

The moon winces as it surveys the unsleeptime in this Romani refugee camp.

It sees prowling sewer rats tearing the shadows of the night. In one hut, an old man, eyes closed, awash in memories of his youth, mutters the name of his long-gone wife over and over as he lies quietly dying.

In another, a baby, three weeks old, cries at the lack of milk in her mother's breasts. A couple nearby, unsure about each other's dreams, argue about their future. In other huts, children sleep with empty stomachs as their parents lie awake, unable to end the nightmare.

It is late, and through a chink in the wall the moon notices Cinka praying for sleep. Outside the ramshackle structure she and her family call home, someone walks by whistling. A sick child next door moans, the mother trying to comfort it. Further away someone hushes a cat in heat.

The whole camp world is audible through these symbolic walls of scrap plastic, metal sheeting and wood secured with rope and wire. This pathetic excuse for a bit of privacy, like all the other camp huts, could easily be demolished by the kick of a policeman's steel-toed boot or his nightstick weighted with racial intolerance. Not even a wish from the moon could save it.

Cinka lies on an old carpet under another old carpet, staring into the darkness all around. Her sister and mother sleep close beside her, the three crammed tightly together. Her brother sleeps apart in two rolled mats.

The wind rattles a piece of tin beside her head. Ignoring her own growling stomach, Cinka argues with herself:

He is cute. And he gives me butterflies. Am I falling for this charming Italian boy? I know he likes me. Antonio's so obvious. And I like him. Maybe too much. But I have to be careful. That old witch keeps an eye on me. She causes trouble for all the other girls. She'll do it for me, too. And I need to work to make money to feed us. I don't have time to go out with boys. Even if he is special.

Her sister turns and places an arm around her, snuggling closer.

I can't forget about my family. We have a better future somewhere. A real house again. With beds, furniture, a garden, and a fridge with food. Our father would have provided this. Now it's my responsibility.

I can't fall for this *gadjo*. It won't work. I have to tell him. But not right away. I like him too much. And my body wants him.

THE YOUNG ACCORDIONIST

It's late afternoon. High in the blue sky, a series of gently puffed out clouds resembling giant Buddhas float serenely. Below, working men and women with circles under their eyes and aching feet in their shoes board the train at every stop from Rome's Fiumicino Airport to Monterotondo, homeward. The lucky ones find a seat.

In one car, a woman closes her eyes, pulls down the window shade to keep out the sun and rests her head. Another plugs in a set of earphones and nods off. A group of loud male high school students run in laughing and joking. They've been shopping and each carries a brand-name paper bag with trophies.

"Check these jeans! Super deal!"

"Look at me! Rock star T-shirt!"

"I got these cool shoes on sale! You believe it?"

A well-dressed, middle-aged man sits down with an equally well-dressed woman. She wears a wedding band; he doesn't. Her dyed hair is not quite in place, as if she just woke up. They whisper to each other. She hands him a piece of paper, he writes something down, she smiles. She carefully studies it, folds it and places it in her purse, then kisses him on the cheek. He smiles and kisses her back.

Cinka's unsmiling younger brother, Corvu, boards the train with his accordion. His father gave it to him when he was seven years old. The boy learned quickly and played together with Cinka and the other relatives for fun. That was before, when Corvu could enjoy childhood.

He's noticeably darker-skinned than anyone else on this train and very thin with longish hair. His sad, twelve-year-old, night-filled eyes scan the car, checking the passengers and the exits. He misses nothing. His baggy pants and sweater are torn. His dirty sneakers are laced with string.

But even if the bellows of his battered instrument wears a masking tape patch job, and the shoulder straps hold together with wire and twine, he can still play spirited Italian melodies effortlessly, skilfully.

He works the car, eyeing every passenger left and right, pausing only for a moment, awaiting something, but never interrupting his tune. A man in work clothes hands him a coin. Corvu nods briefly, pockets it with one hand, then sees the students sitting just ahead, laughing, joking. They stop talking, look him up and down, and something is not quite right on this beautiful sunny Italian day.

He retreats quickly to another car, remembering what his older sister said:

"Smile a lot. Say thank you. Be very polite. Keep an eye out for idiots, crazy ones, racists, and police. Don't talk back. Don't stare or swear. Don't give them any reason to pick on you. Move fast. Watch your back always. Wrap your coins in a sock in your pocket so they don't jingle."

Now he can add a few pointers of his own. Like always have an escape route. Look for allies in the crowd. And stay away from teenagers. He admires Cinka. When they play together, it is safer for both of them. But when they split up, they can make more money. Ever since their father died, Cinka has been the main breadwinner for the small family. But Corvu's catching up.

He remembers his dying father in the hospital:

"You're the man in the family now, Corvu. Look after your mother and your sisters. I'm counting on you. Make me proud. I'll be watching you."

Corvu didn't go to school. His younger sister did. Corvu was counting on her.

"You should become a doctor, Celina. You can help everyone and make lots of money."

"I don't want to be a doctor," she said. "I want to be a teacher. I can still make lots of money."

"You're just a girl. What do you know about money?"

"I know that one day, if I'm a teacher, I can make more than you."

"Now I'm working so you don't have to, so you better become a doctor or I'll beat you up."

Corvu rescued a starling once. It had a broken wing. He built a cage for it out of an old hubcap and chicken wire. He'd feed the bird worms, bugs and breadcrumbs and try to teach it to speak. At night, he'd sing to the bird before covering the cage and putting it to sleep. His father taught him the lyrics:

> The postman's on his way / He brings me a letter / Oh he
>   brings me a letter / From my son in chains
> Out I'll come, my mother / The life in prison's hard / I'll
>   live it / For five black years
> I'm all alone, mother / In front of the mess tin / When I
>   eat it, mother / My heart splits in two
> I don't eat by day / I don't sleep by night / And all for
>   what, mother?

NEWS, 2008, Rome: New security law enacted . . . "Clandestinos" who commit crimes to receive more severe penalties . . . Government deploys 3,000 troops in streets to clamp down on security threats, i.e., illegal immigrants . . .

ROME'S *CLANDESTINOS*

Off *Via Togliatti*, in Rome's early morning darkness, a crowd of two hundred multiracial *clandestinos* desperate to earn a few euros, wait patiently in a parking lot to be chosen by subcontractors for day jobs.

"Did he take you yesterday?"

"No. Not for the last three days. I've been here, but nothing."

"I asked him why not me, and he said, 'Why not one hundred others?'"

"Last week he ripped me off."

"How much? Half a day's pay. Said I didn't do a good enough job."

"I heard they don't want to take any more Africans."

"Before that it was no more Indians."

"Tomorrow, maybe no more Roma."

"Does he know?"

"I don't think so."

"But you heard the news? The new laws? Why would he want to hire us?"

"Because my kids haven't eaten for three days."

CINKA CAN'T BE SEEN WITH HIM

The young couple sits in the shade at an outdoor café. She has her back to the wall and whispers as she scans the busy street behind him.

"Please understand, Antonio. I can't be seen with you in public. For now."

"But why, Cinka? What's happening?" Antonio throws his hands up in the air. "I just want to take you out for lunch or dinner. Go watch a movie or a concert. Normal things everybody does. What's wrong with that?"

She purses her lips and tries not to roll her eyeballs. He's not making this easy.

"You don't understand. It's complicated. I have a mother, sister and brother. I'm the one who brings home money to buy the food. I have the responsibility to feed my family.

"It's not that I don't enjoy spending time with you and don't like you. I do. And I appreciate the opportunity to work in the studio and get paid. I am very grateful and always will be. But at this moment, for more, it is not OK. Do you understand?"

She stands up and is about to leave. He leans forward and grabs her arm:

"Wait, Cinka. Please sit for a bit more."

"I can't spend more time with you. Don't you hear me? And I can't come home late now because of all this . . ." She tries to stifle the tears but can't help herself. "All this anti-Roma feeling."

Antonio grabs both her arms, but she pulls away.

"It will be OK, Cinka."

"No, it won't. It's too dangerous now for me to be out alone at night. There are gangs of angry Italians, hooligans looking for trouble. Looking for people like me to beat up. I hear the stories—you don't. You don't have to worry about this. I do. People come back to the camp and tell us frightening things. I'm sorry for being like this." She wipes her face with her sleeve.

Antonio searches for a kleenex and hands it to her. Fuck! What do I say? I'm such an idiot. How do I keep her here? I don't want to lose her. *Cazzo!* This is fucked up.

"Please excuse me. I must go." She grabs her violin case.

"But Cinka. If I can do anything to help . . ."

"Thanks. I know. You're very kind. You're the first Italian I've met who is different. You care. You give me hope that maybe this ugliness will pass."

Walking home quickly, she thinks: I can't have a *gadjo* boyfriend. I can't bring him home and say, "Mother, meet my new boyfriend. He's Italian. But he's different." Is he really? Does he want what every boy wants, or something else? Something I want, too? What will people say, especially that witch?

He's not Romani, so what am I thinking? I can't spend time with him anyway. I need to make more money to feed my family. And it's too dangerous to hang out with him then walk home late. Forget about him. Jesus Maria! It's not fair. Other girls can have boyfriends. I'm old enough. Why can't I? *Gadjo* or not? *Cazzo!*

At home, she confronts her mother.

"I need to talk to you. Let's walk."

PART III

AGAINST DARKNESS

GREAT-GRANDFATHER: MUSSOLINI'S POPULARITY

Why was Mussolini popular at the beginning? He stepped onto the stage at just the right moment with a winning combination:

"I am a tough guy, and patriotic. I will restore Italy's greatness. Follow me."

I heard him speak. He had a way with words. He could sway crowds of people. The unthinking ones, especially. Not me!

At first, he used his experience in the socialist movement to advocate anticapitalist positions. A shrewd man he was. He spoke about workers' control of the factories, promised jobs for the unemployed, land for landless peasants. Poor people saw nothing wrong with that and cheered him on. I had my doubts.

Mussolini knew that Italy had sacrificed much in World War I. We supported the Allies and their war. Then the Allies humiliated Italy and gave nothing in return. So many had died, for what? Everyone was disgruntled and fed up with the government. Me too! The Communist and Socialist parties were divided and fighting, so Mussolini shifted to the Right, into the welcoming arms of landowners and industrialists. Like I said, a shrewd man was he.

Italy's wealthy wanted a strongman to restore domestic peace. Nationalists looked for a saviour, too. Mussolini seemed like a capable military leader. One who could lead us out of the postwar slump into a bright, shining future. No one knew it would become a nightmare. But I had my suspicions.

A violent man himself, he attracted the most brutal army veterans, the *Arditi*. Bloodthirsty wartime heroes, postwar good-for-nothings, they loved to fight and wanted action. Mussolini provided it. He formed them into his Fascist squads and armed them. They became his loyal bodyguards. With the financial and political support of the big landowners and industrialists, the Fascist movement grew more powerful. Italy's ruling class was all smiles. The Fascists started to crush the opposition like so many cockroaches underfoot.

In February 1921, an Italian anarchist newspaper said:

> Every day armed bands, the Fighting Fascisti, selected from the dregs and scum of the Italian gutters and recruited from the jails, the most savage, bloodthirsty gangsters, set fires to working men's Leagues, Circles and Chambers of Labour . . . They fight the poor at the order of the rich . . .

GREAT-UNCLE RICARDO: LIVORNO BEFORE WE WERE ARMED, 1921

What was I doing in this sleepy, pretty seaport of Livorno? Visiting a cousin, Alphonso.

How did I know the Fascists were about to attack? No one knew. It was 1921 and we didn't have our own armed defence organization, our own militia, not yet. We relied on ad hoc groups to resist the attacks of roving gangs of Fascist thugs.

Alphonso lived in the working-class neighbourhood of *Il Borgo*, where bulging tenements lined the narrow streets. He was a trade union activist on the docks.

In the middle of the day, I heard the banging of a kitchen pot. I poked my head out the window. Further down the block, more pots, creating such a din! Our midday peace now broken.

"It's the alarm! The Fascists are coming!"

Alphonso grabbed my arm yanking me out the door.

"Quick! Outside now!"

Downstairs on the street, he pulled me around a corner.

"Here, take all these bricks to the intersection over there. The others will build a barricade. It's our only hope. Our only defence to slow down the trucks transporting the Fascists."

Together we loaded a wheelbarrow full. Back and forth I ran, dumping my loads.

Other young men and women were pouring out of workshops and houses carrying furniture, building supplies, boxes. Above us, older women leaned out of kitchen windows still banging pots and pans.

I could see the whole neighbourhood mobilized like an ant colony scurrying around with bricks and stones, heaping them into larger piles in the intersections.

"We'll keep them out! We'll teach them!" Alphonso yelled.

I heard the low rumble of a truck behind me. I turned. It was full of Fascists standing in the truckbed brandishing staves. Then came the screams and curses as bricks, bottles, and stones rained down on them from the tenement roofs. My cousin and I took cover in a doorway and watched.

More screams as cauldrons of boiling hot water were emptied on the heads of the thugs from above. The truck backed up and disappeared. A victory. A cheer.

"They'll be back," Alphonso swore, "and next time it won't be so easy."

A few days later the Fascists returned and attacked a nearby union centre, the *Camera del Lavoro*. Workers from the neighbourhood surrounded the invaders, but then had to fight off the army sent to rescue the Fascists. After two days of fierce combat the Fascists captured and burned down the centre.

Two weeks later I received a hand-delivered letter from Alphonso:

We lost those battles because we had no arms. But with
our presses we kept printing leaflets and posters against
Fascism and distributing them widely across the town.

Some of the younger comrades kept the police busy by painting graffiti on the walls. "Fascists get out of Italy!" "Fascists are not true Italians," "Fascists can't read." One night, comrades attacked the Fascist Party headquarters with bombs, blowing out huge sections of the walls. Another night they attacked the Militia barracks, driving out the soldiers like cockroaches. Our resistance is ongoing. How about yours?

GREAT-UNCLE RICARDO: EARLY ANARCHIST ANTI-FASCIST OPPOSITION

Long before Mussolini took power, one of my friends, Lugo, an intellectual from Turin University who attended our anarcho-syndicalist meetings in the *taverna*, spoke about the coming Fascist counterrevolution.

He was a tall skinny guy with glasses, a beard, and bushy black hair. A likeable fellow. Always carrying a big bag of books, giving out pamphlets for us to read—or to read to those who couldn't read.

"Fascism is inevitable," he'd say in his high-pitched voice at our meetings. He'd look directly at each one of us, right in the eyes.

"The First World War aggravated all the natural class hostilities that already existed in our society. Common people were forced to endure more hardships in the name of war, while the bourgeoisie reaped the benefits and grew richer."

True enough. We all nodded.

He said, "Fascism leads to the inevitable class war between us, the proletariat, and the bourgeoisie."

We listened to his explanations. We had just lived through the great factory occupations of 1920 with six hundred thousand other workers across Italy.

"Comrades, we know that at this very moment, as we sit here and try to determine our next move for a better future for all working people, there are others who sit behind closed doors in fancier settings, sipping their brandy, smoking their cigars, and discussing how to crush our workers' movement. They need to defend themselves from us and won't hesitate to use the most violent means at their disposal."

A murmur of agreement swept the room.

"Just as we study history to learn how others battled for their emancipation, so do our oppressors, the ruling class, who study counterrevolution. It's a cat-and-mouse, life-and-death struggle between those who hold power, and we who believe we have none.

"It is repeated time and again. We must learn from it if we want to avoid the bloodshed that will come. Remember the crucifixions after the rebellion of Spartacus? The fall of the Paris Commune? Every uprising in between and since? The ruling class will respond violently. They will use others and will supply them with the means to crush our movement. We must prepare to defend ourselves."

He would then quote one of his favourite authors, Errico Malatesta: "If we do not carry on to the end, we will pay with tears of blood for the fears we now instil in the bourgeoisie."

When Lugo first talked like this, some of us wondered: "Is he exaggerating?" We soon found out.

One black night, a gang of Fascist thugs came knocking on our union hall door with iron bars and clubs. They smashed their way in. Elsewhere in the city, simultaneously, they destroyed our offices, libraries, and meeting places. They threw our books, newspapers, typewriters, and printing supplies out the windows. Beat anyone who tried to stand in their way. This was only the beginning of the backlash against our "Red Biennium" and factory occupations. In Turin, as elsewhere across Italy, we were taken by surprise.

GREAT-UNCLE RICARDO: PROPHETIC WORDS

The next morning, a workmate came rushing into the café and dropped a newspaper on Ricardo's table.

"You see this?" Carlo asked, sitting down.

FASCIST SQUADS DRIVE INTO BOLOGNA AND ATTACK CITY

HALL . . . CALL IT A "PUNITIVE EXPEDITION" AGAINST ALL
THE "RED" TOWNS AND VILLAGES.

"They want blood! People were terrified and the police did nothing. Many comrades were injured. The Fascists smashed up the union halls. They hit Trieste, Modena, Livorno, and Florence, too. The cooperative offices, leftist papers and meeting halls, all attacked by truckloads of thugs. We can't let this go unanswered. We must stop them."

Ricardo looked Carlo in the eye and asked:

"But how do we know where they will strike next? And how do we get there before them? They have trucks, army vehicles. And the army gives them weapons. What can we do?"

Carlo leaned forward, pulling Ricardo closer to him, and in a lower voice, whispered:

"We fight them. However we can. We go to every village and town and organize self-defence groups before they get there. We go to every union hall, recruit and prepare the comrades. We find them weapons. We arm ourselves and everyone at risk of attack. They leave us no choice."

"I agree. We can't turn the other cheek and hope the Blackshirts will disappear."

We had no idea of the ferocity of the attacks, the depth of the anger behind them. And the incidents worsened, the level of violence increased, while the police and the authorities stood aside, hands behind their backs, and watched—or participated, lending the Blackshirts arms and transportation, encouraging ex-officers to join and train them.

Only then did we understand fully what Lugo was warning us about. His words were prophetic. We were forced to respond to save ourselves.

THE ARDITI DEL POPOLO, THE PEOPLE'S COMMANDOS

Fifteen of us were present that lazy summer night at the first meeting in a stone farmhouse on the edge of town. We were anarchists and others on the Left. To be safe, we posted three armed guards outside, war veterans, just in case. We trusted the moon to help us, because it shone brightly, surrounded by a pale halo.

"A good luck sign," a comrade suggested.

Two comrades, building trades workers, spoke first. One had a black eye; the other wore his broken arm in a sling. Both had bad bruises and cuts to their faces.

"When we tried to talk to the Fascists, to reason with them, this was their response."

"When we tried to resist them with our bare hands, they used weapons."

Another comrade missing his front teeth stood up and added:

"They knocked these out and said next time, if I don't stop talking, they'll cut off my tongue."

"They put Lugo into the hospital. We don't know if he will survive."

"They beat me on my back and forced me to drink a bottle of castor oil. I'm still puking every day," an older anarchist said.

Her eyes burning with rage, a young woman—one of three present—said, "I was beaten and assaulted after I denounced them in the street."

The room turned stone quiet as the men tried to absorb this last bit of news, shaking their heads.

"Each of us can tell more stories like these." Gino Lucetti was speaking. "We must answer their violence with an organized response of our own. All agreed?"

Everyone grunted approval. Carlo, one of the anarchists, added:

"Whatever group we set up, it must be independent of any of our official organizations. There can be no connection at all. Agreed?"

Fourteen heads nodded. A new armed anti-Fascist umbrella group was born: the Arditi del Popolo, the People's Commandos. The days of ineffective responses were over.

It was time for many guns to answer. The AdP would speak.

Mussolini's Fascists were organized into hit squads with

a special uniform and a military hierarchy. We, the AdP, had our own form of organization, with battalions, companies, and squads, including a bicycle squad to serve as a communication link. There were ten of us in each squad and a group leader. We didn't want to wear uniforms, but some liked to wear a red rose in their buttonhole.

Our symbol was simple: an axe smashing the fasces symbol. Unlike the Fascists, we workers and peasants couldn't obtain arms permits, freely given to the Fascists without questions.

We didn't have access to police or army arsenals willingly shared with the Fascists. There was no shortage of guns or ammunition for this new anti-labour movement. We had to find our own illegal sources. We weren't bankrolled by generous industrialists and landowners.

They were gloating over their own private army of armed thugs to crush labour unions and popular unrest. We were a grassroots, working-class organization. Our base of support: poor urban workers, farm labourers, and some war veterans. The odds were unequal, but we had no choice. Resist or die.

So we organized. Quickly. All over the country. By the late summer of 1921, we numbered about 150 groups totalling twenty thousand members. But Fascism was spreading, too.

KEEPING LIVORNO CLEAN

"No Fascists welcome in the streets of Livorno!"

Hundreds of students were belting out chants, waving black and red flags and blowing whistles and horns as they marched through Livorno's Venezia district near the anarcho-syndicalist trade union office.

They had just encountered a smaller group of Fascists standing on the Marble Bridge, trying to block their path. The students overwhelmed them, beat them, and tossed a few into the canal.

"Livorno belongs to us and don't forget it!" they yelled at the floundering Fascists.

For now, yes, great-uncle Ricardo's cousin, Alphonso

thought, thanks to well-organized students and the AdP. But for how much longer?

He strolled along the seafront, enjoying the brisk breeze but watching the horizon where ominous dark clouds regrouped over the ocean, headed for land.

When the big National Congress of the Socialist Party took place in Livorno in 1921, we anarchists and our allies beat off gangs of Fascists who tried to stop it. Those were the days we showed the Fascists we were not afraid, Alphonso thought. The days we proved we could fight and defeat them on their own terms. Then came the reprisals.

BLACKSHIRTS INVADE CITY HALL

It was a glorious August morning. A cool, refreshing sea breeze swept through the streets of Livorno. Fishing boats bobbed at anchor in the port. Children played on the sidewalks. A major strike had just ended and workers reluctantly returned to their jobs. According to the bosses, there were to be no more strikes. Ever.

Then five army transport trucks, bearing dozens of armed Fascists, rumbled into town. Knives and guns flashing, the Blackshirts stormed city hall and murdered the unsuspecting leftists inside. There had been no warning. The screams could be heard in the streets below, now filled with bloodied, gun-toting Fascists looking for more victims. News spread quickly.

Alphonso was at work in a factory when a young boy came running into the shop, whispered into his ear, and ran off. Alphonso dropped his tools and ran into an adjacent shed to rally his comrades.

"They've killed many at city hall and are now looking for others. We have to stop them."

Carlo and two other men dropped their tools and quietly walked off the job.

"Hey, where you going?" the foreman barked. The men didn't reply.

"We can get them as they turn the corner."

Alphonso, Carlo, and six other men and women armed with rifles and homemade bombs were lying belly-down on a hot warehouse rooftop at the edge of town. Pigeons in a coop nearby cooed softly. Four other Arditi del Popolo members were across the street on another rooftop. A short distance from them, another six AdP cadre were settling into position on two other rooftops. A crossfire.

As the convoy of Fascist trucks came rolling up the hill, Alphonso lobbed a bomb into the first truck. Another comrade lobbed a second bomb into the final truck. The explosions rocked the trucks, men shouting and screaming. The AdP opened fire from above.

It was a short, quick attack. The anarchists succeeded in killing several Fascists, but lost three of their own. It was the first of many armed skirmishes.

Later, as the ocean welcomed another flaming sunset and mothers tucked their young into bed, Livorno was mourning too many dead. Church bells rang. Families swore vengeance. In soft voices and dark corners, groups of young men and women talked about joining the AdP.

A LIVORNO SURPRISE

Dusk, and the sky above the ocean was overcast, heavy with low-lying grey clouds, glowing orange and red on their bellies, as if the disappearing sun had left them burning.

The wind ruffled the leaves of the tall palm and cypress trees outside the open windows. We were finishing our fish stew in Santino's little house beside the Ligurian sea on the edge of town, and emptying the last bottle of wine.

Out there on the waves, where gulls still paddled and fished, there was no talk of how to best eliminate the Fascists. Inside, around the table, we were nine anarchists from Livorno, Carrara and Piombino comparing notes and planning joint actions. It was a rare regional gathering of comrades from the AdP.

"We've stockpiled machine-guns, submachine guns, and even a piece of small-calibre artillery. It's well hidden."

"*Cazzo!* How did you manage that? From the armoury?"

"One night, after a few bombs near the barracks, we were ready."

"You were either very drunk or incredibly courageous."

"Well, we needed it more than them, yes?"

The men laughed.

"We have our eyes on the barracks here in Livorno, but so far no luck penetrating it. We're too busy organizing aid to anti-Fascist prisoners. We have lost many comrades rotting in those Fascist 'hotels.'"

"In Carrara, we meet high in the mountains in safe houses. They watch us too closely in the mines."

"For us in Piombino, we've had to kill so many Fascists who infiltrated our groups, it's becoming a weekly ritual. Another pig, another Fascist, one after the other."

A sharp-pitched whistle came from outside. Santino swore.

"Hurry! We must scatter! You two—up that ladder, onto the roof. Sergio will show you the way. Keep low and to the back. You three—down those stairs and into the cave. The tunnel is behind the barrel that I showed you. Keep going to the end. Another comrade is waiting there beside his boat. He'll take care of you. Hurry!"

It wasn't a moment too soon. A Fascist patrol with a truckload of soldiers braked outside Santino's house and the soldiers surrounded it, guns ready. Santino and his three remaining friends looked at each other and shrugged. Prison, torture, endless time in a cell—or fight and risk death now?

AFTER THE RAID

The Cararra anarchist lay on his bed in the Livorno safe house staring at the ceiling. There was a knock on the door: two short, followed by two long knocks. He got up and opened it. A heavyset fisherman, a comrade, walked in.

"We lost three men yesterday. We think we killed about four or five of theirs."

"Alphonso?"

"Dead."

"Anyone arrested?"

"Two comrades."

"And the rest?"

"Hiding on boats and in other houses for now. We want to get them away by tonight. More soldiers are coming. You should leave also."

"But we haven't finished our business!"

"It can wait. We don't want to lose any more lives. And it's dangerous for us, too, if we have to hide so many at once."

"We will win this, you know. We must."

"For now I will be happy if no one else is killed. It's difficult enough to lose friends to the sea, to disease, to old age. But to die at the hands of a Fascist thug?"

AND IF THE FASCISTS COME AT NIGHT?

Rafaele and Massimo Discordia finished eating their late dinner of soup and pasta at a nearby *trattoria*, and returned to their tiny room to prepare for bed. It had been another exhausting day at work followed by a tense union meeting.

Massimo bathed at the washbasin, then his brother. Each was silent. All day their workmates had talked furtively about the increasing strength of the Fascists in power.

In Milan as elsewhere in Italy it was the same. Fascist reprisals against union militants were more common, from beatings in the streets to being sacked on the spot at work. The workplace had its own ever-present mechanical dangers, but now, other concerns were equally worrisome.

"I didn't want to say so at the meeting," Massimo said, drying himself off with a towel, "but I am really frightened. They have spies everywhere—in the plant, in the bosses' offices, on the street. I have no idea when they will strike next or how."

"My brother, I'm scared too. We are marked targets. It's only a matter of time. Then what?"

Rafaele crawled into the shared bed. The springs protested and the mattress sagged, but this shabby, cold room with one bed was all they could afford. Wages had been cut and uncertainty reigned at work.

Massimo lay in the opposite direction, arms folded behind his head, looking up at the ceiling and the one bare lightbulb.

"There are Fascist informers around every corner with the biggest of ears that catch even a whisper of dissent. I find myself holding back now when I speak at meetings."

"Me, too, Massimo, but it's too late. The question is not if they will come for us, but when."

"A beating in the street, if we stand together, we might have a chance. But if we're caught alone, they can kill us off one by one."

"They prefer to haul people in, to beat them out of sight in prison, torture them, extract information, then murder them. This is what I'm hearing."

"My brother, what are we going to do? We can't hide."

"We hold onto our jobs as long as possible, save a bit of money, and prepare to flee like the others. Exile or the mountains. It's our only hope. Our family will help."

Massimo raised his head to look directly at his brother: "And if the Fascists come here at night?"

"My gun is under my pillow. Where's yours?"

"I'm still frightened."

WE LOOK DIFFERENT, SO WHAT?

Antonio tapes a hand-scrawled sign to the outer door: *Back in 30 minutes.* Then he and Cinka undress and lie naked, side by side on the couch in the recording studio.

Their legs intertwine, arms wrap around each other, eyes lock. She traces his face ever so lightly with her fingers. He kisses her repeatedly as his hands explore her entire body. She twitches at his first touches, then relaxes. She strokes him, grips him, and he presses closer into her. They roll together, sliding slowly off the couch on a blanket. She crouches above him, arms pinning him down. Her long hair dangles in his face as she positions herself just so. He pulls her down, she moans. They lip-lock, their bodies lock, and the world stands still.

Twenty minutes later, they are both panting on their backs on the floor.

"You are handsome and angelic. Your eyes are happy and sad. Your lips are like a ripe fig. I could eat you for breakfast, Antonio." She whispers: "Lunch and dinner, too."

"And then you would have indigestion and many bones to throw away."

They kiss and make love again. And then again as thirty minutes turns into more than an hour.

A week before, they had agreed after much discussion that they would become surreptitious lovers.

"Only during the day, you understand?" Cinka insisted.

"Sure, whatever you say." Antonio nodded vigorously, his cock almost bursting out of his jeans.

"Only between the time I need to busk and your own paying jobs. Not every day, either. And it must remain a secret—for now. Understand?"

"Oh yes, absolutely, completely, I swear," Antonio was all smiles. He could handle restrictions, rules, whatever she wanted. He would obey. Anything to keep her.

The "not every day" restriction soon became the obvious challenge. Once they started, they couldn't keep their hands off each other, but she insisted. He did his best to respect the agreement.

Now, as she stood and dressed, Antonio noticed a tear falling.

"Why, sweetheart?" He pulled her close, lifting her blouse and kissing her stomach. She sighed, looked down at him, caressed his hair and tried to smile again.

"Because I can't forget. You and I share a love that many of your people would never approve of. Nor mine."

"What are you talking about?"

"I'm sorry. It's been so long. So long since I felt comfortable, secure this way, just being with you. And it reminds me: you are special and unlike the others." More tears fall.

"Darling, what's wrong?"

Cinka leans on his shoulder then slides onto the couch.

"We look different, that's what. Your people have been brainwashed to hate us. To feel threatened by us. And you ask what's wrong? *Cazzo!*"

"Cinka, I understand, but . . . I love you so much."

"Antonio, that's not the point!" She pulls away from him. "That's not what we're talking about." She stands up, facing him.

"In Romania, people would give us food laced with rat poison! Poison! In Switzerland, they gave a box of toys to Romani children, booby-trapped with a bomb. And everywhere I see the graffiti: *Get out, Gypsies!*

"Do you know how it feels to walk around in fear because you are feared? To fear people who smile and offer gifts? Not to trust anyone, anywhere, who appears to be nice?

"Now I have to walk back to the camp. Every time I walk the streets, day or night, I have to remember: be careful. I can call no place home. There is nowhere I belong, nowhere I can feel safe. I am an outcast, from an entire race of outcasts. Everywhere I go, I am a stranger."

Antonio covers his mouth with his hand, looks at her, and exhales. This is not going to be easy.

After she leaves, he opens a beer, paces the studio, then sits down and strums his guitar. *What can I do? Nothing. What does she want me to do? Beats me. What am I getting into? Shit if I know. It's not like getting laid by a local girl. It's fucking challenging. Complicated. She's special in so many ways. It's more serious for her. Me, too. But what do I know about Gypsies? I mean Roma. I'm such a moron.*

Now I'm totally hooked on her and I think it's mutual. She's taking a huge risk opening herself up to me, allowing me into her life, despite the danger. And what can I do about her situation? Fuck if I know.

GREAT-GRANDFATHER: ANTONIO
Let me tell you about one of my great, great, great nephews, Antonio Discordia. He was born in the small village of

Miglianico near Chieti. When he was thirteen years old, he joined a punk rock band playing drums. By fourteen, he had read the complete works of Dante. At fifteen, he fell in love with a girl who lived across the street. He smoked his first—what do you call it, a marijuana cigarette?—at sixteen. He lost his virginity at seventeen. When he turned eighteen, he left home to study philosophy. By nineteen, he had his heart broken three times. I kept track.

At twenty, he travelled to America on a student exchange program. He was arrested for possession of one marijuana cigarette and speeding. He returned to Italy a year later, vowing never to visit America again. A smart boy.

At twenty-two, he discovered the joys of cooking. A late bloomer. He proposed to the same girl who lived across the street, but she said it would be better if they waited. A smart girl. He grew tired of waiting and at twenty-six fell in love with a long-haired, bass-playing, punk rock girl called Charlie. She had multiple piercings all over her body—I peeked—bright colourful tattoos of Greek goddesses on both arms, and always wore black skirts and combat boots. Antonio learned Japanese and moved to Japan for one year.

He returned to Italy vowing to marry Charlie. But Charlie told him she was no longer a woman; she was now a he. Antonio was slightly confused. Then he met Cinka. With her, he is completely himself, the happiest I have ever seen him. How I wish them luck. How they are going to need it!

ONE NOSY OLD WOMAN

One particular elder in Cinka's refugee camp had nothing better to do than spy on everyone else. A large woman with thick overhanging eyebrows, a bulbous nose and dishevelled grey hair, she sat on a box outside her hut every day from morning to night, leaning on her cane, spitting into the dust, and paying attention.

Who's going where, with whom, at what times? What are they wearing or carrying? Are they smiling or sad? Troubled or carefree? And why?

She tried to overhear all conversations, imagine everything else, then opened and maintained files in her mind on everyone. She paid special attention to the young women, married or single, for their own sakes of course, since they never knew better. She was extra-vigilant around the head-turning Cinka. She had her reasons.

By asking a few questions, she discovered that this one had been promised to a certain young man back in Romania. A man related to the cousin of the nephew of a friend of hers. Cinka was already a taken woman? Or so it seemed. But recently, she noticed Cinka walking through the camp smiling all the time with that certain, I'm-in-love kind of haze. But who could it be?

The old woman sent a young spy to follow her. The spy reported back. The camp gossip slapped her thigh and congratulated herself. Then she started to spread the poison. First one neighbour, then another:

"That Cinka girl has been raped. By an Italian. Now she is lovers with him. You know she was promised to a young man in her home village? I have his name. We must tell him. This is outrageous. An injustice. We must act."

THE ROOSTER STORY

It's a lazy, visit the zoo at the *Villa Borghesi* kind of afternoon.

Cinka and Antonio walk in step, wear matching smiles and hold hands and waists the way new lovers do. They take turns pecking each other's cheeks, then sit on an ornate bench to share ice cream cones.

In the distance a rooster crows. Cinka tugs Antonio's sleeve.

"My grandmother once told me a story:

"Hundreds of years ago, the Turks wanted to destroy our people by killing off all Romani children. They went door to door to carry out the massacre. To protect her two children, a Romani mother killed a rooster and spread the blood on the door of her house. The Turkish soldiers came by, saw the blood on the door and thought that other soldiers had already been there and slaughtered the children. They left. The children in that house were saved. Ever since, we give thanks and celebrate this as the Day of the Rooster, another day that we have survived. One more day of life. Wherever we are, even here in Italy."

She kisses Antonio long and hard.

"I give thanks for you. My red-headed rooster."

MAKING LOVE IN THE *VILLA BORGHESE*

Cinka and Antonio make love whenever and wherever they can, as often as humanly possible for two desperately amorous souls living with a curfew and an agreement that demands ingenuity and flexibility.

Unlike other couples, they don't have the luxury of uninterrupted nights together. She always has to return to her family, with enough time to get home safely. So when the band's practice studio couch is unavailable, weather permitting, they turn the lush 148-acre gardens of Rome's elegant *Villa Borghese* into their open-air *boudoir*.

Over the months, Antonio and Cinka's passion grew, as did their resourcefulness. Like thousands of Romans before them, they improvised secret garden love beds: beneath the canopies of compliant, tell-no-tales trees; in the shadows of sculpted, ornamental bushes; between rows of immaculately trimmed hedges—wherever they could find enough privacy, Antonio would spread his jacket or a blanket.

In silence they love each other, quickly, breathlessly. Only once are they interrupted.

Antonio is about to ejaculate when Cinka taps his shoulder hard, points, and whispers, "Look!"

Breathing heavily, Antonio turns his head, laughs, and collapses into her arms. A pair of gawking geese honk and wander off.

A JOURNALIST VISITS A REFUGEE CAMP

"Hi. I'm Marek, the journalist."

Antonio extends a hand. The lanky, bearded journalist

with long hair and glasses standing outside the music studio shakes it. He has a camera slung over one shoulder.

"I'm here to write some stories about Romani refugees. My younger brother is a big fan of your music and suggested I contact you guys. I heard from one of your bandmates, Massimaxo, that you have connections and could possibly get me into a camp?"

"Possibly."

A few days later, Antonio gives the journalist directions. Marek heads for the camp.

MAREK

I step off the tram at the Nomentana train stop and walk quickly along *Via Etopia*. Antonio said to meet a friend of a friend, a doctor, at 9 AM. I'm running late. A bus will be too slow. I hop into a cab and direct the driver. He looks over his shoulder and repeats the address:

"*Via del Baiardo*, 50, *a Tor di Quinto*?"

Racing along *Via Olimpico*, we cross the *Tor di Quinto* bridge over the Tiber River. The driver eases the cab off the overpass, turns right and hits a small dusty gravel road. He slows down as we enter a no-man's-land of scraggly trees, shrubs, and dry grass.

Looking into the rear view mirror, he asks, "You're sure?"

I look around, hesitating, then see the ramshackle collection of huts behind a wire fence.

"I'm sure, this is it. I get off here."

The driver gives me a final quizzical look.

They say two hundred families, over a thousand people, live in this Romani refugee camp. I walk through a large opening in the fence and follow a dusty, potholed roadway. Laughing children run around playing, looking at me wide-eyed, while mothers hanging laundry stop to stare. Older people sitting outside small huts eye me suspiciously.

Antonio said this was a good opportunity, because a human rights group, *Gruppo EveryOne*, was coming here today from Milan, to stage a press conference and fact-finding tour.

A mutual friend, a Romni doctor, also from Milano, would guide me and other visitors around the camp.

"She won a scholarship and studied for ten years at the University of Rome, but actually grew up in this camp," Antonio had said.

The stunning dark-haired woman in the white lab jacket flashes a huge smile and extends her hand as she greets me.

"You must be Marek? Welcome. I'm Selena."

We join a gaggle of fifteen other journalists and press photographers surrounding a small group of Romani refugees sitting under a tree. They're telling their stories one at a time to a visiting member of the European Parliament, a Romni herself. She listens attentively. The photographers jostle for positions and keep clicking. In the background, other camp members sit silently in front of their doors and watch.

A young girl walks by carrying her baby sister on her hip. The cameramen all turn in unison to photograph her. Then a cherubic pair of girls no older than five saunters by, all curious, and plop themselves into a chair. Again, the photographers turn together, switch lenses and cameras, and start shooting. It's photo-op heaven, but I abstain and wonder how many photos of cute refugee children the magazines and dailies will take.

A tall, thin, shy girl brings out a coffee tray laden with teacups and saucers. An older Romni smiles and motions for me to sit at a table covered with a plastic blue cloth under the tree. The girl pours coffee and hands it to me. The normally bucolic electronic symphony of Italian summertime cicadas is now dominated by a disturbing nonstop "thump-thump" of cars roaring across the overpass above, a reminder of the "other" world out there. Here I notice all is eerily peaceful.

Outside the wire fence, cyclists ride by leisurely on the bike path staring at the refugees within. Still more unwelcome onlookers manoeuvre carefully along the gravel road outside the fence in shiny new cars, watching the inhabitants. No doubt: this is a human zoo, a prison, a ghetto, where people could easily be rounded up and loaded onto cattle cars.

I tag along with the walking tour led by the doctor. First stop: a sad, low home right under the overpass. It's a ramshackle shack of scrap wood and metal with a corrugated plastic roof, cobbled together by one of the original campers who came here long ago thinking it was just temporary. He's an older man, barrel-chested with a gold chain showing through his unbuttoned shirt. He sits on a folding chair, arms crossed over his chest while his wife fries red peppers on an outdoor stove and glances at us over her shoulder.

"Thirty years I've lived in this camp, finding work here and there. Never anything steady. And now, nothing. Look around. We live like animals. We have no choice."

He gestures toward the children playing on a pile of cast-off broken furniture under the overpass.

"This is our life. The police drive by constantly just to intimidate us. We do no wrong. We only try to survive."

Makeshift but tidy little houses built of scrounged wood and metal are scattered haphazardly around the camp on the dry, barren, rubble-strewn soil. It's a wasteland of untended patches of dirt and gravel, and piles of refuse—but around each house, the attempted landscaping and orderliness is apparent.

Women sweep outside their doors, tidying little yards, washing windows and walls. Small flower or herb gardens surround the homes. Rare paint helps to brighten up the walls. Inside, some floors are tiled. A few terraces belonging to the more established inhabitants have poured and polished concrete floors. Under a tree, an old mattress is covered with an even older carpet.

Overall, there are few trees to offer shade. Everywhere I see broken, repaired, useable furniture salvaged from the garbage. A man gives a haircut outside his hut. A woman cooks on a stove. A few houses actually fly the Italian flag high on poles. Men repair a roof, hammers busy. Boys play soccer. Women and children line up at the communal water station, filling buckets and containers with drinking, cooking, and cleaning water to lug back to their homes.

Nearby, a line of bright blue plastic outhouses stands starkly against the wire fence. A minimal concession from the authorities.

This camp sits within Rome's city borders, a short drive from pricy condos and shopping malls, yet these people live in absolute, abject poverty.

We walk down a pot-holed gravel road toward a small, neat, bright-yellow home sitting under some trees. Unlike the others, this one looks solid. A clothesline sags with today's wash. A tall thin girl hangs clothes on a second line as her mother hand washes more in a large plastic tub.

The mother dries her hands and smiles. In front of the house, under cover of an overhanging roof, I spot a small table covered with a crisp white tablecloth. A shrine. On it, a bouquet of fresh flowers, a lit candle, a large bottle of Peroni beer, and a framed photo of her late husband—the father of her four children. All were born in Italy.

The mother invites the doctor and a few of us to sit down at a large homemade picnic table under a tree. Her children surround us and are silent. Her face is drawn as she tells her story.

"He died last month, in the hospital. They couldn't tell me why. He was a carpenter. Now what do I do?"

What can we do but thank her and walk on?

Outside the next house, a tired, worn, quite thin woman cries.

"In Romania," she says, "I cleaned hospitals for very little money. Our rent each month for two rooms was almost three times my salary. I have two children. When they were old enough to work, they had to quit school so we could have money for food. But we couldn't earn enough. So we came here. And now? Nothing. We will return to Romania. I'd rather die in my home country than far away."

She introduces us to Viktor and Elena, two visiting Romanians. They resemble the living dead, their faces drained of all life. He speaks Italian, Romanian, Polish, and does manual labour. So does his wife. But they have no work. They live in a hut under a bridge in Pisa. During a tragic fire in Livorno set by Fascists, they lost one of three children.

We walk on.

Outside another hut, an elderly survivor of the Auschwitz concentration camp—tattoo still visible on his arm—is deep in conversation with Rebecca, a twelve-year-old Romni artist. He is part of the human rights group delegation. She proudly shows him her drawings, including artwork that won a UNICEF prize as poster material for their children's rights campaign. Her work depicts the persecution of the Roma in Italy. One graphic drawing shows her parents in tears, their makeshift shelter just destroyed by the police. She tells the older man how she tried to intervene physically when the police were beating her father in the streets of Milan. The Auschwitz survivor dabs away a tear.

In this camp, the residents come from Croatia, Macedonia, and Romania. Their stories, one after the other, repeat the same message:

"This is not working. We cannot find work. The government does not want to help us. The police harass us. What do we do? Where do we go?"

No one has answers.

On the covered terrace outside Selena's home, her mother sits in a plastic chair and watches the tour pass by. Selena, a former resident of this camp, invites me inside to show me her artwork. Her paintings are large watercolours, on paper, in a basic, simple, symbolist style. Powerful images of arms and hands reach out and are handcuffed. Bodies are chained together. Fires engulf homes.

"Last winter after a police raid when they beat our people in the camp, arrested them, then razed every home to the ground, I was so angry and tired of crying, but I had nowhere to turn. I pulled out my paints and for five days all I did was paint. I didn't want to eat. I didn't want to talk to anyone. I didn't want to go outside. I felt violated by the raid. We all did. I had no words to express my sorrow and anger. So I painted. One painting each day."

TWO GIRLS ON A TRAIN

"Those two Gypsies! They stole my wallet!"

The man pointing the finger and scowling was a stylishly dressed Italian businessman in his thirties, carrying an expensive leather satchel over his shoulder.

The train stopped at a station and four young male police officers boarded. Two Romani girls, no older than thirteen and fourteen, were cowering in corner seats. They were penned in by a handful of older, jeering Italian teenage boys.

"OK, you guys get out. Everyone else off this car except for you, sir," the officer in charge said. Once the car had emptied, the officers questioned, then started to pat search both young girls. They found nothing, so ordered each terrified girl to strip naked in front of them. The girls pleaded and cried, but there was no sympathy. Nor was there a wallet.

ANTONIO OVERHEARS

Antonio is waiting on a bench in a park for Cinka. He watches a group of Italian boys kick around a ball. One yells at another jokingly, "You play like a Gypsy!"

The other replies, "Up yours! Your family must be Gypsies."

"You're still a fucking Gypsy!"

And Antonio remembers how in his adolescence, he and his friends would insult each other using the same words. *Cazzo!* he thinks, were we stupid or what?

"Hey guys!" he yells. "Yes, you!" The teens look at him.

"Can't you come up with another word besides Gypsy?"

BETROTHED TO A ROMANI MAN

"Who told you this? You're sure it's Cinka? Positive?" Luca, a chain-smoking, tattooed young Romani man with a shaved head and a large bushy moustache slams down the phone in the bar and storms out the door. Someone had said:

"Call your cousin in Rome. It's important."

He sits on a bench hunched over and stares at the potholes in the main road of the Bukovina village. He exhales and sees his breath in the cold mountain air. He spits and crosses his arms. "Shit! What is she thinking? She's making a fool of me."

A lone, creaking horse-driven cart rolling on old car tires passes by. It carries honking geese inside two wire cages. The sad, calf-faced driver looks at Luca.

"Fuck you!" Luca yells and scowls. The cart crosses an ancient narrow bridge that spans a noisy stream.

Luca is twenty-two, the same age as Cinka. When they were both fourteen, Cinka had been "promised" to him by his parents. Everyone knew. She was destined to be his wife. It was the agreement. The way of their people, as old as their people. He waited for her to return. She was supposed to work in Rome, save some money, and move back. She had been gone for years. He was almost on the verge of forgetting about her, writing her off—until the phone call.

And now she is seeing a *gadjo*? It's embarrassing. Why would his relatives lie to him?

"Impossible! How could this happen?"

He kicks over the bench and walks across the gravel road to the edge of a sloping meadow. A peaceful green valley dotted with small houses and a white church lies below. Nearby, a few sheep graze.

With the toe of his boot he dislodges a rock and throws it at the sheep. Then another. And another. They protest loudly and scatter. He returns to the bar and drinks himself into a screaming rage before he passes out. Someone loads him onto a creaking cart and takes him home.

HOTHEAD COUSIN

Luca's cousin, Nicu, aka "Tiny," is twenty-three years old, tall, and dangerously obese. Since moving to Rome two years ago, his Big Mac addiction has gotten out of control.

Hence, the more comfortable American gangster rapper look with oversized T-shirts and baggy pants, bright sneakers, exaggerated gold neck chains, shades that hide his tiny eyes and a ball cap.

Among the refugees, Tiny is known for his short temper and penchant for fights. People avoid him.

Both his parents were killed by Romanians. A crime of hate. A village mob set fire to their house, then as the parents ran out, murdered them with axes. The culprits were never charged. Tiny vowed to avenge their deaths. He's promised it will be an act of mayhem.

Now he heads a gang that pulls off small jobs outside his refugee camp: petty drug dealing, finding and selling everything from car parts to whatever falls off the back of a delivery truck.

But there's a price: he pays off a local Mafia crime boss. He also lends money. And for a fee of special favours, he offers protection to other Roma. Into his circle he recruits teen boys eager to reap the rewards.

Nicu lives comfortably enough by himself in a small trailer in the camp and has a car. He also has a small library of books that he lends out to his gang members. Russian classics by Tolstoy, Dostoyevsky, Gogol.

"Read this," he orders one teen boy and another, "then tell me what you learned from it."

"Luca," he says to his cousin over his cell phone, "I can take care of this for you. Fix it. Nothing messy . . . Why not? . . . Save you the trip. It's a long way to come for a girl . . . So what if she was promised to you . . . Listen, she's not worth it. She's slept with a *gadjo*. Leave it to me, OK? . . . Come on! Be smart! . . . No? OK, I won't do anything. I'll wait until you get here. I'm sending you some cash for the bus. Don't drink it up."

GRANDFATHER'S BEAR STORY

When Rafaele was a child visiting his grandfather in the ancestral home in Ripa, he looked forward to a prebedtime ritual. Grandfather would light his pipe, sit in a rocker in front of the kitchen fireplace, and take the boy on his knee. Then he would tell him the most incredible true stories. Like the one his own grandfather had told him about the bear and the boar.

"As a young man, your great-grandfather used to hunt the Abruzzo chamois to help feed the family. One day, in the woods, high up in the *Gran Sasso-Laga* Mountains where golden eagles and golden owls fly, he spotted bear tracks. This was when the big Marsican brown bear roamed far and wide in Abruzzo.

"He followed the bear's tracks for a kilometre or so, then spotted him beside a mountain meadow. This bear was old with a grey snout. Great-grandfather slowly raised his rifle to shoot. But at that very moment, he heard a terrible noise, like the roar of a monster. He turned to see a huge wild boar grunting and charging him from behind. The boar had two sharp tusks. One was broken and shorter than the other. By this time, the bear had spotted Great-grandfather, and he too let out a roar and charged him.

"Frightened out of his wits, Great-grandfather ran faster than he had ever run before, leaping over rocks and fallen trees, and somehow escaped uninjured and alive.

"One week later, Great-grandfather decided to try his luck again and returned to the mountains. This time, he spotted the trail of a wild boar. He followed it and found the very boar that had charged him, with the one broken tusk, happily wallowing in the mud in a bog beside a lake. Ever so quietly, he raised his rifle to shoot.

"But once again, he heard a loud roar and a crashing through the trees. This time, to his horror, he saw the same old big brown bear with the grey snout charging straight for him. He had no time to shoot, but again, ran for his life all the way home, losing his rifle along the way.

"Great-grandfather told this amazing story to one of his neighbours, who kept nodding all the time until the end, and then revealed to Great-grandfather a long-held secret which he had never told anyone before.

"His father, too, was once interrupted in the middle of a hunt. First, by a huge wild boar with one tusk shorter than the other, protecting a bear; then by a big old bear with a grey snout, coming to defend the boar. And his father's father had told him the same story, once a long time ago, saying that he had never told anyone else this story either."

"But Grandfather," Rafaele asked, "how could it be the same bear and the same boar all these years?"

"My little one," Grandfather replied, "the mountain is the same mountain all these years. The rocks are the same rocks. The oldest trees, the same. The water in the lakes, streams and falls, the same. Why not the same bear, the same boar?"

NEWS, 2008, Verona: A 29-year-old Jewish man of Romanian descent dies after a beating by a neo-Nazi gang, the Veneto Skinhead Front . . .
Napoli: A refugee hut set on fire by a gang of racists. Thirteen Roma, including children and babies, suffer burns and almost perish . . .
Napoli: A six-year-old Romani boy attacked by a "street patrol" of Italians, slapped, insulted and thrust under a public fountain . . .

ROME, NEO-FASCIST CENTRE

Behind the high iron fence looming ominously in the rain, Rafaele sees the one-story, fortified, heavily graffitied neo-Fascist social centre—Rome's newest.

Anarchists and others on the Left have to fight to have any space for their own use, he thinks, but here, a whole city block owned by some wealthy right-wing asshole is given to Nazi-skin goons to plan their dirty work.

He circles the block in his car to get a good look at the men coming and going into the building: racist skinheads and others, young and old, arms around each other, laughing, some carrying boxes or suitcases. Here, they plot their attacks on the Roma, gays, lesbians, and other minority groups. Here, the fuckers drink, sing, chant, and slap one another on the back to fuel their rage and give them courage to mindlessly attack the innocent in the street. Who funds them? The owner of IKEA? Fiat? Peroni?

If only I had a large Molotov—or better, a bulldozer—I'd raze this fucker to the ground.

These fuckheads are the poisoned tip of the arrow pointed at all of us. They're the shit in the water, the germs in the air, the smog above. Rafaele rolls down the window and spits in their direction. If we don't stop them now, who will, and when?

GREAT-GRANDFATHER: AN ASSASSIN?

An assassin can be an ordinary man, or an ordinary woman. This we know. A would-be anarchist assassin is something else.

In the bourgeois press that fuelled the historical popular imagination—yes, even all the way back to my time—anarchist assassins were supposed to resemble the caricature: beard, long black cape, black hat, crazed look on the face and bowling ball-sized bomb in hand.

Few would-be assassins ever looked like this. Certainly not most anarchists. And history's most effective killers wore fancy robes and crowns, or funny feathered hats and rows of shiny medals that decorated their uniforms.

Today's murderous presidents and prime ministers wear only the finest Italian tailored suits when they sign on the dotted lines that send men off to war. Other killers wear embroidered robes when they spout the religious mumbo-jumbo that misleads believers to mass murder . . .

Then there are the common people who sometimes get so fed up that they either daydream about it or act. We look like everyone.

GINO LUCETTI, 1926

It's a beautiful, sunny, end-of-summer morning. Not too hot and not a cloud in sight. A tall young man with fine features strolls lazily through *Piazza Venezia* in the centre of Rome. He wears a slightly rumpled brown suit; he's clean-shaven and handsome, slender with intense blue eyes, calm and composed. A ladies' man is what his comrades call him. Around him the *piazza* is alive with men and women hurrying to work. But today he can take his time, stop to smell the flowers.

Gino Lucetti, twenty-six years old, born in 1900 in Carrara; a marble worker, anarchist, and anti-Fascist, who has returned from living in exile, is about to enter the annals of history. Consciously.

He crosses the street, then walks in the shadow of the grand, fifteenth-century *Palazzo Venezia*. He pauses not far from the first floor balcony where Benito Mussolini, the world's first Fascist dictator, gives his most important speeches. Gino spits on the sidewalk and thinks, *Ha! It would be so easy to toss the bomb from here*. His right hand moves ever so slightly with a flick of his wrist. *Poof! Boom!* He clenches his teeth and smiles. But this is not the plan.

He keeps strolling. Ever vigilant, but with a slight swagger and his head held high, he whistles a popular tune and passes right under the balcony, observing the two armed guards at the entrance chatting on his left, the two attack dogs and their handlers, and the three army transport trucks parked in front. A little further along, he stops to light a cigarette. He leans against a wall and waits.

Soon enough, *Il Duce's* unmistakeable big black limousine turns the corner and comes rolling by. People cheer. Gino's heart quickens, his eyes grow wide, and he tries not to glare as he follows the progress of the car.

"Another day, *Il Duce*, another day," he mutters to himself. This very ordinary-looking man drops his cigarette and grinds it out with his shoe.

Alone, back in his tiny rented room on *Via Novara*, shirt sleeves rolled up, he sits by the open window, smoking, listening to the sounds of the street. He peers out. A newspaper boy is hawking papers. Two young lovers are quarrelling. Street workers are hammering, shovelling, and whistling as they rearrange the sidewalk. The rattle of the streetcars dominates. Rome enchants and scares him, seduces and repels him. So unlike the peaceful charm of Carrara, his small hometown in the mountains.

As he reviews the events of the past months, a blur of intense mixed emotions and unwavering resolve compete for his attention. He tries to keep everything in perspective. Have all his years of dedicated anarchist activity inevitably led to this final act? This enormous personal risk? This ultimate, logical, and necessary conclusion to a painful chapter of Italian history?

His heartbeat quickens and for the first time since he was a small boy, he feels alone and frightened. But there is no need, he assures himself. Dozens of people know what he is about to do, including some of Italy's most respected anarchists. He has their tacit, unwavering support, even if they are not present in this room with him.

He retraces his years in the south of France, the countless, heated, endless debates with other anti-Fascist comrades in exile. He remembers the final unanimous decision the group took in an isolated farmhouse, and how he leapt up at the table, the first to volunteer. It was a spontaneous gesture. He felt compelled in a way he had never felt before. And now he has no regrets, just a burning passion to see justice done.

He smashes his fist on the window ledge.

"I will not fail. *Il Duce* will pay."

He flicks his cigarette stub out the window and watches it spin in midair.

In France, anarchists and everyone else had agreed: *Il Duce* had to be eliminated. And the time is now. This is not to be another "propaganda by the deed" to inspire the masses. It is an obvious necessity, an act of humanity. Thousands have already been terrorized, arrested, imprisoned, tortured, beaten, and killed by Fascist Blackshirts in *Il Duce's* name. Thousands more will die unless someone stops him and his murderous machine. Gino will do it.

He has convinced himself that it is no different than volunteering to distribute flyers for a meeting, or putting up posters for a demonstration or clearing away the chairs in a hall.

The job has to be done, and Gino has never avoided the tasks necessary to build a better world. Doesn't every gesture, however small, however daunting, however menial, repetitive, or backbreaking, bring everyone closer to the final goal? Doesn't everyone have to step forward when duty calls, regardless of the risks, before anything can change?

He furrows his brows, purses and licks his lips, as he contemplates the perplexities now before him. Was it courage that propelled him into this abyss of longing for a better future? Or a pure and simple wish to mete out the revenge of the people, to redress a colossal, unending wrong that the masters have unleashed to protect their interests? Gino knows that their guard dog, Mussolini, has his supporters, yes, even among the working class—deluded, confused, ignorant people looking for an easy answer to Italy's economic and political woes; a saviour, a "strong man" to make things right . . .

He shakes his head. He walks to the metal washbasin. Looking in the mirror, he runs his finger over the scar in his neck. A memento from a Fascist bullet acquired during a bar fight in Milano three years ago. How could he ever forget? What had once been a friendly anarchist bar where comrades would meet after work, changed the moment local Fascists decided to move in and "get rid of the scum."

It was another one of Mussolini's "solutions." Eliminate the opposition and no one will ever complain again about working conditions, cost of living, human rights, freedom. One night, a heated argument broke out in the bar. Gino knew as well as anyone what could be the outcome.

"Fascists like to talk. How they boast. But when they don't make sense, when they are losing an argument, they use the club, the knife, the gun."

A particularly stupid Fascist was losing an argument with Gino, and in an explosion of anger, pulled out a gun. Gino grabbed a chair and smashed it in the Fascist's face, then fled for his life.

Outside on the street, he fired from his own gun as he ran, but took a shot to the neck. Comrades had to smuggle him onto a ship for France to find a doctor who would remove the bullet. Doctors in Italy were too afraid of Fascist reprisals. And who could blame them? He curses out loud, *"Cazzo!"*

Since the snivelling reformists, the socialist cowards and traitors signed the "Pact of Conciliation" with the Fascists in 1921, no one in this country was safe.

And the communists? Ha! They didn't join us to fight the Fascists back then, when we could have built a popular movement of armed resistance across Italy. Why? Because they refused to work with us anarchists. Now today they, too, are dead, exiled or in prison camps with us. What can they say? "Oops, sorry, we were wrong"?

Stupido!

Scowling, Gino makes a "fuck you" arm gesture in the mirror and turns away. He rearranges the window curtains to let in more light and starts pacing in the cramped room. If he could, he would throw the bomb right now and get it over with.

Steady, Gino, steady! he tells himself. Wait for the right moment. And the whole world will rotate forward. Into the light again.

THE MOMENT OF TRUTH

Sunrise, September 11, 1926, and Gino is wide awake. He washes his face, dresses, combs his hair, and makes his bed. Then he slips the dagger into his boot, shoves the pistol into his waistband, and carefully pockets the two bombs—leftover grenades from his World War I days, saved for a special occasion like this. He also grabs a handful of extra bullets, "just in case."

Downstairs, on the corner of *Via Reggio Emiliano*, inside the bright yellow café, he nods "good morning" to the bald man behind the counter. He sips his morning espresso with his back against the wall where he can watch everyone, hoping no one notices his shaking hands.

Then his heart skips a beat as two *carabinieri* poke their heads into the café. He puts down his coffee. One hand slowly reaches for his gun. The police officers take a quick look around and leave. Gino exhales. And finishes his coffee.

Outside, in the brisk autumn air, he tries to walk quickly along *Via Nomentana*, but is suddenly aware of how heavy his feet have become. Each step requires a measured effort.

Forward, damn it! Don't fail me now!

A mischievous gust of wind dances around him and almost steals his hat, but he hangs onto it tightly. His brain processes an unending stream of images, recapping his life:

The comrades in France embracing him, some tearfully, wishing him luck and kissing him goodbye. The girl he once loved and dreamed of marrying, despite his comrades' raised eyebrows. The marble quarry in Cararra where he worked for so many years covered in dust. The green river bank where he took long walks, lost in thought, a book always under his arm.

All the great thinkers he read: Malatesta, Bakunin, Kropotkin—what would they say now? But Malatesta already agreed. The songs of Pietro Gori he loved to sing. Now is not the time to sing. Not just yet. He remembers the noisy workers' bar yesterday where he had a glass of red wine and wondered, "Is it really the last?"

He cannot forget that he has an escape plan, and reassures himself. Every detail carefully considered. The different escape routes, the time it will take, how many knocks on the two doors, the money needed to survive in hiding, the change of clothes—everything is ready and waiting for him.

But who knows, he reminds himself. Who knows?

For the hundredth time this week he debates the question that will not go away, and reassures himself with the only answer he knows.

Destiny? Yes, mine consciously; Mussolini's, unconsciously. Both hands thrust into his pockets, Gino feels the two hand grenades, souvenirs from a pointless war. Today, they will serve the cause of freedom.

To no one in particular, but to everyone in the entire world who should be listening, today, this significant day, he speaks.

"I believe that everyone has the right to live in total freedom. Free from the chains of poverty, ignorance, and power. Free from the tyranny of any dictator. We have only one chance on this earth—to live honourably, with dignity, to serve the cause of truth, justice, and freedom. Or to squander the years and live selfishly, in denial to the grave. I have been entrusted with this, the second attempt on Mussolini's miserable life. One comrade failed before. I, Gino Lucetti, cannot fail now."

He grits his teeth and quickens his pace, secretly hoping that the sooner he arrives at his rendezvous with destiny, the sooner the deed will be completed.

He asks himself: Does a man's resolve come after years of hard work, constant reading, thinking, and discussing with one's comrades, weighing moral imperatives and historic truths? Or was it always already there, hidden under the surface, enduring years of frustration, waiting patiently for the right historic moment?

For a split second, he hesitates and asks yet again: Is this the right moment? Yes! Without question. Now is the time to resist. To strike. To end the dictator's madness.

He picks up his pace and straightens out his shoulders. Up ahead, Gino sees a familiar barber shop. The heavyset man who cut his hair and gave him a shave just yesterday sits outside on a chair under a tree, arms folded, smoking. Gino holds his breath as he tips his hat and nods a quick *"buon giorno."* The barber smiles and nods back.

My last shave and haircut as a free man? He tries to banish the thought. Mario, the barber, was a good man. *"Not too high, not too low,"* I specified for the cut, and he knew exactly what I wanted.

Dear Mario, what will you think after you read the headlines and see the photos? We never discussed politics. Would you ever imagine you cut the hair of a man about to change the course of history? Will you think, "I cut the hair of a monster" or "I cut the hair of a decent man"?

A friendly contact inside *Il Duce's* library gave one of the comrades today's route for *"the daily car ride of His Excellency."* Now as Gino approaches the monumental gates of the *Porta Pia*, he checks his watch. I'm early. Slow down, Gino, slow down. You're an hour ahead of schedule.

He paces back and forth, marking his steps: forty-three

paces to the right, forty-three to the left. He reminds himself to stay calm. But nerves, muscles, flesh and blood don't obey. Above, two giant saints carved out of stone stare down at him. He stares back and waves at them.

Go on! Bless me if you want, me an atheist since childhood. But wish me luck, too, and maybe one day I'll return the favour. I cannot fail.

A tiny hunchbacked nun with glasses and brown sandals hesitates while trying to cross the street, stepping forward, then backward.

Good luck to you, too, sister, he thinks. *Why more reminders of yet another oppressor? You want me to repent? Ha! To hell with you! I am an anarchist!*

Gino's large, calloused palms are sweating. His mouth is dry, his heart pounding like a steaming locomotive.

Concentrate, Gino, concentrate! Do not waver! Do not weaken! Do not fail!

Across the wide street, at a government ministry office on the corner, men in suits with briefcases walk in and out self-importantly. A policeman outside keeps a watchful eye on them.

On them? On us? On whose business, and why?

Luckily he thinks, he is far enough away, and there are cars and trams between. It won't be hard to escape. It shouldn't be hard to escape. I've got to escape.

He checks his watch and realizes he still has another forty-five minutes. He crosses *Via Ancona* and walks through the *Piazza di Porta Pia*, circling the newsstand kiosk, scanning the headlines. He chuckles, imagining tomorrow's front pages splashed with the shocking news:

DICTATOR ASSASSINATED! MUSSOLINI IS DEAD! *IL DUCE* KILLED BY A BOMB! MYSTERIOUS ATTACKER GETS AWAY! NO CLUES WHO KILLED HIM. WHO KILLED IL DUCE? GOODBYE IL DUCE!

They will not know, he thinks. *It does not matter who throws the bomb, pulls the trigger, or attacks with the knife. As long as the task is done, the dictator dead.*

"Oh," but the pacifists will say, *"another one will rise to take his place."*

And I and others will respond:

"Yes, and that one will die, too. As long as no one is free in this country because of one man's dictatorship, we are all obligated to work to rid ourselves of him and his regime."

Gino walks back along *Via Nomentana* to the *Porta Pia*, his hands clasped tightly behind his back.

Be calm, be still! Listen to me, body of mine! Arms, legs, hands, you've served me well all these years. You always helped me do my work. Now help me complete the task here. Pump the blood. Move my muscles. Give me the strength to throw this bomb.

An elderly couple strolls by arm in arm and smiles at him. He tries to smile back but his facial muscles don't cooperate. He has trouble lighting one cigarette, and another. He thinks of all the months of careful planning and preparation, all the comrades counting on him. *I cannot fail!*

He flinches and a facial tic attacks his left eye. It forces him to pause and swear: *"Cazzo!"* Suddenly, he finds himself awash in doubts, wondering what the hell he is doing here.

What? Second thoughts? Me? No! Never! But I am only human. And an anarchist. It is not in my nature to take the life of another. It is not in my anarchist thinking, my anarchist principles. I am not a man of violence. I'm no beast. Ask anyone who knows me. This is not how I live. I've always respected everyone's absolute liberty, everyone's right to enjoy life.

But Mussolini is a dictator who respects no one's freedom, no one's life. He must be stopped. So I have set aside my reservations, and I will act. I will kill him. In the name of all of those before who begged for their lives, who paid with their lives. I cannot do otherwise. This is my task. I cannot fail.

He rubs his eye, but the twitch won't go away. He covers his eye with one palm, swears again, and hopes it won't interfere with his task.

A flock of pigeons flies so close above his head that he feels the wind from their flapping wings. *Like them,* he thinks, *I must fly, flee quickly the moment the deed is done. A safe house awaits me. There is money, food, a change of clothes, and a ticket for a train that will take me far away.*

Somewhere nearby, church bells ring. He checks his watch: 10:06 AM. On time, Mussolini's gleaming black limousine approaches. His blood pumping, his breath heaving, Gino focuses all his attention on the despised target: his enemy, the enemy of the people, of all freedom-loving people.

This is it. Come! Come closer to me, your Excellency! Come and receive your gift from the people! This is the moment of truth! Of justice! Of total, ultimate responsibility! The end to your reign of misery! Now you will pay for all the lives you have crushed, all the families you have destroyed, all the dreams you have stolen! The Masters' guard dog will bite no more! Come, your Excellency! Come closer!

His heart pounding, he reaches inside his pocket for one of the bombs. The car is now within spitting distance. With all his strength he hurls the grenade, screaming, *"Death to Fascism!"*

Then he freezes. He sees the chauffeur's face contort into horror.

"Oh no!"

He watches the windshield splinter into a spiderweb of shattered glass. But the bomb—the well-aimed, precious all-important bomb, the bomb that will change the course of history, that will speak for anti-Fascists everywhere; the bomb that will end the dictator's life here and now—bounces off the windshield and doesn't detonate. Doesn't explode.

"Cazzo! I threw it too hard! I didn't throw it hard enough! What happened? *Che cazzo!"*

The bomb bounces off the hood of the car, drops to the running board and falls to the street.

"Mamma mia! What have I done?"

And then—*Kaboom!* It explodes. Gravel and road debris fly in all directions. The shock of the blast hurls Gino onto his back. But the car speeds off with only minor damage.

Oh no! I've failed! How could I? How could this happen? Run! Run and hide! Run for your life! Gino leaps up and starts running, then . . .

No! Wait! Stop! Walk! Don't run! Che cazzo! Walk away and don't look back! Keep walking!

NEWS, 1926, Rome: *Mussolini survives assassination attempt . . .*

GREAT-GRANDFATHER: MIRACLE MEN AND GINO

When Mussolini survived Gino's attempt on his life, like a few others before and after, it helped feed the legend that *Il Duce* was "The Man of Miracles." Luck, I call it. His good and our bad luck.

Some people also called him Man of Miracles because, they said, he built many roads and buildings. Clarification: he didn't. Skilled, sweating, working men and women did. Their work lasts to this day.

But the dictator left another legacy, less visible but just as important. A brutal Fascist one. He shut down all independent newspapers. Abolished all political parties except his Fascist Party. Ordered the assassination of socialists and anarchists in Italy and across Europe and America. Imprisoned and tortured anyone who opposed him. He "baptized" many dissidents by forcing castor oil down their throats. If they resisted, Fascists added gasoline. You call these miracles? I call it barbarism.

Poor Gino Lucetti. He was caught and sentenced to thirty years. In 1943 he escaped, only to be killed by an Allied bombing raid. To honour his memory, two anarchist anti-Fascist partisan groups fighting near Carrara adopted his name.

After his failed *attentat*, does Gino rest in peace? Ask him.

HELL NATION

Rome and its inhabitants have no choice. *Cazzarola!* Today's scorching white-hot sun chooses to roast rather than bake everything and everyone in sight.

A heavily perspiring Antonio steps off the #19 tram at *Via Nomentana*, turns left and walks on the wide sidewalk in the shade of the towering, leafy *albero* in the direction of the *Porta Pia*, toward one of his favourite indie music stores, Hell Nation.

Last night he'd caught the tail end of a TV news show that recounted the 1926 assassination attempt by Gino Lucetti against Mussolini near the historic gates.

Antonio had heard of Lucetti years ago from his grandfather. "The black sheep" of a distant part of the family, they called him "the dark one" because he was swarthier than other Discordias, according to his grandfather. Antonio had almost forgotten the family connection.

Now he feels a certain pride. He decides to walk a few extra blocks to see for himself where Gino had lived out his last hours as a free man.

Smaller trees, fewer cars in those days. Same tram tracks. Maybe the same barbershop. Another generation of pigeons roosting, cooing, and shitting on people's heads. Another would-be Mussolini in power.

He stops in front of *Via Nomentana* #13—the doorway, according to the TV report, where Gino tried to hide from the pursuing police after tossing the bomb.

Today it's a fancy condominium project for the bourgeoisie. Across the street, the government Ministry of Infrastructure office is still the same: men in suits with attaché cases, talking self-importantly with one another. The cops outside keep a watchful eye on them, on us, on whom? And why? I see no more would-be assassins in the area. Just ordinary people.

A heavyset woman with a huge tattoo on her shoulder speaks on her cell phone:

"I'm right here in front. Can't you see me?"

A man walks up behind her with his cell phone and kisses her on her back.

Scooters, buzzing like oversugared bees and noisier than cars, zig in and zag out of traffic. Antonio stands by a low wall outside the Ministry and contemplates the possibilities.

What would ordinary Italians think of Gino today? Would they think differently if he tried to bump off Italy's current Mussolini wannabe? I could write a song about it.

He passes the pizza places, the *falafel* houses, the corner cafés and turns into the coolness of the music store. Here he feels at home, alive, totally stimulated, head to toe.

Rock, indie, punk, hardcore, soul, reggae, ska, afro-funk. *It's all me*, he smiles as he closes the door behind him.

The rockabilly sales clerk with her retro Betty Boop hair cut, tattooed, pierced, in tight-fitting black top and jeans, smiles back.

"Ciao bello!"

The shop also stocks a small selection of radical political books like *Gli Autonomi: Le storie, le lotte, le teorie* (We Autonomists: The Story, the Fight, the Theory) by Sergio Bianchi and Lanfranco Caminiti, and DVDs like Claudio Lazzaro's *Nazi Rock: Il contagio Fascista tra I giovani italiani* (The Fascist Epidemic among Young Italians).

Textual and visual brain food for music lovers like me, Antonio thinks, as he fingers the rack of new CDs. Keep expanding the horizons. Melodic and cerebral.

This place is the new locus of cultural dissent. Where modern cultural rebels come to replenish their stock of musical ammo. Their little corner of the world.

"Any shows coming up?" the clerk asks.

"Nah, too busy, still recording."

"There was a new shipment of reggae this week. Cool vintage stuff, reissued. I know your cousin likes it, so let him know, OK?"

Back in the day, Antonio used to visit the shop at least once a week. More if he had extra money. But since he met Cinka, less often. Now, as he mulls over what to buy, he stops to consider his music habit.

He can't help it. He's beginning to think of himself as more than a musician. His comfortable little musical world is teetering, showing stress lines, and no longer diverting him from new and troubling truths. With Cinka and her almost unimaginable life situation, he confronts other realities, unknown and frightening.

As a musician, what can I do that would matter? he thinks. What would make a difference in Cinka's life? What would make things change? Regardless, I still need my music, my lifeline.

We consume, yes. We share, too. We band together at shows, on the street, online, at work or school. We give money that we hope goes to the artists, the bands, the groups we support, the stores and distro outlets we depend on. We discuss, agree or disagree, appreciate or diss the products of like-minded, like-spirited, twenty-first-century other-cultured music fiends or artists. Our music is political—in its own way, in the broadest of senses.

I'm not that political, but my music—our music—isn't it a kind of protest, a defiance of what is, a harbinger of what could be? Between the words and the beats, the chords and the fuzz, the distortion and the vocals, aren't we saying that another world is possible? A better one? Recuperated? Sometimes. Co-opted? Occasionally. Commodified? Duh, yeah. We still churn it out.

Now Antonio thinks about it in different terms.

Could it be more effective, more purposeful? When I was younger, I was raging, rocking, railing against the system. I saw myself pounding away at the foundations with a booming bass line. That was punk, right? With Cinka, though, something else is happening, musically, in my head. I think of music as soundtrack, heartbeat, slogan, spray-paint, poster, protest, weapon, bullhorn. Maybe to help change things. Is this crazy?

At home, Antonio opens up his band's online profile and writes:

"Underground" or not, music is our way of saying NO! to the corporate musical pablum Big Business would rather we listened to.

They can't censor our cell phones, our computers, our turntables. Not yet. We long for music to feed rebellious, dissident, nonconforming thought patterns. Music to help us cope. Our drug of choice on the palate of consumer "choices." Music to feed our hunger for something "other," something that we can't find in this crazy new world disorder. A different soundtrack for our lives.

Music to pump up our heartbeats. Music to soothe our wounds. Music for the walking, dazed, wounded who keep searching for something not found on store shelves or on TV or in any shopping mall. Music to replenish the soul they keep attacking, trying to tame, manipulate, brainwash, and control by entertaining us, lulling us into an unconscious state of zombified, wasted, deadened humanity.

Music that demands active, listening attention. Music that isn't background noise. Music that tells us we are still living, breathing, acting individuals. Music, wonderful music. Wonderful beats in a world of fury. Music to combat the lie of Fascism.

Antonio stares at the words on his screen. What would Gino Lucetti say?

THE ALARM RINGS

In his sleep, Antonio dreams around the world, time travelling to famous music stages and moments: Memphis in the 1950s with Elvis, Woodstock in the 1960s with Jimi Hendrix, CBGB's in New York with the Ramones, London with the Clash. And he's playing guitar with all of them, soaking up the adulation and the beer, smoking up, meeting the fans. Then he hears someone grinding coffee in the kitchen.

"Holy fuck!" He's seriously late for work again.

"Hey there!" The boss grabs his arm as Antonio tries to bolt through the front door of the restaurant.

"What's the rush? Slow down," the boss says with a big phony smile. "You know, Antonio, I like you, the customers like you, you're a good waiter. But there's a problem. You decide: are you a student, a musician, or a waiter? Do you not want this job, asshole? Because if you keep walking in late like this, you can walk right back out! I can't afford to keep you here, understand? There are others, also students and musicians, who will choose wiser."

He lets go of Antonio's arm.

"Yes, sir, of course. I'm sorry, sir, it won't happen again." Antonio disappears into the kitchen.

OK, I'll try harder, he says to himself. But when do I have time to see Cinka, read, play, record, and have a fucking life? Bosses don't care. To hell with work.

CINKA'S MOM, LUMINITSA

Cinka's mom, Luminitsa, sits on a plastic crate in the sun outside her refugee hut. She greets passing neighbours as she sews up the rips in one of her son's two shirts. His pants were torn recently, too, but he never really explained how it happened.

"I fell down a hill."

A heavyset, worried-looking woman of forty-five, Luminitsa in her day had been always happy and as slender and attractive as her daughter. Relatives joked:

"Your blue eyes? Your blond hair? You don't look like us Roma."

Now she has arthritis in one leg. Her teeth hurt. Her eyes are giving her trouble. And she has no money to buy food today.

A neighbour, a single mother as well, about her own age, walks over with two cups of tea and sits down beside her. They exchange a few words, then drink in silence in the bright sun. The neighbour sighs audibly.

"My God. Remember years ago, under the Communists? When we Roma were relatively protected? Romania was good, then, yes?"

Luminitsa smiles. How can she forget? Back then, racism was not tolerated and her family had a hard but satisfying life. They rented a little house from the State and always had enough food on the table. In Communist Romania, everyone could go to school, herself included. There were jobs even for Roma. She had been a seamstress. Once she married, her status in the village as *"wife of the best violinist"* meant something.

People treated her with respect, especially if they wanted her husband to play their family functions. Even better, he brought home extra food from the weddings. But when the Communist dictatorship disappeared, it was open hunting season on the Roma. And when her husband died, everything changed. Luminitsa's face showed it.

Now, almost overnight in Rome, the level of intolerance has shot up dramatically.

"I don't feel safe here, do you?" she asks the neighbour.

"No. Me neither. But what to do?"

"I came here for my children, like you. Now, I think it was a mistake."

"Ah, my first mistake was marrying my husband. My second was leaving him. And now, I'm tired of making mistakes. I think, though, it is time to leave. Maybe the wind will tell us which way to go." The neighbour stands up and wishes her a good day.

Luminitsa returns to her mending. Without her extended family around her, she feels completely vulnerable in this new land. *What was I thinking? Back home, even though things were getting worse, we could rely on our family. Here? There is no one. It was a huge risk to come. I gave up everything.*

Sure, I learned enough Italian to get by. But now every time I ask at shops for work, no one gives me anything. Now I'm afraid to speak to any Italian.

Thank goodness for Cinka. She takes care of us the way her father did. And this new gadjo *friend of hers sounds like a nice enough young man who cares about her. He gives her work that pays and food to bring home, just like her father. Can he be trusted? I know better than to press Cinka for details. When she's ready, she'll tell me . . .*

Just then, the camp gossip walks by. She leers at Luminitsa.

"And where, can I ask, is your lovely daughter today?"

"If it's any of your business, she's working. Like always. Maybe you should find something yourself. Keep you out of trouble."

The old woman snorts and disappears. *An evil woman,* Luminitsa thinks. *She gives me goose bumps.* In the distance Luminitsa sees Cinka trudging home, her violin case in one hand and two bulging plastic bags in the other.

She hugs her mother and flashes a huge grin. "Look!" The bags contain fresh fruit and vegetables.

"But where did you get all this?" Luminitsa is incredulous.

"Antonio's cousin has a garden in the countryside."

"Shh! Keep your voice down. This camp has too many ears."

ANTONIO RIDES THE TRAIN

Antonio blinks, rolls out of bed, and throws open his wooden green shutters. The flash of early morning sunlight blinds him.

A new day. A new me? Or do I never change?

He stretches and squints down at the central courtyard. A lone white cat sits on a bench and licks itself. One quick coffee and he bounds down the three flights of stairs, pushes two buttons to open the door and the front gate, and rolls Simona's big borrowed Honda out onto the street.

He guns the bike and roars onto the cobblestoned *Tibertina*, past the *Verano* cemetery and early morning newspaper hawkers, past the corner squeegee refugees, all the way to the train station.

Bike parked, he runs in and weaves around other commuters to the #4 track to catch the early train to Fara in Sabina. On board, he notices a young woman sitting across from him, putting the final touches to her workday makeup: eye shadow, mascara, and lip-gloss. He imagines Cinka sitting in her place. She needs no makeup, he thinks. She's already beautiful.

The stations roll by as Antonio stares vacantly out the window. Roma Nomentana, Salaria, Fidenae. Then the train runs alongside the two-lane Salaria roadway already backed up with the morning rush hour. Beyond the highway, open yellow and green fields end in rolling low hills in the distance. How often he had taken this train as a child to his grandparents' house! Another stop at Settebagni and finally Monterotondo.

With his shoulder bag bouncing on his hip, Antonio runs down the stairs and up the ramp out the station into the early morning freshness of country air.

He loves this place with its smells, its lush canopies of

trees everywhere, its laid-back pace under unobstructed wide-open skies. Ahead, on *Via Monte Amiata*, under the shade of a huge oak, he sees a white-haired city worker in orange coveralls on his knees cleaning out a sewer connection with a shovel.

"*Ciao*, Franco! How goes the job?"

Antonio knows him from years of commuting and nights in a local *taverna*.

"Well," the older man replies, looking up and smiling, "it's the same old shit, but it pays the bills and keeps the wife happy."

Antonio shakes his hand and turns onto *Via Filippo Turati*, heading up a hill. Maybe Cinka would like it here? Then he remembers the firebombing of the Romanian food store recently and scratches the thought. Her family might be a bit too conspicuous for this small town.

If they don't feel safe in Rome, they'd be sitting ducks here. Fuck!

Across the road on his left, he sees an elderly man carrying a wicker basket in one arm and a long metal rod ending in a "U" at one end and a small circle at the other. He's hunting rabbits in the overgrown corner lot that dips just below the intersection. Antonio pauses to watch the old guy walk cat-like among the tall reeds and wild pink, purple, and yellow blossoms, stalking his prey. He snaps a photo with his cell phone.

Inside a local bar, he spots his contact, a bearded young activist with blond dreadlocks and a braided beard, a friend of Rafaele's. They shake hands and order coffee.

"Today, Italy is a strange place, my friend," the contact says.

"Stranger than Dante could ever have predicted." Antonio knows his Dante.

"In L'Aquila, the State is using the earthquake as an excuse to experiment with new forms of social control. The cops have taken over."

"In Venice, I hear, soldiers set up a military blockade to prevent a march called by a local residents' committee."

"Mass arrests of students and comrades in Turin, Bologna, Padua, Naples, and Reggio Calabria—just for demonstrating against the G8 Summit."

"My friends at *La Sapienza* University were arrested during an occupation protesting the arrests."

"The police keep referring to the usual suspected threat of an anarcho-insurrectionalist attack, this time against the railways. And who causes the fatal accidents? They do!"

"Now they introduce a new 'Security Package' to intimidate and criminalize us."

"Not just us, look at the Roma. Illegal immigration is now a crime. They can hold suspected illegal immigrants for up to eighteen months. Renting an apartment to an illegal immigrant is also a crime, punishable by up to three years in prison."

"They want to jail graffiti artists. They're so dangerous."

"And if you apply for a permanent residency permit, now you have to pass an Italian language test."

"But if you can't produce identification on demand, they can jail you for one year."

"Even homeless people are now supposed to be registered."

"And if you go to a hospital and ask for medical treatment, but have no papers, they can report you to the police!"

"Welcome to Fortress Italy. Mussolini would be happy."

"*Cazzo!* So," Antonio asks, "what we can do about it?"

THE LATIN INSCRIPTION, 1930

The scaffolding holds two stone masons working on the building façade. It sits about four metres above the arched doorway of this brand new San Lorenzo apartment block. One worker fixes a crack. The other is chiselling letters into the stonework. He lays down his tools and wipes the sweat from his brow before lighting a cigarette.

"Shit. Do you believe this? Whose idea was it?"

He studies the Latin inscription he is reproducing in the stonework: "*Life is indeterminate. Work and Pray.*"

"Where do they come up with nonsense like this? How much wine were they drinking? And did they get paid for it? Or was it something he found in a book or scribbled on a wall?"

His workmate laughs.

"Just think, a century from now, some poor guy will look up at this, scratch his head and wonder, 'What were they thinking?'"

"Later they'll put this block of stone into a museum. An artifact from yesterday."

"People in the future will pay good money to look at this. And me? What will I get?"

"From up in heaven, a good laugh."

"Oh, don't worry, God. I keep one eye open for you all the time. I don't trust you, real or not. I'm a simple working man. What do I know about religion? I just do my job and feed my family. I say nothing about the Church or *Il Duce*. Except that a few priests probably say their prayers for good measure before they suck his dick."

NEWS, October 1935: Italy invades Ethiopia . . .

March 1936: Italy firebombs the Ethiopian city of Harar . . . Uses mustard gas and other chemical weapons against Ethiopia in violation of Geneva Protocol . . .

May: Italian troops occupy Addis Ababa, Ethiopia . . . 1,757 Italians and 1,593 Eritreans killed . . . More than 275,000 Ethiopians killed . . . Fascist Italy takes Addis Abba and annexes Ethiopia as Benito Mussolini celebrates in Rome . . .

January 1937: Italian regime bans marriages between Italians and Ethiopians.

NEWS, September 2003: Italy's Prime Minister Berlusconi says Mussolini sent his enemies "on holiday in internal exile" and could not be compared to deposed Iraqi President Saddam Hussein . . . Memories still raw in Ethiopia of invasion ordered by Italian dictator in 1935, when his forces used chemical warfare against troops defending the country then known as Abyssinia . . . "These scars you see are a reminder of Italian Fascist atrocities," says an 80-year-old resistance fighter who fought the invaders, lifting his shirt to reveal welts on his torso. "Such scars are carried by millions of Ethiopians. I suggest that the Italian Prime Minister gets his facts straight before uttering such nonsense, trying to absolve a Fascist dictator from his horrendous crimes . . ."

BUS RIDE FROM ROMANIA

It's a sunny day, but a distant wind is sculpting the few snow-white clouds into ever-shifting monumental icebergs crossing the horizon.

Between cuddles, Antonio and Cinka gasp at the atmospheric transformations in the sky. They sit on a low stone wall in the shade of a grove of trees overlooking the city from the *Villa Borghese*. Antonio lightly kisses her cheek and whispers the sweetest of nothings into her ear. Cinka sits, knees pulled up to her chin, smiling but pensive.

Antonio breaks the silence.

"You never told me, sweetheart, how you and your family got to Rome. By bus?"

Cinka stares straight ahead. She doesn't answer for a while. He waits.

"Hmm, yes. The trip was exhausting. But I was excited and happy. Fearful, too, and with some regrets. To leave Romania? The country where I was born? To move so many thousands of kilometres away to a land I knew nothing about? This dream left my stomach in knots.

"It was my father's dream. We were realizing it without him. On the bus, my mother was anxious, but said little. She kept playing with her rosary and whispering her prayers. That is, when she wasn't dozing, or handing us sandwiches and cookies from a bag at her feet.

"For my brother and sister, it was their first bus trip anywhere. It was jammed with other Romanians and Roma, and their suitcases, birdcages, even a fuzzy orange little puppy. He just wanted to play.

"Everyone was heading for Italy, 'the new land of opportunity.'" She laughed.

"I wondered if everyone was as anxious as me. So many questions I couldn't answer."

Where will we live? Will we find work? Will we learn Italian quickly enough?

How will Italians receive us? Will we ever see our families we left behind again?

Will we succeed? Or be forced to return home, embarrassed to show our faces? Will our father's brother be happy to see us, or overwhelmed? Are we making a big mistake?

"I kept telling myself, this is what our father wanted. I can never forget his words before he died.

"He was very sick. He pulled me close on his hospital bed, and with great effort, whispered into my ear."

"Take them to Italy, Cinka. Give the family a second chance. They don't want us in Romania anymore. It will be better in Italy. You'll see. People are civilized and generous there. Our family will prosper. Promise me you will take care of them. You can do it. I have faith in you."

"My father's dream was that Italy would appreciate what our family could offer. In return, Italy would allow us to realize all of our dreams. This gave me strength for the long ride—into our new future."

Antonio hugged her tighter as he listened. As she spoke, he had realized his love for her was greater than any he ever known. Something in her voice, her eyes, resonated deep inside him, stirring something he still couldn't name.

"I watched my younger brother and sister giggling and switching seats on the bus, faces glued to the window, or playing with the puppy. And I kept thinking, we're doing this without our father beside us, to protect and guide us. But he must be somewhere close. Otherwise, how could we do this by ourselves?

"Will we have a big apartment with a bedroom and video games?" my brother asked. "Will you make lots of money playing violin and buy us a car so we can go to the beach like other families? When we get to Italy, I'm going to go to school and get a job, too!"

"I'm getting a job also," my sister said, "in a fancy cloth-ing store where all the rich *gadjos* shop. They'll give me nice clothes to wear that they don't want. And I'll go to school at night and study to become a doctor. Then I'll buy a big Italian house for all of us with a swimming pool. And all our relatives can come from Romania and live with us. And Mother won't be sad anymore. And Cinka will be a famous violinist and play with Madonna. And we will have front row seats at every show."

"And I'll play accordion with Madonna," boasted her brother, "and Cinka and Mother will be proud of me."

"Silly! Boys can't play with Madonna. Only girls."

SUPPERTIME AT CINKA'S

It's suppertime for Cinka's family in their refugee hut. But first, Luminitsa, like every Romani mother, insists that everyone wash up. Outside, she pours water from a plastic bottle into cupped hands that are rubbed and shaken dry. Only then can the meal begin.

A plastic milk crate, adorned with a clean tea towel, serves as the table. It sits on an old rug covering a sheet of plastic on top of the dirt floor. Cinka, her mother, brother and sister sit cross-legged on top of two other rolled up old rugs on either side. Their meal: a bottle of water, a loaf of bread, a lone battered orange, and a container of pasta with tomatoes that Cinka brought back from the recording studio. Antonio always made extra for lunch for her to bring home. There are four plastic spoons.

The family take turns dipping their spoons into the pasta for a mouthful each. Tonight's pasta lasts about seven spoonfuls each. The bread is divided up equally.

Then Cinka carefully peels the orange and hands out segments.

Supper is over.

BUSINESSMAN SEES ATTACK

He is middle-aged, well dressed, with a cell phone in one hand. Two bags of groceries sit at his feet. He stands on the sidewalk face-to-face with one of the local *carabinieri*.

Two fire engines, three police cars, and an ambulance block the street. A patchwork of fire hoses criss-crosses the sidewalk. Flashing red and white lights pierce the night and bounce off nearby apartment blocks. Neighbours line the street opposite watching, commenting. The air is heavy with the acrid smell of smoke. A policeman laboriously writes notes in a little book with a stubby pencil.

"Look, officer, I know what I saw with my own two eyes. I'm a local businessman. A member of the Chamber of Commerce. My hardware store is around the corner. I live a few minutes away. I've got kids. And I won't stand for goon violence in our streets. Monterotondo is my town. I was born here. Six generations. This can't happen here. It's a vile gesture against honest people."

The policeman stops writing, furrows his eyebrows, and looks up at the businessman.

"You're sure you're telling me the truth?"

"What? Why would I make this up? I am telling the truth! Jesus Christ! Why do you think I called the police? Like I told you: I saw five men, all wearing ski masks.

"They pile out of a new black Jeep Cherokee—I know my cars. No, officer, I didn't get their licence number. I told you, the rear plate was covered. I didn't see their faces."

"You didn't see their faces but you swear they were men?"

"Of course they were men! What are you implying, that I can't tell men from women? Come on! They were all big guys, bigger than me. They wore dark jackets, dark clothes. Two of them had long steel pipes. One had a knife. And two had big sticks, about half a metre long, like the one you're wearing on your belt."

"Are you implying that these men were policemen?"

"I didn't say they were policemen, officer. They were thugs. Goons! Hooligans! Understand?"

The officer nods and keeps writing. "And you say you think they were Italian, our people?"

"Yes, of course, Italians!"

"And how can you be sure of this?"

"How do I know? They spoke fucking Italian! Excuse my language. Like me, like you! They were calling the Romanians all kind of names, swearing at them. Look, I'm telling you exactly what I saw and what I heard. Why would I lie to you? Why don't you believe me? Why are you rolling your eyes like that?"

The officer sighs. "I'm just tired."

"Aren't you supposed to be writing this all down? Isn't this your job?"

"Sir, don't tell me how to do my job."

"I'm not telling you how to do your job. I'm telling you I'm a damn witness to what happened here and you don't seem to believe what I'm saying."

The policeman shakes his head slowly. But starts writing again.

"People got hurt, maybe even killed. I called you because I don't want to see those thugs get away with this. See that graffiti over there? '*Die Romanian scum!*' It wasn't here yesterday. It must have gone up last night."

The officer copies the phrase in his notebook.

"Listen. The goons piled out of their car and started hitting the accordionist for no reason at all."

"He must have done something to provoke them, said something, made a face at them. No?"

"No! He didn't provoke anybody. He always sits there in front of the store and plays for money. That's his spot."

"And you know this accordionist?"

"His name is Tony, that's all I know. He just plays and smiles. He doesn't bother anyone."

"And he's Romanian, you say?"

"Yes, as far as I know, he's Romanian. Look! See the blood over here?"

The businessman walks toward a wooden stool lying on its side and points to the red stain on the pavement.

"See this? It's his blood! They beat on him until he fell and then they started kicking him. I yelled at them to stop, but they ignored me."

"You didn't try to stop them?" The officer bends down to look at the blood.

"Hey, five big armed guys? I'm not that young anymore. Then they attacked two other Romanian guys who ran out to help him."

"You saw all this—from where?"

"I was right here, walking back to my car, talking on my phone to my wife, when I saw the thugs wearing masks heading for the store. I knew something was up. I thought it was a robbery. I called you guys right away. It happened so fast. Women were screaming. Throwing things at the guys. The thugs beat all the men, and a couple of the women, and smashed the windows. Then as they were running back to the car—over there—one of them turned and threw a Molotov. That's what started the fire. It exploded inside. I had just finished shopping in that very store, the one he set on fire!"

"You saw one of these 'goons,' as you call them, throw an incendiary device?"

"Yes, I saw him throw it."

"Did you see who was driving the getaway car, too?"

"No, I didn't see the driver. Jesus! Why are you looking at me like that? You don't believe me, do you? You think I'm lying."

"Just trying to get the facts, sir, that's all. And you say your last name is spelled D-i-s-c-o-r-d-i-a?"

"That's right."

"And you knew this was a Romanian store you were shopping in, right?"

"Of course. I shop there all the time."

"Why do you shop at a Romanian store instead of an Italian store?"

"What do you mean, *why?* Because I choose to! Because I always shop here! Because it's my business to shop wherever I want! I don't care if they're Romanian, Indian, Chinese, or whatever. It's a free country. What's the relevance of this?"

"Just asking." The officer closes his little notebook.

"Look. Five goons attacked innocent people. Three ambulances took away the injured. A dozen people almost burned to death in that store. There's blood on the ground. And you ask me why I shop here? *Cazzo!*"

THE GARBATELLA ANARCHISTS MEET

"Take the Metro to Garbatella, walk down *Via Ignazio Persico*, and turn right on *Via Giovanni Battista Magnaghi*. I'll meet you in the office."

Simona, Antonio's raven-haired, heavily tattooed, delightful cousin has invited him to a meeting of her anarchist group.

A gay couple was viciously attacked by neo-Fascists on *Via San Giovanni*, Rome's "Gay Street," near the Coliseum. Simona's gang wants to join in a noisy public response with an anarchist gay collective.

"You can talk about what's been happening to your girlfriend's camp. Maybe get some help."

Antonio walks down polished marble steps into the open doorway of a well-lit but musty basement room smelling of old books and decades of smoke, beer, and *grappa*. This is the historic Garbatella Anarchist Group office. Simona waves him in.

The yellowed walls display photos and drawings of anarchist forefathers and foremothers: Bakunin, Kropotkin, Malatesta, Goldman, Michel. A set of Peruvian pan pipes and an oud hang between. Posters of Fabrizio de André, the most famous Italian anarchist troubadour from the 1960s to the 1990s, are everywhere. A long wooden meeting table occupies the middle of the room. It's surrounded by bookshelves where anarchist literature is piled haphazardly.

Simona kisses Antonio on both cheeks.

"Look." She points to the painted red slogans on the wall. "Leftover from World War II comrades who used this office as a hiding place from the Fascists even before the war."

At the table the compact group of seven men and two women discuss how to support Rome's gay, lesbian, bisexual, transgender, and queer communities. The room fills with smoke. Ashtrays overflow.

People speak respectfully in turn. One man takes notes. Someone whispers translation into the ear of a visiting anarchist from Oaxaca.

"We march with the gay collective comrades in the streets."

"And spray-paint anti-homophobia slogans in that neighbourhood."

"We hang banners from the roofs overlooking the street where the couple was beaten."

"We poster the street."

"We let them know that homophobia will not be tolerated."

"But what about Romani refugees, too? They get beat up all the time. Who will protest?"

Antonio blurts it out. Simona smiles. An older man replies.

"Comrade, you are correct. We need to address the xenophobia, too. It's linked to the homophobia."

"I say we make the connections between fear of gays, fear of the Roma, fear of immigrants and anarchists. Write up a flyer."

"Fear of those living on the margins. Fear of those the media and politicians demonize, render objectified, dehumanized, uncommon, and 'foreign.'"

"It's the same tool the Fascists used before."

"And the Americans, post-9/11."

"And every government today intent on creating a climate of fear worldwide."

Simona proposes:

"We need a concise history of Romani immigration to Italy. The public doesn't realize they've been here a long time."

The oldest anarchist—pipe-smoking, white-haired, and jovial—speaks:

"You know, Roma first came to Italy in the beginning of the 1400s, from the east, after leaving India hundreds of years earlier, in the eleventh century. In 1422, I believe, a group of Roma actually asked for and received a letter of passage from the Pope. But, according to historical records, the Roma were expelled and persecuted from the start. Hospitable people we always have been."

"I read somewhere that in 1500, the Holy Roman Emperor, Maximilian I, issued a decree saying that to burn or kill Gypsies was not a crime."

"Sounds like our prime minister!"

"And the Northern Party senators."

"The fact is that the early Roma who stayed here survived for generations. They integrated themselves into Italian society until the next round of persecutions when Mussolini and Hitler came along."

"Didn't Mussolini call them 'subhumans' in 1926 and start expelling them?"

"Yes, and then Hitler killed more than a million of them in the extermination camps."

"Condense that and put it also in a flyer."

"But you need more than that, yes?" Antonio looks around the room. "It's not enough. They're getting the shit kicked out of them. My girlfriend is Romani. She tells me all these stories. No one hears about them."

"How about a solidarity dinner party?"

"With members of the Roma and friends and supporters. A big public event where everyone gets to speak? Tell all their stories. Your girlfriend, too."

"And we invite members of the gay community also. Show how homophobia is linked to security fears and repression."

Antonio is having difficulty following the discussion now; everyone is jumping in with something to say. Simona puts her arm around him and squeezes. A young man with thick glasses who has remained silent all this time speaks:

"Our message to people has to go further. The State feeds the public fear with warnings that 'the Evil Ones are among us.' They flood the streets with armed soldiers. The public responds by acting out: a mass, knee-jerk reaction to the undesirables—gay, Roma, visible minority immigrants. Then comes public ostracizing, purging, driving out the demonized."

"You got it! Because then the victims, though familiar with it, nonetheless are bewildered by the process! The players all fulfil their roles—the media especially."

Simona finishes the thought:

"And what is left to do? Enact legislation. Legitimize the stigmatization of the 'unwanteds.'"

"The U.S. did it to the Indians, right, corralling them onto reservations."

"And did it later to generations of immigrants, including Italians."

"Europe has done it to the Roma for centuries. And now the State returns to our not-so-distant Fascist past to once again target those perceived as non-Italians."

"Despite the fact that the majority of the Roma, for example, are citizens of Italy!"

"How do you know?"

"It's in all the census reports. I get them at work. I can show you."

Simona looks around the room; everyone is sitting on the edge of their chairs talking at once. Antonio still looks confused.

"OK, guys, do we have consensus? A flyer that speaks to all 'diversities'? Something like, *'The natural, ever-growing Italian rainbow the State and media want to discolour with their campaign of hatred and their climate of intolerance . . .'* or whatever."

"Are you writing this down?"

NEWS, 2008, Milan: *Abdul Salam Guibre, 19, an Italian originally from Burkina Faso, murdered by a shopkeeper and his son after they caught him stealing packets of biscuits from their snack bar near Milan railway station . . . shouted "We'll kill you" as they repeatedly struck Mr. Guibre with iron bars, leaving him lying in blood . . .*

PART IV

FAMILY WEB

GREAT-GRANDFATHER: OUR FAMILY TREE

I came from a large family. There were sixteen of us. My mother's and my father's families each had ten or more children. A spider web of Discordias! We stayed mostly in Abruzzo, but eventually spread out all over the country: Pisa, Napoli, Rome, Torino, Milano, from the mountains to the seacoast, Discordias everywhere!

I never knew most of them. Nor they, me. But our blood was shared and still is. Good strong Italian stuff, our family wine, spilled sometimes for no good reason, sometimes, despite the rivers of tears, with meaning.

My grandfather told me family legends. The kind every family tries to preserve. I do my best to pass them down to my grandchildren. But do they remember? Their memories grow shorter and shorter; mine, longer and longer. But the legends remain. Somewhere.

A SON'S REVENGE, 1931

He was a nondescript, ordinary-looking man, but a wealthy man. Not a worker. You could tell by the way he dressed and the way he walked. Always erect. A fancy walking cane in one hand as he went from his office to his chauffeured car parked in front. He wasn't portly, just stout and bald. Somewhat stern in his face. He had pink cheeks, and rarely smiled.

Georgio had watched him from across the street for an entire week planning this moment.

Georgio's father, a Discordia, had described the industrialist as a tight-fisted, callous, calculating man who drove his employees to work longer hours for less pay. It was "his" factory. He made all the decisions. No gang of anarcho-syndicalist trade unionists was going to tell him how to run his business. Georgio's father had learned this from the first beating by the goons hired by his boss.

"Lay off the union stuff or you won't see your family again."

The second beating left him in even worse shape, but he still went to the factory gate each morning to talk to the other workers before they entered. He encouraged them to support the union demands for better working conditions.

One day, Georgio's father never returned home. The news of his death came later that night from his former comrades. They told Georgio's mother, in front of him and his four brothers and sisters:

"First, they beat him with clubs. Then they tied him to a car and dragged him for a few kilometres outside the factory. There were witnesses. The goons left a sign on his body saying '*Subversives pay.*' We're so sorry."

After that day, Georgio's mother was never the same.

Now it was 1931, ten years later, a cool fall evening. Georgio, the oldest son, never forgot his silent promise to his dead father. He fingered the revolver in his pocket, then walked up to this ordinary-looking industrialist. Facing him, he calmly pumped seven bullets into his stomach as he said:

"This is for killing my father and all the other fathers, husbands, uncles, and sons."

In prison, Georgio was tortured and beaten by the Fascists. He died a few days later.

His younger brothers and sisters joined a partisan brigade.

WHAT DID YOU LEARN IN SCHOOL TODAY?

Three schoolboys in shorts were walking home, kicking a rock in the street. They turned into a doorway and shoved one another aside as they raced up the stairs. Breathless after two flights, one-by-one they said goodbye and entered their apartments.

"So how was school today?" the first mother asked as her son sauntered into the kitchen and sat at the table for milk and cookies.

"OK. We learned that Italian workers think and talk too much about politics. The teacher said that's why Mussolini banned strikes and outlawed labour unions."

His mother kept cleaning the kitchen.

"Uh huh. What else?"

"That boys are better than girls because Mussolini says so."

"And what do you think?"

"It's true because *Il Duce* only speaks the truth."

The second mother in the apartment a few doors away hugged her son as he dropped his school bag on the hallway floor and also asked him about school.

"Oh, today the teacher told us that the Pope thinks socialism is evil and that we should report any socialists to the police."

"That's what the teacher said?"

"Yes. And that women should not wear trousers because *Il Duce* said so. You better change your clothes, Mother."

"What's wrong with my clothes?" His mother looked down at her trousers.

"You could get arrested. Or someone could report you to the police."

"But son, that's ridiculous. Why should anyone be telling me what I can or cannot wear?"

"Well, give me some more cookies and I won't say anything."

The third mother was busy cooking when her son entered the kitchen whistling. He started opening all the cupboards looking for something to eat.

"How is my little devil?"

"Uh, OK."

"And how was school today?"

"Uh, OK. Our teacher was arrested by the police."

"What? But why? What happened?"

"Yesterday she took down the picture of *Il Duce* from the wall in our class. She said it was time to stop praising him. That we should start asking more questions. She told us that she had had enough. That she couldn't keep teaching us lies."

"She said that?"

"Yup. And she said that it is wrong to beat and kill someone just because they think differently from you. Like the Fascists beating up trade unionists and anarchists and stuff. She called it nuts."

"She told you this in the classroom? Holy Mother of God!"

"Uh huh. Today she was telling us that the Blackshirts are no different from criminals, and we should not trust them. That's when the police came into the classroom. They dragged her out. She was kicking and yelling, *'Fight the dictatorship!'*

"Mother, what's a dictatorship?"

GREAT-GRANDFATHER: MUSSOLINI STILL POPULAR?

Many people supported Mussolini in the beginning because they thought he could actually make things better. For everyone. Then everything changed. Mussolini formed a friendship with Hitler. In 1938 *The Race Manifesto* was published. The Fascists passed unpopular new laws like the racial ones against the Jews. Until this time, there had been little anti-Semitism. Then came the Germanification of the Fascists— Nazi Fascism. The Fascists marginalized Italy. It was the first time the nation was united in a project. But it was different from Germany. For example, there wasn't the same genocidal zeal. We Italians could not support that. But it was also the beginning of the end for Mussolini. He screwed himself good.

FOLLOW THE MULE

Don Paolo, the rotund Fascist village prefect, curses loudly as he rides the lurching, uncooperative mule up the side of the steep mountain under a blazing sun.

To his right, the village lies far below the rocky trail, obscured by trees and cliffs. Today he's paying a visit to the charcoal burners' huts high above to collect the money he's owed. No one knows where this money goes. But not to pay it means trouble—from the prefect and his two goons.

"Come on, you useless piece of shit! Keep moving!"

He kicks the mule in the ribs again and again with his knee-high, black boots. The mule has stopped in protest and refuses to budge. Don Paolo pulls out a dirty handkerchief to wipe his drenched shiny face, then slaps the mule on its rear. The animal still doesn't budge but stares unblinking ahead, spotting the slight movement behind a rock just to the left.

Behind an outcrop, the teenage girl crouches silently, waiting. She whispers softly to herself: "One bullet for persecuting my uncle and sending him to the insane asylum. One bullet for threatening our elderly neighbour, beating him and frightening him to his death. And now one bullet for tormenting this poor animal that would gladly pull the trigger if he could."

Don Paolo squints at the bright white burning sun above and surveys the valley below.

My valley, he thinks to himself. *One day, all mine.*

He hears the "crack!" of a gunshot, then clutches his left shoulder as the lead burns his flesh. He winces and groans.

"What the devil? Who? Damn you!"

The crack of the second bullet follows the echo of the first, across the mountain and valley, as the Fascist prefect reels backward, his feet kicking the air as his heavy body tumbles off the mule in slow motion.

The young woman, now standing, fires a third bullet as his body rolls over the edge of the steep trail—but misses. She only had three bullets. She runs over to catch a final glimpse and watches the corpulent mass start a small rockslide as it rolls and bounces down the slope. A few hundred metres below, the lifeless body stops and is buried under the rocks that follow. A black boot sticks up out of the rubble.

One less Fascist to worry about, she thinks.

The mule glances over the side of the cliff, brays, turns around, and walks back down the trail. The young woman follows.

GREAT-GRANDFATHER: REPRISALS

Does anyone today discuss the reprisals after the war, the reasons behind the first war, and why the second? Not really.

I have great nephews and great-grandchildren in North America, and even there to this day people are afraid to speak about these unspeakable things! Fascists and their spies are everywhere. Even in foreign governments!

The U.S. government would send Mussolini names and addresses that he had requested of Italian dissidents living in America. Then Mussolini sent his people overseas to silence the dissidents, the ones who had asked too many questions and publically criticised his regime and organized resistance. Much like the U.S. government does today. But after all his years of terrorizing Italy and beyond, did Mussolini learn that he too, was expendable?

NEWS, 1943: Axis forces defeated in North Africa . . . Allies invade Sicily . . . Bomb Rome . . . Mussolini deposed & imprisoned by own people . . . Nazis stage dramatic commando raid on Gran Sasso mountain-top hotel prison to rescue the dictator . . . Return him to power in German-occupied north & central Italy . . .

SEVEN BROTHERS

Seven brothers once lived on this peaceful hillside outside Rome in Monterotondo. They farmed, raised cows and pigs, goats and sheep, minded their own business, got married, raised families, contributed to the local church and helped their neighbours. They were good people. Related somehow to the Discordias. Then the Fascists came and Italy began to change.

The Fascists espouse their new ideology. They want to "improve" Italy. Build the Empire. Make Italians feel superior. Benito Mussolini marches on Rome in 1922, and with the consent of Italy's traditional elite, assumes power. Fascist jackboots go *"stomp, stomp, stomp!"* Dissidents disappear into prisons, underground or into exile. Books are burned.

Meanwhile, ordinary people, from labourers to lawyers, and even some pro-Fascist Jews, join the party. Some want to wear shiny black boots and have a taste of power themselves.

"I am a Fascist! Respect my authority!"

Others, well, because . . .

"I want to keep my job."

"They're only hiring Fascists now, no one else."

"I want to preserve the Italian race, too."

"If Mussolini is popular with the women, maybe it can work for me also?"

"If I don't, they'll think I'm a radical and I'll be punished."

"Life is permanent warfare. Italy has many enemies within and without. Only the Fascists can protect Italy."

"We must keep the lower classes in check. They demand too much."

"I love Italy. The party loves Italy. That's good enough for me."

"I like to fight. Fascists fight. If I join, they will pay me to fight."

"We need more authority, more order, more control by the State to stabilize Italy."

"Maybe it's not so bad after all. It's like joining a soccer club, right?"

"If I join now, they won't persecute me or my family later."

"Italy must become great again! Like in the days of the Romans."

"Idiot. It's good for business!"

"If the Church supports them, they must be OK. God approves."

"My brother-in-law joined and now he's a big shot."

"Everyone else is doing it. Why shouldn't I?"

Groups of Fascist thugs, the Blackshirts, roam the streets to provoke and intimidate those who might constitute an opposition, those who represent a threat to this all-consuming, all-demanding dominant ideology. On nightly expeditions, Blackshirts attack and ransack radical labour centres, piling up and burning books outside on the streets.

"Disagreement is treason!" they scream in public.

And everyone hears them, because Italy is changing. Ordinary, unthinking citizens say:

"Change is good. Yes?"

Radio stations and the newspapers controlled by the Fascists all agree:

"Bravo loyal, patriotic Blackshirts!"

Bloodstains appear on their boots and shirts. Graffiti is written in blood:

"*Credere! Obbedire! Combattere!*" Believe! Obey! Fight!

"*Tutto nello Stato! Niente al di fuori dello Stato! Nulla contro lo Stato!*" Everything in the State! Nothing outside the State! Nothing against the State!

Their slogans are shouted ever louder:

"Absolute allegiance! No exceptions! You are with us and the State, or you are the Enemy! Hail our dictator! *Viva Il Duce*! Long live the leader! Hail the army!"

They never say:

"Death to Democracy! Death to Freedom of Speech! Death to Freedom of the Press! Death to any individuals, groups, parties or associations of any kind outside of the State!"

They simply say:

"All for the greatness of Italy! Children, mothers, fathers, do your part for the State! Italy is number one! One vision only! Down with dissidence! Jail and execute all dissenters! The Dictator will take care of all! Death to socialism, communism, anarchism! There is no class struggle! There are no classes! Just One People United in the everlasting glory of The State! Italy! Italy! Italy!"

The mantras are repeated over and over again.

"*E' l'aratro che traccia il solco, ma è la spada che lo difende!*" The plough cuts the furrow, but the sword defends it!

Their loudspeakers go *"boom, boom, boom!"* and many (but not all) believe the lies and promises of a new, better, reborn Italy.

Their clubs and whips go *"thud, thud, thud!"* and Italy cries. Italy is terrified. Italy bleeds. And Italy joins hands with Germany and forges an alliance to transform the rest of the world in their own image—whatever the cost, in lira or in lives. Because as everyone knows:

"War is to man as motherhood is to woman."

"Viva la morte!" Long live death!

"Molti nemici. Molto onore" Many enemies. Much honour.

"Se avanzo, seguitemi. Se indietreggio, uccidetemi. Se muoio, vendicatemi." If I advance, follow me. If I retreat, kill me. If I die, avenge me.

Italy changes. Some remember those days fondly. Others not so fondly.

"Oh, but the trains ran on time!"

"Opposition parties were silenced."

"But Mussolini reminded us of our former greatness and gave us hope again! He offered new aspirations to conquer the world, like the Romans did, to restore our former greatness!"

"More dissidents were jailed. Artists who didn't promote Fascist ideals were persecuted."

"But look at all the beautiful new Fascist architecture he introduced: the palaces, the public buildings, the meeting places, the wide glorious modern avenues!"

"The poor remained poor, underhoused, hungry, and unfed."

"But what a wonderful heritage he left behind!"

"He forged an alliance with Imperial Japan and Germany, entering World War II and starting a global killing spree."

Of course the millions of people killed by the Fascists cannot shout out their disagreement. Leave that to their surviving family members.

On the hillside in Monterotondo, the seven brothers challenge the Fascist machine. They speak out against the right-wing propaganda, the attack against all that is human.

They believe in the goodness, decency, and common sense of the people—not the omnipotence of a dictatorship propped up by big business.

Through the grapevine, they hear of others—critical thinkers, socialists, communists, and anarchists—who share the same ideas. They unite and organize themselves into the Arditi del Popolo, the world's first anti-Fascist movement.

The brothers pick up the gun. They go underground to fight the Fascist and Nazi poison. They engage in sabotage and guerrilla warfare. They form part of the multilayered resistance.

At first, they are outnumbered, but they never give up. They are wounded, captured, and one dark day they are all forced to kneel on the ground, Fascist guns to their heads. The Fascists calmly execute them one by one, their still warm bodies left crumpled together.

Eventually, the Fascist governments of Europe are all toppled. People cheer. Former Fascists suddenly become non-Fascists, even partisans, veterans of the resistance. They rewrite their own histories.

"I was never really political. I never really believed it. I did it because everyone else was doing it . . ."

But Fascism, that putrid growth whose roots grow deep in the hearts and minds of some, does not die. Italy has changed.

Here today, on the verdant hillside in Monterotondo, where chickadees sing and lemons grow, and the gentle sun warms the red-tiled roofs of neat villas and gas stations and shops lining the main road, the citizens walk about without having to look at swastikas or drunken goons or officers goose-stepping.

"But beware," say the brothers' spirits. "There is something sinister in the air. You too, will have to fight someday."

C.S.O.A. (EX SNIA VISCOSA) *VIA PRENESTINA*

Nestled in the bushes between the railway tracks and *Via Prenestina* in the centre of Rome, is a sprawling, abandoned industrial complex called Ex SNIA Viscosa.

Huge trees have rooted themselves beneath former factory floors, and their branches and foliage are taking back bombed-out brick and concrete structures, transforming them into living, almost camouflaged ruins. Where the trees once were denied life in the complex, now they dominate it.

An accidental lake on the property is now home to birds. The entire, multi-acre park is testimony to untamed returning urban wilderness.

It's also a hiding place for refugees, a temporary camp for *clandestinos*, the undocumented; and the home of a self-managed Social Centre (CSOA—*Centro Sociale Occupato Autogestito*).

Ex SNIA Viscosa was once a textiles factory that opened in 1908. In the 1920s, the Arditi del Popolo were active here, sabotaging the machinery. Generations of the Discordia family who lived in San Lorenzo also worked here, including one of Antonio's great-aunts. She told him that almost 60 percent of the workforce was women—all union members.

"The factory used to produce rayon silk, but in the 1930s, it produced mustard gas bombs for the Fascists," she said.

"When one of the workers, an anti-Fascist, was caught sabotaging the machinery, she was taken outside the plant and shot in the park. Other factory workers were active in the struggle, transporting stolen bombs on their bicycles to anti-Fascists outside. Were we afraid of getting caught? Of course. But what else could we do? Watch them arrest and kill our friends?"

By 1955, Ex SNIA Viscosa was abandoned and became a warehouse for trucks. Romani refugees camped in it. But by 1994, it was occupied by youth. There were differences of opinion with the Roma, and the Roma left. One member of the Marxist-Leninist urban guerrilla group, the Red Brigades, Daniel Epifanno, was arrested here and jailed. Now diverse refugees occupy it.

Today, on the super-clean floor of CSOA Ex SNIA Viscosa, a one-armed, one-eyed Palestinian refugee breakdancer shows his stuff, spinning on his head. Loud hip hop music blares overhead while a multiethnic group of Albanians, Arabs, and Africans watch him.

In another corner, northern African *Sans Papiers*—the undocumented, without papers—stage an impromptu ping pong tournament. Surprisingly, in the *Tratlosina*, the centre's makeshift but fully equipped kitchen, a group of ten young American high-school girls learn how to make pizza. In another corner, a young black man mops the polished red brick floor. Dozens of young people come and go through the garage-size doorway, in and out of this centre, their place to hang in the community.

The main cook, for example, dropped by the centre one day to get his bicycle fixed, helped to cook, then stayed to fix bikes and cook food on a volunteer basis. He's also a graphic designer and teaches at a local school.

"I work two paying jobs, but seven-eighths of my salaries go to pay the rent. And I'm renting places that are smaller and smaller, with more and more roommates. Otherwise, who can afford to live in Rome anymore? The government keeps selling off public housing to the private market. My next home could be here, under a tree, under a tarp. Move over, refugees. We Italians are the newest homeless underclass. In our own country."

ROME'S DRINKING FOUNTAINS

Antonio walks down *Via Gattamelata*, crosses *Via Prenestina*, and hurries up a gravel path. At the top of a slight hill, he lounges on a bench in the small park just outside the CSOA Ex SNIA Viscosa factory fence and waits for Cinka.

Behind him, from the giant freight yard, he hears a pleasing symphony of steel on steel, the squeak, clank and crank of train wheels and couplers.

In front, children play and laugh on the swings behind a low hedge. A few dozen black men sit together on a wall, talking and drinking. Others kick around a soccer ball on a small field. This welcome patch of green in an otherwise dense neighbourhood is always well used.

Antonio crooks his head backward to drink in the brilliant blue sky above, framed by a row of ornamental, emerald green pine trees. He thinks how lucky he is to have Cinka in his life. *She makes me feel whole, at peace with myself, the world and everyone in it.*

He's enjoying watching the sweaty afternoon joggers pound the path encircling the park, clockwise, then counterclockwise. A few stretch muscles against the towering pine trunks. A dog runs by, tail wagging, a huge pinecone in its mouth.

Almost everyone stops at the cast iron water fountain to cup their hands and drink, wash their faces, soak their heads, fill water bottles, or clean their shoes. Even thirsty dogs lap the cool running water.

A Southeast Asian father walks alongside his young son learning how to ride a bicycle. The father takes his hands off the boy's shoulder. The boy continues on his own, all smiles downhill, then loses control and rams his runaway bike into a wire mesh fence. Antonio winces. Then he spots Cinka on the pathway, carrying her violin and limping. She's frowning as she approaches.

"What happened, sweetheart?" Antonio throws his arms around her.

"Fucking racists!" she spits out as she sits on the bench. She drops her face into her hands and sobs loudly. He pulls her even closer.

"These weren't Nazi skinheads wearing swastikas, no. These were ordinary-looking young Italian guys. Six of them surrounded me on the street and blocked my path. They said I shouldn't be walking in this neighbourhood because 'animals' without a leash aren't allowed here. Can you believe it?

"One of them spat on me, then tried to grab my violin case. They were laughing, too. I swore at them, screamed and tried to fight them off. They called me names. Said Gypsies were less than dogs and were not welcome here. Then they started to kick me! Look!"

She pulls back her skirt to reveal ugly black and blue bruises on her leg.

"Didn't anyone come to help you?" Antonio is torn between wanting to cry, to scream, or go back and beat the crap out of the guys.

"Nobody at first. There were people nearby watching. They did nothing. Then a young Italian woman ran up, swore at the guys and pushed them away. She was smaller than me, but the guys listened to her and backed off. She saved my life. I was so frightened. Thank God she was there. She walked me all the way here to make sure I was safe. I wanted to give her something, to get her address, to thank her, but she said no."

"Those bastards! Where are they? I want to smash their faces in. Fucking assholes!"

"Antonio, what do you think that would do? Stop them from harassing others? No. It will take more than my skinny lover trying to beat up a bunch of idiots to change things."

Cinka wipes her face in her sleeve and smiles faintly at Antonio. He continues to rage: "They can't get away with that! They attacked you! We have to call the police! Report them!" Antonio was standing up now, agitated and livid.

"And whose side do you think the cops will take?"

"But they could be charged with assault!"

His face is beet red. He kicks the gravel underfoot.

"Antonio, you forget who I am. No cop will ever charge an Italian for assaulting a Gypsy."

"But there were witnesses!"

"And they did nothing."

NEWS, August 2007, Livorno: *Six Romani children perish in a fire in a refugee camp. The "Armed Group for Ethnic Cleansing" (GAPE) claims responsibility for the attack.*
September, Rome: *Molotov cocktails dropped from a bridge into a Romani camp burn several homes; next day, 40 masked men armed with metal bars and Molotovs attack the same camp again . . .*

October, Turin: Molotov cocktails thrown at a Romani camp burn it to the ground . . .

CINKA'S MOM SPEAKS OUT

"My daughter's happiness is what's important! Not what was said so many years ago! Things are different now! Do you understand?"

Cinka's mom is yelling so that everyone in the vicinity can hear. She's in fighting form, standing outside the hut of the refugee camp gossip this late afternoon. Her hands on her big hips, chin thrust forward, she scowls at the old woman standing inside, who glares back. A small curious crowd has gathered around Luminitsa.

"I only speak the truth," the old gossip retorts.

"And so do I! My daughter's life is none of your business! You have no right to interfere! I'm warning you! You keep your nose out of her affairs! Do you hear me?"

The old woman mumbles, "We'll see who's right," then slams her door shut.

Luminitsa turns to face the small crowd. The crowd steps back.

"The lies this old woman spreads stop here!" She draws a line with her shoe in the dirt in front of her. "She has said enough about my daughter! If you want the truth, speak to me or to Cinka! Don't listen to this hag!"

LUCA ON THE BUS

Luca is stuck sitting at the back of the hot, packed bus near the toilet. It's his first bus trip anywhere, and between endless mechanical problems en route, the revolting stench from the toilet, crying babies, and passengers who suffer bus sickness, the journey to Italy is a nightmare. He vows to escape this rolling madhouse as soon as possible.

With his last bottle of vodka gone, and no more money for drink or food, he's having trouble concentrating.

I don't want Cinka anymore, he keeps repeating to himself. She slept with another man. She is soiled. Fuck her!

She was supposed to be mine—my woman, my wife, to cook and clean for my parents and me. To give me a son! She didn't honour the arrangement. She didn't honour me. It's not right!

She went to Italy to work. To make money. For one year only. That's what they all said. Then come back to the village. That was the understanding. She made it two years, then three. Her family said she had no work, no money, and they couldn't come back. Now this? Somebody is lying. I'm going to find out who. Nobody makes a fool out of me. Everyone in the village is talking."

At the next bus stop, he calls his cousin collect in Rome.

"Don't do anything until I get there. Just set it up with the elders, OK? I'm on my way."

ROMAN STARLINGS

Rafaele parks his Fiat Panda on *Viale Trinità dei Monti* just below the Medici Gardens. He gets out, and from his favourite vantage point, gazes over the city roofs as Romans head home from work. For Rafaele, though, this is showtime—a Murmuration.

High above the palaces, hills and church spires, he watches the starlings—hundreds of thousands strong—performing their end-of-day acrobatic aerial ballet. It's a centuries-old spectacle. Unlike his family and friends, he never tires of it.

Before bedtime, after feeding in the countryside, the starlings return to Rome, where they group and regroup in complex, mesmerizing flight patterns. From a distance the swarms are so thick they can look like smoke. In fluid airborne waves, the birds come together in complex, geometrical patterns, shift in midflight in any direction responding in unison to currents of air or whims or habit, then separate and reform into something new.

The living tableau resembles a painting by one of his favourite old-school artists, Seurat, the Pointillist. But instead of fixed images, this painting goes through unending changes. It shifts constantly. Instead of primary colours, these thousands of individual pinpoints are all black. And instead of an artists' skilled hand, they regroup out of habit, painting and repainting pictures themselves.

Do the patterns mean anything? Are they trying to communicate with us lowly earth-bounded? Do these birds give a shit what we think? Rafaele shakes his head. North, south, east, west—who can predict their next direction, their next trajectory?

Sometimes groups break away and fly off into the distance, only to return moments later and reform into an even larger, more incredible pattern.

Like us at a rock concert waving our cell phones? Like pilgrims at a mass assembly, or a giant airborne army from some fantasy film, or Fascists at a wartime stadium rally herded into a gigantic swastika? Who is the choreographer? What unseen hands are actually behind the spectacle, pushing arrow keys: Left! Right! Forward! Stop!

Rafaele walks to the *Piazza del Popolo*, watching the pedestrians below herd themselves in small groups, re-form and break away. The compliant, submissive, obedient flock; and "the others," the different ones. The mass, a historic, timeless collectivity; the blip, the anomaly, the dissenting, excuse-me-I-think-otherwise individual.

The one way, which we are led to believe is the only way, is to follow, vision blinkered, no digressions please beyond the approved limitations of living. The other: the endless other possibilities we rarely have the time or courage to consider . . .

The mass consciousness, moulded into consensus all the way to old age. And within the uniformly bland and anonymous urban cacophony this creates, the startling, distinct birdsong. The crash and flash of thunder and lightning during a snowfall. The new stranger, unalike, with another way of being, solitary, or with family, silently, or with the sound system cranked to max.

For all their fluid aerial beauty, the starlings could be emissaries from the Dark Side, sinister and threatening. Maybe following commands, maybe heralding a storm to come. But also, their totally free and seemingly random, wild, spontaneous fluctuations respond to some primal urge, some joyous impulse, and speak to Rafaele about a world without restraint. A world of endless beauty and freedom, where alone or with others, regardless of old ways of thinking and behaving, desire and pleasure rule. And make beauty.

CINKA'S MOM AND THE SHOPKEEPER

Luminitsa always wears her traditional long skirt, billowing blouse, shawl, bangles, and bracelets. She has a friendly face and a kindly demeanour; but today, she's also wearing an extra big smile.

She's en route to visit her old friend in Monterotondo outside Rome—a luxury she allows herself once a month. Her friend's health is failing so she wants to cheer her up with a small bag of fruit, tea and sweets. She stops off at a local grocery store near the station.

In her rudimentary Italian, Luminitsa asks the stern-looking bald shopkeeper behind the counter a simple question.

"But sir, please. Why you charging me more for tea? Same tea I buy last month."

In a loud voice, the shopkeeper answers: "That's the trouble with you damn Gypsies! You want things for free! You don't understand or respect our Italian way of life! You want handouts and when you don't get them, you rob, beat and murder innocent people!"

Other customers in the store turn to look.

"Excuse me? What you speaking about?" Luminitsa is shocked and takes a step back. "Please, I only ask about price of tea."

"Yes, and then you pretend to be ignorant! And you're criminals! You get away with murder! I've had enough of your people! All of you are alike, damn Gypsies!"

By now, every customer is staring at Luminitsa and echoing his comments.

"He's right!"

"You're all thieves and murderers!"

"Damn Gypsies! Go home!"

Luminitsa looks in horror at the customers forming a semicircle around her.

The shopkeeper waves his fist in the air threateningly as he steps out from behind his counter, bellowing, "Get out of my shop! And don't come back!"

Half crying out of fear and disbelief, Luminitsa cautiously backs out the door. She hurries to the train station and doesn't dare visit her friend.

He might come after me with a knife, a gun, or thugs! Maybe he'll phone the police and have me arrested, she fears.

On the train a young man sitting opposite her reads a newspaper. The headline screams:

300 ROMANIAN GYPSIES EXPELLED FOR PUBLIC SECURITY REASONS!

POLICE DESTROY ILLEGAL CAMPS HOUSING 7,000 GYPSIES IN ROME, BOLOGNA, PISA, PAVIA!

She sinks down in her seat and feels dozens of Italian eyes focused on her.

One man commits a crime, she muses, and they blame and punish all of us? Oh Mother of God! Why did we ever come here?

GREAT-GRANDFATHER: WARTIME RESISTANCE

During World War II, the Resistance inside Rome confounded the Nazis. Where do these damn people come from? Who supports them? Who keeps them armed and alive? Who will snitch on them?

They bought spies among our own people. Traitors. Scoundrels who betrayed the Resistance. Eventually, the Nazis targeted three working-class neighbourhoods in the city as bastions of anti-Fascism: San Lorenzo, Quadraro, and Il Pigneto. Then they went hunting door to door, terrorizing everyone in sight. Children, too.

Our family was mainly in San Lorenzo. Generations

grew up there working in the factories. The ones, that is, who couldn't handle all the fresh air, scarce but tasty food and backbreaking fieldwork in Abruzzo. As early as 1922, when Mussolini's Blackshirts marched into Rome through the *Porta San Lorenzo*, the locals—many of our family's neighbours, and us Discordias too—resisted and were killed. During Mussolini's reign and the occupation of Rome by the Germans, our kind of people never adapted to Fascism and never stopped resisting. Thank goodness.

Quadraro in the southeast was home to *Cinecittà*—Cinema City—our own Italian Hollywood. We had our stars, too: voluptuous peroxide blonds and brunettes with all the makeup. Suave, pale-skinned, moustachioed men of the big screen. How the young people loved their films!

The huge film studio complex was set up in 1937 by Mussolini as a propaganda facility. He was thinking ahead. The Fascists proclaimed that *"cinema is the most powerful weapon"* and released films glorifying Italy's military victories and the benefits of Fascism. More than one rotten tomato was lobbed at the screen, I'll tell you.

In 1944, one thousand men were arrested over two days by the Germans in this so-called hornet's nest of anti-Fascism and deported to Germany to work in weapons factories. Half died in captivity; others escaped and joined the partisans.

Il Pigneto was north of Quadraro, south of *Via Prenestina*, through the *Porta Maggiore*. Many local men who wouldn't give the Fascist salute in a bar were arrested and deported, never to be seen again. We lost them by the hundreds. Others who rescued people from Fascist beatings were arrested and disappeared. Many homes hid escaped prisoners of war. My family, bless their souls, would hide people behind false walls built into cupboards. It was a nerve-racking existence. If you were caught, you were shot. In 1945, Il Pigneto was the site for one of my favourite postwar films, Roberto Rossellini's *Roma, Città Aperta*. On and off the screen the resistance continued.

RAFAELE'S MOTHER BORN IN A PARTISAN CAMP, 1944

As the first snow started to fall during a gunfight in the mountains, I, Loretta Marcella Discordia, chose to be born. My father and his partisan comrades were trying to repel a Nazi-Fascist patrol sent to kill us. My pregnant mother—also a partisan, and our partisan midwife—both with rifles ready at their sides, were on the verge of cursing me.

"Why now? Here in the middle of this attack? Mother of God! What is this baby thinking?"

I admit my timing was a bit off, given that my father, Enrico, could not be present, but wanted to—or so he told my mother, Elisabetta. The damn Nazi-Fascists were closing in on our no-longer-secret mountain base, because of a traitor giving us away (another story, of course). Little squirming me was diverting the attention of two necessary fighters.

But as the gunfight raged in the heavily wooded valley below us; and my mother, lying on straw and blankets, bit hard on a rolled up rag to stifle her screams; and the midwife with one eye on me emerging and one on the door in this shepherd's stone hut heard the *rat-a-tat-tat* of enemy machine guns getting closer—I popped out. Surprise! Another girl for the front!

Within minutes, the midwife (a journalist who had given up her job to join the Resistance) and my mother (a former factory worker) had me bundled up in a knapsack and slung onto my mother's chest. Driven by fear and the ever-approaching sound of gunfire, the two women scrambled down a rocky trail that encircled the mountain camp and headed for a second hideout to wait for my father and the others. It was a long day.

TWO PARTISANS SAT ON A ROCK

Two partisans sat on a rock, side by side, busy with their own thoughts of family and war, death and survival. Each smoked a cigarette and scanned the valley below, watching individual house lights slowly disappear into the blackness as inhabitants went to bed.

They listened to the silence infused with a steady chorus of crickets, interrupted only by the bellowing of a distant lone frog. Like the early night sky, they watched and waited patiently for the moon, their signal to act. The older one spoke softly:

"When I was a boy, I used to come here camping with my father. He taught me how to build a fire, how to choose a spot out of the wind for sleeping, how to catch wild pheasants and rabbits, how to clean and roast them over the fire. Nights like this, he instructed me how to tell directions from the stars. Then, as we huddled together close to the fire, he told me stories about ancient slave and peasant revolts. About Spartacus in Greece, and Corsican pirates who settled islands in the Caribbean and started new colonies of free men, free of any authorities."

"How did your father know all this history?" the other asked.

"He read books, talked with others. The usual way."

"I'm afraid I have nothing to offer to teach you other than how to make a good pizza dough."

"You make pizza?"

"The best in my village, or so my sisters say."

"When this war is finished, you can teach me how to make your dough."

"Only if you teach me how to read the stars."

"OK. Pay attention. See up there?" He pointed. "That is the Archer, Sagittarius."

"I don't see an archer."

"Look carefully. It's where the Milky Way is brightest. The Greeks said Sagittarius is shooting the Scorpion, just below, which bit the Hunter, Orion, causing his death. But we can't see Orion when Sagittarius and the Scorpion are in the sky."

"You mean . . ."

"Shhh! Listen!"

They both sat upright, guns raised as they heard footsteps in the dark.

"Relax! It's only me, guys. Time to blow up the bridge," said the skinny bearded musician, code-named Skunk, as he barged through the bush wearing a big grin. He walked with a limp from a gunshot wound.

"We got word from the other brigade. We need to act now. There's a big convoy of Nazi tanks heading this way. You ready?"

The older partisan slapped his companion on the back. "Let's get the scorpions!"

BLOW UP THE BRIDGE

The task was simple. Blow up the bridge spanning the river to stop Nazis tanks from crossing. If Allied planes can't do it, anarchist partisans will.

"We'll show them what we're capable of, and maybe they'll drop more guns for us, like they promised."

Skunk scratched and shook his head.

"You think the Americans want to see more guns in the blackened hands of Italian anarchists? I think they'd rather see us dead than better armed."

"But if we don't have enough weapons, how can they advance? We're cannon fodder, I agree. Dirty Italian sacrificial lambs. But they need us alive for now, to do their work for them. Of course they'll take all the credit and forget about us. Just watch how they write the history of this war. I can see it now: *Allied bombers destroyed a key mountain bridge, paving the way for total Allied victory.*"

"Not a word about us."

"Ha! As long as they and the Nazis leave our country after the war, I'll be content to mop up the leftover Fascists myself."

"You and twenty anarchist comrades, right? Sure! With pleasure!"

RESIST OR DIE

The bridge blown successfully, the partisans retreated to their base camp. A pimple-faced, rail-thin partisan of twenty years, code-named Mouse, was stirring the pot of coffee on the campfire. Skunk and a third much older partisan, The Bear, were sitting on a log cleaning their guns.

"Why did you join up, Skunk? You never told me."

The bearded musician replied:

"No different, I think, from everyone else, or at least from all my friends back in Milano. We never had a choice. It was simple: resist or die. What were the options?"

"But you could have gone into exile, to France or Spain."

"Sure, and some of my friends did and survived. Others were tracked down and assassinated. Some of my other friends tried to blend into the general population and pretend they never had any 'subversive' thoughts ever. 'Oh no, not me, I never said that, sir!' Like disobedient schoolchildren caught in the act."

"I could never do that." Mouse poured out a round of coffee.

"Me neither. When dissent becomes a crime, the crime of thinking, it's time to resist."

"But it wasn't always like that, was it?"

"No," Skunk replied. "I was still a student ten years ago when it started to change. If they suspected you were at all favourable to dissident thought, you'd get a knock on the door. Then an interrogation, a beating, and a warning. If you still refused to lick Mussolini's boots, they killed you."

"But they didn't scare you off?"

"Of course I was scared. Like everybody else. But we kept on meeting, sharing our ideas about resistance, in a park, on a boat, or even in prison. Now I'm here with you, on this mountaintop, with a bullet in my leg and no more stories to tell. For now."

A LOVELY DAY TO EAT GREEN APPLES

In the centre of Torino, the summertime afternoons were white with a great heat that barely diminished by sundown. Sometimes at dusk before curfew, Ricardo Discordia would walk through a local park to escape the confines of his room.

He could hear the concert of the crickets fill the air with song. The park was also handy for the occasional rendezvous.

Today, a young *staffetta*, one of thousands of women in the Resistance, pedalled her red bicycle down the path. Ricardo was already sitting on a bench, legs crossed, reading a newspaper. The woman parked her bicycle beside the bench, then sat down to join him.

"It's a lovely day to eat a green apple," she said as she pulled one out of her bag.

"It is a good season for apples," Ricardo answered smiling. He stood to leave, taking not his bag which contained food and newspapers, but hers. A few metres away, he reached inside the bag beneath the food and fingered the concealed gun. He walked for a few minutes out onto a busy street and stood on a corner.

A man in blue coveralls, a factory worker, approached on a bicycle. The cyclist stopped and greeted Ricardo.

"What a great day for pizza, yes?"

"A very good day for pizza, certainly," Ricardo replied as he held the bag closer to the bicyclist, who reached in and quickly took out the gun, pocketed it, and rode away. Ricardo watched.

At the end of the block, a German command post. Across the street, two other comrades stood beside their bicycles in conversation. As a big black gleaming officer's car drove up, the man on the first bicycle rode by and glanced at the car without stopping. At the end of the street, he returned pedalling slowly. Meanwhile, the other two cyclists started pedalling toward the car.

As two German SS officers exited the car, shots rang out. A guard appeared from the building pointing his rifle. More shots. In less than ten seconds, three Germans were lying dead on the street; the chauffeur was slumped over the wheel of his car. The three cyclists had disappeared.

Ricardo met his man around the corner where the gun was placed back in his bag. A few minutes later he was back in the park, where the young woman was still sitting.

"A lovely day for green apples, indeed."

"Truly, a lovely day," she answered, as they exchanged bags and left in opposite directions.

THE BOMBING OF SAN LORENZO

It was a hot day, July 19, 1943. The church bells chimed 11 AM. Then the terrifying wail of air-raid sirens pierced the streets and skies of Rome, provoking a tidal wave of panic. In San Lorenzo, as elsewhere, horror-stricken residents fled deep into the nearest bomb shelter. Others, far from any shelter, dropped to their knees in the streets.

"Oh, Mother of Jesus! Help us!"

Rafaele's great-grandmother and dozens of other women yelled out the open windows on *Via dei Sabelli*, into the inner and outer courtyards where the children were playing.

"Grab your brother! Your bag! Come quickly! We must go down!"

Two younger children, sitting on the floor playing, were puzzled.

"But what is it, Grandmother? Where are we going? What is that sound?"

"Don't ask questions. Come with me now!"

She grabbed both children by the wrists, yanked open the door, and joined the stream of neighbours shuffling hurriedly down the apartment building's marble stairs.

They heard the ominous drone of the Allied Flying Fortresses overhead. Then the horrifying blasts from the first bombs dropped on the nearby Tiburtina train station and freight yards. More bombs fell, this time on their own working-class residential neighbourhood just east and north of the train station. A deafening blast rocked the building and shattered windows. Adults and children screamed. Holding one another tightly, one-by-one, the families pushed through the iron grilled gate leading into the basement of their building, then down the stairs past the *Refuge* sign on the wall pointing to the air raid shelter.

There they huddled in the shadows with the other frightened mothers, children, and elderly. Many were in tears and incredulous as they held their breaths and trembled in the cool dankness of the stonewalled rooms. Two exposed lightbulbs hung above them, illuminating the arched ceilings. Another nearby blast, and the bulbs flickered. Everyone screamed. Apart from muffled cries and sobs, no one spoke.

They prayed softly, crossing themselves, fingering rosaries, not knowing that their beloved *Basilica di San Lorenzo fuori le Mura*, far from the train station, had also been hit. Fear and incomprehension reigned. Mothers rocked infants in their arms. Little brothers and sisters clung to their grandparents.

"But I have to pee! Now! Please!"

"See the toilet over there?" She pointed to the hand-painted sign and arrow on the wall. "You're a big boy. You don't need me. And wash your hands after in that bucket, OK?"

"But Grandmother, who is dropping the bombs on us?"

"It's the Americans. The Americans."

"But why, Grandmother? Why are they bombing us? We didn't do anything to them did we?"

"No we didn't."

Tears welled up in her eyes but she immediately brushed them away. She never read the flyers dropped over Rome just moments before these bombs fell, explaining that the Allies were "*not going to bomb any cultural monuments that are the glory of Rome and the civilized world.*"

Nor did any of her thousand dead neighbours.

SAN LORENZO MOTHER

In San Lorenzo, a distraught mother kneels over the body of her young son and wails. She curses the Fascists, curses God, then begs his forgiveness and curses the Fascists again.

"You swine have taken my only son! You scum, you filth!"

Cradling the boy's head in her lap, she kisses his forehead tenderly, tears streaming down her cheeks. She rocks back and forth on her knees, saying over and over,

"I loved you like I loved no one else. Now be with God."

MAMA'S BIG WOODEN SPOON

Under the blanket of a starless, foggy night, a small group of partisans snuck up on the German command post. Each took position under a window. Massimo Discordia walked up to the front door, cleared his throat, knocked loudly, and entered. The Germans inside were startled to see one smiling, armed Italian anarchist partisan in their office and started to shout and grab their guns. In perfect German, without flinching, Massimo announced:

"Gentlemen, your command is surrounded. You have five minutes to release all your prisoners or suffer the consequences. We will leave no one alive. Do you understand?

"But you're joking!" a German replied.

"Not tonight," Massimo said, "Take a look."

And he pointed to the windows where the other comrades now stood, their rifles and machine guns aimed inside. After a lightning-quick consultation, the Germans inside fell for the bluff, and agreed instantly to the release of the prisoners. It was Massimo's boldness, his calm and authoritative manner that convinced them.

The rest of the group admitted later that they were scared shitless of what might have happened had the Germans refused. They quickly hustled the freed comrades out and into the forest where they disappeared into a waiting truck. Later they asked, "Massimo, how did you do it?"

"Oh, I kept thinking of my mama's big wooden spoon when I was a child. It was always waiting for me if I failed to finish a task. That helped."

GREAT-GRANDFATHER: THE SO-CALLED ALLIES

What our poor partisans did not know during that tortuous, difficult winter of 1944 was this: while partisans froze to death or died in battles because of lack of support, the generals and politicians, the Churchills and their cohorts, met safely behind closed doors to sip whisky, play with their toy soldiers, tanks, and planes, and tally the number of little people they were prepared to sacrifice.

We know who writes the history books. Not the slaves, grunts, or sheepherders—pawns and cannon fodder all. Who takes credit for "victory" and "mission accomplished"? Not the dead sons and daughters of the poor, the ones who actually fight for freedom.

Thousands of partisans will never forgive the so-called "liberators," the traitorous Anglo-American so-called Allies, for stalling their advance in Italy during that winter. The Allies wanted the Germans and the Fascists to do their dirty work for them: to rid Italy of as many radicals as possible. To kill those fighting in the Resistance. To make their job of setting up a compliant postwar government all the easier. The swine. All those men and women sacrificed by Churchill and his friends.

Not only did the Allies needlessly bomb partisan positions, but also they refused to give them weapons to fight to defend their own lives. From afar, in comfort, they knowingly watched poor partisans in their broken boots try to resist the well-equipped overpowering Nazi-Fascists, then die.

Our future was denied by calculating murderers who never stained their hands with blood, but gave others the order. This we should never forget. In my sleep, and my children's sleep, and the sleep of the generations to come, this can never be forgotten.

ARE YOU HAPPY?

The two partisans walked through the woods and came to a small clearing at the edge of a cliff. They stood side by side and gazed across the vastness of the deep purple valley below. It was their shift on this high mountain post.

In the distance, a dog barked. Another one answered. Above, the pale blue moon outshone thousands of scintillating stars vying for attention. A slight breeze stirred the pines behind them. The older partisan spat into the void below, then hummed the melody to one of his favourite partisan songs, *Fischia il vento*—Whistling in the wind:

The wind whistles, the storm rages / our shoes are
broken but we must go,
to conquer the red spring / where the sun of the future
rises
to conquer the red spring / where the sun of the future
rises.

"Hey, are you happy?" the younger one asked.

"What? Happy? What kind of question is that?"

The older partisan scratched his beard and leaned his
rifle against a rock.

"I have no time to think about that."

The younger one persisted:

"But all these years of struggle, you know. Debating, fighting, hiding, and planning. Why do we do all of this if nowhere
we can find a bit of happiness? Something to make us really
happy."

"You mean a girl, a wife?"

"Maybe. Maybe not."

"I would love to have a girl or a wife, but how? Where?
When? Maybe later."

"Why not here and now?"

"You crazy? Instead of looking for ways to stop Fascists,
we concentrate on finding girls?"

"Why not make some time for that too?"

"Huh? Because you say so?"

"Because we all need a bit of happiness. Not in some
distant future, but sooner."

"But can't we wait until we have secured victory? Until
we know we've won? Defeated the Fascists?"

"And how long could that take? In the meantime, what's
the point of all this if not to make ourselves happy? Is this not
why we struggle and sacrifice?"

"We fight hard so that we can find some peace and
freedom."

"And happiness, yes? Why not?"

The two partisans lay down on their backs to rest under the midnight stars. They used rocks for pillows. A sudden brisk wind blew and they shivered. Neither of them had enough warm clothes. It was a cold but peaceful night. No one would have known a war was raging on. An owl hooted somewhere. They heard the flutter of wings in the distance.

"Look! A shooting star!" the younger one pointed.

"Make a wish that this war will end and we can go to the inn and celebrate."

"Did you hear about the innkeeper's brother? That greedy good-for-nothing rat who sold out the unit across the valley?"

"Yes, everyone is talking about him. They say he got extra food and cigarettes from the Fascists, and who knows what future favours."

"The traitor should be shot the next time he shows his face."

"Him and all the others who infiltrated us only to betray us for a reward."

"Everyone says, '*support the glorious, romantic partisans, our heroes.*' Then the knife in the back. The dogs. No one ever talks about our own scum."

"It's a war. What do you think? There are hungry, desperate, selfish, and fearful souls out there. Hunger can sometimes erase any thoughts of compassion and solidarity. It can turn a decent person into a heartless ogre."

"We'll make that scum pay later. If any of us are still around to identify them."

"But then they'll just lie low, waiting for the Fascist resurrection."

"Not if I can get to them first."

"You watch. The Allies have a high tolerance for Fascists, in and out of war. More than we ever suspected. In fact, it seems they would prefer to let Fascists run the country instead of having it fall into our hands. The dogs!"

"Traitors usually come with a smile. Smelling them out is never easy. So-called 'allies' or not."

GREAT-GRANDFATHER: MUSSOLINI'S CAPTURE AND EXECUTION

How did the monster, *Il Duce*, Benito Mussolini, finally die? Ignobly. Italian partisans apprehended him trying to escape Italy into Switzerland. He was in a German convoy travelling on the road on the edge of Lake Como, disguised as a German soldier, cowering in the back of a troop transport truck. Hiding like a naughty boy!

How the once-mighty can shake in their boots and piss their pants when the people rise up and spit in their face. The partisans couldn't believe their luck when they dragged him out. They found his mistress too.

The next day—a grey one it was—Benito and his mistress, thinking they were being rescued by friendly forces, were hustled into a car that sped off. A bit later, the car stopped outside a villa on a quiet mountain road. They were told to step out. She was asked to move away from Mussolini. She wouldn't. On the spot, they were both gunned down, executed.

There is still controversy about the circumstances surrounding this event, whether someone was acting on orders to kill Mussolini before any trial, to spare the Allies the embarrassment of having all his secret dealings with the British government exposed.

A day later, April 29, 1945, the citizens of Milan gathered in *Piazza Loreto*, one of the main city squares, to see an extraordinary sight. From the roof of an Esso gas station, hanging upside down, side by side by their heels high in the air in plain view of everyone, were the corpses of several dead Fascists, including Mussolini and his mistress. Like pigs in an *abattoir*. It was a gruesome, sorry sight. But the butcher, the Fascist dictator, "The Man of Miracles" was now, himself, carrion for vultures.

PART V

THE LEGACY

THE WOMEN IN THE RESISTANCE, 1965

"You want me to tell you about the women in the Resistance?"

Enrico Discordia was rolling a cigarette at the kitchen table in the yellow brightness of his small apartment. Enrico, a sad-faced, fifty-five-year-old widower, was a millwright, like his father, and his father before him.

His only daughter, Loretta, a twenty-year-old university student with a pixie haircut, horn-rimmed glasses, jeans, and sneakers, put her tape recorder on the table.

"Please, Dad? It's for a paper for my history course. I'm writing about the women who risked their lives to save the lives of partisans. The women who fought alongside you, behind the barricades or on the mountain ridges. Remember? You used to tell me the stories when I was younger. You just talk into this thing, Dad, see?"

She placed the microphone in front of him and waited.

Her father sighed and managed a feeble smile. He lit his cigarette, took a long drag, then stared out the kitchen window.

Loretta was used to these long pauses. She watched his face as he gathered his thoughts, saw the furrow in his brows, saw his eyes glaze over slightly, and she wondered again how deep he had to search for memories like these. It had been a while since he had talked about his war experiences.

"OK, I'll tell you some things. There were women—mostly young—who rode their wobbly bicycles down treacherous roads, past Fascist checkpoints, to bring us food, warm socks, ammunition, and weapons. They risked everything for us. Without them, we couldn't survive. They were our lifelines. These women we adored. And they were many. Students, peasants, bakers, seamstresses.

"But there was one in particular I loved with all my heart. She was ingenious. Brave. Resourceful, cunning, defiant, indefatigable and charming. She spilled out of my dreams day and night. How could I not love her? A dazzling smile as white as snow, a pair of enchanting eyes, and the voice of a seductive forest nymph. She was only nineteen years old, like you, but already a veteran fighter. She came from an entire family of partisans who joined after their father was tortured and killed by the Fascists, years before.

"Her partisan name was Rosebud. She was a *staffetta*, a courier in our region. She rode a red bicycle and always wore a black flowered kerchief on her head. When she undid it in front of me, I got goose bumps watching her long brown hair fall to her shoulders. She would shake her head to untangle her curls. Each time I almost fainted from the sight. As did every other man nearby. I swear even other women were in love with her, too. Can you imagine? But who could blame them?

"She used her beauty and her charms to talk her way past enemy soldiers. But I know she was acutely aware every moment, every day, of the dangers and the risks she took. If your mother was alive today, she could tell you so much more. Is that good enough?"

"That's fine, yes. Thanks, Dad." She shut off the tape recorder.

Loretta's father remembered how Rosebud once confided in him a horrible secret. He had never repeated the story to Loretta, at his wife's request.

"I was riding my bicycle late at night, carrying documents for a partisan brigade just outside the city. Around a corner, a known local Blackshirt leaped out of the dark and yanked my bicycle to the ground. He pounced on me. He pinned me to the pavement and

*slapped my face a few times. Then he dragged me screaming into
an abandoned building and tried to rape me. He called me a dirty
subversive, a whore who didn't deserve to live. He tried to muffle
my screams with one hand. I had no choice. It was either his life,
or mine. I pulled out a concealed knife strapped to my thigh and
stabbed him repeatedly in the back. I'll never forget the look on his
face. He rolled over dead. I hid his body under some old machinery
and completed my mission."*

CIVIL WAR POSTWAR

Loretta brought her father a cup of coffee and a plate of
cookies and sat beside him. His face lit up.

"My favourite! Chocolate Supremes! When did you buy
these? Thank you. Just like your mother."

"You know, Dad, the teachers in high school tell us that
after the war, all the Fascists supposedly disappeared. That
you and the other partisans crushed them and wiped them
out. This was the official line. But it was never true, was it?
You won, but not really?"

The elder Discordia sipped his coffee and took a long
drag on his cigarette. Then he whistled a bit from one of his
favourite Partisan songs, before he spoke:

"Loretta, after the war, only the blind and the foolish
would believe that the hostilities were over.

"In the months after what everyone called the 'liberation'
of April 1945, we were all heady with victory. Big changes
are coming, we thought. Sweep out the old regime! Time for
something new! Radical even. We were naïve. Right under
our noses, a civil war was raging all over Italy. Fascists used
their positions of authority in the new government to exact
revenge on us Partisans. They had us beaten, imprisoned, and
killed. To this day, the cruelties, the indignities, the everyday
Fascist-inspired violence scars the faces of Italy.

"Take a look around. They break up strikes with police
and hired guns. They mistreat the poor unemployed from the
south. They rail against peasants in the fields and workers in
the factories.

"It breaks my heart. No amount of tears will stop them. No pleas for compassion will touch them. No cry of hunger from any child walking the street will change them. They will crush human lives and never flinch. They will try to fulfil a Fascist legacy as dark as the sewer that they crawled out of.

"And every time they raise their heads high, the rest of us must stop them. Because they can only rise while standing on the bodies below."

He kept whistling the song as he looked up at the wall where the photo of his wife was hanging. She knows what I'm talking about, he thought. She paid the ultimate price. Loretta saw her dad wipe back a tear. She hugged him tightly.

"So to answer your question, honey: no, we didn't crush them permanently. We won, but not really. It was a temporary victory of sorts. And short-lived. You kids must continue where we left off. Where your mom and I stopped."

GREAT-GRANDFATHER: A LEGACY

Fascist Italy—a sad and dangerous legacy. After the war, in the 1950s and since, the Italian talking picture boxes, television, tried to forget our terrible Fascist past. Everyone tried not to discuss it or figure out what had happened and why. But public memory, I say, is a priceless thing. It helps shape our values. Who we are and who we become. And what we choose to remember about our history, and what we choose to forget as a people, says a lot about our civilization.

We Italians prefer to forget our Fascist past. Is it too painful? Too embarrassing? Too troubling and too close to today? Perhaps. So instead, we remember the war, but not Fascism. We remember the Resistance, but prefer to forget about the Blackshirts. This reflects how little progress we have made as a civilization. This is a sad and dangerous legacy to hand to our children.

SAN LORENZO PARK MEMORIAL

Antonio is late for work again and takes a short cut through a little park in San Lorenzo. He walks quickly alongside a long, low wall of cold black granite following the curved path. One thousand names of local men, women, and children are inscribed in the stone—the dead of San Lorenzo, victims of a ferocious American bombardment of Rome during the Second World War.

He hums an '80s song with beautiful piano lines written by Francesco De Gregori about the bombing:

"And that July 19th, the bombs fell like snow . . . a thousand dead."

Today, he thinks, the American government would call all of them "collateral damage," like broken pieces of plastic and fibreglass from a car accident. Like dead Iraqis or Afghans—all collateral damage from wars waged by madmen.

If every city in the USA suffered what countless cities in Europe suffered during World War II, and what cities from Vietnam to the Middle East suffered since . . . If they wrote the names of the dead in stone so that future generations would never forget the horrors of war . . . would America still be so enthusiastically warlike?

Come over here, all you American patriots. Run your fingers along this memorial in San Lorenzo. Hear the voices of the dead singing,

"And that July 19th, the bombs fell like snow . . ."

CINKA'S NEWS

"Antonio?"

"Cinka! Where are you? Is everything OK?"

"Yes. I'm at a pay phone near the camp. Listen, we have to talk. It's important. Meet me outside the Euclide train station in the *Piazza Euclide* in front of the big Basilica at 6 PM. Same spot under the trees. We can walk up to the park at the *Villa Glori.*"

Two hours later in the square, Antonio grabs Cinka, kisses her on the lips, and studies her face. She takes a deep breath, holds both his hands, and looks away.

"Antonio, I'm pregnant."

"What?" His jaw drops. "You're kidding?" His knees buckle.

She smiles faintly. "No, I'm serious. Really." Her smile grows.

"You're sure you're pregnant?"

Cinka rolls her eyes. "Antonio, it's my body and I'm telling you, I am pregnant, yes."

"Oh my God! Sit down!" He motions to a bench. Antonio's head is spinning. "You sure? I mean, wow! Oh man! That's fabulous!" He pulls her close to him and hugs her. Then his voice changes. "Um, what are we going to do?"

Cinka looks away.

"You know we can't get married, Antonio. For now. Marriage to outsiders is strictly forbidden. I told you this before. And I told you that in my culture, premarital sex is strongly forbidden. This is very bad."

She moves away from him.

"Whoa! OK, I know." He lifts up her chin. "So? What do we do? Run away or what?" He's grinning.

"There's something else, Antonio."

Cinka swallows hard. Her eyes brim with tears.

"Before I met you it had already been arranged for me, when I was fourteen, to be married off to someone else. A boy back in our village. The same age as me. He's on his way here."

Antonio's jaw drops. He throws up his arms.

"What?" His eyes turn dark with anger; his voice, too. "Now you're really kidding, right? It's a joke, tell me, yes?"

"No, I'm not joking. I'm serious. But I don't love him. I never did. I don't want to marry him. I was just a young girl. I want you. And our baby. Together."

She throws her arms around his neck, but he pushes her away.

"What the fuck!" he shouts. "How do I know it's our baby? Have you been sleeping with him, too?"

"Antonio! Don't be ridiculous! How can you say such a thing! You know you are my first and only! You know I have never been with any other man! Why don't you believe me?"

"Well, a guy has to be careful sometimes. But frankly, I don't know what to say. *Cazzo!* What's going on?" Antonio scratches his head. "Like, how is this going to work? You marry both of us?"

"Antonio! Don't be stupid!" It's her turn to crank out some rage. "This is serious, and all you can do is joke about it?"

"Shit. I don't know what to do. It's a big surprise. First a baby. Now another guy. What do you want to do?"

"I don't know. I really don't. But it's my problem and I'll deal with it. You don't have to worry about it. Just forget it."

She starts to walk away but he grabs her and spins her around.

"Listen. If it's our baby, let's run away, sweetheart. Far away. I'm serious."

"Antonio, I can't. I'm scared."

DISCUSSING CINKA'S LOVE LIFE

"I followed her. She didn't see me. I saw her sit down at an outdoor café with the Italian redhead. I saw him kiss her on the lips, reach out and hold her hands, stroke her hair."

"No! This can't be!"

"Shame! Shame!"

The old Romni is speaking in a low, hoarse voice to five other camp elders crammed into a ramshackle refugee hut. A lone candle casts flickering shadows on the walls. They all shake their heads in disbelief, cluck their tongues, and one by one, state their disapproval.

"This is very bad. She has no idea."

"She's in trouble now."

"How could she do this?"

The old woman nods, holding back a smile, as she embellishes her tale.

"I saw her rub her tummy the way a woman does when she carries a child. He put his hand on her tummy as well. The way a man does when he first finds out his woman carries his child."

"Mother of Mary! This cannot be!"

"She's pregnant with a *gadjo*?"

"What is she thinking? She is defiled!"

"It will be the spawn of Satan."

Again the group murmurs their undisguised, collective disgust.

"I swear on my mother's grave. How I hate these Italians."

"If what you say is true," an old man says, "this means she is carrying his baby, and we all know this cannot be. She is betrothed to someone else. And if they want to marry? This cannot be."

A woman speaks up. "Yes, she is betrothed to my cousin's nephew back home, Luca. He is already on the bus coming here. I am sure he will kill the Italian."

"But that young hothead, Nicu the Fat One—" another elder adds. "Luca's cousin from the other camp, he will kill the Italian first."

"That Nicu is an evil one. His business makes all of us look bad."

"But at least he provides jobs for the young ones."

"He's no better than the Mafia."

"He's with the Mafia! It's true!"

"He is no good."

"Blood will be spilled. This is certain. She was promised when she was fourteen years old."

"Will they kill her, too?"

"They might."

"Then someone here will avenge her, no?"

RUNAWAY LOVE

The night after Cinka discloses her pregnancy and tells him about the other man, Antonio heads home thoroughly dazed and confused, as if a train had hit him.

He yanks a few beers from the fridge, grabs a bottle of wine, locks the door in his bedroom, and gets smashed, alternately crying, laughing, and screaming into a pillow.

He's consumed, tormented, and confounded by three inseparable thoughts.

First: This is fabulous! I'm going to be a father! I have to tell everyone. We must celebrate!

Second: This is crazy! I can't be a dad! I'm too young! I

don't want a snivelling kid on my hands. How can I play music or have a life? *Cazzo!*

And third: And how can we ever be together? Her people won't allow it. Who the fuck is this guy and what is he going to do? Say he's royally pissed and comes after me. What do I do?

His final solution: Cinka must run away from her family, change her name, cut and dye her hair, wear makeup and new clothes, look like an Italian girl, and live with me far away.

And if the other guy shows up, well, we'll call the cops and get him deported. Antonio feels better now.

Then we either keep the little bugger, or give him up for adoption. Or have an abortion and no one will ever know. Just Cinka and me in a love hideaway. Cuba, maybe.

He curls up into a ball on the floor hugging a pillow, smiling, and passes out.

Next morning, hung over and no clearer, he meets her in their favourite Russian tea house on *Via dei Falegnami*.

"Ugh, Antonio!" Cinka makes a face. "You reek of alcohol! You look terrible! Where have you been?"

He props his head up with both hands.

"Sorting it out, sweetie. Listen, this is what we do. You know I love you. So we run away. You, me, and the baby. Forget this other dude. It's the only way. You and me together. And our baby, of course." He burps. "Excuse me."

Cinka shakes her head. *Cazzo!* Does he not understand? Is he this dense?

"Are you out of your mind? I have my mother, my brother and sister. I can't walk away from them."

"But you love me, yes?"

"Of course! Don't be silly. It's not a just a question of love for you. Put yourself in my place. I'm responsible for them. I take care of them. There is no one else. Look, if it seems complicated at this moment, it won't stay like this forever." She strokes his hands and tries to convince him. "I can deal with the other boy. I need to speak with him with my mother present. She's good at sorting these things out. He'll listen to her. Everyone does. One day we'll all be together. One happy family. Trust me."

Antonio searches her almond-coloured eyes with his sad reddened ones. The most beautiful eyes on the planet, he thinks, full of love for me. How can I not trust her? He doesn't have the heart, nor the energy or the mind to argue. Besides, his head throbs.

"OK. We'll wait. Maybe once the baby is born things will be different. Your people will accept me and forget about the other guy. We'll all be friends."

LUCA ARRIVES

After shining itself out, the tired mango moon is now reduced to a quarter of its full size. It kicks back and reclines in the sky. Below, it observes the final stragglers trying to make it home from Rome's late-night bars. Sanitation workers pile out of city trucks to clean up their mess.

Luca's bus pulled into Rome way behind schedule. Now lost, exhausted, and hungry, he's been walking for hours from the bus station after his gruelling journey. Someone's leftover pizza in a garbage can beckons, so he eats it. A few hours later, he staggers into his cousin's refugee camp. He bangs on the trailer door, yelling: "Nicu! It's me! Open up, damn it!"

Nicu, a gun in hand, peers into the early morning blackness from a window.

"Luca?" he whispers.

"No, it's the fucking devil, you turd!"

His cousin unlocks the door and embraces him. "You made it, man! I was worried."

"I want to meet that old hag! The one that saw everything! Take me to her! I want to settle this now!" Luca smashes his fist on a table. Then he vomits on his cousin, blacks out, and collapses on the floor.

The next morning Nicu leads Luca to a large shack in the camp where a group of elders sit in a circle. Luca coughs, removes his baseball cap, and pokes his head through the door.

The oldest man taps his cane on his chair. Everyone stops talking. He speaks in a raspy voice as he squints at the young man.

"Are you Luca?"

Luca bows his head and nods.

"Enter."

Luca fidgets with his cap and scans the group of elders without raising his head. They all stare at him. An old woman clears her throat.

"You were right to come. We know the story. Cinka was promised to you. She is at fault. She has not honoured the arrangement. She has dishonoured you and brought shame to your family and to our people. You must confront her. However you wish."

The others nod.

Luca mutters "Thank you," then leaves.

He walks quickly toward the camp exit with his cousin.

"Here." Nicu hands him a switchblade. Luca pushes it away.

"Don't need it. Brought my own."

"This is the address. I drew you a map. It will take you thirty minutes by foot. These guys will go with you." He points to two Romani teens who fall in behind them.

"Don't need them. I need a drink."

CINKA'S MOM KNOWS FIXERS

"Antonio, it's me, Cinka. I spoke with my mother. She's going to work it all out . . . Yes, it's OK for me to keep the baby and keep seeing you . . . Of course it's true! Listen, my mother knows people. They can fix things for us . . . No, don't worry. She'll take care of everything. It will be OK. And she wants to meet you soon . . . Why? To talk about the future . . . Our future, silly! I'll see you tomorrow . . . Love you, too."

AN ABRUZZO FAMILY STORY

Simona, her dad Augusto, Antonio, and Cinka pile into a little blue stuttering Nissan en route to a family dinner in the mountains. Simona sits beside her dad. Cinka and Antonio hold hands in the back.

Augusto is a jovial, middle-aged, bespectacled journalist in a rumpled, untucked shirt and baggy pants. He has two pens clipped inside his shirt pocket and sings his favourite Italian partisan songs for Cinka loudly and proudly.

> One morning I woke up
> Oh goodbye beautiful, goodbye beautiful! Bye! Bye! Bye!
> (O bella, ciao! bella, ciao! bella, ciao, ciao, ciao!)
> One morning I woke up
> And found the invader
>
> Oh partisan take me away
> Oh goodbye beautiful, goodbye beautiful! Bye! Bye! Bye!
> (O bella, ciao! bella, ciao! bella, ciao, ciao, ciao!)
> Oh partisan take me away
> Because I feel death approaching

"Maybe you already know some of these songs. Maybe not. I know you'll appreciate them."

Driving on the A-24 toward L'Aquila, they head for the blue mountains of Abruzzo. Augusto plays tour guide for Cinka, pointing out the "*acacia,*" little oaks, the *Gran Sasso* mountain on the left, the Maiella mountains in the distance, and more.

Four songs later they reach Bazzano. The sign announces *Gran Sasso Gran Shopping.* They visit the artisanal bakery and leave with freshly baked almond cookies.

"My favourites, soon to be yours!" Augusto hands the backseat lovers a whole bag. They cruise past lush cornfields, and just outside the village of San Dimitrio, they spot a few partridges on the road.

"Roasted with rosemary and fennel, delicious birds!" Augusto exclaims before a repeat rendition of his preferred driving song, *Bella Ciao.*

> And if I die as a partisan
> (O bella, ciao! bella, ciao! bella, ciao, ciao, ciao!)

And if I die as a partisan
(O bella, ciao! bella, ciao! bella, ciao, ciao, ciao!)
You must bury me up in the mountain

"Now we are approaching the village of Campo Santo where everyone sleeps all the time! With this new construction on the highway, it's the most activity anyone has seen here since the war. Imagine the stress!" He honks his horn a few times and laughs. It's only three kilometres to the village of *Fagnano Alto* now past the *Orso Marsecano*.

You must bury me up in the mountain
In the shadow of a beautiful flower
And all those who will pass by
Will exclaim: "What a beautiful flower!"

That is the flower of the partisan
Who died for freedom

In the hereditary family house, the party enjoys an impromptu lunch of panini, prosciutto and melon, a glass of white wine, and an espresso. A shot of *Genziana*—an Abruzzo liqueur made from juniper berries and genziana roots—rounds out the meal. Outside on the terrace there is birdsong.

Simona points to the cold fireplace.

"Once, an owl fell down that chimney and flew around the house. Dad trapped and released him, but not before naming him Goofo."

"Like the prime minister!" Antonio laughs.

Augusto makes a face.

"Argh! He's a fool surrounded by fools."

"And now he calls the soldiers coming back from the Middle East '*the heroes of Italy.*'"

"Argh! I don't like heroes. Never did. Never will. They spoil my appetite and contribute to wars. You think I want to fight a war? I had to do two years of compulsory military service, but I opted to do noncombat service and was a chauffeur." He shakes his head, pointing to Simona.

"You know your grandfather, Fabio, like millions of soldiers, fought for the king and was a monarchist to his death? In the 1946 referendum, the Republicans won by a slim majority, but your grandfather never forgave them. Every election thereafter, he went to vote, but would spoil his ballot."

"Was he an anarchist?"

"Ha! Definitely anticommunist. See this photo?"

He pulls down a framed photo of a large, big-boned man, with thick red curly hair and a bushy red beard. On the wall are more framed photos: him as a student in Abruzzo in 1932, and in Africa in 1937 in uniform, sitting proudly astride a donkey. Rifles on their shoulders, Ethiopian soldiers run to keep up with him.

Other photos show him standing under a tree beside a miniature but fully functional tank, or posing with a camel and Ethiopians who collaborated with Italian Fascists.

"See him serving his king and country, contributing to the genocide of this campaign? He met your grandmother there, though. She was an army nurse. And just after she gave birth to your mother, they all ended up in a prisoner of war camp of the British Army. That was 1943. Both your grandfathers were friends from the same village in the same army. Enough talk. Time for some fresh air!"

Augusto leads everyone on a quick tour of the property surrounding the house.

"We're on the edge of *Sirente* Park. Here, wild boars scratch themselves against the tree trunks. Like this." He demonstrates. Everyone laughs.

"See the tufts of hair? Up in the mountains, foxes, deer and bears roam. Down by the river at night, you can hear the wolves." He impersonates one. More laughter.

"Local dogs howl right back, trying to reach their brothers and sisters. Remember, this is the land of truffles, where people educate their dogs to find the delicacy. More lucrative, I'd say, than just walking Fido around the block."

Augusto guns the protesting Nissan as they climb the winding, bumpy gravel mountain road back to the highway.

"That village on the next ridge? It's San Demetrio. One summer, your Aunty Isabella asked Grandpa for some white paint and a brush. Said she saw some neo-Fascist graffiti on the wall of the post office. This was in the 1960s. She drove her Fiat 500 with a broken exhaust pipe over there, waking up all the farm animals, covered that graffiti, then painted a slogan of her own: *"Work less, live more!"*

"What a scandal! All summer long, she and the Fascists competed for attention on that wall. She knew the guys doing it and they knew her. Old school friends. But she stood her ground. No one could intimidate her, Fascists or not."

"Why do you think Aunt Isabella rebelled in the 1960s?" Simona asks.

"Oh boy! Imagine! Postwar Italy is a deeply moralist country. The Church has a lot of influence. The government, too. It's stifling, too controlling. People, young people, need to breathe, to grow. Especially after twenty years of censorship imposed by the Fascists. Books, films, from around the world were banned. People here were hungry for contact with international culture. And what are young people in the rest of the world doing in the 1960s? Rebelling! Against the church, the government, universities, old values, tired ways of thinking. How could we Italians ignore all that?"

DEPORTING IMMIGRANTS

Today's news: another special report about the new emergency decree to deport immigrants. Rafaele listens while he cooks. Between chopping, stirring, and boiling, he runs into the bedroom to work on his computer.

When the government starts scapegoating Romanians and Roma, he thinks, it's no different from any far-right group or anti-immigration Northern Party line.

Cazzo! He's burned the sauce! He removes the pot from the stove, places it in the sink and tastes it. Salvageable.

The wave of xenophobia following Giovanna Reggiani's death highlights the unease many Italians feel about the transition of our country from a place people used to leave to seek a better future abroad, to a destination for immigrants trying to improve their lot."

Rafaele rolls his eyeballs. Are they nuts? The State doesn't respect or want to integrate immigrants, to turn their presence into something positive. They don't want to use it to increase understanding and better relationships with others. So now people take out their anger on them and blame them for everything: bad wine, bad weather, burnt sauce.

He chops up more garlic, adds it and a splash of red wine to the sauce, tastes it, then adds more wine. Better! He's successfully made burnt sauce taste unburnt.

Three days ago, the Minister claimed that 75 percent of all arrests in Rome last year were Romanians. Then yesterday he retracted this, saying that he erred, that it was an "accidental" exaggeration. Too late, *douche*-bag! Rafaele thinks. Damage done. Every Romanian now labelled "criminal." It's first impressions that count. Everyone knows that. No one reads or hears the corrections.

Rafaele carefully dumps the measured pasta into the boiling water and stirs. Then he starts washing and drying salad greens. The report continues:

> Romanians have long come to Italy to look for work, largely because they speak a Romance language similar to Italian. A minority are Gypsies who live in ramshackle camps at the edge of major cities—and their reputation as criminals has spread to the entire Romanian population.
>
> The situation for Romanians is very tense. "Some are afraid to go out on the streets or to work," said Italy's Romanian Association president. Others, he said, are considering returning to Romania for good. Romanians comprise one of Italy's largest ethnic groups, with 560,000 registered officially, or about 1 percent of the population.
>
> The association of Romanians in Italy says the actual number of Romanians is closer to 1.5 million, not includ-

ing Romanian Gypsies. That takes into account those who entered the country illegally, working off the books as caretakers, house cleaners, or janitors.

Italy's Romanian immigrants are generally highly educated—with nearly two-thirds holding a high school or university diploma, compared with one-third of Italians.

PART VI

RISING

GREAT-GRANDFATHER: THE 1960S AND *LA DOLCE VITA*

We Italians say it lasted from the end of the 1950s to the end of the 1960s. Skipping of course the troublesome *quarantotto* of '68 with those annoying student and labour protests. So unpleasant!

Foreigners called it *la dolce vita*—the sweet life. And sweet it was, for some. You might have seen the movies. But it wasn't all champagne and roses for those who lived in the tough suburbs of Rome, like *Pietralata* or *Tor Bella Monaca*. Read some of Pier Paolo Pasolini's novels. Or in the forever impoverished south, the poor buggers. It was mostly for the bourgeoisie. Who else! Capitalism is their game.

In postwar Italy we went from rural to industrial very fast. There was a big economic kaboom! Money flowed into—and right out of!—the pockets of comfortable Italians, the workers with better salaries, white-collar people, all the upwardly rising sorts. Families started buying the talking boxes—those televisions—and two-wheeled machines, those Vespa scooters. *Mamma mia!* I would have loved a turquoise one! They took holidays and spread the word:

"Italy is a fun, relaxed place! We don't rush but enjoy ourselves! We like our wine, too. Come visit and join us!"

The foreigners, especially the well-moneyed jetsetters, flocked to the sun-drenched beaches of Sardinia or Capri, or to the quiet villages in Tuscany, or the lively centre of Rome. All of a sudden Italy was full of loud Americans and Germans—

louder even than us Italians! They revved up their red Alfas and raced through narrow old streets, tops down, all smiles, hair and neckerchiefs flying in the wind, shouting to one another:

"Let's go to *Trastevere*, eat some pizza, and ogle the girls!"

"No, my friend has a villa in Umbria with a pool, we'll go there!"

"I heard Gregory Peck and Elizabeth Taylor are staying in a hotel on *Via Veneto* again. Let's take a peek!"

Our cinema flourished. American record companies released albums like *Holiday in Rome, Italian Paradise, Fall in Love Italian Style*. As if anyone else could do it just like us!

All of North America discovered Italy and fell in love with Sophia Loren. I was already in love with her, as were all my friends, and we resented the competition! Our wives knew, too. It was no secret and they understood why. *"La dolce vita"* beckoned.

Marcello Mastroianni was irresistible. Italian "beat" music was, as the youth say, "the coolest." We were what everyone in the tourist industry called "a happening place." We already knew that, too!

Then 1968 arrived. *Cazzarola!* What a surprise! Behind the smiling faces of waiters serving happy tourists were angry scowls. Conservatives in power were viciously attacking the hard-won social programs of the decade. Students and workers were getting restless. Unemployed farm labourers revolted. Poverty and hunger marked too many faces. Factory strikes multiplied, and the *spumoni* bubble burst. Pop!

"La dolce vita" faded and gave way to the *anni di piombo*—the years of lead—marked by bombings and shootings. Italy was no longer the "in" place to be for the jet set. But for our youth, it was an exciting time to build a new world out of songs and dreams, love and rage. Of course our family was part of the action. It's in our blood.

THE HEADY DAYS OF 1968-1969

The heady year, 1968, shook both France and Italy to the core as students and workers spilled out of universities and factories, into the streets, questioning and challenging all authority, demanding reforms and radical changes.

"Be realistic, demand the impossible!"

"Take over the city! Make it ours!"

Their slogans appeared overnight, graffitied or postered onto walls. A wildfire of imagination tore through campuses and factories, inspiring workers and students *en masse* to dream and create a new world here and now.

"Live without dead time, enjoy without chains!"

"Arise, you wretched of the University."

Across Italy the young and the restless were hoping this was the moment to finally rid the country of old guard Fascists who still held positions of authority in key institutions.

"Strike! Strike! Strike! Occupy the factories! Occupy the schools!"

Challenges to Fascist mentalities swept across Italy, provoking the inevitable reaction from the forces of the Right. By 1969, the bloody and murderous "strategy of provoking tension" came into play:

Turn public opinion against this new wave of radical thinking, against these know-nothing youthful "intellectuals." Fight their ideas, their newspapers and their books. Convince ordinary citizens that the Left is populated with dangerous nuts who would destroy Italian society and kill innocent people in their quest for radical social change.

Instill widespread fear in the public. Get them to pine for the days before 1968, when right-wing positions were predominant. Stage spectacular, horrific bombings, then blame the Left. Specifically, scapegoat anarchists. Unlike the socialists or communists, they have no major political party machine for self-defence, and everyone knows anyway: anarchists, at heart, are violent.

Violent—like "the monster," the anarchist ballet-dancer Valpreda, who was targeted, framed, imprisoned for a crime he never committed. His case, a *cause célèbre* in Italy that drew worldwide interest even long after his death, left many questions unanswered about the real perpetrators of a horrendous crime.

GIUSEPPE PINELLI

December 12, 1969, the *Piazza Fontana* in Milan. A deafening explosion rocks the headquarters of the national Agrarian bank. Sixteen people die from the deadly terrorist bomb. Immediately, the police accuse anarchists of the bombing and arrest almost one hundred.

Among the accused anarchists: a dancer named Pietro Valpreda and a railway worker, Giuseppe Pinelli. The police say it was a "routine interrogation." They say that Pinelli committed suicide by jumping from the fourth-floor window of the police station.

"Suicide"? Highly implausible. Too many discrepancies in the police account of the incident remain unanswered. Many Italians believe Pinelli was murdered by his interrogators and pushed out the window or thrown to his death.

The prosecutor, "for lack of evidence," drops murder charges against one of the interrogating officers. Dario Fo writes his celebrated play, *Accidental Death of an Anarchist* based on the murder of Pinelli.

Later, it is demonstrated that the anarchists had nothing to do with the bombing. After serving three years in prison, Valpreda is finally acquitted and released. Many years later, Italy learns the truth: Fascist groups carried out the bombing with the complicity of Italian intelligence, NATO and CIA operatives, including a U.S. Navy officer. No one is ever prosecuted.

BALLAD FOR THE ANARCHIST PINELLI (*BALLATA PER PINELLI*)*

> Quella sera a Milano era caldo
> ma che caldo, che caldo faceva,
> "Brigadiere, apri un po' la finestra!",
> una spinta . . . e Pinelli va giú.

* (From the album Canti Anarchici Italiani—Italian Songs of Anarchy, 1974, by Gruppo "Z," written by Anonymous, Eliseo, and Luciano Francisci. Translated from the Italian by Davide Turcato.) www.chiavedisvolta.org/anarchia/

"Sor questore, io gliel'ho giá detto,
le ripeto che sono innocente,
anarchia non vuol dire bombe,
ma uguaglianza nella libertá."

"Poche storie, confessa, Pinelli,
il tuo amico Valpreda ha parlato,
é l'autore di questo attentato
ed il complice certo sei tu."

"Impossibile!" grida Pinelli,
"Un compagno non puó averlo fatto
e l'autore di questo delitto
fra i padroni bisogna cercar."

"Stai attento, indiziato Pinelli,
questa stanza é giá piena di fumo,
se tu insisti, apriam la finestra,
quattro piani son duri da far."

C'e' una bara e tremila compagni,
stringevamo le nostre bandiere,
quella sera l'abbiamo giurato,
non finisce di certo cosí.

E tu Guida, e tu Calabresi,
se un compagno é stato ammazzato,
per coprire una strage di Stato,
questa lotta piú dura sará.

Quella sera a Milano era caldo
ma che caldo, che caldo faceva,
"Brigadiere, apri un po' la finestra!",
una spinta . . . e Pinelli va giú.

That evening it was hot in Milan
how hot, how hot it was,
"Brigadiere, open the window!",
a push . . . and Pinelli goes down.

"Mr. interrogator, I told you already,
I am repeating that I am innocent,
anarchy does not mean bombs,
but equality in liberty."

"No more nonsense, confess, Pinelli,
your friend Valpreda talked,
he is the author of this bombing,
and you certainly are the accomplice."

"Impossible!" shouts Pinelli,
"A comrade couldn't possibly do that,
and the author of this crime,
must be sought among the masters."

"Watch out, suspect Pinelli,
this room is already full of smoke,
if you persist, we'll open the window,
four floors are hard to do."

There's a coffin and 3,000 comrades,
we were all clasping our flags,
that night we swore,
it won't end this way poor Pinelli.

And you Guida, you Calabresi,
if a comrade was killed,
to cover a State slaughter,
this fight will just get harder.

That evening it was hot in Milan
how hot, how hot it was,
"Brigadiere, open the window!",
a push . . . and Pinelli goes down.

ANTONIO AND CINKA IN THE TEA HOUSE

It's a driving rainstorm, destroying umbrellas and soaking everyone to the skin.

Cinka and Antonio sit face to face in the small Russian teahouse, cupping their teas, waiting to dry out. Classical music plays in the background. The dour-faced Serbian owner sits knitting behind the counter. Two students discuss their exams. A white-haired man peruses a Russian newspaper with a magnifying glass.

She's too sad, too quiet, Antonio thinks. This isn't like her. Did I do or say something?

"Cinka, is everything all right?"

"Sometimes I don't want to burden you with my problems. It's just too much for anyone."

"I'm here for you, honey. Tell me."

"You won't think I'm just complaining again?"

He kisses her hand. "Tell me."

"Antonio, so many of our people are being attacked in the street by right-wing vigilantes. They are leaving Italy. Frightened. Whole families are being uprooted. They won't return. Some are going back to Romania. Others to Germany and the UK. They say Roma are treated better there. Who knows?"

"Does your mother want to stay or go?"

"She's not sure. All her friends are leaving. Our camp is slowly emptying. People fear a raid by the police any day, or worse, an attack by vigilantes. They've started to burn camps. We could be next."

"Shit! I mean, I'm sorry, Cinka. What can I do? Tell me."

"Change the attitudes of Italians? No one can do that. It won't happen."

"Cinka, I'll do what I can. I just joined an antiracist action group."

"A what?"

"They're activists. It would be good if we could link up with activists in your community, yes?"

"Activists in my community? What are you talking about? Antonio, please. My people are all activists every day. Active trying to survive. Italians have no idea. The looks of disgust people give us on the street!

"You don't see this or hear the poisonous words behind our backs, to our faces. The fear of our elders, our children—

even in the schools, afraid of other children, afraid of . . . What am I doing here?"

Cinka was shaking and sobbing out loud. The other clients turned to look. The tea house owner turned up the classical music. The white-haired man coughed.

"But Cinka . . ."

"Antonio, what am I doing here? Don't you see?"

"What are you saying, sweetheart?"

"I'm saying, one white Italian woman is murdered. And please understand, I am very sorry about this. Revolted by it. And whoever is responsible should be punished. I agree. But one Italian is murdered and the entire government reacts."

"I hear you, Cinka."

"They use this as a pretext to terrorize thousands of innocent Roma and Romanians. Suddenly it's a question of "public security." Do you know how many Roma have been murdered over the years by vigilantes in Romania and even here? Not once did any official ever speak out about it or denounce it. Not once did anyone demand government action, or pass a national emergency decree to arrest or deport the criminals. Not once! Is this fair? Civilized? Is this Italian justice? Is this my future?"

Cinka's tears stream down her face into her cup of tea. She tries to wipe them away with her arm.

Antonio reaches across the table. She pulls away. He bites his tongue and says nothing. Fuck! What can he say?

Other customers are staring at them. He's seething with waves of rage and frustration. He feels totally helpless.

I'm fucking useless. She's the one putting up with it. I just want to mitigate her pain. As if I could. I want to make things right. As if it were possible. I want to give her something to look forward to, a bit of hope. But how? Undo centuries of racism? Kick the government in the balls? Slit the throat of every neo-Nazi? Start a war against the ignoroids? Cazzo!

NEWS, 2007: *Rome authorities tear down Gypsy camp . . . Expel 100 Romanians from Italy while condemning "racist" attack in Rome triggered by murder of Italian naval officer's wife . . . Romani man of Romanian*

nationality squatting at immigrant shacks near station arrested . . .
Clothing stained with what investigators say is the victim's blood.

CINKA PAYS

It's late in this punishing, sweltering afternoon as Cinka busks at a new location beside a sunken fountain in *Piazza della Chiesa Nuova*. She is feeling slightly nauseous and decides to take time off and go to Antonio's rehearsal studio to lie down.

He's so lucky, she thinks, walking to the bus stop. *He's Italian with white skin and he has everything. A part-time job. He can take classes at the university. He has an apartment and the studio. He can stay with his family in their big house or with his friends. Now he's got me. And what do I have? My family, my violin, our little hut—and now him. I'm so grateful. Without him, I don't know how we could survive.*

As she turns down a narrow street, she hears an aggressive *beep! beep!* behind her. *Cazzo!* The police car pulls up and the driver waves her over.

"Come here, Gypsy girl. We need to talk."

Cinka freezes. She can't run away. She can't hide. She has her passport, but they are still police.

"Your papers?"

There are two officers. One flips through her passport while the driver looks her up and down, a disturbing smile cracking open his face.

"You're new around here."

The other cop leans over to get a better look.

"Oh, yeah. She's fresh all right."

"What do you mean?" she asks nervously.

"You've never played the *piazza* before. We know all the musicians who play here. There's a price, you know." He smirks.

"That's right, baby."

"What are you saying?"

"You can only play here if you obey the rules. We have special rules. A smart, pretty girl like you should know that. You want your passport back? Here."

"What rules? What do you want?" Cinka is momentarily stunned.

"Don't play stupid." The officer changes his tone of voice.

She unzips her violin case and pulls out a few euros wrapped in a sock.

"Is this what you want?"

The officer seizes her wrist and grabs the money.

"For now. Next time it will be more. Understand?"

RAFAELE VISITS CAMP

A soft, gentle sun filters through the lemon trees in Rafaele's backyard garden. He sits under the largest one sipping his morning coffee, laptop open, scanning the daily *La Repubblica* online. His stomach turns as he reads the headline: *The Romanian Threat.*

Rome's mayor declared that *"Rome was the world's safest city until Romania's entry into the European Union."*

The interior minister added, *"The inflow of Romanians is very strong and many delinquents are part of it."*

Wave after wave of xenophobia, Rafaele thinks, *and who will stop it? Easy for them to blame immigrants without looking at the real problems. You want globalization, you got it. Now deal with the results. More people, but no increase in public services. More cheap labour, but no decent jobs, no affordable housing, no social support system, no educational programs. And how can new people "fit in" if they aren't provided with the basics we take for granted?*

Rafaele remembers the day Antonio took him on a tour of one of the camps where a Romani violinist and her family lived. The violinist was doing studio work with Antonio.

"You gotta see this for yourself, if only once, Rafaele. You're an architect. You'll appreciate it," Antonio had said.

The shantytown camp was one of two on a hillside just above the Tiber River in the suburb of *Tor Di Quinto*, not far from a train station.

Antonio led him along a mud path past a collection

of lean-tos made from cardboard, plastic, scrap metal, and wood—all with dirt floors. Third World hovels minutes from the twenty-first-century metropolis of Rome, he thought. This was home for Italy's poorest.

Dozens of families with kids, crowded together with no adequate sanitation facilities. No basic services. It was a sight out of impoverished urban Brazil or the Philippines, places he had visited before. At least in Charles Dickens's times people were lodged in buildings with real roofs, he thought. These structures—miserable excuses for shelter—couldn't protect anyone from cold, wind, or rain. Yet metres away in plain view, commuter trains roared past, filled with Italian citizens, none of whom had to live like this.

Did Rome city officials care? Was the neglect deliberate? What was the excuse? Then you blame the Roma for more crime? This is the crime! You who allow this are the real criminals!

He traded glances with Antonio as they walked, but said nothing. Occasionally he smiled at the young Romani children laughing and playing on the paths, curiously eyeing the tall, bearded stranger and the red-head carrying a guitar case.

Then it hit him. *I could design a house. A small but roomy family house. Two stories. Wood. Based on something Eastern European, but Italian too. Something solid, cheap to build. Something with an aesthetic that would reflect who the Roma are, how they lived before and how, ideally, they would want to live now here.*

I could get my firm to work on it, with Romani artists, artisans, carpenters, engineers. Design it with them, based on what they want. Something traditional yet modern. Then build it with Romani labour. Show Italians something. Make it a community effort. A model Romani house for families in Rome.

They built the model home. With Romani artists and labour. Everyone was so proud. It was beautiful, contemporary, solid, airy, and spacious. The Department of Architecture at the University honoured it and brought students to study it. Then, before any Romani family had the chance to move in, Rome's finest neo-Fascists burned it down.

THE FASCIST GRANDDAUGHTER

Alessandra Mussolini, Fascist grand-daughter of the Italian dictator, looks into her makeup mirror, arranges her dyed dirty-blond hair and stares at her blood-red fingernails.

She reminds herself: *I must write a thank you note to that darling footballer, Paolo Di Canio, from the SS Lazio team, for saluting me during that game. What a delightful straight-arm Roman salute. I was deeply moved. Thank goodness we have decent Italian Fascist boys playing. All those swastikas in the stands. Grandfather would be proud.*

She is awaiting her turn to speak in the European Parliament (EP). She is bored and this morning's session seems endless. On her agenda for today: another short but vicious attack against foreigners. It's not hateful. Just part of a calculated strategy to soften people up with the smile. Then the slam-dunk message Grandfather so often preached: *"Italy for Italians."* It's not racist. Just logical and Fascist. To each their own country.

This is the bread and butter of the xenophobic miniscule far-right group in the EP called Identity, Tradition, Sovereignty (ITS). She smirks to herself. *Thanks to that filthy Gypsy murderer, we now have that Romanian riff-raff by the balls. Running scared. And we won't let go.*

Only recently, she left the National Alliance to start a new far-right party, because the NA wasn't Fascist enough for her. Now it's her turn. She rises and babbles on about noble, peaceful Italian traditions, a country once free of violence. She pauses dramatically:

"And then the Romanians came!"

She pounds the desk, her voice rising, as she speaks about the insurmountable problems Italy has had to confront since "these people" entered the country, suggesting that all Romanians live like delinquents: "Breaking the law became a way of life for Romanians. However, it is not about petty crimes, but horrifying crimes, crimes that gives one goose bumps."

On cue, her Italian colleagues applaud loudly while shouts of audible disbelief and *"Shame! Shame!"* emanate from among the five racist members of the Romanian contingent of the ITS. How dare their Italian "ally" paint all Romanians with the same brush.

"Just like her grandfather!"

And now the entire EP is in an uproar, some members laughing. It's a catfight within the extreme Right, a diverse group of Europe's most vocal anti-immigrant and Euroskeptic parties and politicians. Mussolini sits back and glares at the Romanians, thinking: they're all alike. Cavemen and criminals.

RAFAELE'S GRANDFATHER'S REQUEST

"You know why I like to visit my mom's parents' house in the mountains? To clear my head. It's peaceful. Clean air. No distractions. Just me, the wind, and the birds singing outside."

Rafaele and Antonio were en route to a meeting with an antiracist organization and Romani refugees. Rafaele zipped in and out of rush hour Rome traffic with unbelievable daredevil moves. Yellow lines? Forget them. Long lineups? Pass them in the no-go zone. Someone won't move? Honk, swear, glare, and force your way in. Jockey aggressively for position. Employ the killer manoeuvre.

Antonio, equally known for his own cowboy driving habits, braced himself with outstretched arms against the dashboard and repressed gasps. He had learned a lot of his moves from his cousin, but Rafaele could still scare the crap out of him.

"When were kids, we'd chase each other around the outside of the house, yelling, slipping on the grass and gravel until we were completely exhausted. Grandma would call us in for egg sandwiches and milk, and plates packed high with home-baked treats. I can picture her sitting in the kitchen, stoking the fire, all the battered pots and pans hanging on the walls.

"She'd go from sink to stove to the big wooden table covered with a flowered oilcloth, churning out the best pasta, soups, and breads. On the terrace out back, Grandfather would be discussing the latest news with his neighbours.

"Once they took on a big chemical company trying to build a plant in the valley just outside the village. The city lawyers were so slick, lying to everyone, promising no big changes to the valley. All bullshit. Grandfather and his neighbours were no match. Big money bought off the local politicians, who stabbed the villagers in the back.

"Eventually the plant shut down. But the villagers never forgave those politicians, and would spit on the ground whenever one of them came to visit. Sitting by the fire, smoking his pipe, Grandfather used to say, 'Never, never trust the government. Or guys who wave around money. They come from the same place. Self-interest. And greed. Don't you be like that.'"

"And look! My Ferrari does it again!" Rafaele toots the horn. "Take that, big SUV polluting asshole."

He outmanoeuvres an SUV for a parking spot, slams on the brakes, and parks.

ANTONIO ASKS RAFAELE TO HELP

Two in the morning? Who the fuck? Rafaele rolls over to answer the phone.

"Pronto?"

"Rafaele, sorry. It's me, Antonio. I'm parked outside your house. I'm with Cinka, her mom, her little sister and brother. They got chased out of their refugee camp tonight. Their place was bulldozed. They lost everything. Can you please help out? They need a place to stay. Just for tonight."

"You know what time it is?"

"I know, I'm sorry. But this just happened. And you know there's not enough room in my apartment. Just one night, please? I promise. Tomorrow I'll help them find another camp. It's so late now and the kids are crying and . . ."

"OK, OK. I'll be right down. Let me get dressed."

GREAT-GRANDFATHER: SALVATORE DISCORDIA

Sometimes I lose track of all my great-great-nieces and nephews, the ones that multiply like rabbits. My friends have the same problem. So we number them. We also keep lists and use modern computing machines with Excel charts, arrows and tiny smiling faces.

My great-great-niece Loretta, for example, Rafaele's mom, aunt to Antonio, etc., had a charming younger brother, Salvatore. Born 1951, died too young, 1972.

He had long thick black hair, big bushy moustache. Incredible intellectual curiosity. Wore blue and pink striped bell-bottoms, flowered yellow shirt, and a bright green silk scarf around his neck. He loved that recorded music by those young people's orchestras: *The Black Sabbath*, *The Iron Maiden*, *The Stepping Wolf*. Drove his neighbours crazy when he played it full blast on his hi-fidelity stereo system. Wrote good poetry, too. Well, pretty good.

He helped set up a "Red Market" in a working-class neighbourhood where they sold fruit and vegetables at affordable prices. Also worked on a committee to free the anarchist dancer, Pietro Valpreda, who had been framed by the police.

He was in love, my poor Salvatore, and in the prime of his life when the police murdered him. Swine! I never forgave them. It was a horrible crime.

First, they beat him at an anti-Fascist demonstration. Then they drove him to the prison and beat him again. No prison doctor treated him. The prison authorities didn't give him any medical attention. Two days later, in agony, he lapsed into a coma and died. How that poor boy suffered!

The autopsy showed that not an inch of his body had been spared. There was a huge demonstration to protest his death. The anarchist marble workers of Carrara donated a monument that was placed in a small square to honour him. But the courts made sure that no police were ever brought to justice.

NEWS, Rome, 1970: *Over 500 secondary schools, one-third of Italy's total, closed or occupied by protesting students . . . students demanding revised programs and decision-making power . . .*

IN THE GARDEN, 1970

Salvatore's uncle Rafaele, one of the Discordia triplets, is talking with two old friends sitting on the wrought-iron benches in the backyard. They're under a lemon tree heavy with fruit, this lazy summer afternoon. Salvatore fetches another bottle of wine, then sits on the ground at their feet to listen to their stories.

These old retired men, who smell of aftershave, tobacco and leather, wear a lifetime of lines crosshatching their walnut brown faces—souvenirs from sun and wind, hard work and worry, families and wars, tragedy and happiness. They gesture with large, gnarled hands—hands that caressed women's faces and held babies, but never used a typewriter or received a manicure.

Mimmo, the oldest, had been a bricklayer; Primo, a metal worker; Salvatore's uncle, a machinist. They were the last of their small group who lived through World War II together, from prison camps to the Resistance and the Liberation, or "the Deception" as they called it.

They survived Fascists and Germans, and police and government orders to hunt them down. They found work, rebuilt homes, raised families, and had children like Salvatore—a nineteen-year-old with many questions and never enough answers. Looking from face to face, trying to understand, Salvatore feels compelled to ask:

"So what was it? What helped you, Uncle Rafaele, and you, Primo and Mimmo, survive the war? Luck? Cunning? Willpower? What?"

The three men smile, look at one another and shrug. For a moment, Salvatore is embarrassed and wishes he hadn't spoken.

"Was it luck, boys? Or the girls and the wine?"

They laugh. Mimmo, with his bright blue eyes and snow-white hair, leans forward and puts his hand on Salvatore's knee.

"I swear, Salvatore, it was the garlic. Lots of it. Raw, every day." They all laugh again.

"Yes," his uncle adds. "Garlic so strong it turned away bullets, knives, and Germans."

"I say it was my feet," Primo said. "Not the smell, you understand. But the way they helped me walk or run away from bad situations."

"Seriously," Salvatore asks. "What did you guys do that was different from the others, the ones who didn't make it?"

His uncle licks his lips, pours another glass of wine for his friends, and raises his.

"First, a toast to all our comrades and family who can't be with us here in this lovely garden today, relaxing without fear."

"To them, yes!" Mimmo and Primo raise their glasses reverently.

"I think it was patience. The endless patience of ordinary people like us, waiting and thinking before we acted," Rafaele said.

"We often thought about to how to remain sane in a world gone mad," adds Primo, "but it wasn't easy."

He places his glass on a small table and speaks with his big hands:

"Then as now, the politicians decided, the people applauded, and we who disagreed . . . well, we did what we had to."

"We did what we could to avoid being slaughtered," said Mimmo. "We had will. We had opportunities. And we had our friends: the mountains, the caves and the deep forests to help us. We had each other's solidarity, each other's support. Yes, it took individual courage for each one of us. But in the end I'd say it was the collective enterprise and initiative of our little group. No?"

He looked at the other two men nodding their heads.

"And a few smokes, right?"

"And some wine."

"We watched out for each other and helped each other like brothers and sisters."

"We shared the little bit of food we scrounged when times were difficult."

"We consoled each other, encouraged each other, and stood together always. Were we lucky? Perhaps."

"We can't thank God, since we don't believe in him, do we boys?"

"Nope, never did."

"Never will."

"Maybe the devil was on our side, since the priests always preached patriotic sermons and blessed all the Fascists' weapons of war."

"Remember that priest who joined us on the street barricade?"

"The one riding by on his bicycle who saw us building it?"

"And said he was one of us, and not a Fascist?"

"Him, yes! He stopped to watch us working and said, "Come back to the church with me. I have lots of empty pews that would be more useful right here."

"He helped us load them onto wheelbarrows and stack them in the street."

"He sweated with us. Then stood beside us."

"Imagine the parishioners cursing the devil who stole their pews!"

"Let's drink to that devil of a priest!"

RAFAELE IN MOM'S BELLY, 1977

I was born a few hours after my mother, Loretta, and some trade union bureaucrats were chased out of La Sapienza University of Rome by hundreds of masked protestors. What could I say? I heard shouting, glass breaking, tables and chairs being overturned, and my mother screaming at someone: "I'm pregnant, can't you see? Don't you dare touch me or I'll smash your face in!"

My mother has an authoritative voice and people tend to listen. Pregnant or not. It happened to be another young woman she was addressing. No one touched her, but she was forced to back up out the conference hall and make her escape with others.

Why the fuss? Students protesting the police killing of a student in Bologna were occupying La Sapienza. He'd been a member of the radical group *Lotta Continua*—The Struggle

Continues. Someone thought it would be a good idea to invite a top union bureaucrat, a real pork-chopper who was buddy-buddy with the Communist Party of Italy (PCI) to address the occupation. Bad move.

Never invite a high profile so-called leftist sell-out to speak to a radicalized student body—especially since his good friends, the PCI, opposed the occupation. The PCI opposed anything that remotely challenged their aspirations to govern and their historic compromise with the Christian Democrats. This was the position of Euro-Communism back then: keep the lid on any non–Communist Party dissident movement. Let no one rock any boat and the Party will eventually achieve power.

My mother just happened to have a summer job working for the trade union and was present as one of the researchers. How did she know the ever-ready-to-party *Autonomia Operaia* cadre would crash the event?

They stormed the hall with sticks and steel rods, bandanas covering their faces, and clashed with the trade union security people. The *Autonomia Operaia* outnumbered and overpowered the unionists and chased them away.

I was kicking inside my mom's belly, desperate to see all the action, and she was screaming out of pain and anger. Angry that the job description never mentioned anything about dangerous working conditions, especially for a pregnant woman! Angry that she had to miss another episode of *Charlie's Angels!* Angry because none of her colleagues stayed behind to help escort her out to safety.

In fact, she screamed so loudly, for so long, that her boss personally drove her to the hospital. En route I decided that the excitement of a new radical social movement clashing with the old institutionalized Left was just too good to miss. I popped out in the back seat of the car, bloodied and early.

PREFERRING THE 1960S
Personally, I would have preferred to be born during the 1960s instead of 1977. Italian music was so much better in the 1960s. Design, too. I love it!

In the 1960s, people weren't afraid to advance critiques of modernism and the cult of the "object." They dared to challenge traditional, boring concepts of architecture! Cool or what? They were concerned with social problems and had radical ideas about what to do to solve them. They were even criticizing globalization way ahead of the times. Did tons of theoretical work about it, too.

I love how they came up with theories about anti-design. For a future engineer like me—this was an exciting new direction.

But then I can't knock the '70s completely. We Italians reinvented ourselves politically in the streets, face-to-face, or at least face-to-mask. Call it another level of excitement with a different kind of aesthetic. Another challenge for the collective imagination. The once voiceless and forgotten from below— not just the intellectuals, artists, architects, and designers—were now advancing their own ideas for designing a new world.

Take my uncle, Luciano Discordia, for example. Born in 1960, he was one of those late 1970s longhaired, long-bearded, bell-bottomed, guitar-playing university students. Looked like Jesus. He knew the famous singer Fabrizio de André. Told me stories about hanging out on the beach with his buddies, drinking wine, singing radical songs, talking radical politics. Then they'd hit the streets in those crazy heavy-duty demonstrations, Italian style.

LUCIANO: *AUTONOMIA OPERAIA* MARCHES IN ROME

May 1977, 6 PM. I assemble with several thousand other *Autonomia Operaia* (Workers Autonomy) members in *Piazza della Repubblica* and tie my red bandana around my face. Cops are visible in the distance, riot gear ready, but they only watch for now.

We prepare our gear. Some pack pistols inside their waistbands; others, Molotovs and hammers in backpacks. Gloves pulled on to better wield long iron bars and wooden staves. Spray-paint cans in pockets. I recognize comrades from the university, fellow students from political science, from the women's group, from the antinuclear organization and many others. We will march together, shoulder to shoulder, and watch out for one another.

Our own *Servizio d'ordine* (security people) march in formation at the front and the rear, holding bars and staves end to end as we take position. They demarcate our line: keep your distance, police, or else. Today, here and now, the streets belong to us. An agitated voice crackles through a megaphone: "We march!"

We walk quickly, purposefully heading into *Via Torino*. Passers-by glance at us nervously, uncertain of what will happen, and walk the other way. In the distance we hear the "clang! clang! clang!" of metal shutters dropping as shopkeepers close their businesses. No one takes chances.

Out comes the spray paint. We give the tired, dirty grey metal shutters a new life with poetic slogans in red:

"Work less, love more!"

"Beneath the pavement, the beach."

"Refuse to work! Agree to live!"

As we pass the freshly decorated shop exteriors, comrades with a musical, rhythmic bent, transform the metal sheets into percussive instruments, beating out rhythms with bars and sticks.

"Oom pa pa! Oom pa! Clack clack clack!"

The beats bounce off the pavement, climb the walls of the buildings in the narrow street, and disappear high into the grey sky above, or echo into the empty streets behind us. Their message:

"Autonomia Operaia was here!"

In the middle of the demo, comrades raise their arms and give the "pistol salute"—two fingers tight together—the barrel of a revolver. If the police try to stop us from marching by using force, comrades are ready to use their weapons, including their pistols, to defend our rights. It's our violence versus State violence. The only equation they respect and fear.

We aren't crazy enough to believe in a full frontal attack against the armed might of the State. Some of us actually disapprove of the use of guns. But in a narrow street, during this demonstration, if individual officers try to harm us, if they dare try to attack us with their riot sticks or other implements of repression, we will defend ourselves with the weapons at hand. This is certain.

Along the route, comrades stock up on roadside construction material: pieces of wood, metal, chunks of brick and stone. Steel bars help to dislodge the *sampietriono*—the black stone underfoot that paves Rome. This stone that has borne the weight of the city for centuries might find itself freed, sailing above the streets, arcing in the sky, gracefully, purposefully, with a new vocation: a messenger from our generation to the decaying, corrupt, bankrupt old order. In our hands, these rocks will talk loud and clear:

"We've had enough! To hell with all your parties and politics! Step aside and make way for the revolt of the desperate, the unemployed of today and tomorrow! Enough of your cutbacks, your austerity, your attacks on our lives! We want a new world—now! Out of our way!"

There is a palpable tension in the air. Everyone is nervous. We never know the outcome of an action like this, the potential for a violent clash, injuries, or even death.

Behind me marches a group of *Metropolitan Indians*, wearing colourful costumes and war-paint. They poke fun at everyone, leftists included, and lighten up the mood.

They chant: "More work, less pay! More work, less pay!"

I recognize one "Indian" as a student from my class.

"Hey Ignacio! I didn't know your family was from North America!"

"*Ciao*, Luciano! Yeah, we immigrated here to teach you guys how to grow corn and party!" he replies, waving a plastic tomahawk decorated with bright ribbons.

"Get your free bus tickets yet?"

"No, from who?"

"*Autoriduttori*—the self-reduction guys—are handing them out. Here. They did a great print job. Who can tell they're fake? They printed a few thousand to distribute."

"Thanks. I can use them. When bus fares go up, I find myself walking more. It's tiring, man."

"You heard about that supermarket raid over in San Lorenzo? About twenty housewives were shopping, buggies loaded with food. When they lined up at the cash register and saw all the increased prices, they refused to pay, shouting, '*We can't pay! We won't pay!*'"

"They loaded the food into bags and walked out the door. A bunch of students were in the store, too, and followed their example.

"Cool!" said the "Indian." "They raise the prices, we counter with price reductions. I like it. Good for the housewives. So what do you think of the demonstration?"

With his tomahawk he motioned to the crowd around us, now packed tightly together as the street narrowed.

"I like that everyone can have their own voice, that every voice is equally important. We can all have our say and no bureaucrat, no sectarian politico is going to shut us up. This is the way it should be."

"Long live Sacrifice!" he chants derisively, waving his tomahawk wildly and jumping up and down. His friends and I join in, laughing.

The future, Luciano is thinking. *No more partisan politics. No more bickering among leftoid groupuscules. Just us, taking to the streets, determining our own fates, figuring out what to do. No leaders, no bosses, no party hacks or fucked-up politicians of any stripe using us and the issues for their own self-interest. Just us reshaping this world according to our needs. Our vision. Yes, I like it.*

NEWS, 1977, Rome: *Over 100 Fascists invade Rome university campus . . . Shoot and wound students . . . Faculty of Letters occupied . . . Thousands of students demonstrate outside neo-Fascist party offices of MSI . . . Police open fire . . . 20,000 students demonstrate in streets of Rome . . .*
Bologna: *Local pirate radio station, Radio Alice, accused of obscenity . . . denies charges . . . vows to fight . . .*

RADIO ALICE, 1977

"You are now listening to the only pirate radio station in Bologna, Radio Alice, with a special report on the recent obscenity charge.

"What do we say about this charge? We say it is obscene. Why? For centuries, we have repressed our bodies, our sexuality, our desire to stay home, sleep in, and not go to work. To be deliberately nonproductive. We scold ourselves. We say, 'Satan, do not speak to me. Do not tempt me. Go away!'

"We at Radio Alice say, enough! Enough of working eight hours or more a day, commuting maybe two hours every day, and coming home to have a short nap, a family dinner, and a bit of television before we need to sleep to repeat the same routine again and again, workday after workday, week after week. Enough! We refuse to stay within the prescribed limits of this boring, life-sucking routine. Enough! For our stated opposition to this, they call us obscene? Enough! Their order is the real obscenity."

A WARNING FOR FASCISTS

Six of us sit on the floor in Giuseppe's cramped apartment above a bakery, smoking, drinking coffee, and eating. The aroma of fresh bread fills the room and Fabrizio D'André sings for us on the turntable.

We are all Turin University students from "the movement." Romano and Giuseppe are two soft-spoken, best friends from Abruzzo, now studying mathematics. Both wear horn-rimmed glasses. Giuseppe is a cousin of Luciano Discordia, a known student activist in Rome. Ricardo and Carmela are the almost inseparable raven-haired twin brother and sister from the Political Science Department. Southerners, they are olive-skinned with large mussel-black eyes. Loretta and Alberto, just married, are in engineering. They hold hands all night long.

"Enough talk," says Ricardo. "We know the Fascists are escalating their violence in the street. After the last demonstration, Fascist thugs beat three of us on our way home. What's next?"

"If we don't try to stop them, I guess more of us will be injured. Maybe killed," his sister adds.

"Are we agreed? It's time to respond to them on their own terms."

"Why should we be the only ones who no longer feel safe in the streets? They should taste their own medicine."

"That bar is the best target. They meet there all the time. Everyone knows it." Loretta is referring to Bar Domenico, a popular Fascist hangout.

"But how will we know when it is empty? We don't want to hurt anyone. Just burn it and send them a message."

"And hope they get it."

"Giuseppe and I have been watching it for the past week every night until closing time. The last guy leaves by 2 AM. Always."

"You're sure?"

"Positive."

"And no one lives upstairs?"

"We don't know for a fact. It seems empty."

"But we're agreed we do it? Now? Yes?"

"Let's do it this week."

"It's not hard to figure out. A few of us stand watch on the corners. Another rides by on a bicycle with a rock. Two more on a scooter with the Molotovs. Everyone wears gloves."

"No fingerprints. No evidence. Not a word to anyone else."

"It stays in this room."

"I can write the communiqué."

"With gloves. No fingerprints."

ATTACKING THE BAR

It's 2 AM. The moon is peeping out from behind a cloud. Still slurring their unending stories, the last Bar Domenico patrons are zig-zagging home supported by a straight arm to a wall or the shoulder of a compliant friend.

One couple and one individual linger on the corners bookending the bar. The couple is making out, but watchful.

The solitary person smokes a cigarette and eyes the street up and down.

"You nervous?" Alberto asks Loretta, squeezing her hand.

"No, you?"

"No, but I imagine they are. Look, here they come."

A red scooter, two-up, slowly cruises past. Eyes meet, and the scooter continues around the block. A bicyclist now approaches, waving his hand. Alberto waves back. Ricardo, the cyclist, pulls a bandana up on his face, then slowly pedals toward the bar. He hears the scooter coming back around the corner. The scooter blinks its lights. Ricardo pedals faster, then brakes suddenly in front of the bar. He throws two fist-sized chunks of cement through the plate glass window, shielding his eyes as it shatters, then pedals away.

The scooter drives up and stops. The rear passenger dismounts, lights the first Molotov, and throws it through the hole. It explodes. He lights and throws the second one. The flames dance, lick, and roar, and the students speed off into the night.

THE CONSEQUENCES

The Turin courtroom is jammed with noisy spectators. The judge bangs his gavel, calls for order, and addresses the five defendants standing before him. They look haggard and frightened. The sixth member of their group sits apart. He is a police informer.

"You are five young students with promising futures. Why did you do it? Why did you throw the Molotovs? You knew you could end up in jail, your careers ruined?"

The courtroom erupts in jeers and catcalling and the judge calls for order again.

"Because we all knew it had to be done. Because if we didn't do it, the Fascists would grow fearless."

The spectators cheer.

"What else could we do? Send a polite letter: *'Please stop your violence'*?"

More cheering.

"Because the police do nothing. They won't stop the Fascists. The government does nothing. They turn a blind eye."

The spectators stamp their feet and hoot.

"Because everyone talks about how terrible the Fascist violence is, but no one tries to stop them. We are through with talking. The time to act is now."

Wild applause, whistling and yelling breaks out in the courtroom.

"Because we can. We have nothing to lose. If we don't try to stop them, who else will?"

"We will! We will! We will!" the spectators chant in unison as guards try to restore order and the judge continues to bang his gavel. But no one listens. No one obeys.

NEWS, 1977, Rome: Italian Communist Party (PCI) members provoke scuffle with students . . . Police clear out students occupying Rome university . . . PCI applaud actions . . . 30,000 students demonstrate against PCI and police . . . Fascists shoot and wound students . . . Bologna police shoot and kill young activist . . . Prime Minister says this killing is "normal and inevitable" . . . 100,000 protest in streets of Rome . . .

JOURNALIST GETS HIS HOT SUMMER OF '77 STORY

The twenty-four-year-old émigré Polish anarchist journalist, Marek, paced in his bed-and-breakfast room in Turin. He set up this meeting a month ago from London, where his family now lives. It promises to be an interview unlike any he has ever done before. The ground rules:

> You will leave a written message about where you are
> staying on a piece of paper taped to the message board
> of the anarchist bookstore. It will be addressed to Pippo.
> You must say: Pippo, contact me at this address. Give the
> agreed date and time. Then wait. Someone will come and
> get you. You will have 15 minutes to ask your questions.

It was the "hot summer of 1977," that followed the "Italian spring of 1977." Italy was witnessing some of the fiercest, bloodiest street fighting in its major cities since World War II.

On one side, the cops. On the other, politicized members of Italy's growing underclass: the desperate, the unemployed. It was a radically diverse movement intent on totally autonomous action, independent of all parties and politics, but united in resistance to cutbacks. These cutbacks affected people in universities, at work, in housing, transportation, and basic social and public services. Economic attacks that penalized mostly the poor.

So the youth took to the streets in sporadic guerrilla actions, mobile and spontaneous urban warfare. "Anti-politics" was their watchword. And their weakness. No one knew if this movement would last or burn itself out spectacularly for lack of any long-term organizing to build a broader mass base.

The sweat-soaked journalist was about to get his interview. There was a knock on his door. He opened. A well-dressed young blond woman wearing oversized sunglasses smiled at him. He smiled back.

"Hello there!"

"Come with me, please. And don't forget your notepad and your recorder."

He fumbled nervously with his knapsack then followed her down the stairs, into the street, and to a busy coffee shop full of students.

"Sit here please. Someone will come for you."

Soon enough, another equally stylish young woman with sunglasses tapped him on the shoulder from behind and told him to come with her. He smiled again as she crooked her arm in his, walked him out the door, around the corner into the backseat of a waiting car and slid in beside him.

"Excuse me while I place this blindfold on you. It's a security precaution."

Marek was anxious, but excited. The car lurched forward. For the next ten minutes, it bounced and turned on the cobblestoned streets. When it finally stopped, she led him outside and into a cool, dank building, down some stairs. Another young woman removed the blindfold.

"Follow me please."

They walked through a series of dark corridors and entered a dusty basement room. It was lit by the feeble light from a dirty, sidewalk level window. Inside were two men, both wearing red bandanas concealing their faces.

"Sit here please." They pulled up a wooden chair for him.

"Sorry for the precautions, but you will understand. These are tense moments. This is the blossoming of a new resistance movement. We need to protect ourselves. The forces of repression are everywhere."

Both of the men—"spokespeople" they clarified, "not leaders"—for one of the new autonomous groups, spoke rapidly in turn, and at one point, raised the fronts of their sweaters to show pistols tucked into their waistbands.

The wide-eyed journalist was already two pages into his notebook scribbling madly to keep up. All he could think of was, *Holy fuck! Holy fuck! This is a story!*

"The State can't control us. The police can't control us. Now the Communist Party is trying to show that it can tame us. But they are mistaken. As the new police, they will fail. We have new cells, armed cells, springing up everywhere. We are about to enter a new phase of struggle. An unprecedented insurrectionary phase. You will see. Tell your readers. This is just the beginning."

NEWS, 1978: Italian authorities spread dragnet for woman charged with complicity in Red Brigades kidnap slaying of former premier Aldo Moro . . . Has been living with the man who rented a hideout used by the Red Brigades . . .

GRANDMOTHER'S BOOK CLUB, 1989

Tall, thin, and elegant, with sparkling eyes, snowy white straight hair pulled back tightly in a long braid coiled on top of her head: This is Rafaele's grandmother, Consuessa.

She has unsurpassable culinary skills, a way with words, a wicked sense of humour, and an ongoing concern for Rafaele's education. He loves spending time with her and will do anything she asks, from running errands to helping her in the kitchen and the garden. She taught him how to grow and cook food.

Today she invites him to join her in the cool darkness of the dining room. They sit side by side at the polished mahogany table for lemonade and cookies. She pours him a glass. He gulps it down, then notices the two large piles of old books neatly stacked at the other end the table. She smiles at him and puts an arm around his shoulder.

"Now tell me, Rafaele, what kind of books are you reading these days outside of school?"

"Ahhh . . ." He happily recites a list of popular boys' books about the adventures of a youthful soccer-playing gang. "They're so cool."

Consuessa squeezes his shoulder.

"Rafaele, you're twelve now. Old enough to start reading more seriously. The great thinkers and writers."

She slides over the two piles of books.

"Look! Dante, Plato, Descartes, Petrarch, Ovid, Virgil, Shakespeare, Dickens."

She pulls a book from each pile—Italian and non-Italian— flashes the cover, describes the contents, then places it on the other side, starting two new piles.

Rafaele follows the deconstruction and reconstruction of the piles, left to right, trying to make a mental note of each.

"You need to familiarize yourself with the thoughts of the great minds of the past. So that you can advance your own ideas about the human condition and help make the world a better place."

"Yes, Grandmother." Rafaele swallows hard. It's the first time she had ever spoken in this tone to him.

"In school they will only teach you certain things. Not everything. You must educate yourself outside of school. Understand?"

"Yes, Grandmother."

A look of consternation crosses his face. He needs more time after school, not more homework, he thinks, but says nothing.

"Here we have Elio Vittorini, Vasco Pratolini, Cesare Pavese. Some of our greatest writers. I think you will enjoy them. They wrote the best Italian literature in the 1930s and the 1940s."

She holds up one book with an illustrated cover.

"This one, my favourite, *Bread and Wine*, was written by Ignazio Silone when he was in exile during Mussolini's time. A significant book. A great book. You must read it. All his others, too."

Rafaele nods hesitantly at every recommendation, his head slowly spinning as he munches cookies and sips lemonade.

Jesus, he thinks. *I had no idea Grandmother read so many books. Where does she find the time? I only see her cooking, cleaning, and working in the garden.*

"This one," she continued, "*Time of Indifference* by Alberto Moravia, was censored by the government. Do you know what *censored* means?"

He shakes his head.

"They did not appreciate his attacks on the Fascist regime and tried to stop people from reading his work. This is how important a book can be. The government feared what the author was saying. They were afraid that people might take his words to heart and act on them. I have more favourite books, but we'll look at those later."

Rafaele nods, still not sure what to say.

"For now, start with these."

Seeing his mouth open wide, she modifies her expectations.

"Or only a few of them if you wish."

Rafaele closed his mouth. He didn't want to displease his grandmother.

"Yes, Grandmother. I'll do my best."

"Good boy. Take a few of them home today. Next time you visit me, we can discuss the books. Over more lemonade. This will be a special book club that only you and I belong to. No one else. Agreed?"

ANTONIO: CORSANO SUMMER HOLIDAYS

Every summer, our parents would load my sister and I into the back of the car and drive south for a weeklong holiday in Corsano.

They rented a small whitewashed house a few kilometres from the beach. Each glorious day from morning until supper we spent on the sun-drenched sand and rocks or in the crystal blue water.

Father would plant a large yellow beach umbrella in the sand and spread out a blanket. Mother would open a picnic basket filled with cool drinks and fruit. Then beneath the cloudless happy sky where seagulls roamed, my sister and I would attach our snorkels and dive into the clear warm waters searching for treasures.

I would often wade into the ocean up to my knees, defying the waves rolling in from Greece, trying to block their path.

"Halt! In the name of Antonio the Great, ruler of all Italy!"

I imagined hundreds of the Greek gods—Poseidon, Aegaeon, Ceto, Nereus, Thetis—all of them disguised as miniature water spirits, standing upright in fantastic little speed boats, waving their sceptres, thunder bolts, and tridents as they rode the crest of each wave, avoiding direct contact with my giant forbidding knees, to land safely behind me, burrowing themselves into the sand. There, they would construct magnificent new kingdoms beneath our feet.

Later, in the name of my Empire, I tried to excavate the buried fantasy worlds with little luck.

Sometimes I was the Madonna in the water, stretching out my arms over the entire ocean, healing all the sick and disabled creatures of the sea, the one-legged crabs, blind fish, or ailing shrimp.

Other days I was the unmoving and mammoth Rock of Gibraltar, or a Corsican pirate plotting my next move, or a half-human sea monster ready to prey on my unsuspecting younger sister.

Our grandfather and grandmother sometimes met us on the beach. Grandfather once said to me:

"Take a deep breath, put your face in the water, and look into the ocean for signs of life."

I did, came up gasping for breath, and he asked:

"So, what did you see?"

"Nothing but rocks. That's all."

"You didn't look close enough, long enough."

I'd look again and still see nothing but the rocks.

"Don't give up. Keep looking. Be patient," he said, "prepare yourself for the wait. Take a deep breath."

A few attempts later, I spotted the tiniest of sea creatures crawling right before my eyes.

There was a local boy, my best summer holiday friend I met over many visits. A beach towel draped around his neck, he would wobble his way through the grass and sand on his bicycle toward my family's umbrella.

"Hey, Antonio! Wanna come and see some super fat Germans wearing tiny bathing suits? They look so gross. Like white whales flopping out of the water."

"Nah, let's go over to that spot by the rocks and snorkel. Remember, there's a cave, right?"

"There are some pretty German girl tourists there, too. Come on, let's go look!"

I was starting to be embarrassed because of the growing erections I would get every time I ogled a girl in a bikini walking by. How do you hide a twelve-year-old's erection in a tight bathing suit? I'd lie on my stomach on a towel, but it only seemed to make the problem worse. The bulge grew. My father didn't seem to have a problem, dozing on his side under the umbrella. Only me.

Once, I noticed a man in a wet suit with a harpoon who plopped himself ass-first into the water. As he sat there near the shore, he crossed himself with his free hand, then kicked off, tugging an inflated orange and white plastic float that bobbed in the water. I feared for the poor creatures that would die at the end of his deadly arrow.

Every day my sister and I would wander off into the dry

grasslands bordering the beach, to explore an ancient shepherd's hut. The small, almost conical structure, hundreds of years old and built of field stones, was still standing in the tall grass, now home to field mice and snakes. Our mom warned us to always wear shoes:

"Vipers sun themselves on the rocks or sleep in the shadows of the hut."

In the distance I could see sailboats rocking their way forward across the horizon, dipping and rising. That steady line marked the end of the world that I knew or imagined I knew. How many times I touched it with a fingertip, saying:

"Beyond is the beginning of another world. A really cool world. Where parents don't fight over money and stuff. Where no kid comes to school hungry. Where every kid can get whatever new sneakers they want. Because they're not so expensive, and parents won't say, "You can't have them." Where girls don't giggle at me every time I try to say hello. And where you can eat all the ice cream you want, 'cause it's OK."

I would beckon it, shouting: "Come closer, other world! Come closer so that I can see you!"

There were days I would hunt small crabs in a tidal pool. I'd catch one, and watch it, helpless in my plastic bucket as it circled the perimeter looking for a way out. I never noticed the terror in its eyes, nor sensed the fear in its movements, trapped, a victim of my superior size and intelligence . . .

Today, in a park in San Lorenzo, with Cinka beside me, I read in the newspaper that the Interior Minister proposes to house Romani refugees in giant metal containers. To stack them up and eventually ship them out to sea, to float past my favourite beach at Corsano.

What monster sees this as a solution?

GREAT-UNCLE'S SECRET, 1994
One haze-filled fall afternoon, Rafaele's beloved grandmother, Consuessa, asked him to follow her from the house into the back storage shed. The low stone building was dug halfway

into the side of a slope, sheltered by a few tall pine trees behind the ancestral Ripa home. It served as a root and wine cellar. The stone walls and floor kept everything at an even temperature through hot summers and freezing mountain winters.

"Sit here please."

Consuessa motioned to a squat stool beside a small rough-hewn wooden table. She pushed a second stool close and poured two glasses of red wine.

"I never told you this before, and nor did my brother— your great-uncle—because you were too young to understand. Now that he's gone and you are a young man, it is time you knew."

She disappeared into the shadows behind a row of stacked wooden barrels and returned with a long object wrapped in an old blanket. She placed it on the table, and looking Rafaele in the eyes, said in a low stern voice:

"This was my brother's, your great-uncle Antoniolo's. I kept it hidden for him."

She pulled out an ancient bolt-action rifle, polished and oiled, gleaming in the faint light in the darkened cellar.

"But Grandmother, this isn't his hunting rifle, is it?"

"No, Rafaele. This was his other gun. When he was your age, seventeen,—he used this one to defend his family. And to kill Fascists. He was part of the AdP and later, the resistance movement here in the mountains. You know we were very close and he often confided in me. He told me stories I would rather not repeat now. Maybe later. But before he died—bless his soul, I still can't believe it—he made me promise I would show you this and tell you the story behind it."

She drew a white handkerchief from inside her sleeve, daubed her eyes and composed herself, sitting upright.

"He said he thought he would never see the day when he had to kill others, to save his family and his friends, but that the Fascists left him no choice. The Fascists were killing anyone who disagreed with them, hunting them down like rabbits in the forest. For Antoniolo, it was either kill or be killed. He was part of a small group of local young men and women, all anti-Fascists since the beginning of the war. I met some of them later. This was his group."

She slipped a worn, creased, black and white photo from an old envelope that had been concealed in a pocket sewn into the blanket. Five young smiling people stood arm-in-arm. One had her fist raised in the air. Another held his rifle above his head.

"On the left is Antoniolo. These other men and women were his closest companions, his "resistance family" he called them. Two of them were killed in the fighting."

"This is the same rifle in the photo?"

"Yes. He wanted you to have it. As a memento of what he fought against, and what he fought for. He would be shocked to hear about that young witch who now sits in the government extolling the virtues of her butcher grandfather.

"Like many of us, your great-uncle despised that man and what he did to our country. So many suffered and paid with their lives to stop him. So many more today still suffer because of his vile ideas and what he left behind.

"Antoniolo asked me to ask you to promise never to allow men like that, men who espouse that kind of thinking, to take power ever again. Can you promise me and your great-uncle this, Rafaele?"

"I'll do my best, Grandmother."

"Good. Now you know it's here."

She rewrapped the gun in the blanket and returned it to its hiding place.

"Antoniolo always kept it in good working condition—in case he ever had to use it again."

PART VII

LIES, HOPE

WHERE ARE THE OLD CADRE TODAY?

Rafaele pauses outside the bar on *Via dei Volsci*, one of three local alternative social centres in San Lorenzo. In the 1970s, this brightly painted building with an anti-Nazi steel sign above its door was home base for *Autonomia Operaia*—a countrywide, extraparliamentary organization of disenfranchised youth and workers. They rocked Italy's streets with headline-grabbing prerevolutionary action.

They thought the future was theirs, Rafaele muses, *but they didn't hang onto it long enough, and we haven't scripted it yet.*

As loud reggae blasts through the open door from the sound system, Rafaele scans the faces of the patrons nursing their beers on the sidewalk terrace.

Which of these grey-haired oldsters was once a former *Autonomia Operaia* street radical? Who hid their face behind a kerchief while marching during a noisy demonstration with ten thousand other *Autonomia Operaia* members?

Who stood, a pistol clutched with both hands, aiming at cops trying to break up the demo? Which one joined several hundred others all carrying long steel bars and chased Communist Party bureaucrats out the door of the university? Rafaele couldn't tell, scanning the bar patrons, who were peacefully puffing on cigarettes, chatting with each other amicably.

On the nearest street corner, youthful dealers peddle

their drugs. Wheat-pasted high above them on the stone wall is a giant poster decrying the gentrification of San Lorenzo.

Inside, Rafaele orders a beer, then sits down with a heavyset black man with dreadlocks and a bright yellow T-shirt. Rudy.

Rudy is part of *Radio Onda Rossa*—Rome's alternative radio station, housed next door. He also teaches at Rome University's Department of Political Science—still the most activist sector of the university. Recently, its students occupied the Rectory to protest a scheduled visit by the Pope and effectively prevented him from coming.

Before that, they prevented the Fascist *Forza Nuova* from organizing a "revisionist history" conference intended to blame leftists for killing Italians in Tito's former Yugoslavia. The Fascists later beat five students outside the university gates.

Radio Onda Rossa reports all the news the dailies and commercial radio stations ignore.

"Hey, Rudy, what's up?" Rafaele extends a hand. Rudy's engrossed with his laptop.

"Working on a new documentary," Rudy replies, not looking up. "An oral history with survivors of a century of Italian racism. Maybe you can help me."

He stops. Looks up.

"I'm looking for older Italians and immigrants who remember incidents from way back. We're talking early twentieth century, when all the Calabrisians suffered 'cause you pearl-white northerners never accepted them 'cause they were darkies like me. Then the waves of internal racism, Italians mistreating other Italians because of dialect differences until the 1980s when the Poles and Turks came here. They were targeted, then the Albanians, the Arabs, the Africans. Today it's the Romanians. Tomorrow? It's a long list."

"And the Roma?" Rafaele asks.

"Shit, man, they've always been persecuted. Just ask your grandfather and his grandfather. Nothing new. Just a little more intense now, 'cause there are a few more of them around. But there's no one to defend them. Typical, I'd say. The State always picks on the weakest. Those who can't fight back. Then uses the poorest of the poor to attack them. Keeps their hands clean. Motherfuckers."

MONTEROTONDO MORNING

Antonio awakens in his cousin's Monterotondo house to morning birdsong. He throws open the bedroom shutters and breathes deeply.

Above him, a leftover half moon, like a forgotten slice of blanched lemon from last night's party, is stuck to the clear blue sky.

A toilet across the narrow street flushes loudly. A young mother opens her shutters, leans out, breathes deeply, then closes them. White-breasted swallows convene on an adjacent rooftop and begin chattering. Up and down this street, people start their cars and motorcycles and speed off to work.

Antonio stretches and scratches his back, enjoying this bit of fresh-aired, suburban tranquillity where the morning cacophony of Rome is replaced by scattered, uncrowded solo audio statements. Every singular sound breathes on its own in the composition. He wishes he'd brought his recorder to capture the sparse beauty of this soundscape.

In between the silence and revved-up engines, he hears snippets of early morning conversations from open windows. A pair of loud-mouthed caged parakeets argue on a balcony below him, while a mini garbage pickup truck putt-putts down the street.

Two city employees in bright orange pants get out and empty garbage cans into the back of the truck. A cigarette dangles out of one woman's mouth, sunglasses rest on top of her head. She grabs two bags at a time and tosses them in as she hums and sings a popular romantic song:

"I was yours, yours, yours, until you threw me out with the garbage..."

Antonio descends the stairs and walks into the verdant tree-shaded yard. An overweight grey and white cat sits perfectly still on a hammock slung under two apple trees watching birds flit just above its head. Both cat and birds know: the feline is too lazy and too heavy to pose a threat. In the garden, tiny cherry tomatoes ripen. Antonio nibbles on a few.

A strong aroma of blossoming thyme fills the morning air. Behind the tomatoes, giant zucchini and peppers dangle from branches like new babies about to drop.

Next door, a vivacious, middle-aged woman, decked out in a yellow straw hat with a pink ribbon and matching pink top over her flowered skirt, busies herself in her immaculate flower garden. She bends down to weed between clown-faced pansies and bluebells and notices the shirtless Antonio.

All smiles, she booms out a "Good morning! How are you? Good! Good!" before returning to her task.

Satisfied that all is well with the flowers, she returns her empty garbage container to her house, and with a purposeful stride, heads out her gate and down the hill. Antonio breathes the fresh air deeply and wonders: will Cinka and I ever find this kind of peace?

THE NORTHERN SENATOR SPEAKS

The greying millionaire senator from Florence, Roberto Fancazzista of the Northern Patriot Party, parks his SUV in the underground parking lot, then strides into his gleaming downtown office at precisely 7 AM.

"Good morning, Senator," says the secretary. "You have three interviews with the press: 8 AM, 8:30 AM, and 9 AM. Would you like your coffee now?"

"Yes, with some of those biscuits from yesterday. Is Bruno in?"

"Yes sir, he's waiting for you in his office."

"Hold all my calls until after the interviews. Bruno, come in! Let's finish this speech, pronto."

The much younger aide grabs his laptop and sits opposite the senator "I went over what you wrote," he says, "but I made a few changes last night. What do you think?"

The senator adjusts his green necktie and reviews the changes.

"Fine. Good. Let me see how it sounds."

He clears his throat, coughs, and looking into a mirror, switches to his mellifluous public speaking voice. Bruno shifts his chair, watches, and listens.

"For all of Italy, this is a difficult moment. According to a recent poll, three out of four Italians today feel insecure. Is this normal? No. This used to be a country of happiness, of respectful, law-abiding Italians. Recently, we've noticed a sharp increase in crimes against property, and now this—a heinous crime against an honest, god-fearing, hardworking, devoted Italian housewife. Killed because we Italians have failed to protect our own country from the invasion of . . . *people*—I don't want to say *immigrants* just yet—who don't respect our religion, our culture, our civilization, our hard-won values, etc., etc. Hmm. I haven't quite decided how to end that sentence yet."

"Um, sir, how about just ending it after 'hard-won values'?"

"Good. Keep it simple. These *people* have brought a crime wave. And the public response is one of disquiet, shock, disgust, and a growing anger. We, the guardians of all that is Italy, will no longer stand by and watch our culture, our people be subjected to the disrespect, the indecencies, the rapes, murders and robberies, the acts of barbarism committed by these *immigrants* . . . There, I said it!"

The senator slaps his notes with the back of his hand.

"The press will love this! Timing, my boy! The right word, the ripe situation."

"Yes, sir."

The senator smiles broadly. "*Il Duce* would have approved. What did he call it: '*The moment—we have everyone by the balls.*' I'm on a roll. Yes?"

Bruno nods vigorously, "Yes, sir, absolutely."

"We have to milk that unfortunate murder for everything we can. It won't be in the headlines for long. Now listen to this!"

He clears his throat and resumes his stern tone, glaring into the mirror and jabbing two fingers at an imaginary press scrum.

"There are those who claim that our party is leading a witch hunt against foreigners. Witch hunt, no. Housecleaning, yes. Long overdue, the kind any good housewife performs all the time . . . I axed that part about vigilante patrols for now. We can use it later."

"Yes, of course, Senator."

"The practices, values and attitudes of many recent immigrants, particularly the Romanians, render them incompatible for integration into our society. Romanian and Gypsy refugee camps across Italy serve as gathering places for thieves, prostitutes, muggers, and rapists. They must be cleaned out. Our party is not afraid to demand that the government expel all these troublesome foreigners from Italy immediately for reasons of public health or security—without trials. We're talking 250,000 expulsions countrywide—no less—of all foreign criminals, Gypsies, anyone committing offences, and people who are homeless or can't support themselves. It's time for them to leave."

Bruno stamps his feet, applauds, and whistles.

"No, no. Hold the applause please, Bruno. I'm not finished yet."

The senator places one hand over his heart.

"We Italians should not have to walk the streets of our own country in fear of violence. Only yesterday, my own dear mother said she was afraid to walk alone at night, afraid that a Gypsy might mug her. We cannot tolerate the Romanian rabble any longer. I propose that if any immigrant commits a crime against an Italian, then we should punish ten immigrants for every slight against one of our citizens. We must make Italy intolerable for them."

The senator adjusts his tie, chuckles, and faces a smiling Bruno, who rises to shake his hand.

"I got the idea about the reprisals from the German SS during the war. It's what they did here. Like it?"

"Sounds like a winner, Senator. Another winner. Congratulations."

PARROT RADIO

Driving back from a gig in Florence, Antonio keeps thinking about how much he misses Cinka when the band travels. He can't stand not seeing her for even one day. She's supposed to call him later. He cranks up the car radio while Agnesia and Massimaxo talk loudly in the back seat.

"Shh! Listen!"

> And in other news, Senator Roberto Fancazzista of the Northern Patriot Party described the Gypsy camps outside Florence as "a gathering place of thieves and prostitutes, muggers, and rapists," and called for all Gypsies to be prevented from entering Florence. Further, the senator said his party was not afraid to demand that the government expel foreigners from EU countries for reasons of public health or security, and that under the new emergency decree, no trial of any suspect is required.

Massimaxo lets out a long whistle.

"Assholes!" Antonio pounds the steering wheel. "I don't fucking believe it! Fan the flames, Senator! Send out a message of contempt. Fuck you! You and your hate-filled messages! You're the problem!"

"A royal prick," Agnesia says.

"One of their biggest," Massimaxo adds.

Antonio continues. "Didn't we Italians once migrate? From the south to the north? And to North America, South America, France, Belgium?"

Massimaxo nods. "We ourselves were the exiles. The refugees. The strangers who spoke a different language, with different customs, trying to better our lives."

"And weren't we fucking discriminated against? Beaten and spat on? And even killed? This is *our* history, too, Senator Fuckhead!" Antonio screams.

"What happened to Sacco and Vanzetti? Where's the collective memory? The sense of justice? They used to call us Italians '*thieves, prostitutes, muggers, and rapists.*' Like the Roma and the Romanians. All we wanted was a better life, too. *Cazzo culo!*"

He swerves off the highway into an Auto-Grill to gas up and get food. Massimaxo and Agnesia visit the washrooms while he orders.

"Three espressos and three panini, please."

At the counter, he overhears three men having a heated discussion behind him. He turns to look.

"I tell you. Italy is taking the lead in Europe. Finally, we're showing the rest of them that we don't want all these fucking immigrants."

"Good riddance. You see that damn Gypsy squatter camp bulldozed to the ground? Beautiful, just beautiful."

"Yeah, and with any luck, these new laws will apply to all those Africans and Middle East people. Don't want them. Don't need them. Go home!"

Antonio is about to say something, just as the third man disagrees.

"What the hell are you guys talking about? Listen to you. Bunch of racist boneheads. My own cousins too. I swear, if your dad could hear you now . . ."

"Fuck you! What do you know?"

"Remember Uncle Tommaso? Went to Canada to work ten years ago? You don't remember? Called Dad crying, telling him the Canadians wanted to kick him out. They called him a dirty wop stealing their jobs. Told him to go home. He wasn't welcome. Remember?"

"That's different. Uncle Tommaso, he's like a skilled engineer. They'd need him in Canada. It's not the same."

"Lots of these people are skilled too. We can use them here. And they want to work. What's wrong with that?"

"Bullshit! They just want to steal and rape and live off of us."

"You're so full of it. Didn't your dad hire that Romanian computer dude?"

"Yeah, so?"

"And that Tunisian mechanic? Nothing wrong with them, right?"

"Ali? He's OK, he's different."

HER TEACHER TOLD HER

"Rafaele, it's Antonio. I'm fine, thanks, you? Listen, remember Cinka's sister, Celina? The smart little eleven-year-old? She tried to kill herself last night. Slashed her wrist. I'm serious.

"Her teacher told her that her mom was a criminal like other Romanians. Said a Gypsy mother was not fit to raise her. That the police should take her away from her mom. Put her in an Italian home. She's in the hospital now. This is nuts, man. What can we do?"

SAN LORENZO THE RED

San Lorenzo was once Rome's solid "Red" neighbourhood, Left to the core. But its traditional political colour is fading as the housing crunch drives up prices and forces out the working poor, the moneyless students, and the ever-struggling but assertive dissidents. A new generation is replacing them. One that brags about more "green" in their pockets and has so much less "red" on their minds—or in their hearts.

San Lorenzo, where the Nazi-Fascists once faced their greatest opposition, where mass arrests, beatings, and murders couldn't stifle the resistance before and during the war, where even the Allies pummelled the poor neighbourhood with bombs, killing their own staunchest supporters, leaving orphans, widows, and widowers behind to reconsider wartime and future allegiances.

San Lorenzo, where graffitied and postered walls scream out for attention, but can't make the current inhabitants blink for longer than a microsecond. People are too busy working more hours for less pay or desperately searching for work, fearful of days ahead without an income.

San Lorenzo, where students from *La Sapienza* University study the films of Pier Paolo Pasolini and discuss war and peace and where to buy the cheapest dope.

San Lorenzo, where the homeless now sleep on ever-thinner cardboard and eat the tasteless-as-cardboard leftover junk food tossed their way by today's good Samaritans.

San Lorenzo, where the peal of the cathedral bells still consoles, where ever-cooing pigeons still reign, where the markets in the square still offer surprise bargains, where one can find the best pizza at a decent price, where hope still peeks around the corner in the big brown eyes of a child, where the red ghosts of generations before still haunt the cafés and bars on *Via degli Equi, degli Etruschi, dei Volsci, dei Lucani,* in *Piazza dei Sanniti*—their voices distant but discernable amid the chatter in the shadows; their vision for a red Rome, a red Italy beyond the walls of San Lorenzo, still lingering long into the night under the pale moon and even into tomorrow's yawning orange sunrise.

"San Lorenzo, my love!" they cry. "Don't leave us behind! Don't forget us!"

San Lorenzo, where Antonio holds hands with Cinka as they walk and whispers into her ear: "You are the love of my life. I'll never let you go."

MASSIMAXO VISITS A REFUGEE CAMP

"Wish you'd been there, Rafaele!" Massimaxo said, describing his first visit to a Romani refugee camp. "It was so moving and so awful!"

Massimaxo had helped a documentary filmmaker friend that day. He wore headphones and carried the sound boom.

"It was a combo press conference and guided visit—to document conditions for an European Parliamentary delegation. There were Italian, American, Polish, Belgian, French, German journalists, and cameras, man—tons of telephoto lenses bumping together! And, like, a dozen or more EU politicians, human rights people, translators, and staff. Must have been fifty of us! And Roma from Milano, Livorno, Romania, and Trieste. All telling their stories to the parliamentarians.

"The refugees in the camp were kind of overwhelmed, but super polite and hospitable. They brought us water and coffee and gave us chairs to sit on. All the kids were posing for the cameras. The photographers went nuts 'cause these kids, man, they're so photogenic!

"There was an old Italian Jewish survivor from Auschwitz— one of the last, I think—with a hearing aid and a blue tattooed number on his forearm. The Nazis carved it into him as a kid. He said this camp reminded him of his days behind the barbed wire in Poland. Can you believe it?

"He's sitting beside this beautiful little girl, a Romni. She's an artist, maybe eleven years old, and she's beaming, showing him page after page of her artwork. Watercolours, drawings, touching stuff about life as a refugee. She won some UN-sponsored art contest for refugee kids. But get this: the cops in Milano beat her when she tried to stop them from beating her father in the street!

"He had given interviews to journalists about how his family was having a tough time in Milano. The cops found him, beat him and her, and told him to go back to Romania or next time they would kill him.

"There was a young husband and wife from Livorno. They lost a child in a fire set by Fascists a month ago. The saddest people I have ever seen.

"The stories of police raids, police brutality, Fascist attacks—the fear these people were living with sent shivers up my spine. And all the time while people were giving these heavy interviews, and camera guys were clicking away, these gorgeous little kids, many of them barefoot, ran around playing, laughing, chasing each other.

"Some of these families have lived here for thirty and forty years! I couldn't believe it! They flew Italian flags from flagpoles on top of their roofs! Who does that anymore?

"I tell you, some of these Roma are more Italian than us. Flags, pictures of the Pope, crucifixes everywhere. One of the girls who lived here went to university and came back to the camp as a certified doctor.

"But it's a real hellhole. Their houses are just shacks. The whole camp is surrounded by wire mesh fence. On the other side of fence is a row of about thirty Porta-Potties. A gift from the city. They have no running water in their homes. There's one communal hose outside. No toilets inside."

SAN LORENZO: PAY THE RENT

The tattooed young woman hanging laundry in the sun-drenched courtyard is angry with her boyfriend. He sits on the stone stairs in runners and shorts and listens. The San Lorenzo church bells chime 1 PM.

"I told you. We won't have enough money to pay the rent. They're cutting back my hours and you still don't have a job. What the hell?" She glares at him.

"Yeah, yeah, I'm trying. But no one is hiring. Read the papers."

"You're not trying hard enough, and I'm getting fed up."

"I can't force anyone to hire me. They're not interested."

"You better make them hire you, because next month who is going to cover our rent? Get off your ass and find something."

"Fuck, OK, I will. Don't worry. Look, I'm going."

He heads down the street and walks all the way through the *Porta Maggiore* and into his favourite bar, a small neo-Nazi hangout. Inside, among the dozen young men in jeans and polo shirts, sunglasses perched on their heads, he looks for a friend.

"Hey, man, I'm having a hard time now. You know anyone hiring? I'll do anything for some cash."

His friend, a short wiry guy, pats him on the back and pulls him close.

"Good timing. I've got something for you. A small job, a few hours at night. You ride with us. We rearrange the outside and inside of a 'non-Italian' store. Know what I mean? Nice and quick. Then leave. Easy cash in your pocket. There might be bigger jobs for you later."

THE BEAST PUNKS

With Conflict blasting out of the bar sound system, two of the Beast Punks, a punk band from Genoa visiting Rome, sit on a bench and write the text for a leaflet and a poster announcing an anti-racist, anti-Fascist night of music and speakers.

"Keep it short and to the point. No big words. No long sentences."

The two twenty-year-old students with shaved heads and tattoos hunch over a laptop.

"How's this?"

Who are the real criminals? Fact: Foreign migrants are less likely to commit crimes than other groups. In London, they make up 27% of the population, but commit only 20% of the crimes. Source: London Metropolitan Police.

"I like it. Keep going."

Fact: the majority of immigrants move to Italy in a state of poverty because they want to become less poor. Fact: Italy's low birth rate means our economy is dependent on a constant flow of new arrivals to survive. Fact: many immigrants work in the illegal sector and live in poor accommodations—but not from choice.

LET THE DEVIL DANCE ON MY TONGUE

It's midnight and a reddish moon glows above Rome. Massimaxo and Antonio pack up their guitars after a long studio practice and step out into the humid night. The pavement underfoot still radiates the day's heat. Everywhere, young Romans sit on curbstones, drinking and talking.

"Where to, my dear? Pizza time? Want your *Diavolo*? Or some gelato?"

Antonio scratches his beard and, putting his arm around Massimaxo's waist, drags him into the street.

"Let's go!"

"Where to?"

"Georgiano's—the hottest and the best at this time of night. If we can get in."

They shoulder their instruments and inch their way through the nightlife throngs into a jammed pizzeria a block away. Hunched over the tiny marble table, squeezed among a hundred or more other customers, they order beers and pizza.

"Extra hot, please!" Antonio winks at the burly waiter who winks back.

Two beers arrive. Extra cold.

"Massimaxo, I've been thinking and I just don't get it."

"I think a lot and I don't get it either."

"No, seriously. Some people can realize the obvious—that we all have rights. Or should have them, right?"

"If you say so."

"People fight for these rights, end up in wars and in prisons to defend them. Others extol them in books, speeches, and works of art. Everyone assumes this, lives their lives accordingly, and never questions it. Right?"

Massimaxo twirls his beer bottle and shrugs. Then in his best singsong voice, imitating an orator in front of an audience, he launches into a response:

"We are born. We enter this world from between our mama's thighs. We have the right to live, breathe, burp, feed, and clothe ourselves. The right to think—or not—for ourselves. To house ourselves. To find meaningful—or totally shitty—work to pay for the basics like beer, pizza, and dope. We have the right to fall in love or not. Smoke up or not. To plan for our future, go to school, or drop out and freely enjoy the wonders of life around us. Yes, I agree."

Antonio rolls his eyes. "But we also have the right to walk our streets in peace and security. Yes?"

Massimaxo's order arrives and he stuffs pizza into his face. Then he answers:

"For the most part. And we can fuck for pleasure and get married if we want—unless we're gay in this backward country of ours."

Antonio helps himself to an olive off Massimaxo's plate. "We take these rights for granted."

Massimaxo nods, burps, and leans back in his chair until he bumps into a large guy sitting inches away, his back to them. The guy turns and growls, "Hey, *cazzo!* Be careful!" It's their recording engineer. He pretends to strangle Massimaxo and laughs.

"Hey, guys! You know that Roma chick you brought in to record that violin track? She is fucking awesome. You lucked out with her. It's gonna be a killer CD now. She clinches it. I want to record an album of hers, just solo violin with some of my beats. You tell her I'll do it for free."

"You're on!" Massimaxo shakes the engineer's hand.

Antonio continues. "Who could enjoy the sun, the moon, weddings, good bread, wine, love, spring, a songbird, a sea breeze, without these rights?"

"Comrade, I agree."

Massimaxo notices that Antonio has been nibbling away at his pizza when he wasn't watching. "*Cazzo!* The philosopher/pizza thief strikes again!"

Antonio's pizza arrives. He tastes it, frowns, then motions to the waiter.

"I need more garlic, hot peppers, and chili please. I want the *Diavolo* to dance on my pizza and my tongue. Bring him to me and let him dance!"

"Two more beers!" adds Massimaxo.

"So why do we deny others these rights? Because they speak a different language, have different customs, and maybe wear a bit more gold than the average hairy-chested Italian man? Shouldn't this be considered a crime? Not the hairy chest, but the denial of rights?"

"Antonio," Massimaxo sighs, "you ask the toughest questions at the latest hour, even before we've smoked up."

HOPE IN A REFUGEE CAMP?

Marek, the middle-aged Polish journalist from London, smokes a cigarette under the tree with a younger Italian photographer.

"In this dusty, hot, pathetic refugee camp, Italians, Romanians, Macedonians, Americans, Jews, Roma, young, and old are able to sit and talk like civilized people. To trade stories. To laugh and cry. To empathize and discuss problems and solutions. Here, today, there is hope. Hope for change. Wouldn't you say?"

The Italian is uncertain. "You call this hope? Take a good look." He gestures with one hand. "I call it a media event. A moment to capture the despair and the injustice on camera and tape to tell the world once again: Wake up! There's something wrong here. Do something."

The Pole from London shrugs. "That's helpful, no?"

INTERVIEWING THE SENATOR

The secretary knocks hesitantly on Senator Roberto Fancazzista's closed office door. Good moment, bad mood, she could never tell.

"Come in."

"Senator, the reporter from the *La Repubblica* is here to interview you. Are you ready?"

"Yes, send him in please."

"It's a woman, Senator."

A striking, tall, young black journalist in a grey pencil skirt and stiletto heels walks in.

"Hello, Senator. I know you are a busy man, so thank you for your time."

"Please be seated, my dear. It's always a pleasure to be interviewed by a beautiful journalist. What did you say your name was?"

He was trying not to show it, but even at his age, he got an instant erection the moment she walked through the door. He started to undress her in his mind. Like the prime minister, he had a reputation among his peers, and if he could bed this one, the boys would be impressed.

"Chirasella Andante, Senator."

The journalist sits, pulls out her recorder, and places it on his desk.

"Your Italian is excellent, Ms. Andante! Where did you learn it?"

"I was born here, Senator, and I have two degrees from Rome University. First question. A lot of people believe that you and your Northern Patriot Party are leading a witch-hunt against foreigners. Is this true?"

"Can I pour you a drink first, my dear?"

He smiles and motions to an assortment of bottles in a cabinet behind him.

"I like to make these kinds of one-on-one journalistic experiences as pleasant as possible."

She declines. He decides to forgo the drink.

"Now to your question, yes."

He holds his fingertips together in front of his lips and leans back in his large leather chair.

"Hmm . . . I would not call it a 'witch-hunt' as you say. Housecleaning perhaps. You see, we Italians have been too slack, allowing all the dirt to accumulate in our house."

"Are you saying that immigrants are 'dirty'?"

"Oh, no, not at all. I'm only saying that a lot of the, um, attitudes of many *recent* immigrants, particularly the Romanians, render them incompatible for integration into our society. And to deal with this, we need more law and more order. For a safer Italy."

He stares at her breasts, then catches himself and looks away as she clears her throat loudly.

"Senator. Do you perceive immigrants as a threat to Italy's 'national identity'?"

He smiles at her again, noticing how her hair frames her beautiful face, her eyes, her lips . . . but to the question at hand!

"In the past, we expelled troublesome Muslims, Albanians, and the like, for similar reasons, to preserve and protect our beloved Italy from threats within. I believe we must act now, swiftly, decisively, to safeguard what is historically the goodness, the decency of our own home."

Decency. That's always a good angle.

"Who exactly do you want to expel, Senator? All Romanians?"

Certainly not you, my darling. I have something else in mind for you . . .

"Who, did you say? Only foreign criminals, Gypsies, anyone committing offences. And people who are homeless or can't support themselves. Our cities, our people, our country can't support them any longer. It's time for them to leave."

"What do you say, Senator, to those who call for more integration and better services for Roma living in the camps?"

"I say more laws, more police, and get them out of Italy now. It's that simple."

If only it was that simple to bed you, honey, but I can see that you will be a challenge . . .

"Have you noticed, Senator, that crimes committed by Italians do not receive the same treatment as those committed by foreigners?"

"No. I haven't."

"For example, Senator. If an Italian kills someone—as occasionally happens—you wouldn't say that Italian *people* exhibit criminal tendencies."

"Of course not. Romanians are much too different from Italians to be lumped into the same category."

She is exciting me, pushing my buttons, and I like that. Jesus! I'm still hard . . .

"What is your opinion on the recent beatings by vigilantes of Romanians in the streets?"

"My opinion?" The senator begins to raise his voice, then catches himself, lowers it and smiles. Keep cool, he tells himself. He rises and walks from behind his desk to the front, and sits on a corner, for a better view of her cleavage.

"Like many, indeed most, loyal Italians frustrated with a weak-kneed government, I say vigilante action is a legitimate form of self-defence. How else can we rid Italy of undesirable elements?"

"Senator, in a recent housing debate you had some harsh words for immigrants in general, saying: '*You work your whole life and then we give a house to the first bingo-bongo that arrives? You must be kidding.*' Who, or what exactly, is a bingo-bongo?"

"Uh, I mean by that, an uncivilized or unlawful person. A savage, an intruder."

"Like a black journalist?"

Oh, well, he thinks, *you can't win them all . . .*

"Do you have anything more to add, Senator?"

"Frankly, my dear, I think if our government has any guts, and wants to prevent any more heinous crimes carried out by those who don't respect our way of life, then any boat carrying illegal immigrants should hear the blast of cannons, and after the second or third warning, boom!"

WHEN SKINS MEET SUITS

It's Saturday night under a forlorn, emaciated moon. A squat grey building that resembles an aborted gargoyle gone bad sits alone and menacing on a boulevard island in central Rome. Pricy real estate. It's surrounded by high security cameras and a high wrought-iron fence topped with spikes. Heavy metal grills encase its tiny windows, while its walls are saturated with racist posters and graffiti.

This is a neo-Fascist bunker hangout. Inside, about thirty noisy white power skinheads are drinking beer. The sound system pounds out racist punk rock. Organizers have set up a podium and a microphone on the small stage. Tonight's special guest: a speaker from Italy's biggest Fascist party. He's the well-dressed, cherub-faced youngish businessman who just walked in. His job: wind up the boys. But first, he shakes hands and passes a fat envelope stuffed with cash to Gino, the grinning skinhead leader.

Gino's a scar-faced, steroid-muscled, intense, and intelligent thirty-five-year-old smothered in tattoos. By day, he pretends to work part-time in a local *pizzeria*. The rest of his time is dedicated to recruiting young toughs across Rome. He has an expense account and takes them out for lunch, supper, or a drink. These are opportunities to bond with them and inculcate them with the white-power philosophy. He also gives them someone to look up to. And he helps them land flexible jobs with white power–friendly bosses. In other words, he hooks them and reels them in. His keepers recognize and reward his talents.

An early bout of polio left him with a pronounced limp that other kids always ridiculed. So he learned how to fight with and without a knife. He did time in juvenile facilities, then prison at eighteen. His face carries a long scar from one lost jail fight. After that, no more losses.

Inside, he met an older white power racist who coached him, gave him books to read, and hooked him up with neo-Fascists outside recruiting young toughs like himself.

"The system kicks you, kid; you kick back, harder. But we do it together so we change this country and get rid of all the foreign scum behind the mess."

It was his lucky break, he remembers. Gave him something to fight for.

"One country, one nation, one people," reads the tattoo across his back.

All these punks running around trying to show how tough they are, when really, they're scared and weak—I see myself a long time ago, he thinks.

"Alone, you'll get nowhere," he tells them. *"You'll get arrested or beaten up. Join us Nazi-skins and you'll have a family and a future. We'll look out for you, take care of you. Trust me. Remember: Life is permanent warfare. There is no room for the weak. Fight with us and you'll be stronger."*

As he pockets the envelope Gino leaps onto the stage.

"Guys! Please give our honoured guest a warm skin welcome!"

The skinheads roar, raise their mugs of beer, stand and give Nazi salutes. The businessman beams, waves back, then launches into his tirade. As he speaks, an overhead projector flashes newspaper headlines and photos about the recent murder of an Italian naval commander's wife. In between are pictures of immigrants arriving in Italy by the boatload, in line-ups, and in squalid camps. One shows the alleged Romani murderer with an X marked over his face.

"You men, the best of Italy, are the frontline against the hoards of immigrant scum. You are the defenders of Mother Italy and our Italian way of life. You are the protectors of innocent Italians. Italians who walk our streets day and night in fear of being attacked, robbed, beaten, raped, or killed by Romanians, Gypsies, Africans, Muslims, and Albanians."

The skinheads boo, bang their mugs on the tables and the heels of their boots on the floor.

"You know our country has recently been overrun with unwelcome, parasitical, lazy, good-for-nothing cavemen and cavewomen."

"Woo! Woo! Woo!" The skinheads grunt in derision. "Bingo-bongos!"

"Their sole objective is to take over our Italy and remake it into their own barbaric country."

"Hoo! Hoo! Hoo!"

The skinheads jeer some more. The businessman rants for thirty minutes, working himself into a sweat while the images play over and over to a slowly building skinhead punk soundtrack. As the music crescendos and the images appear on screen faster and faster, the Fascist on stage wraps up. It's a tightly orchestrated presentation. Everyone knows his part.

"You, stalwart defenders of Italy! You soldiers of Italy! You men of Italy, you know what you have to do! In the name of a free, pure Italy, get out there and do it!"

The skinheads roar in unison. One stands up, yelling, "We gotta kill the fuckers! Get rid of them and their families!"

The room is now a seething mass of skinhead testosterone and beer-driven rage as they bang the folding chairs on the floor and pound their mugs on tables. Gino grabs the mic.

"You've seen it on TV. You've read about it in the papers. You just heard what our speaker said. Now, in the name of our country! In the name of our people! It is time to strike! Time to teach all motherfucking immigrants a lesson! Time for all loyal soldiers of Italy to kick Gypsy and Romanian ass! We have a plan of attack. Who's in? Who's out?"

He scans the room. The skins stand, grunt and hoot as one cohesive mob. They salute their allegiance to the cause and to Gino, chanting, "Gino! Gino! Gino!" He waves them to stop.

"Where's the graffiti posse?"

A group grunts and waves.

"Here's the paint. You know the slogans. You know where the immigrant scum live. Get to work. We need to organize a big march against them. Giuseppi, you taking charge?"

He points to a skin in the front row, who makes a face and shrugs his shoulders.

"Posters, flyers, banners, callouts. Yeah, it's a lotta work, but you can do it. Giuseppi, don't be a jerk!"

The other skins chant, "Giuseppi! Giuseppi! Giuseppi!"

Giuseppi nods.

Another skinhead waves an opened a switchblade in the air and calls out: "What about the faggots? We getting them, too?"

"Leave the faggots for later. It's immigrants, got it? There's a football game coming up with that Romanian monkey playing against Lazio for Fiorentina. We need a huge posse in the stadium, to chant against him and throw bananas. Spread the word. Everyone clear? Now, who wants to do the 'other' stuff?" He makes quotation marks in the air with his fingers as he studies the crowd. His eyes settle on a quieter group of six skins sitting in the back.

"You guys get the Molotovs. It's Romanian and Muslim grocery stores. Pick your targets. Monterotondo or Pienta. Use safe vehicles and scooters. Wear gloves. Remember: no evidence. No trail. No witnesses. No licence plates. No ID. Nothing to trace it to you or back here. Understood? Put that gun away, you idiot! How many times do I have to tell you?"

Gino jumps off the stage and seizes the wrist of Ox, a huge, grinning skinhead in the group of six, who is brandishing a small silver-plated pistol.

"Yeah, but Gino, how am I gonna waste some Romanians if I don't use this?"

"Use your fucking brain, stupid. Listen! Once you've finished, split town for a few days. We've got some safe houses and some cash. Nick is in charge of all that. Play it cool. Keep your mouths shut. And when you're using bats or knives, wear gloves. And ditch the weapons and the gloves—separately. And Ox—hide that gun!"

In the days that follow, this misguided crew of misfits, thugs, alcoholics, and a few sons of immigrants, make the news and sow fear within Rome's immigrant community and beyond. But as they exit that night through the only gate, someone sits in a parked car nearby snapping everyone's picture.

PARKING LOT RENDEZVOUS

Next morning, Rafaele waits in his car in a supermarket parking lot for his rendezvous. He spots his man in a black hoodie picking his way between the rows of cars. The guy slips in beside Rafaele. It's a tight fit. His head is compressed against the ceiling. Big grins and a handshake.

"The shit's hitting the fan, Rafaele. Last night, Mr. B from 'the Party' came to preach. He's one twisted scumball. Gets the skins to do all his dirty work. So here's the deal, a citywide anti-immigrant graffiti campaign. You'll see it everywhere. We have to counter it. Cover it up real quick. There's a plan for a big Fascist march in one week. It's got to be blocked. Stopped.

"Worst of all, they'll be torching a few Romanian markets. Here are the names and the addresses. I'll try to water down the Molotovs. It's going down in the next day or so. Warn the shop owners. Get people ready to watch outside. Have fire extinguishers inside.

"And finally, more random beatings are coming. I don't know when or where, and I'm not sure how we can stop them. But they're out for blood. We need an alternative strategy real fast. A public info campaign, whatever. Got it?"

"Yup, all written down."

"I gotta run. Take care, brother. And good luck."

"Thanks. Keep in touch, and hey—be careful."

"You know me."

They knock fists and he disappears.

ANTI-RACIST ACTION MEETS

That afternoon, Rafaele meets up with a group of ten anarchist antiracists at someone's apartment. Italians and non-Italians, students, professionals, men and women, they sit on the floor, the couch, the windowsills, and listen. The mood is tense. Rafaele recounts what he heard from his skinhead mole, word for word, reading his notes. People shake their heads.

"He was really specific. All this goes down in the next few days, maybe even as we speak. There's no time to lose."

A young lawyer speaks, then many voices join in.

"As much as we resent it, we have to react. Fast. Again, the Fascists are ahead of us. They're riding the newest wave of xenophobia."

"With the mayor and the government bending over backward to placate public opinion, they're also promoting the racist agenda of the far-right."

"It's more of the same crap. Inflame the hatred of Roma and Romanians."

"And provide the Fascists with a convenient, timely platform to spew their poison and provoke violence."

"So what's the counterplan?"

"Who's in touch with our Romani friends?"

"They're coming later. They said to start without them."

"Late again? Somebody has to talk to them about this."

"But what do they want us to do?"

"How can we decide without them being here?"

"They said do whatever was necessary to stop the skins. They'll get word back to their communities."

"Come on guys, there is no time to waste. We have to get cans of spray paint to the Romanian kids down at the social centre. They can take care of the Nazi graffiti."

"Someone has to pay Mr. Big a visit. Redecorate his party office. Let him know he has to pay for this shit."

"I know somebody who'd love to work on that. It's taken care of."

"We should also disrupt his public appearances. Shadow him. Make it difficult for him to speak. Picket his gatherings."

"The football game? Everyone should be there and lead the anti-Nazi chants. I'll email the list."

"Wait, wait! One at a time! Who's bottom-lining the Mr. Big actions? You? Good."

"For the march, we need to outnumber them like we did before and stop them from marching. Send a 'Stop the Nazis!' call out tonight. We assemble in the same spot before them."

"What about the arson attacks? That's kind of a priority, no? Who can organize flying squads with cars and scooters? Put everyone on high alert?"

"Me. I'll get people to park out front in shifts, with cell phones and fire extinguishers, and backup teams."

"Don't you guys think someone has to meet with the Romanian shopkeepers right away? Warn them?"

"They're our people. My sister and I can speak with them. Who can drive us? It will be faster."

"What about the random beatings? What the fuck are we going to do?"

"How about 'Stop Nazi Violence' posters, graffiti, and flyers?"

"That won't prevent people from getting hurt."

"There's nothing we can do."

"Don't we have photos of all the goons from last night?"

"Yeah, but for now, the pictures won't do us much good."

"We should use those photos. Put them online. Make a giant WANTED poster or something."

"I don't think we can actually do anything in the short term tonight, tomorrow, or whenever to physically stop the random attacks, unless we target the individual Nazis beforehand. We have to beat the shit out of them—in advance—when they're alone."

"We have their photos. How do we track them down?"

"It's not up to us."

"I think we should encourage Roma in the camps and the community to fight back. Offer them physical support. Set up people's patrols, like monitoring groups. Hang out with them and keep an eye open for attackers."

"Um, we got to be careful about this."

"I think we ask them first if this is what they want."

"We're running out of time, guys."

Cell phones and Blackberries start buzzing. People break out their laptops and hunker down in corners of the apartment sending out communiqués and appeals for help. The host hands out cups of coffee. It's only 6 PM, and already every anti-Fascist in Italy has received the news: "Stop them now."

ANTI-FASCIST MOLE

Rafaele's skinhead contact, aka Ox, is an old family friend. Their mothers were both student activists at university and studied law. Now they're labour lawyers. Rafaele and Ox attended the same high school and played soccer together.

Ox leads a double life. Once a PhD student in anthropology, he's now on a break. More like a mission. Ox attends white power meetings and feeds information to anti-Fascist groups through Rafaele and another contact. It's a dangerous game, a whole new lifestyle underground. He has a black belt in karate and tries to keep a low profile, but he always worries.

The charade demands razor-sharp wits and putting up with a lot of bullshit. So far, he's kept his identity and his real politics well hidden. No one pries and he doesn't divulge. He bites his tongue often and keeps a secret online journal. He's taken out a hefty life insurance policy and leads a Spartan life. He's always looking over his shoulder. Or so it seems to Rafaele, who worries about him constantly.

OX QUESTIONS

As Ox walks quickly through the empty dark field, the dewy grass remembers each footstep. The field lies beside the tangled, wild and accidental urban park in Pigneto—the park that has overgrown the former Ex SNIA Viscosa factory complex. It's a peaceful early summer dawn and most of the park's inhabitants, like most of Rome, still sleep.

Ox pauses on a hilltop to breathe deeply and watch the awakening sun climb inch by inch above the horizon. Its rays strike the roofs of a row of yellow, pink, and peach apartment blocks opposite the complex, setting them aglow like candles on a cake. Still climbing, the sun aims its rays at the tops of trees across the street. The trees guard the edge of the urban lake that sits still and silent amid the ruins of the once giant complex. The rays glance off the trees and touch down on the blue green water, warming its surface, filling it with shadows and reflections of the wild bushes and shrubs lining its perimeter.

Birds now sing uninhibited. Some already catch the glint and hum of bug-winged breakfasts that flit past. Sleeping creatures, feathered and furred, stretch, preen, and arise from within the tall grass, greeting one another. Feral dogs and cats begin to hunt. The hunted search for cover.

The stunning cityscape reminds Ox of a favourite Impressionist painting by Pissarro or Seurat. He can't remember which. Now he has a rendezvous with another antiracist activist, his backup contact when Rafaele isn't available. It's critical inside info about a significant impending neo-Nazi action.

As he walks, hands in the pockets of his baggy pants, head under a hoodie, he plans his next move. He's always thinking each day through, way ahead. Stay cool. Stay stupid. Stay in character. Watch and disguise every action, every conversation, inside and outside the group. Memorize faces, names, information. Focus and breathe. Don't get caught. One slip-up is dangerous. Two, a death sentence.

Ox has been a mole inside the neo-Nazi group—one of the most violent on the Right—for almost a year. He knows his time is running out. The stress is wearing him down. And he fears the inevitable: having his cover blown.

This is no state-funded Secret Service operation. No one pays him. He has no licence to kill. No network of earpieced, weapon-carrying, hidden-in-the-parked-van, computer-hooked-up, microphone-guided, SWAT–equipped backup team. This is a DIY infiltration, a lone wolf operation of utmost risk. His choice. Friends warned him, but he didn't listen. This was personal.

"Ox," the big dumb goof, always good for a laugh, not the brightest of the dim bulbs within the neo-Nazi organization, but smart enough to take orders and follow through.

"Ox," the guy who likes to brandish a pistol and talk up getting tough with immigrants and lefties.

"Ox," the runner, the driver, reliable and strong, always there to help with heavy lifting.

"Ox," the PhD student, undercover anarchist, risking his life—for what?

It's personal.

Several months earlier, a close friend, an immigrant PhD student from Tunisia, an antiracist activist, was almost beaten to death by a gang of Nazi-skins. He still lay in a coma in a hospital. Ox swore to get even, not by a simple physical retaliation, but something even more damaging, he thought. Infiltrate the skinhead group. Destabilize them by feeding information to the antiracist activists. Use his acting experience—he has a degree in theatre—and rely on his martial arts expertise, his size, his meditation and yoga practice to help him survive. He also bought a gun.

He told other friends and family that he was taking a break to travel around the world. Then he shaved off all his long hair and his beard. Stored his important personal belongings in a locker. Rented a tiny furnished room for a year. Hid his personal computer in a safe place. Found a part-time job as a deliveryman. Got a gym membership.

He went underground and disappeared. Swore that at the end of the year he would quit the group, move somewhere else and finish his PhD. His doctorate was about the neo-Nazi movement.

As he waits for his contact on the jogging track beside the park, he does his daily deep breathing and stretching exercises.

Maybe now is the time to leave, he thinks. Eight months is enough. I can't tough out twelve. I'm sick of this shit. The isolation is killing me. I'm breaking. I've been lucky so far, but how much longer?

I can't keep up the violent actions. Can't help them do it,

then rationalize the morality of it. It's fucked! Immoral. Now I'm part of the problem. It's wearing me down. I'm losing myself. This wasn't the plan. The bullshit acting? Can't take it. The pressure inside? The recurring nightmares? The screams of victims? Skins bragging about it? Sometimes I want to rip them to pieces. Break their necks. Plant a bomb in the club-house and watch it light up the sky. Boom! Yeah, sure. There will always be others to take their places. So shut the fuck up, jerk. Never forget who I am, why I'm here, and stick it out. And watch my back.

NAZI-SKINS IN NAPOLI

Ox is driving Gino and two other Rome Nazi-skins to Napoli to participate in a big neo-Fascist demonstration. They're also delivering a few boxes of neo-Nazi literature to their sister group. The sun is shining, the SUV stereo blasts white power punk, and the guys sing along.

Gino sits beside Ox, slapping his thigh in time. His jacket is festooned with patches and badges of the Italian Ultras tri-colour. One slogan above the old *Ardidti* logo of a skull head clenching a knife in its teeth reads, "Smash the Reds."

In the back seat are two of the bigger Nazi-skins from their group: Pino and Tony.

Pino is twenty-five, with a protruding red goatee and bulging steroid-enhanced biceps. A skull-and-crossbones is tattooed on one arm, above the words "*Natural Born Killer.*" Shades perch on his pink shaved head. His fingers are adorned with large stainless steel rings. Four skulls on one hand; four triskelion supremacist insignias on the other. His fists can do a lot of damage. Under his army camouflage jacket is a blue T-shirt emblazoned with the words "*Italy, 1934 champions.*" Above is an image of the Italian national soccer team giving the Nazi salute.

Pino grew up in Primavalle, a poor northeastern suburb of Rome. A Fascist-built neighbourhood finished only in the 1950s, it has a reputation of churning out gangsters and bank robbers. Pino himself comes from a proud family of Fascists.

From a young age, he was a small-time crook, stealing and selling cars and involved in the drug trade, until Gino brought him into the Nazi-skin group as his personal bodyguard. It's a job that pays and comes with perks and prestige.

Oddly enough, Pino's older brother is an anarchist. And he hangs out with Simona Discordia. The brothers don't get along.

Tony, the other Nazi-skin, is a twenty-one-year-old part-time university student and a huge fan of Ezra Pound, the long-dead American expatriate poet turned Fascist cheer-leader. At school, Tony wears a baseball cap to cover up his "Skinhead, white forever proud" tattoo encircling his head. Nothing hides the black widow spider tattoo on his face, the diamond stud in one ear, the heavy gold chain around his neck, or his fingertips-to-neckbone tattoos. He wears a black "Italian Pound House" T-shirt with the words *"Shield and Sword of Italy"* in large letters. He works part-time for a publisher of neo-Nazi books. Always a cigarette in his mouth.

Tony was born twenty kilometres southeast of Rome in Frascati, a town where anti-Semitic mayoral candidates, close to the local Nazi-skin organization, would run for office. As a teenager, he handed in white supremacist essays to his teachers that read:

"We skins are hundreds of people, hundreds of heads, united by a sole source of pride—the race, defending our rights, the rights of white Aryans, the rights of Italians."

Now he writes racist tracts and articles for the group. Gino mentors him.

Both Tony and Pino describe themselves as "street soldiers."

"We're the guys who like to fight and get our hands dirty. We don't stand on the sidelines."

It's true. They wade in, with clubs, fists, chains, and other weapons flailing. Their targets of choice are "blacks, Jews, dirty people, and Third World immigrants." They've also set people on fire who sleep in the street and torched the homes of Third World immigrants.

Pino is nicknamed *The Butcher.* His concealed weapon of choice: a compact butcher's cleaver that he wields expertly. Once, he and Tony beat and sliced up a Muslim religious leader. Arrested, they got off with suspended sentences. Thank the well-paid lawyers on retainers who never ask where the money comes from. They're just grateful.

The four enter a local Nazi-skin hangout not far from the Napoli Italian Pound House, for a few drinks before the big demo near *Piazza Carlo.* It's light banter back and forth about Napoli women and beer. Ox never drinks alcohol, only tomato juice.

"They're pretty ugly, right?"

"No, they're nicer looking than Roman chicks."

"The beer tastes like piss."

"Southerners don't know how to brew."

The guys are all laughing. Gino sits opposite Ox. Pino and Tony sit on either side of him. At one point Ox notices that Gino is staring up at him. Even sitting, Ox's huge frame rises above Gino, Pino, and Tony. As Gino's eyes narrow and he keeps staring at Ox in an odd way, the others stop talking and the conviviality suddenly disappears.

"I heard the attack on that other Romanian grocery store had a problem, Ox. What happened? Can you explain?" Gino glowers at him.

Ox shifts in his chair, scratches the back of his large shaved head, and speaks in his usual but affected slow drawl with a bit of a nervous laugh. It's his actor's voice.

"Huh? I dunno. I was sitting in the car with the engine running. I was the get-away driver, remember?"

"Yeah, but the bottles didn't ignite like they were supposed to."

"Bad gas? That was weird."

Ox's mouth goes dry and he starts to sweat. Gino leans in closer to him over the table, inches from his face, his eyeballs now almost popping out, and in a lower voice says, "One of the cops on the scene called Mr. B. Mr. B called me. The cop told him that the two Molotovs were watered down. Water in the gas."

"No way! I filled them myself!"

"You're sure about that?"

"Absolutely. Positive."

Gino looks at the skins on either side of Ox. Pino and Tony now both stand on either side of Ox, real close, hemming him in. Each places a hand on one of his shoulders.

"Well if you filled them, how come they had water in them? And how come there was a gang of anti-Fascist assholes hiding inside the store waiting for you guys? A fucking welcoming committee. How did they know where to go and what time to be there, huh?"

Gino has raised his voice. The rest of the bar patrons back away.

Ox looks down at his glass, lays his two palms out flat on the table to steady himself, sighs, takes a deep breath, and slowly says,

"I really don't know Gino. Honestly. I can't say."

In the blink of an eye, Pino uses his cleaver to cleanly chop off Ox's little finger. Ox screams in pain. With two quick powerful flicks of his wrists, left and right, he smashes both skins with two backhands, breaking their noses.

A half second later he leans forward to head-butt Gino in the face, sending him reeling. He then swings around and grabs Tony by the arm, flipping him over the table like a rag doll into Gino, shoving the table on top of them. With his big boot he gives a side kick to Pino's kneecap and breaks it.

Blood is everywhere. Guys are moaning and screaming in pain. Gino is on the floor pinned under Tony and the table, holding his flattened nose. Ox stomps on Gino's hands and kicks Tony in the ribs. He gives another boot to the head of Pino lying on the floor.

Less than nine seconds of mayhem and Ox is bolting out the open door, running, dodging people and cars, squeezing the bleeding stump of his finger. He hails a cab and speeds off, his cover blown.

GINO PUTS OUT A HIT ON OX

A few minutes later, Gino is holding an icepack to his nose and trying to speak on his cell phone.

"Listen, fuckhead! I said find Ox and waste him! Understand? I don't care how many guys it takes. Just find him and get rid of him. He's probably headed back to Rome. Put the word out. I want him dead. Got it?"

CINKA'S BROTHER WALKS HOME

A giant cloud that resembles a loping bear drifts in front of the pale moon, hiding it. Cinka's brother, Corvu, walks home alone. He's on a dimly lit street in *Tor di Quinto*, whistling a happy song. He had no money for bus fare, it's been a long walk, but he's almost at the camp.

For the last few minutes he's been focused on kicking an empty can along in front of him. He hears voices, looks up, and under the streetlamp ahead, sees a small group of teenagers. Italians!

Instinctively he crosses the street to avoid them, desperately looking for shadows to blend into, a doorway to hide in, or an escape route, hoping they don't notice him. Too late. They've spotted him. Someone yells,

"Looks like a fucking Gypsy boy! Get him!"

Corvu turns and runs for his life. They give chase.

"Run, you little fucker! Gypsy scum!"

A bottle flies by his head and shatters in the street. Another bottle arcs overhead and hits a parked car. The alarm goes off.

He keeps running, turns a corner and sees a short, waist-high wall to his left. He leaps over it into the blackness. He drops and screams "Mama!" then finds himself rolling, rolling, rolling down a steep dirt embankment littered with refuse, rolling and bouncing headfirst, then feet first, then sideways, rolling and bouncing until he comes to rest at the bottom, landing against a thick but prickly hedge, smothered under a pile of plastic bags full of garbage.

He spits out a mouthful of dirt, coughs up some more, and scrambles on his bleeding hands and knees right into the hedge to hide. He's hurt, breathless, and shaking all over, but alive.

He keeps spitting out dirt as he hears voices far away up above. Another bottle crashes somewhere. Laughter. Jeers. He waits until it is absolutely quiet, then limps into the darkness.

Above him, the moon sheds a tear.

PORTA TIBURTINA

As Antonio walks near the ancient wall of the *Porta Tiburtina*, he sees a man with long unkempt grey hair, a beard, and a dirty T-shirt, trying to sleep on the sidewalk in midafternoon, tossing and turning under a filthy blanket.

The man sees Antonio and bolts upright. He points and yells, "Hey you! Got any money? Any food? I'm hungry."

He jumps up holding the blanket around his shoulders.

"Come on, help an old man. One day you might be here. Once I belonged here. Now they chase me out. Where to next? There is no room at the Hilton. No room at all."

Antonio smiles meekly and drops some coins into the man's outstretched hand.

Further along *vial Porta Tiburtina*, a lone anarchist has left his red circle @ on a white wall. A few metres away, a Fascist has also felt compelled to leave his circle.

And the average person, Antonio wonders, who walks by, thinks what? Whose slogan, whose circle will challenge and change his mind, fill it with memories of other days or thoughts of a new world? Will someone one day spray-paint a new circle, square, or hieroglyphic?

DUSK VISITS *VIA SABELLI*

Antonio cooks up a simple pasta of "little ears," mixing in some *ricotta*, fresh basil, and tiny halved sweet tomatoes. In this shared apartment, once again he sits to eat dinner alone.

Staring out the kitchen window at the ragged skyline he thinks about Pier Paolo Pasolini's film *Accattone* and the lives of the main characters. They lived their own precarity, he muses; we live ours.

He looks at the pile of dried bread on the corner counter, the collection of missing-handle coffee mugs, the cracked but still intact dinner plates in the dish rack, the rickety wooden table he sits at that refuses any remedial attention, the problematic fridge that ices everything inside, and he thinks about the sometimes nagging futility of it all.

Never enough money. The rent keeps rising, the bills are put off, his day-to-day insecurities mount, his love life is not so simple anymore, his dreams seem further away than ever. *Cazzo!* What to do? He reaches for the last Peroni in the fridge.

Beer, my old friend, I can't resist you. You can't save me. But together, we are magic.

He remembers the shrine at a friend's apartment, with photos of the dead uncle, a lit candle, a few little mementos, and in the centre, an empty Peroni bottle.

This friend is one of the Roma—the hidden Roma, he remarks. Our blinded culture tries to deny the real world of change, and pretends it's 100 percent pure-bred Italian north, south, inside, out. But his friend is more patriotic, more Catholic, a more fanatical football fan, an erudite Italian history, art, and geography buff. Fuck, he's more Italian than any other Italian I know!

This guy flies the flag from his window. He plasters his bedroom wall with photos of Italian soccer stars, his living-room with Italian movie posters, yet he will never be accepted as Italian by other "real" Italians. He will never pass.

Italy's war against so-called "outsiders," will continue until the day we are forced to admit: it is a wrong—not only against others but against ourselves as well.

He hears a mother yelling: "What are you doing, child? Get to bed, right now. No dessert! You hear?"

Someone is knocking out coffee grains from a pot against a sink. Dusk visits, and *Via Sabelli*, San Lorenzo, Rome, prepares to call it a day.

Italian husbands, wives, lovers, fighters, children all refuse to go to bed, and so someone is chiding them. Upstairs, downstairs, all the voices, loud and soft, pleading and arguing, coaxing and enticing, drift out of semishuttered windows and blend into the crescendo and diminuendo, the ebb and flow of the night-time choir this old four story building has heard for generations.

A plate crashes on the floor. Someone applauds.

"Bravo, sweetheart, bravo." Then laughter. Forgiveness. A kiss and an embrace.

Bedsprings creak, slowly at first, then with gusto and wild passion. A baby cries. A TV is turned on, too loud, then turned off. Somewhere, an overly cocky and too-eager cockroach is crunched underfoot then kicked under the stove. The end of a short life.

Bring on this night, Rome, we are ready for you!

Night, the great Peacemaker, the Calmer of emotional storms. The Bearer of a blanket of silence. Night tells all: it's time to forget, or at least to try to, to breathe slowly, to turn off every digital gadget other than the alarm clock, dim the lights, wind down the frenzy of the day, and enjoy the comfort of a welcoming pillow and bed—if you're lucky.

A lone woman sings the words of a hit love song. She only knows the first three lines. She tries to remember the rest of it, but massacres the song. Night winces. She stops singing. Night triumphs. In the end, all obey.

For those trying to sleep far away outside the protective walls of this building, Night gives different instructions:

Find a quiet, safe spot, lie down on a piece of cardboard, a few newspapers, a sleeping bag or a dirty mattress; or better still, sleep with your head inside an empty box so no one can see your misery. Close your eyes. Pray for a few hours of peace and no disturbances from ugly drunken youth with untamed boots and sticks and empty bottles directed your way.

Forget this day of hunger, humiliation, frustration, and no generosity, no compassion. Shut out the intruders, the suicidal thoughts, the waning will to continue. Try to dream. Try to remember the way it was before.

Who dares defy the wishes of Night commits a terrible *faux pas*. Who dares disturb the peace of darkness is cursed by one and all. A loud drunk friend trying to console another? A couple arguing? A cat in heat? Unforgiveable by Night. Even the waves slow down their assault on the beach.

Under cover of Night, Rome sleeps and dreams of better days long ago, and better days to come. But everywhere, in every corner of the city, the question is: when?

Two blocks away, a small Romani family huddles together for warmth under a plastic tarp tucked hidden away in the crevice of a church facade. They pray.

AN ANTI-FASCIST DEMO

A hundred metres from the square where the neo-Nazi party *Forza Nuova*—New Force—is holding a poorly attended public meeting, a group of two hundred anti-Fascists gather to drown them out. Riot police stand in between. Rafaele has a bullhorn in his hands. There are no Nazi or Fascist symbols displayed during the FN meeting, just Italian tricolours and FN flags.

It's so aggravating, Rafaele thinks. Months away from the date Italy commemorates its "liberation" from Nazism and Fascism, and we still have to stand up to these neanderthals. Nonstop acts of provocation and intimidation by bands of neo-Nazi-skins in public places against our friends and immigrants. Beatings. Graffiti. The media doesn't care. The cops don't respond. And a right-leaning government makes this all acceptable. How do normally rational people become imbeciles?

CINKA TOUCHES HER BABY

The sun peeks over the horizon wearing a giant grin. Its ritual daily baking of the roofs, streets, sidewalks, and denizens of Rome is about to begin.

Unwanted or eagerly awaited, it sneaks unannounced into people's homes through cracks in the shutters, a slightly opened curtain, dirty skylights, and easiest of all, through holes in the walls, doors, and roofs of the refugee camp shacks.

"Awake sleepyheads! To work! To school! To beg in the

streets! It's me again, and I'm giving you another new day! Another chance! Today, life might be better! But I promise it'll be hotter, too! Look out!"

Romans hide their faces in their designer pillowcases, or under cardboard, newspaper, or a dirty coat. Some moan,

"Go away! Get lost! You're too early!"

Others, like Cinka, obey the first rays. She rises quietly, slips on her shoes and exits the camp. Her stomach protests, but she refuses to listen. The few pieces of bread left from yesterday tempt her, but she leaves them for her brother and sister.

While other young women her age window shop Rome's trendy clothing boutiques, Cinka's gaze always lingers on butcher shops and bakeries.

How often she's dreamed of gathering a few dozen Romani children together to swarm a fancy food shop, take what they want, and scatter.

The consequences? She knows them too well. Forget the slap on the wrist for any Romani kids. More like abduction by the State into foster homes, with parents also arrested and jailed for child neglect. Of course it would be different if the miscreants were Italian children.

She walks along the dusty sunlit camp road joining other silent early risers. Birds chirp. Cars thunder across the bridge above. And one hundred or more refugees—some barefoot—form a long line of hopeful hunters and gatherers, men and women alike, all trudging into the city centre to spread out and look for work, money, and food.

She notices a few young camp mothers pushing baby strollers. Smiling, she touches her own belly. Nothing shows yet, but she knows it's there and it must be hungry.

—Soon, it will be my turn. If others bring their babies while they work, so can I. But I'll need more than bread and water to nourish it. It's one thing to feed my family, but now—my baby. Antonio's baby. How can it be his, too, if I'm carrying it? It's pretty much mine. And I can take care of it—alone if I have to. Oh my God!

Overcome with a sudden bout of panic and dizziness, she holds her forehead and reaches to support herself against a tree. She leans against the trunk, slides down, and slumps onto a patch of grass. The whole world is spinning.

Oh Mother of Jesus! What have I done? What will I do? What will everyone say? I can only hide it for so long. Antonio will have things to say. And now Luca. I have to tell him. But how? I haven't seen him for years. I won't even recognize him.

She watches her camp neighbours walk by. A young mother pushing a stroller yells:

"Cinka! Are you OK?"

"I'm fine thank you." She slowly stands up and starts walking.

To hell with Luca! To hell with all of them! It's my life. Is it so wrong to want to have my own life? To decide myself what I want? With Luca, it wasn't my decision. I was just a child in a village where people live in the past. I never loved him. How could he love me? And we are no longer in Romania. I'm not a young girl who has to obey old village rules. That was yesterday.

This is Italy, today. I look after my family now. I'm about to become a mother. It's a new beginning for everyone. He has to understand that. If only Antonio weren't a *gadjo*!

LUCA FOLLOWS CINKA

Luca is waiting for Cinka to exit the camp gates. He spots her from afar and hides behind a tree. The whore! She looks beautiful, though, he thinks. And different. Something has changed. She doesn't look like the girl I remember. Of course not! Now she's been defiled. By a *gadjo*. Fuck him! Fuck her! But she's still beautiful.

RAFAELE AND THE NEW DEMOGRAPHIC

With a steaming morning coffee in one hand, and his purring cat cradled in his other arm, Rafaele peruses *Il Repubblica* online:

According to the Roman Catholic charity Caritas, there are some 3.7 million immigrants in Italy, making up 6.2 percent of the population and providing much needed labour in a rapidly aging nation. An estimated 560,000 of the immigrants are from Romania.

We need and want them to do the dirty and dangerous work, but don't let them live in peace, he thinks. Rafaele sees the new demographic especially on his job sites. Fewer Italians are labourers. It's the immigrants—African, Muslim, and East European—who scramble up and down the scaffolding, wheelbarrow, the gravel and cement, dig the foundations, place the rebar, and lay the bricks. They work hard and for less than what Italians would accept. He keeps reading:

> The Romanian and Italian ministers have written a letter to the European Commission asking for help for nations that receive immigrants from other European countries and for a strategy for integrating the Roma in Europe.

Hypocrites! he snarls. *The Romanian government allows the perse-cution of the Roma. It's not like before. That's why they come to Italy. For a future. Our own damn government could have done something long ago to prevent the tensions. They didn't. Now they're talking "more Romanian police officers in Italy" and "better border controls"?*

Cops and borders won't do it, Rafaele thinks. *We need com-passion and cold cash.*

He throws open the kitchen window and lights his first cigarette of the morning. Sunlight pours in as he exhales into the fresh air. On the hill opposite, he sees a neighbour per-forming his almost hourly, daily outdoor ritual.

The man lights up and walks back and forth, fourteen paces exactly each way, on the roadway in front of his peach-coloured house. He smokes three cigarettes, his head bowed deep in thought. He wears the same long blue coat, rain or shine, summer or winter. Rafaele returns to the newspaper:

> After the killing, Gianfranco Fini, leader of the opposi-tion National Alliance (NA), directly took on the delicate question of criminality among the Roma, saying that they "are not able to be integrated into our society."

"Fuck you!" Rafaele says out loud. *As if your gang of post-Fascist Alleanza Nazionale loonies could ever be integrated into our society. You, who once praised Mussolini as "the greatest statesman of the twentieth century." You who decorate the walls of your party's headquarters with pictures of the Duce and recruit skinhead neo-Fascists as members. You who say we should expel at least two hundred thousand immigrants from Rome alone. When can we deport you and your fucking AN?*

THIS SAN LORENZO APARTMENT

Puffing a cigarette and sipping his beer, Antonio sits at his desk listening to the rattle of supper dishes and cutlery being cleared away in another apartment. There's the clang of pots being washed then dropped on a floor. Someone is watering plants on the terrace.

Every little sound echoes off the dirty, sun-dried, orange walls of this building and gets snagged on the overhanging gutter on the roof. The gutter is the resident Keeper of Sound. The wind and the rain mix the sounds, the decades of noise, conversation, music, and birdsong. The sun warms it, shapes it, and bakes it.

If you hold your ear to the gutter drainpipe running down the side of the building, you hear this remixed symphony, this captured aural history of days and nights and conversations and fights and sighs and yawns, racket and dulcet sound. It's the soul of the building. It tracks the sins and the wonders, the deeds and the joys, the pain and the lust that escape windows and walls. It's everything accumulated in snippets of speech and entire operas of the past.

The doorbell rings. It's his cousin, Simona, a gorgeous black-haired former punk rock girl, now an immigration lawyer. She's giving him a lift on the back of her big Honda. Helmet on, he sits behind her as she guns the bike toward the train station.

For whatever reason, the figure of Gino Lucetti haunts Antonio. He tries to imagine Gino on the back of the Honda, bombs in his pockets, ready to throw.

If only Gino'd had a bike. And a helmet to hide his face. And a way to ride right up to that limo. But if Gino was a *clandestino*, today, what would he be doing right now?

On Antonio's right, the cathedral bells chime 10 PM.

At the train station they head inside for coffee—and wait for Cinka.

"You know, Antonio, the longer I practice this law stuff," Simona says, "the more I want to cry. Today I tried to help a Ukrainian woman, a housekeeper who came here first and now wants to bring her husband to join her. She doesn't make enough money to support both herself and him, but what to do?

"Then a young unemployed Albanian guy wants to bring in his wife, and again, where is the money? They'll do anything: housework, hotel, home care, but are having a hard time nailing down a job. At least the woman seems to have more opportunities than the guy. Don't ask me why. But she's a live-in, sending all her money home. So where is her husband going to live? In the closet?"

PART VIII

FOREVER

WEDDING BOUND

Four wedding guests crammed into a tiny old Fiat leave Rome and head north to Umbria's mountains on a sun-drenched afternoon.

Outside the city they pass magnificent flatland fields of regimented sunflowers. Each yellow head faces exactly the same direction, nodding in unison, obeying the wind's instructions. The wedding guests drive past tired dusty tobacco farms and archaeological excavations dug into olive grove–checkered low hills. The Fiat protests as it begins to climb the mountains. Centuries-old silent churches, castles, and monasteries on either side rise imposingly from the ancient rock.

Their love ever-fresh, Cinka and Antonio hold hands in the back seat and take turns sneaking kisses. Simona's new chain-smoking husband, Alberto, nicknamed "the Bear" because he's big and hairy, drives while Simona lovingly caresses his cheek and reads out directions. Her brother is having a lavish mountaintop wedding at the family's restored Roman castle.

Cinka thinks Simona looks dazzling in a low-cut black dress, heels, and a huge amber necklace. It's a startling change from her usual punked-out attire when she's not appearing in court. Cinka had to borrow a dress from Simona for the occasion and now wears it ever so carefully.

Pre-wedding day, an anxious Cinka, kept checking with Antonio:

"You're sure it's OK that I accompany you? No one will be offended or angry?"

"I told you, these are my second cousins. They are family and you are my girlfriend, the mother-to-be of our child. Why should anyone be offended?"

"Because we're not married yet? Because I'm a Romni and Italians hate us? Because you don't know the other guests or family members? And because some of them might be angry that I am with you and pregnant?"

"Sweetheart, you don't look pregnant, do you? And who cares what anyone else thinks. If anyone says anything, I'll handle them. This is a wedding, remember? Everyone will be on their best behaviour. Don't worry. Everything will be fine."

Easy for him to say, she thought. He doesn't see what I see: the stares and dirty looks, the whispering behind the hands. He doesn't have a clue. It's not his fault, how can he— he's a *gadjo*. Sometimes I think our lives are so far apart, how will it be possible? But still, I love him.

Cinka is doing her best now not to crease or rumple the gorgeous borrowed dress, even sitting in the car, for fear of somehow ruining it. Never in her life has she ever worn anything so revealing, so form-fitting, showing off her legs in public too, something a Romni is forbidden to do. But she had no choice. There was no other dress that fit.

Forgive me, Father; forgive me, Mother; forgive me, ancestors all, she thinks. *There won't be any other Roma at the wedding, that's for sure.*

But today, I'm breaking barriers. My first Italian wedding. My first western dress, plus shoes, a necklace Simona insisted I wear, and luxury of luxuries, lipstick! Simona applied it for me. I even stepped into her shower this afternoon, another first. Hot water, soap, hair shampoo, conditioner, beautiful clean towels, a gorgeous bathroom full of perfumes, lotions, and creams for hands and legs. Simona told me to help myself. It was heavenly!

It's as if I'm in a dream. Never did I imagine ever setting foot in a real Italian home. Simona's apartment has beautiful furniture, paintings on the walls, shelves with books, tables with plants and lamps, floors with gorgeous carpets. My family will never believe me. I even smell different.

I feel guilty dressed like this. Antonio says there will probably be more food at the wedding than I have ever seen in my life. If only I could bring some back for my family. Would that be wrong? But I can't embarrass Antonio. Stay invisible. Keep my mouth closed. Just play the violin.

AN ATYPICAL ITALIAN WEDDING

High atop a dry, sun-kissed Umbrian mountain, the wedding—and what a wedding!

"An atypical Italian wedding," the groom's father says, raising his eyebrows.

For this fairytale fantasy, the bride chose her family's centuries-old remodelled Roman castle. It sits at the end of a steep, winding road, surrounded by fruit trees and towering conifers, decorated inside and out now with thousands of multicoloured flowers.

The minister is Polish. He attends with his hot Italian girlfriend and equally hot Japanese male friend. An Egyptian three-piece band with *oud*, keyboard, and *tablas* accompanies a scantily clad belly dancer. A Chinese acrobatic team performs daring high-wire acts at the edge of the forest, high in the trees.

Family and friends, hundreds strong, arrive from Rome, Tuscany, Egypt, Turkey, England, and North America.

The bride's father and the groom cleared a forested mountain slope for the ceremony. For three months they felled trees, chopped brush, yanked out stumps and roots. The landscaping was completed the day before the wedding. Now the mountain meadow yields an awe-inspiring Umbrian vista of verdant valleys, endless ridges, and a sparkling Lake Corbara below.

Cinka takes her violinist position. She stands nervously on an ornate burgundy carpet in the shade of a white wedding canopy near the meadow's lower end. As she tunes up, she scans the huge number of people seated on the slope above. She's unusually self-conscious in her new outfit and wobbles on her heels.

Every woman here, she thinks, *wears a stunning dress with shoes and jewellery to match. They all look amazing. They all belong in a movie! I own one pair of shoes, a sweater, a coat, two blouses, a few necklaces, two skirts and two Romani dresses. Beautiful in their own way, OK, but . . . One day, I too will own a dress like this. And another pair of shoes. And get my nails and my hair done. And have a wedding!*

For now, breathe deeply. Stay calm. Guests are still arriving. It's just another performance, yes? But what are they thinking? They must know I'm not one of them. They'll ask. Will they be shocked once they find out? Disgusted? How will Antonio react? Will he defend me? This could be more than he asked for. I don't know if he realizes it.

So far, everyone is well behaved. They are exceedingly polite, smiling and nodding at me. Very formal. A bit stiff even. It's different from our weddings. Maybe this is how Italians do it.

In this natural mountainside amphitheatre, walled off with trees and bright blue sky, transformed now into a full marital reception with hundreds of perfumed, after-shaved, and coiffed guests sitting on terraced rows of rustic wooden benches lining the slope, the Polish officiant gives the signal and Cinka launches into a traditional, joyful, and spirited Romani prelude.

The guests immediately begin to murmur their approval.

"Ooh! She's good. Very good. Who is she? Italian?"

"I don't know, but she's with Antonio, my sister's nephew. He has good taste."

"She must play with the symphony."

"So pretty, too."

This striking violinist, the most amazing violinist anyone present has ever heard, a veteran performer of several hundred Romani wedding celebrations and daily street shows, transforms the mountain setting into a concert hall . . .

Cameras flash. Videos roll. Antonio, resplendent in an

electric pink suit borrowed for the occasion, watches proudly as Cinka works her music magic. He was worried, very worried all night and day, but said nothing to her.

I don't know these people that well. Many are strangers. They could be racist assholes. In our family, too. Thank God my parents aren't here. I would have died. But Cinka looks so hot! When she stepped out of Simona's bedroom in that dress I didn't recognize her. How can anyone not love her? And her playing? She's smoking! I love her more and more each day.

Meanwhile, both mothers-in-law are knowingly directing the last of the wedding guests to appropriate seats on the rustic benches.

Cousins with cousins, aunts with aunts; your family left, our family right. They take care to avoid seating feuding relatives too close to one another, ex-husbands and wives too close to unknown new spouses, especially the ones with plunging necklines, backlines, tight outfits, enticing red lips, and killer stiletto heels.

The sun beams down on the wedding. Guests are already loosening ties and removing jackets or fanning themselves with purses, hands, and handkerchiefs; but the scorching afternoon heat rules.

When Cinka transitions into a sweet, captivating Romani bridal processional, all eyes and cameras turn to focus on the giddy, gaudy, handsome couple approaching from above the slope. They slowly descend the long red runner over dirt and mountain grass to the canopy below.

The bridal party stands stiffly on the Egyptian rug, flanked by vases filled with giant sunflowers. Curious swallows fly zigzag patterns above. The ceremony is over in minutes—short and sweet—punctuated by giggles, cheers, and camera flashes.

Cinka plays a traditional recessional, and the couple slowly retraces their steps up the red runner, laughing as guests shower them with pink and orange rose petals.

Then, where ancient Romans once led pack mules loaded with goods and supplies, everyone follows on the uphill hike along a narrow, winding road to the wedding castle fifteen minutes away. Antonio blows Cinka a kiss. But she's too busy to catch it.

Aunts, uncles, cousins, and friends—Italians all—crowd around, congratulate her and take photos with her.

"Do you have a card? How can we reach you?"

"You are fabulous, my dear! My son is getting married in two months. Are you available?"

"Would you come to Milan to play my parents' anniversary?"

"Put us on your mailing list, please. We don't want to miss any of your shows!"

She blushes and poses affably as she has done for tourists so many times before. But this, her first Italian wedding, leaves her wondering.

No one said anything! I can't believe it! No dirty looks, nothing! They just accept me as one of theirs. The way my people would accept a gadjo *guest at one of our weddings. Now comes the real test. I have to sit with them and eat. Please let me not make any mistakes.*

She finds Antonio and whispers into his ear: "If this is a typical Italian wedding, I want one, too!"

WEDDING LEGENDS

A few hours later, under the glow of lanterns, a slow setting sun and the eyes of the hungry, the sumptuous banquet feast takes shape on the outer grounds of the castle. The wine keeps flowing, as the servers bring out tray after tray of sausages, ham, roast beef, pork, grilled lamb, fish, and mountains of roasted, steamed, boiled vegetables, surrounded by overflowing pots of pasta and sauces.

The serving tables are ready. Someone gives a signal. Guests rush the spread elbowing each other out of the way, loading their plates with everything in sight, especially the *prosciutto*.

Cinka's eyes bulge as she politely waits her turn, then gingerly serves herself; but not too much in case people whisper, *"The Gypsy is hungry."*

At each table the conversational material for more wedding legends takes shape. Families, reunited after a long time, catch up on gossip, clarify blood connections for the young ones, and entertain new listeners with old tales.

The groom's father: "My grandfather was a simple country man with one bad leg, not really curious about politics, but able to tell good stories, all night long . . ."

The bride's father: "Wild pigs around here can cover up to thirty kilometres a day searching for food. Once I saw a mother and father pig shepherding ten baby pigs across the road, when a black bear popped out of the forest . . ."

The bride's uncle: "A friar from a local monastery was excavating in the night for treasure, when he felt someone pulling his shirt from behind. He looked, and it was the devil. He ran screaming down the mountain to the village and never spoke again . . ."

The bride's drunken aunt: "In the village where we're from, near Todi, there is the jawbone of a dragon they found in the Tiber River. They say he killed many a traveller on the river for decades, including one of our family members . . ."

The groom's father: "A great, great, great-uncle was doctor to the Pope in the eighteenth century. A single man, he left no heirs. But someone in the Vatican who knew another doctor, who knew a woman, arranged to give him a son to inherit everything. He owned palaces and vineyards. He was a rich man. I can show you the palaces in Rome that belonged to him. Our family contested the inheritance and lost . . ."

The bride's great-aunt: "Your great-grandmother was an artist. Made the most beautiful dresses for wealthy mine-owners right until the day she died. And Father was a marble worker. Came home every day covered in dust. At night and on special occasions, he played accordion for feasts and friends. He loved his accordion . . ."

The bride's grandfather: "He was a local hermit, a hunchback. He built a small stone house on the hill over there. Never spoke to anyone for twenty years. Entirely self-sufficient. Until he met a beautiful young farm wife recently widowed . . ."

The bride's great-uncle: "Down the mountain, one kilometre from the castle here, is the entry gate and the gatekeeper's house. You passed it coming in. One day my children found a snake in the woods just behind the house and stomped it to death. The next moment, ten snakes came out of a hole hissing at them. My kids pounded on the door of the gate-keeper's house to let them in . . ."

The groom's uncle: "Our father was a socialist. He was beaten and tortured by the Fascists. You were not supposed to have your own ideas in Aspoli in 1939. When he was fifty years old, Father joined these radical groups. After being beaten, tortured and imprisoned, he was obliged to leave the groups for the sake of his family. But there was no work. The Fascists blacklisted him. No one was allowed to hire him . . ."

The bride's father: "My grandfather raised me here. He taught me everything: how to graft trees, apricot, plums, and peaches. Every branch of his fig trees had a special fig: brown, black, or white . . ."

The groom's uncle: "All of our uncles immigrated to Argentina in the 1930s looking for work. They sold land here to buy land there, and became a famous family. There is a television show made about them, a soap opera, the *Dallas* of Argentina . . ."

By cell phone, Massimaxo discovers he's an uncle. Guests at his table toast his new status. Guests toast his new job. Guests toast his new shoes. Guests toast the fact that everyone is all together again, able to toast one another. Guests toast the number of toasts, seven in the last twenty minutes.

Guests eat wild boar, drink a *Grechetto Umbri* and a *Falesco* and a *Vitiano* red, then toast the wine and the boars that have been sacrificed for the wedding, and toast the new Uncle Massimaxo again.

At the outdoor tables under the stars, Antonio and Massimaxo debate the identity and perspectives of the ever-brightening moon.

"Does it not resemble the letter C?" Massimo asks.

"So sorry to disappoint you, but it's the letter D," Antonio contends.

"Tonight's moon stands for Courage—of the groom and the bride."

"Or is it Doubt—of unnamed guests?"

"Is the moon brave enough to shine all night and illuminate all the injustices of the world it sees?"

"Or does it doubt the right of humankind to continue?"

More wine, and the debate continues. The final consensus, according to Antonio:

"It is a courageous moon to illuminate all that we need to see in order to move forward as a civilization in these troubled times. It is also a wise moon. It is casting doubt on the pronouncements of the idiots currently in power, allowing the people to challenge their decisions."

Massimaxo grunts. The other guests toast this realization. And this coterie of like-minded wolves howls loudly for all the other wedding guests to hear.

Cinka listens, watches and smiles as she holds Antonio's hand under the table. She says little but thinks, *No one will ever believe me.*

THE MINISTER'S HOT GIRLFRIEND

Table candles now illuminate the expansive outdoor dining beside the castle. It's surrounded by towering sentinel trees at the edge of the blackened forest.

Some guests are already making their way home. Others

grab drinks from the bar in both hands, ready to party. Large ornate candles ring the castle's outer stone courtyard as the Egyptian band plays an irresistibly hypnotic, sensuous rhythm beckoning all party animals.

The alluring Egyptian belly dancer, shimmering in thin orange saffron and abundant gold bangles, gyrates her hips and torso. Smiling broadly, she searches out the limp hands of ogling men and leads them onto the dance floor. Slack-jawed wives and girlfriends stare.

One young couple—she, in a tight red dress, he, in an equally tight grey suit—both well toasted, flirt openly, with smouldering looks and hands that wander. She smiles nonstop, eyes flashing. He returns her intensity and grabs her around her waist to draw her closer.

In half a dozen quick steps, a man of the cloth walks up to them, places one hand on her shoulder, an arm around her waist, and quickly spins her sideways toward him. He marches her off the dance floor into the night.

"What?" the spurned grey suit sputters. "I haven't had a girlfriend for seven months, and now a priest steals this one from me? God, what have I done to deserve this injustice?" He looks into the star-laden sky and moans.

A circle of aunts and uncles on the edge of the dance floor knowingly discuss the belly dancer's technique while they finish off a few bottles of wine.

"If my wife could dance like that . . ."

"If my husband could dance like that . . ."

"You couldn't . . ."

"Oh yeah? Watch me."

A middle-aged woman grabs her sister and improvises her own belly dance. The husband winces.

"You know that village past the bottom of the hill? Locals used to call it the Village of the Crazies."

"Why?"

"Because they danced all the time, more than they worked."

"Doesn't sound crazy to me. Especially if they had hot dancers, like her, showing them how."

Locked together, Antonio and Cinka dance slowly. She's never danced like this before, and has to constantly watch her feet in the unfamiliar high heels. She feels awkward and self-conscious, but at this late hour, after so much booze, no one notices, no one cares.

Antonio strokes her hair. She leans on his shoulder and ponders the impossible.

I still feel like I'm living a dream. I'm with a man who makes me happy, *gadjo* or not. I'm in the middle of a crowd of *gadjos*, and no one is giving me a hard time. I feel like an enchanted spirit from a children's fairy tale in another world, but this is a real dream, I think. When will I wake up?

"Will you marry me?" she asks Antonio.

"Fucking hell. What do you think?"

POSTWEDDING HANGOVERS

As the early morning sunlight floods through the window, Antonio rolls over to hug Cinka. He jolts awake. She's not there. He rubs his eyes. She's standing at the foot of the bed, naked and giggling.

"You look so beautiful while you sleep. Like a little cherub on a cathedral ceiling—but with a red beard," she says, laughing.

He jumps up grinning, and pulls her down onto the bed pinning her on her back.

"And you resemble a naked Madonna trying to seduce the cherub. Bad Madonna!"

"Bad cherub!"

She rolls him onto his side. They look into each other's eyes. Ever so lightly he strokes her hair, her forehead, traces her eyebrows, cheekbones, nose, lips, and chin. He notices how her skin glows in the soft sunlight, how the magic blue of her eyes draws him deeper into the mystery of her world, and how he can lose himself forever in her, with her, face to face, lying beside her.

She caresses his hair, his ears, his neck and shoulders. They breathe together, eyes still locked. He places his hands on her ass and pulls her into him. She grinds against him.

He tells himself, then tells her, that he is the luckiest man in the world, and kisses her lightly on the lips. She kisses back harder, her hands all over him, squeezing him, pulling his nipples, grabbing his ass. He caresses her everywhere.

They keep kissing each other breathlessly and make the kind of mad, intense love that forces the bed to reposition itself a few inches. She finally calls out his name, he swears, and they are left both gasping in wonder, relaxed in each other's arms, drunk with love.

Once dressed, they walk down a long stone hallway to join the rest of last night's still groggy wedding party.

Everyone congregates on a large rooftop terrace just off the castle kitchen, sipping espressos and smoking cigarettes under the morning sun. The bride's father is explaining the origins of a wicker basket full of broken pieces of pottery.

"These are two thousand years old. We found them in the woods nearby. See the stamped initials ZSMS? He was Zosimus, a slave the Romans freed because of his artistry as a potter. The family who originally lived here hired him to come and work for them. A poor artist finds a patron and becomes a rich man. Nothing new, right?" He looks at Cinka.

"And you, my dear. You're a rare talent. I'd like to invite you to come back here to play at one of our musical poetic *soirées*. Writers from Rome come for weekend retreats and read with guest musicians. You'd be perfect. There'd be proper compensation as well. You'll meet important contacts for future engagements."

Cinka beams.

"If you could arrange it, I'd love to, thank you."

The bride's father hands her his business card.

"Call me when you can."

She looks at Antonio. He winks. She thinks, *The dream is not over. My family won't believe it. I can't.*

Antonio and Cinka lean on the stone parapet with others to feast on the magnificent view. Mountains defining the Tevere valley stretch for kilometres in every direction, with Lake Corbara in the distance and the Tiber River below. Orvieto and Todi are at either end; this castle sits between them. The bride's father points out two local landmarks opposite.

"A countess from a very old family lives in that twelfth-century castle there. See the chapel tower? It's part of their estate. Inside those walls is a small village. A few dozen families—the hired help—live on that slope below tending the vineyards, orchards, olive groves, and forests the way their forefather probably did for a few centuries. Now they, too, live in the same little stone houses with the same small gardens. The countess lives in her hundred-room castle above.

"The countess's land stretches for several kilometres each way up and down the mountain to the river. At one end are ruins from another ancient Roman watchtower—the sister of this one here. The central stone tower of this castle is two thousand years old. The walls are still intact with the insignia of the original architect chiselled into a name stone."

The castle is nestled in a thick grove of trees, including figs, hazel nuts, oaks large and small, and pines with edible nuts in the big cones.

"Wild pigs, a metre long, rub themselves against the bark of the pines to disguise their smell and fool their predators. It's the pine resin."

Beside the pigs, fox, rabbit, and bear were known to visit the castle gardens, as well as snakes, poisonous and not. White wild pigeons, the *Paloma*, nested nearby.

"We keep cutting back the bush and the trees, but while we sleep, Nature grows."

Despite the predominance of hangovers, guests snap photos left and right. A brilliant Umbrian sunshine beams in the background. Antonio and Cinka pose with friends crowded tightly together laughing. Among them are the hardcore Romans from last night, the *über*-partiers who never wanted the night of revelry to end. They crashed outside on this terrace and another, on improvised beds of pillows and rugs, catching their two hours of sleep before the sun rose and others started brewing the coffee.

Words were few; smiles, many. People were content to breathe in the fresh mountain air, take in the vista, and listen to the omnipresent birdsong.

"Like it?" Antonio places his arm around Cinka's shoulder.

"It's paradise. It's the magic carpet ride I want to never end," she whispers. "So beautiful, peaceful, perfect. It's like a movie or a painting—a moment from both the past and the future. I haven't felt like this for a long time, ever since I was a little girl in the mountains of my village with my family.

"This is a future I want to know. Free of any worries, ugliness, hatred, or hardship. It's how all people should be allowed to live. In total peace. With friends and family together. All the love, too. It's so unreal! Yet I am so happy to be here with you and your friends. I never want this to end. I only wish my family could be here. They would love this."

"Maybe after you play for those writers, we can come back with your family," Antonio hints. "There's tons of room here and the bride's dad is very generous. I'm sure we could work something out."

"You'd make me the happiest woman in the world. My family and I could clean the grounds. We could sweep, chop wood, paint, cook—do any chores in return!"

Cinka imagines the unimaginable. *My family? Here? In this castle? Incredible! Then she really starts to fantasize. It could house half the refugee camp, and the other half could camp outside in the yard. And there'd still be room for visitors. For kids to run around and play. All this land and forest! Land to grow food. We could call it "The Roma People's Paradise" and fly our flag.*

POSTWEDDING PROPOSAL

In the kitchen someone slices a gigantic watermelon in two, then carves the sweet red flesh into smaller pieces for the gang of wide-eyed kids standing by.

Three generations: white-haired father—a former

Partisan; son—a former punk rocker; and grandson, sit side by side at the huge wooden table.

Someone else secures the monster wedding gift prosciutto onto a special carving board ready to be served to drooling guests and family. He uses an ultra-sharp knife to cut off the thick outer rind, then slices paper-thin, salty, pink cured flesh. The hungry morning guests, plates in hand, line up. An uncle brings three large steins of cold beer to the breakfast table.

"The kegs are still full from last night and we have to finish them today," he announces.

One of the grandfathers throws a captured imaginary butterfly from his cupped hands into the air, egging on his grandson to catch the insect. The three-year-old doesn't quite understand, but eagerly participates in the game, running around the table trying to find the elusive object. When a real butterfly actually flies into the kitchen the grandfather shrugs his shoulders while the kid screams with pleasure.

Outside in the courtyard someone has cranked up the sound system and it's blaring reggae and the Stooges.

Cinka kisses Antonio and asks,

"Can we be married here?"

"I thought you wanted to do it in the camp, in front of your people?"

"I have to think about it some more."

"Don't your people do it differently anyway?"

"Sort of." Cinka cups Antonio's hand in hers and smiles. "If we got married according to my people's tradition, the wedding ceremony would be simple. We join hands in front of one of our camp elders and promise to be true to each other. Like you Italians do. Be true, then cheat, fight, the usual. We would have a big celebration with music and lots of food, like here.

"It would be outside. Everyone would come. All the women and girls would wear brightly coloured bows in their hair, tied back, with their best skirts and tops, and dance together in a circle around me. Of course I would wear a white dress. I might change to a red one after. And have my hair done, and my nails. And wear new shoes. The band would play nonstop and we'd dance nonstop. The men would sit or stand around the edge of the circle watching and drinking with you—the groom.

"You and I would break bread with our guests. The guests would pin lots of money on my dress. We would use it to buy furniture for our new home, like a proper bed, things like that.

"For the wedding, we would party, sing, and dance for as long as we can stand on our own two feet. We could do that here, no?"

POSTWEDDING GHOSTS

Antonio and Cinka stay behind with the bride's father and the closest friends for the next two days to clean and restore the wedding site. They stack chairs, disassemble tables, collect the garbage, empty bottles, broken glasses, and wash and sweep the tile and stone floors. Wedding guests partied in every corner of the multiroomed castle.

Late one afternoon on the terrace, Cinka points excitedly and yells, "Look, spirits!"

Ghostly solitary formations, small, thin, wispy trails of white mist resembling human forms, are following one another, one-by-one, in a wind-driven procession, coming from the lake single file, floating up the valley between the mountains to an unknown destination.

"The older people around here," says the bride's father, "believe that these wisps of mist are the spirits of ancient Roman soldiers who died while they were away fighting battles, now returning to search for their loved ones. They float between the watchtowers on the mountaintops and ask if anyone has news of their families. It is said that in ancient times, soldiers in the towers would answer the ghosts, sometimes honestly, sometimes not.

"Once, a watchman refused to admit that he was seeing the wife of a soldier. She crouched below the parapet in fear when she heard her dead husband's voice calling her name.

Later that night, a dense cloud enshrouded the tower. When the watchman and the unfaithful wife walked outside, they were attacked and eaten by wolves.

"They say, too, that when these clouds reach Albania, the soldiers descend and march all night on the deserted beaches moaning and wailing, leaving odd tracks in the sand."

Soon enough, the entire valley below was enshrouded in a thick cloud with the jagged top of the mountain opposite floating above.

"Remember, my dear Antonio. When I come back after death looking for you, don't duck behind a chair because you are sleeping with someone else."

"Ha! I would never hide from you, and don't you ever think of hiding from me."

They embrace and kiss as the disparate clouds behind them unite into one.

CINKA'S MOTHER SPEAKS

On a bright afternoon in *Piazza di Spagna* hogged by the sun, Antonio searches for precious shade at the edge of a crowd. As he claps in time to Cinka's music, someone taps him on the shoulder. He turns but doesn't recognize the older Romni smiling at him.

"Hi. Do I know you?"

"Yes." She looks a bit bewildered.

"Oh . . . are you a friend of Cinka's?"

"I'm her mother! Don't you remember me?"

"Oh, oh!" he stutters. "I mean, why yes, of course I remember! How are you? Good to see you!" He extends a hand and blushes, cursing himself for blowing this so badly.

"Antonio, yes?"

He grins sheepishly.

Luminitsa smiles broadly, a gold tooth glinting.

"Can I speak with you, please? Come."

He follows her to a darkened doorway nearby. She puts her hand on his shoulder and fixes her large brown eyes on his.

"Antonio, you are a good man. A kind man. You help my daughter and you help us. No other *gadjo* has ever done anything like this. For me, you are like family. I think of you almost like a son. Cinka speaks about you highly. You make her happy. And I know you love my daughter. And she loves you." She lowers her eyes and her voice. "We will discuss this later."

"Ahh . . ." Antonio is about to blurt out something stupid, but catches himself.

"For now, I only want to thank you for everything you do for us. I know not all Italians are bad. But I tell you, in my heart, I believe—and I never thought this before—that all of Italy is Mafia. And the government? They are the biggest Mafia of all. You must be careful. Do you understand?"

"Yes, of course. Certainly."

"One more thing. There is a slight complication in our family right now." She looks over his shoulder, quickly scanning the square. "A fly in the soup, as we say. Do not worry." She smiles. "I am taking care of it."

LUCA WALKS ROME

For three days, Luca stalked Cinka through the streets of Rome, waiting for just the right moment. It never came. There were either too many people nearby, or she'd scamper onto a bus or train, or she'd blend like a fish into a sidewalk school of tourists and disappear. Each day that he lost her, he'd chastise himself.

Idiot! What's wrong with me? It's a question of honour for my family. Damn it! She lied to us. She's made a fool out of me. Either she comes back with me—by force if necessary—or it ends here.

Yet still, he hesitated. Why? Was it the steaming heat he couldn't handle? The incessant din and chaos of Rome that overwhelmed his village boy senses? He'd never visited a city before. Was it the hundreds of omnipresent police who seemed to watch him from almost every corner? He felt intimidated and unsure of himself within this urban crush of strangers.

These Romans speak another language. They don't look like me. They are well dressed, they flash money, they drive fancy cars. And there are blacks among them! I don't like blacks.

He was self-conscious and still unsure of how to negoti-ate Rome's labyrinth of *piazzas*, stairs, sidewalks, passageways, and car-choked streets. His head turned everywhere at once, fascinated by statues, fountains, pulsating bars, tourists, and the women. His libido kicked into overdrive. The ever-present smells of food lured him this way and that. He was far from the tranquil, empty village roads, where he, the local young tough, ruled, walking carefree.

Fuck this place. No one knows who I am. I get no respect!

So he'd deliberately knock into people who didn't get out of his way. Romans gave the rude stranger dirty looks. And he still didn't get it.

"Fuck off!" he'd say, but nobody understood him. He'd repeat it louder and make threatening gestures. One more unwanted, dishevelled, disrespectful Gypsy to avoid. One more conspicuous, undesirable foreigner for the police to target.

And always each night when he returned to the camp trailer, Nicu would ask, "Is it done?"

And each night, the reply: "Not yet."

"What's the problem, Luca? Get your shit together. You're not a fucking hedgehog."

And Luca would answer, "Fuck you! Leave me alone!" He refused all offers of help from Nicu. "This is my business, not yours." Instead, he borrowed money to go drink and try to forget about her.

And every morning an elder would ask Nicu, "Is it done?"

And Nicu would shake his head, and the elder would pass the message on to the old gossip at Cinka's camp, and she would pull out her charms and amulets.

SOCCER'S ULTRAVIOLENT

Tens of thousands of soccer fans pour into Rome's *Stadio Olimpico* for the big match between SS Lazio and Firenze's ACF Fiorentina. The air reverberates with chants and singing: traditional Fascist songs lead by the Lazio fans; old communist and anarchist songs by the opponents.

Historically, the SS Lazio team has a connection with Italian Fascism. It was founded by Italian army officers in 1900, and later became the favourite club of Benito Mussolini. The ultra-right affiliation continues. ACF Fiorentina's fan base is the polar opposite—Left. In today's game, sparks, insults, and fists will fly.

Rafaele looks outside the stadium for his group. He winces when he spots the extreme supporters of the Lazio club known as the "ultras." Within them are the *Irriducibili*, a dangerous gang of ultraviolent hooligans. They occupy and dominate the northern curved portion, the *curva* of the stadium. Rafaele wonders why, year after year, no police officer ever ventures into this territory or stakes it out in advance.

It's an ugly, lawless no-man's-land, where the neo-Fascist Lazio fans, becoming bolder over the years, openly chant racist slogans, wave Nazi flags, unfurl hateful anti-Semitic, anti-Roma banners, and make the international news. Even though the law in Italy—as in Germany—prohibits encouraging Fascism, no one ever tries to prevent or stop them.

The stadium is a very public place where anyone and everyone has the chance to express their views and can be joined by hundreds or thousands who share them. One of the Lazio team darlings, Di Canio, will even occasionally reward the fans from the field with a smile and a Nazi salute. Among their supporters: Daniela Fini, wife of the former Italian foreign minister, Gianfranco Fini, leader of the "post-Fascist" National Alliance party. Ex-members of the Italian Social Movement, a group led by former Blackshirts from Mussolini's Fascist regime, founded the National Alliance.

Scum attracts scum, Rafaele muses, and Fascists love to revel in their collective muck.

He spots the huge anti-Fascist contingent finally arriving, waving flags and banners. Soccer is a national fever. Left or right doesn't matter. Rafaele shares the passion. He runs to join them and sits in the southern curved section staked out by the loudest leftist hardcore supporters of the ACF Fiorentina.

This *curva* is a Fascist-free zone; its fans described as *"neither red, nor black—only red-black."* Now the chants of fans in the stadium become deafening. Rafaele joins in.

> Fascists always lose! They suck big ones!
> The dick of a Fascist is not a stick! It's a baby carrot!
> Fascist mommas wipes their noses! Fascist goons swing from branches!

And now thousands sing an anti-Fascist punk song from the redskin group, *Los Fastidios:*

> Come on, come on antifa hooligans
> In the streets, on the terraces
> We are singing and we scream
> All our hate for the Nazi scum
> We are coming: start to run!

Early into the game, the anti-Fascists unfurl their first gigantic banner in the southern *curvas: "Fascists make lousy lovers."*

There is a swelling of cheers and boos across the stands as fans express themselves in response. The neo-Nazis jeer, sing their own songs, wave their flags defiantly and set off flares.

Minutes later, a giant anarchist banner is unfurled: *"Fascists smell bad,"* and again the stadium erupts in cheers and boos. By half-time, the third anti-Fascist football fan banner comes out. It's a response to a previous Lazio banner that read *"Rome is Fascist."* This one says: *"Rome is anti-racist,"* and now the Lazio ultras go berserk, storming the field waving Nazi flags. The game is stopped. To a crescendo of boos from the north and cheers from the south, police chase, grab, and escort the neo-Nazis off the field. The game continues.

THE PROFESSOR

This night in San Lorenzo is the hottest and loudest of the week. Students spill out of bars, arms around one another, clowning, kissing, laughing. Everywhere, conversations are animated.

Antonio, Rafaele, and Massimaxo meet up at their favourite *trattoria* off *Piazza dei Sanniti* late after work. Everyone is smoking and drinking at the packed tables outside. An old acquaintance sits with them. He's a visiting former professor of communication studies at Rome University, home after a few years in Belgium. They all took a class with him, a class that usually ended late, like this, in a bar. The bar talk was always the professor's forté.

He's fifty, balding, tall and robust, with a bushy black beard, thick glasses, and a pipe dangling from his mouth. Rafaele swears his eyes are the blackest he has ever seen, large, searching, and full of fire. An occasional correspondent for an Italian newspaper, he now teaches a course on Media and Europe Today.

A pitcher of beer is rapidly emptied. A large pizza has just been served, but more beer and pizza are ordered. Always animated, the professor speaks with both arms outstretched and waving.

"What is happening here? How could you allow this?"

"What?" Antonio asks innocently.

"This is my neighbourhood! San Lorenzo! Where I grew up! Where I feel most comfortable. Where my mother still lives and hangs her laundry to dry on the balcony above the street." He points down the block.

"All my childhood friends still live here. My old haunts like the Autonomia Bar are still here. But I hear about what happens from my colleagues in Brussels." He shakes his head in dismay.

"What do you mean?" Rafaele and the others are puzzled.

The professor growls like a hungry bear, shakes his head again, and between mouthfuls of pizza, continues:

"Italy is perverted now. Perverted, I say! My neighbourhood is being swallowed up by the rich. This is what I mean. And why aren't you youth doing anything about it? What are you thinking about?"

"Um . . ." Massimaxo speaks up, "apart from some of us wanting to get laid?" Everyone laughs.

"We know we have to do something about the rest," Antonio ventures.

"This is a start!" The professor smiles. "I have friends in the European Parliamentary press gallery. They tell me things. In the European Parliament, my journalist friends ask parliamentarians about the irregularities in Italy. Irregularities? Racist reactions, I tell you! And these knuckleheads must answer. What do they answer? The usual crap full of contradictions and excuses. Any good journalist can then write a story. A story that brings shame to Italy on the European and world stage. So what is obvious?" He gestures with his pipe.

"Uh, that we're in trouble?" Antonio suggests.

"Precisely! An Italy that can't stand up to international scrutiny is a country in trouble!"

Rafaele speaks. "You heard that the government now wants to stop trains from France because they contain Romani passengers? They want to conduct special police searches of the passengers."

"Imbeciles!" The professor is in fighting form. "Will they demand a special permit from these passengers? Will they try to fingerprint their children, too? What an international scandal! Is this what the new, restyled Fascist Italy wants? To isolate itself on the European stage? To return to a darker period? If my grandfather, an anti-Fascist, was still around, he would grab his gun."

"Mine, too," Rafaele adds.

"But how are these new politicians any different from the old?" Antonio asks.

"Exactly! They're not! They resort to the same old tricks. Like trying to get the people to forget their own history!"

For Antonio it's personal. "Do you think the Roma stand a chance? I mean in this kind of climate of fear?"

"The Roma? This word no longer exists for the State and its servile press. We now say "nomads," to give the false impression that the now-criminalized Roma are forever a carefree, habitual race of nomads, content to keep moving, to never have a place to call home. Forget that they are people like us! When will we give our Roma their badge of shame to wear on their sleeves in public?"

A young Romni in a pink fleece top wanders by selling roses. Her hair is pulled back in a ponytail and she wears sweatpants that are too short. She scans the customers sitting on the terrace, her eyes imploring. She doesn't say a word. It's 10 PM. She's no older than twelve.

The professor waves her over, asks for a rose, and hands her two euros. She flashes a huge smile and scampers off into the night.

"Now she and family are two euros closer to being able to eat tonight. This is the new family breadwinner of Italy—a child! Because no one will hire her mother or father! Is this the new Italy that we want? That we are proud of? That the whole world can see?"

The other three purse their lips or just shrug. They haven't heard one of his lectures for a long time. He growls again, taps his pipe on the table, peers into it, then downs another mouthful of pizza and gulps his beer.

"Boys!" he roars, "I believe Bakunin was right! He was the real hero for Italy. He walked that middle road, between the authoritarian Marxists and the republicanism of Mazzini. A free libertarian Italy. '*Complete liberty within complete solidarity.*' Was that Bakunin or was it Malatesta? Hmmph! I'm not sure. But Malatesta had it right, too. None of this centralized strongman authority of the State. To Malatesta! To Bakunin!"

They all clink glasses.

The professor relights his pipe and puffs. He's on a roll and has three former students whom he likes, listening.

"Citizenship, Italian style, means tune in to the nightly news and shake your head. Right?" They nod.

"Sleep on it, citizens, then in the morning, regurgitate what you witnessed on the TV last night, and exchange inanities about it with your neighbours and your workmates. Yes?"

The three grunt their approval.

"Discuss this view of the world—the TV magnate's view of the world—around the dinner table and inculcate your children with it. Is this the fate of Italy? To die through indifference? Because of a lack of caring about our neighbours and ourselves? *Cazzo!*"

He bangs his fist on the table and all the beer mugs jump.

"Do Italians today give a shit about our future? These are not Italians!" he roars. Other terrace patrons turn their heads.

As he speaks, another Romni no older than ten, approaches with a handful of roses. This time Rafaele gives her two euros for a rose.

"Thank you, sir." She bows her head and turns to Antonio with a smile that reveals missing front teeth. "And you, kind sir?" He also hands her two euros. "Thank you, bless you." She bows again and runs off.

"I've come back to this?" The professor shakes his head. "Children forced to support their families?"

By now, the evening crowds have thinned. Tired waiters in black vests lean against counters and count their tips. Dishwashers sit on plastic boxes for a moment and pray there are no more dishes. Sewer rats poke their noses out, sniffing for the next meal. Rome's lights flicker off.

GREAT-GRANDFATHER: THE BIG DIPPER

When I was young, my father took me outside to look at the stars.

"See the Big Dipper? Everything that belongs to the landowners fills the Big Dipper. Now see the Little Dipper? What spills over from the big one, ends up in the little one, which belongs to the friends of the landowners, the generals, the priests, people like that. And everything that spills out of the Little Dipper"—he cupped his hands—"are the crumbs that fall to us peasants, if we're lucky to catch them."

That was then. But now, I don't understand. After all the industrial growth, with all the inventions, the advances in science and medicine, when people should be living even better than before, it seems to me that today's "new" Italy is not much different from the one I grew up in. In fact, it even seems poorer! It makes no sense!

In 1913, an old Russian anarchist, Peter Kropotkin, calculated that with all the new existing machinery, the majority of people needed to work only a few days a week to live well. Our civilization had everything it took to make that possible back then! We were wealthy already! What happened?

There is almost as much poverty now as before. You see it everywhere! In people's faces, on the streets. You hear the rumblings of emptier stomachs, see the thin children and can imagine the skimpier meals around the dinner table. Just like us before. And that was a long time ago! We were peasants!

Today, look at all the painful efforts to economize. The majority have learned to cut and cut some more. People double up in apartments. Sell off their possessions. They don't save money in the bank. They can barely survive with what they earn. Precarious? I'll say!

And always the same demons knocking at the door: pay the rent, pay the bills, feed the children, and try to keep hunger and homelessness away. Those living precarious lives before, now have nowhere to turn. They live in the shadows of their former lives. They have bread, yes. Pasta, yes. A bit of cheese, a bit of meat. Usually yes. And coffee of course. These are the essentials. The rest? Ask any storeowner! The third week of every month, people no longer buy as much food as they used to. The last week of every month, the sales of milk are down. Children learn to drink water and to eat less. They can ask for more, but it will not appear.

Never has our country been so poor economically and socially, so bankrupt morally. This is why we Italians look for scapegoats. The new face of our country is not Romani nor African, but the darkness of Hunger. This is today's Italy. Hurting and fearful of the future. Living off the crumbs from the dippers above. So where did all this wealth go?

Look up. It's being hoarded in the Big Dipper.

SMASH THE TV

Rafaele opens his eyes and finds himself sunk into his armchair, the TV watching him. How long has he been sleeping? His sweetheart isn't home yet and it is getting late.

He blinks at the footage of a long row of police cars, blue lights flashing outside Romani camps. More cities across Italy are razing the camps, blaming the mass influx of migrants for rising crime. The anchorman, wearing a fluorescent green tie, delivers the news in his habitual take-me-seriously phony voice. His eyes are fixed on Rafaele, who switches off the TV and swears. *This is messed up. A kick in the face, get-out-of-here Xmas present solution to the problem. We can't help them. Won't help them. So why don't they just get lost, and presto! An embarrassing social problem solved! You morons.* He throws an empty beer can at the TV.

ANTONIO REMEMBERS THE WEDDING

Antonio lies awake in his bed, studying the jagged, lightning-bolt like crack in the ceiling. Where my dreams come from and disappear, he thinks.

As the local church bell chimes 8:30 AM, he counts 130 rings. He replays the weekend wedding in his head: the music, the chatter and gossip, the crying of someone's newborn baby, how everyone marvelled at Cinka's performance. How they shook her hand and never commented that she was a Romni.

Maybe they saw her as just another immigrant from Romania, but a talented one. No one said a word—openly at least. No one asked. Everyone was on their best behaviour. But then, many of them were strangers, too, at this atypical Italian wedding overflowing with foreigners.

Maybe Cinka blended into the unusually exotic mix of Arabs, Asians, and non-Italians, where everyone got along. Cinka herself noticed it. If only everyday Italy was this accepting.

Today he's meeting her at a jazz bar to finalize a gig for the weekend ahead. A gig that came from the wedding.

At the bar, Antonio slumps into a lime green couch parked just inside a wide-open window facing *Piazza dei Campani* and a construction site. Two workers—non-Italian—joke back and forth as they roll up orange plastic fencing and sweep the street. Behind him, Maria the server rearranges cakes in the glass display case.

Antonio reads the provocative poster plastered on an apartment wall across the square. It features a scantily clad young woman staring vacantly back at him, above the words, *"All I wanna do is clubbing."* Another piece of street art.

These walls, always alive with images, colours and messages, are available to anyone with a piece of paper, wall paste, a magic marker or a can of spray paint. They are either in-your-face or subtle, a scream or a whisper. Each has a few split seconds to capture the eye and the imagination. Better this, he thinks, than the sterility of naked concrete.

As he sips his soda, the sounds of a low-key Sicilian free jazz ensemble escape the sound system. Trumpet, sax, and drums drift in and out of deep conversation, sailing, sailing, punctuated and percussive. How he loves this group. It reminds him of the Sicilian street person he passes by almost every day in the same spot a few blocks away, below the massive San Lorenzo city wall.

The first time he noticed the guy sleeping, he saw a pair of dirty sunburnt feet sticking out from under a piece of cardboard. An aging former truck driver and boxer, Silvio, was lying on a filthy mattress on the sidewalk. His upper torso and head were hidden inside a cardboard box. A pigeon picked its way through the pizza crusts and crumbs scattered around the makeshift bedroom.

Antonio often left him food and spare change and chatted. Now as he waits for Cinka, he thinks how Italians will tolerate their own homeless, but not those from afar. The double standard, a national disgrace.

"Today, no one should be homeless. It's not the nineteenth century," Silvio would shout.

As would Antonio's friend, a Palestinian refugee, who works nearby.

"Look at my face. Palestinian, Etruscan, it's the same shape. What is the difference? We Palestinians are the real

Italians. We exported our culture to Greece, then to Italy. We taught your people how to cultivate land and tend livestock.

"And now, look at all the hungry, homeless refugees, your own brothers and sisters. Palestinians, yes.

"How can you be safe if you don't have food, if you go hungry, if you live with constant risk? It is not right. Life in Italy is not easy. And with a child and no food, it is even harder. All we want are basic human rights. Like what you have. Me, I don't call myself a refugee. I'm a Palestinian motherfucker who came from shit to shit."

NICU HAS LUCA TAILED

"So what'd you see?"

"Your cousin followed Cinka, then lost her. He ended up in a bar."

One of Nicu's teen soldiers is reporting back to him. Same stupid thing day after day, Nicu thinks. What's Luca's problem? He makes me look bad, too, like we can't take care of our own family business.

"Follow him again tomorrow. But this time, don't lose her. Call me."

ROMANIAN GROCERY STORE

There is only one Romanian grocery store in Monterotondo, on *Via San Martino*. Modest, clean and bright, it serves the entire East European *émigré* population and savvy locals. Here, immigrants can find their favourite imported pickled vegetables, canned preserves, chocolates, and rings of spicy sausages.

Rafaele will often buy their fresh meat and non-Italian food as surprises for his girlfriend. He enjoys the loud Romanian music blaring from the speakers and singsong conversation as Romanian tongues mingle with other Eastern European languages—none of which he understands. He's on good terms with one of the owners, a jovial, muscle-bound former Romanian Olympic athlete.

Today, the owner is restocking shelves. Rafaele greets him with a friendly pat on the back.

"How you doing?"

The owner turns, smiles, and shakes Rafaele's hand. His eyes are red.

"Not so good, I'm sorry to say. All this terrible daily news about deportations, and now I have bad family news. The doctor diagnosed my wife with cancer. They'll operate on her soon. This is the second time in our family. My first wife died of cancer. What can I do? Just go on. It's life, right?"

Rafaele takes his arm.

"I'm sorry. You must be strong."

"I have no choice. But now we have to worry about the deportations. When does it end?"

KILL IMMIGRANTS

"Three cheers for our local police and the bulldozers!"

The small crowd of respectable, well-groomed suburban citizens, young and old, raise their wine glasses and shout, "Hear hear!"

The white-haired old man in the green windbreaker smiles at his friends and neighbours as he speaks into the megaphone. It's an outdoor picnic in a small park in Rome's *Centocelle* district to celebrate the bulldozing of a nearby Romani refugee camp.

"The hunting season in Italy has officially begun," he announces, "and not just of the Gypsies. All those non-Italians. We don't want them. We will never accept them. And we will not tolerate them."

The crowd cheers again. A young man yells out,

"We're with you, Mr. Minister!"

The old man continues.

"There is now a bull's eye on all their backs. We heard the prime minister himself say this. So what are we waiting for?"

"Hear hear!" the crowd cheers again. The old man smiles broadly, showing his tiny pearl-white teeth. A TV reporter makes a beeline for him.

"Mr. Minister, a few words for the TV audience please?"

The cabinet minister speaks directly to the camera.

"If those good-for-nothing immigrants—Gypsies, Romanians, blacks, browns, yellows—whoever—don't get the hint that it's time to leave, then all patriotic Italians should use their fists to make it clear. Got that?" He winks.

THE BANGLADESHI

"The guy went berserk. No reason. One minute he's leaning against a wall outside the café reading a newspaper. Next minute he's screaming."

"Goddamn darkies! Fucking immigrants! Get outta my country! We don't want you! Go home, you brown scum!"

Two middle-aged neighbours, in T-shirts and shorts, are talking to each other on adjacent balconies. It's a scorching summer afternoon. The heavier man sits in a chair, legs splayed, fanning himself. The skinny one leans on the railing and points to the street below.

"The guy crosses the street still yelling. We're watching him. What's he gonna do? He walks up to the Bangladeshi shop and—*Wham!*—kicks in the window! The owner runs out and this big guy—I've seen him before—kicks the owner's leg. The owner screams in pain. The big guy shoves him aside, walks into the shop and starts yanking down the shelving. *Crash! Bang! Boom!*

"The owner's wife is screaming on the sidewalk, holding their baby who's also bawling. The owner—he's a little guy— tries to drag the big guy out of his shop. We see it all through the window. The big guy comes barrelling out holding a chair, and heaves it through the broken window from the outside. The whole thing comes crashing down.

"We're standing on the sidewalk watching, but the big guy just keeps going. He walks to the next Bangladeshi shop and again—*crash!*—kicks in that window. Then he runs off. Smashed the windows of three other Bangladeshi stores around the corner, too."

The horse-faced neighbour keeps fanning himself and frowns.

"Later, he walks into the cop shop and tells the guys—I

heard this from my brother-in-law who works there—he tells the police that he's the one! He did it! He admits this and says he's not sorry for it either. He tells them they can jail him or whatever, but that he would do it again because he can't stand the darkies in our neighbourhood and wants them out. Says he's not sorry. He just wants to clean up the city before they take over. The cops let him go because no one has pressed charges yet."

THE CHINESE GUY

The retired teacher was speaking to his son on the phone.

"He was just a wisp of a boy about nineteen years old wearing a jean jacket. Could have been a student, I don't know. I was on my balcony smoking. I saw the whole thing.

"The Chinese kid was carrying a bag of groceries in one hand, walking down the sidewalk minding his own business. He stepped into the street to walk around this group of six young toughs. They're standing on the corner. Suddenly, one of the guys pushed the Chinese boy from behind. The boy goes flying, tomatoes rolling out of his bag into the street. He gets up and yells at the others—in Italian: *'Why did you do that? I didn't do anything to you!'* Then the young toughs start screaming, *'Go back to China, slant eyes! Get out of here!'* It was horrible. I never thought I would hear this in Rome, in my own neighbourhood. I yelled out: *'Assholes! Leave him alone! I'm calling the cops!'* I wanted to throw something at them. One of the kids—I've never seen any of them before—yells up at me: *'Fuck you, you old geezer! Want us to fix you, too?'*

"I called the cops. The Chinese boy was trying to back away, but they surrounded him. He tried to break through and one of the guys slugged him in the face. He spun around and another guy punched him in the head. Then they all jumped him, arms flailing. He was screaming but he didn't have a chance. I'm on the phone, telling the cops this as it's happening.

"They knocked him to the ground and kicked him in the back, the head, everywhere. By now, this Chinese kid is lying face down, crumpled like a rag doll, motionless. It happened so fast. The guys took off running and laughing. I'm thinking: They've killed him! Where are the cops?"

IMMIGRANT RIGHTS?

Antonio remembers that his cousin spoke of a huge demonstration in Rome not long ago.

"It was mega, man! Two hundred thousand people marching through the streets. From *Piazza Esedra* to *Piazza Navona*. Blocked the whole downtown protesting a new anti-immigrant, anti-labour law. There were hundreds of groups: anarchist, trade unionists, and tons of immigrants from everywhere. People carried banners reading: *'No Borders—No States—No Nations—No one is illegal.'*"

Antonio calls Rafaele.

"Remember that big antiracist demo? With all those immigrant rights groups? How do I contact them?"

SUNBURNT ORANGE

A massive fireball of sunburnt orange is dropping into the horizon, its descent cushioned by the hot purple haze smothering the city.

From the balcony of his friend's apartment off *Viale Leondardo da Vinci*, in Ostiense, Antonio scans the flat rooftops before him, empty except for a million grey stalks of TV antennas poking the sky, bent every which way, searching for a signal. He keeps searching, too.

An ambulance races below, its siren droning an almost polite honk-honk-ha-excuse-me-as-I-pass-you-by singsong salute. Two city buses spew out spent workers hurrying home to enjoy the few hours of their own truncated lives before sleep overtakes them and leads them to another day on the job away from themselves.

Antonio closes the door and returns to the cool darkness of the kitchen. He sits hunched over on the edge of a chair, chin in hand, elbow on knee.

Rome, my Rome! Where are you going and where are you taking me this sultry day?

He is tired. Tired of everything he can think about. The needle-pricks of ever-present despair remind him of a painful and deep sadness.

Is it too much to ask, to be happy? To savour what was once easier to find? Where does that joy go when it leaves you? How to retrieve it, bring it back?

He looks at the scuff marks on the wall in front of him, the faded posters of punk rock shows, someone's memories in black and white photos, and feels the beat of his heart in his stomach, carving out a hollowness.

He stands and gazes out the window at rooftops, the skyline, the bridge, train tracks to everywhere else, the odd balcony green and alive with tomato plants, palms, or cactus. A lone crow struts on a ledge, looking for something as well. Back and forth, left and right, it criss-crosses the hot roof, finding nothing. It hops into flight, wings flapping.

Day and night, back and forth, searching for a way to make things work with Cinka. It keeps him awake, distracts him, interferes with his daily rhythms. He notices a bronzed fat man in an obscenely tiny blue Speedo stepping out onto a balcony to lie face down on a cot in the burning sun.

Rome, my Rome.

NEO-NAZIS MARCH IN ROME

Antonio is on the phone.

"Turn on your TV news, Rafaele. Neo-Nazis are marching today. We're counterdemonstrating. I'm here with Cinka."

Cazzo! Rafaele watches the live broadcast. The camera pans over a huge demo of neo-Nazis of all ages assembling in the *Piazza della Repubblica*, chanting racist slogans. Easily a thousand marchers wearing Nazi paraphernalia. The reporter says:

> Today's march serves a dual purpose according to spokesmen. It will celebrate the Nazi campaigns from the past, and denounce what organizers are calling the new Jews of Italy: immigrant Romanians and Roma . . .

Assholes! Rafaele thinks. A hateful, brazen march on this cold, grey, November day—the anniversary of *Kristallnacht*— the "Night of Broken Glass." In 1938, Nazis ran wild through Germany's Jewish areas, ransacking homes and shops. When will they stop?

> We estimate the counterdemonstration a few streets away to be several thousand strong . . .

The camera shows an even larger gathering.
"Yes!" Rafaele punches his fist into the air.

> We can hear the anti-Fascists chanting their angry slogans as they prepare to march toward the neo-Nazis. As you can hear, they're getting louder and louder. Here we have a group of Italians, Jews, Muslims, and immigrants, including, as you can see, a sizeable contingent of Roma marching under their flag. There will definitely be a confrontation at some point. Now to our helicopter coverage from the sky . . .

The aerial view: Rome's riot police on foot and horseback amassing at a midway point between the two demonstrations, blocking off streets. The huge anti-Fascist march is moving. The neo-Nazis stay put.

The police, either nervous, pumped for a fight, or blasé, stand by watching, awaiting orders. Police spotters move across rooftops with cameras. Backup officers by the hundreds sit hunched over in police vans parked off the main routes. As the anti-Fascist marchers turn a corner on *Via Nazionale*, a huge splinter group of about three thousand masked anarchists and anti-Fascists breaks off and runs, charging and yelling toward the assembled neo-Nazis a few streets away.

A police line armed with water cannons forms to block the surprise manoeuvre. But the wave of determined anti-Fascists splits again and detours around the police line. Within minutes, the anti-Fascists reach their target.

The neo-Nazis, uncertain about how to respond, huddle

together. A hail of bottles and rocks flies over the heads of police and connects with neo-Nazi skulls. Dozens of neo-Nazis clutching their wounds retreat. Others seek refuge inside doorways.

The anarchists push through the first police line, past the water cannon and cops on horseback, overturning street barriers in their way. Within seconds they engage individual Nazis in hand-to-hand combat. The clash is bloody and quick. A blur of boots, fists, brass knuckles, metal rods and flag poles.

The overpowered, outnumbered neo-Nazis flee. The anti-Fascists cheer and disperse before police reinforcements arrive. The final tally: several dozen bashed and bleeding neo-Nazis writhing on the ground. Police and anti-Fascists both suffered injuries. Hundreds of anti-Fascists were arrested. But the neo-Nazi march was aborted.

The phone rings again. It's Antonio.

"We beat them, man, we beat them! Did you see?"

CARLO GIULIANI FROM GENOA

Ciao! I'm Carlo Giuliani, twenty-three years old, from Genoa. Excuse me. Must finish brushing my teeth. Shit. Damn phone always rings at the worst time. Excuse me again.

"Pronto!"

. . .

"No, Mom, I told you already. I thought I might go to the beach today instead of that G8 demonstration. It's so hot out and we had a great time there yesterday."

. . .

"Yes, I know there are like twenty thousand cops out there. It's a ring of steel around downtown. Besides, I did so much work helping paint the banners the last few weeks, I thought I could slack off for a day. Not like they're going to miss me. There are a hundred thousand other protesters around. OK. See you and Dad for dinner later. Love you too. *Ciao.*"

As I was saying. I'm a student, I write a lot of poetry, I work in the North East Genoa Social Centre. I'm an anarchist and my friends and I have a band called the Beast Punks. We promote the whole DIY punk rock attitude and do a lot of political actions together. Demos, helping with strikes, putting up posters, spray-painting—that kind of thing.

I've been living in this squat for a year now. My dad and mom are political, too, so they understand, even if they don't totally like where I live. But I go home often for supper and to do my laundry, so I guess it's OK. Excuse me, sorry.

"Pronto!"

. . .

"Hey, honey! How are you?"

. . .

"Uh, no, I wasn't planning on going to the demo."

. . .

"You want to go? Um . . . wouldn't you rather go to the beach? It's so beautiful today."

. . .

"No? OK. Let's not stay long and maybe later we can slip away to the beach. Meet you downstairs in ten minutes."

CARLO'S GIRLFRIEND, GINA

I'm Gina, Carlo's girlfriend. I'm a student. I'm twenty-two years old, I have red hair, a few tattoos, and a nose piercing.

It was my fault, I swear. I brought him to the demonstration. We could have gone to the beach like he wanted to, but no, stupid me.

One moment, it's a huge, festive, multicoloured sea of people. It's a clear blue sky in the bright sun. There are giant puppets, banners, flags, costumes, drums, chanting, and singing. Everyone's in a good mood. A huge helicopter then appears and hovers over us.

We chant, *"Bastardi! Genova, Libera!"*

Then all hell breaks. Tear gas canisters fall from the sky. People are screaming trying to get away. Many of us had no masks and no protection. Canisters explode all around us. The *carabinieri* on the ground fire more tear gas. People lob the canisters back. The cops start beating demonstrators. Carlo and I run away, but we get separated.

"Carlo! Carlo!"

I'm calling his name but I can't see him through the tear gas. Then I hear him.

"Gina! Gina! Where are you?"

I still can't see him. I'm coughing and choking, my eyes are burning. Someone grabs my hand and leads me away. I keep running but I can't really see. I lose sight of our friends, too.

Then the counterattack. People grab wood, pipes, and materials from a construction site and start fighting with the police.

I'm looking for Carlo in the crowd. The police are running away. In a small square, people surround one Land Rover full of *carabinieri* and attack the vehicle with sticks and rocks. The Land Rover lurches forward and smashes an overturned garbage bin. People are screaming. It's totally crazy.

A row of riot police stands and watches not thirty metres away. I'm thinking we'll be outnumbered in moments and beaten. A huge red fire extinguisher pops out of the rear window of the jeep.

Then I see Carlo. I yell. He doesn't seem to hear me. I see him bend to pick up the extinguisher. It looks like it weighs a ton, and he struggles to lift it up. He's holding it in front of him—about three metres behind the Land Rover. People are running past me. I scream his name again. He turns to look. Then I see one of the *carabinieri* inside the back of the Land Rover. He wears a black ski mask and points his pistol through the open window right at Carlo. I scream:

"Carlo! Drop it! Run!"

He drops it and turns to run. Too late. I hear gunfire. Carlo falls to the ground. The police Land Rover immediately backs up over him, then drives forward over him again.

Photos of Carlo lying in a pool of blood travel online around the world and onto front pages of newspapers.

Weeks later, on the beach, I throw some of his ashes into the beautiful blue sea.

CARLO'S MOTHER, YEARS LATER

I'm Carlo's mother. I'm now a senator in the Italian government. My husband is a trade union organizer.

It's been years since the police murdered our son. Medics on the scene said during the trial that his heart was still beating when the police drove over him. The trial settled nothing. The officer who killed Carlo was never found guilty or punished.

Since then, our son's friends in Genoa hold annual commemorative marches to mark the anniversary of his assassination, and the brutal attacks on demonstrators during the 2001 anti-G8 days of action. About fifty thousand people march each year.

Some Italian and foreign punk bands and poets have written songs and poems about Carlo. Filmmakers made documentaries. Plazas all over Italy were renamed after him. There are even websites in his name.

Someone screwed a little brass plaque on a wall near the spot where he died. It reads: *"I was born in this square. Today, someone was killed here."*

I think about Carlo every day. My husband and I miss him incredibly. We often wonder, knowing the kind of boy he was, would he be just a little bit embarrassed by all the attention? Would he say something, like,

"Mom, Dad, I'm one white European boy who died. Look at all the nameless, unmarked nonwhite dead across Asia, Latin America, Africa, and the Middle East. They also died fighting neoliberalism and globalization. No marches, no websites, no songs, no films, no plaques for them."

The *carabiniere* who shot our son had all the charges dropped. The judge said the bullet that killed him was aimed at someone else and that it was *"deflected toward Carlo by a rock in midair."*

In a later trial involving other demonstrators in Genoa, a forensic doctor testified that Carlo was the victim of *"a direct hit."* The press challenged the earlier judge's decision. They also challenged his decision not to charge the police driver of the Land Rover who ran him over twice, saying that he was already dead when they drove over his body.

To add to the confusion, two years after our son's death, the cop who shot Carlo said he was being used to cover up the responsibility of others, claiming that the bullet they found in him was not a standard *carabinieri* bullet, and that the shot came from elsewhere. They're still investigating.

Later, other police admitted to fabricating evidence against antiglobalization activists. One officer said he faked a stabbing of a cop to help frame protestors. Other officers admitted they were trying to justify their brutality against protestors, so they planted Molotov cocktails in a school where Genoa Social Forum activists had been sleeping.

The Molotovs were used to justify a brutal raid on the school where they beat sleeping activists in their beds. The walls and floors of the school were splattered with blood.

They arrested ninety-three people that night, seventy with injuries. Twelve were carried out on stretchers. All were later released with no charges. Almost a hundred police officers were investigated on brutality charges. None were ever found guilty or punished. But they call protestors like our son "violent."

PART IX

DIFFERENCE BETWEEN

NOT ALL ITALIANS THINK LIKE THAT

As dusk overtakes the *Piazza di Spagna*, tens of thousands of starlings perform their acrobatic aerial dance.

Below them, a played-out Cinka, the lone violinist busking near the Spanish Steps, bows the final notes to her last song, a fast and furious Romanian folk dance. The impromptu audience claps in time. As she leans forward on her toes for the grand finale, flashing a show-woman's smile, she bounces her bow off the strings and sweeps it into the air for a dramatic end flourish. Then she bows gracefully, tossing her long mane of hair.

People roar and applaud. Cameras click. Coins and bills drop into her open violin case.

"Thank you, thank you." She acknowledges each fan with a smile.

"Please, a shot with my husband!" An American matron's oversized husband edges close to Cinka.

"Folks back home won't believe we heard a real live Gypsy! So talented, too!"

Cinka accepts the extra tip graciously. As she packs her instrument, she senses someone behind her.

"You blow me away each time." A crouching Antonio offers a huge grin and kisses her.

"Oh, I was a little distracted today. I didn't play my best. You've seen me better."

"You're always at your best. Always on fire. You make it

look so easy. You're the hottest violinist around! People love you! And so do I!" He kisses her again.

"It's my job. I try. How are you?"

"Now that I'm here with you, great! And you?"

She slumps to the ground.

"If I could, I'd buy my family a one-way ticket to Germany or Spain right now—anywhere to get us away from here."

Antonio frowns.

"Darling, it's got nothing to do with you. Please understand." Cinka places her arm around his shoulder.

"Look what's happening. Did you see today's headlines? How can we live here in peace? In fear constantly? Always worrying about who might attack us, when, where. It could happen anytime."

"Cinka . . ." He pulls her closer. "It's just fucked-up hysteria. It'll pass. Believe me. The stupid media is trying to sell more papers, sensationalizing stuff. It'll go away. You'll be OK. Trust me."

"Easy for you to say. You're Italian. What's here for my people? There's no work. Unless you want to clean houses. Or be an under-the-table, underpaid *muratore* construction worker. They pay nothing. And social benefits? Forget it. This poverty is crushing my people. Then the government blames us for the increase in crime? As if all Italians are angels? And the Mafia doesn't exist? *Cazzo!*"

"But Cinka . . ."

"No one cares if Roma are beaten or killed, or if the government passes special laws to get rid of us, or . . ."

Antonio throws his arms around her and pulls her close to kiss her. She pushes him away.

"Cinka, please. Not all Italians think like that. It's just a small group of right-wing assholes in the government."

"A small group? They talk about deporting foreigners who commit crimes. About deporting all of my people!"

"Cinka, I'll help you and your people. Others will, too. We'll make sure nothing happens to you. I promise." He embraces her again.

"Last night the police came to a camp near ours. They arrested people without permits."

"What? I didn't hear. It wasn't on the news."

"I was visiting. I saw it. People were screaming at them to leave. Children were crying. Everyone had to answer to the police. It was terrifying. This is what they did to Jews in the ghettos. It's how the U.S. treats people in the Middle East. How Israel treats Palestinians. Antonio, it's a war against my people."

He holds her tightly, looks away, and tries not to swear.

ANTONIO SCRIBBLES ON A NAPKIN

Alarm clocks ring, showers run, kids protest about going to school, while dogs whimper and scratch at doors, desperate to go out for a pee. It's a typical Roman workday morning.

Everyone chugs instant liquid breakfasts except those running too late, like Antonio. He grabs an espresso in the bar beneath his apartment and is about to run out the door when the glaring headline stops him. He snatches the newspaper from the countertop.

> Government vows to return 5,000 Romanians to their home country in next few weeks. The commissioner for Justice, Freedom and Security, said: "What has to be done is simple. Go into a nomad camp in Rome for example, and ask them: Can you tell me where you live? If they say they do not know, take them and send them home to Romania. It is simple and safe. Romania cannot say they will not take them back, because it is an obligation that is part of being a member state of the European Union. We should also pull down the camps to prevent any Romanians from returning."

He shouts, "What the fuck!" and asks the barman, "Can I borrow a pen please?"

He scribbles on a napkin:

> Sticker/poster/graffiti ideas. Roma. Italy's largest immigrant community. 500,000. Deport an entire ethnic

289

group? Stupid. Illegal. Deport all Americans? All British? Human rights laws. Respect Roma. Screw Fascists. Bulldoze Fascist bars. Just because someone shoplifts once, it doesn't make them a bad citizen. Deport all corrupt politicians. Fuck politicians. Deportation. Circle it. Draw line through it. Jews 1930s. Roma today. Who tomorrow? Small posters. Graffiti. Everywhere.

He returns the pen and races back up the stairs to his computer. To hell with the job, he thinks. Who cares if I'm late. He starts writing:

Roma are not the problem. The problem is bigger. Two-thirds of Italy's sentenced criminals are Romanians. Why? Are they more criminal than anyone else? No.

No more, no less than us Italians. When people emigrate, it's because there is a problem in their home country. They emigrate and look for better opportunities to live. Here we give them no chances, no opportunities. No basic needs are met. Nothing is done to welcome them and help them be part of Italian society. We let them in our house, but shut all the other doors. We prevent them from using the kitchen, the bathroom, the bedroom, the living room. Where can they go? What can they do? We screw them . . .

He dashes down the stairs, runs after the bus that is pulling away and pounds on the door until it opens.

ON A *PIGNETO* BENCH WITH CINKA

Under the spotlight of a blinding fluorescent yellow lunchtime sun, all of Rome wilts.

Antonio waits on a shaded bench in a tiny square off *Via Pigneto*, scanning the street for Cinka. With the noticeable increase in random attacks against the Roma, he worries about her constantly, but has no solutions.

She can't move in with me. Impossible. I can't follow her around to protect her.

A heavily perspiring woman carrying one purse-puppy under her arm, drags another on a leash behind, admonishing it, "Hurry or mommy won't feed you."

On a balcony, billowing pink curtains make a desperate escape attempt out two open windows. Opposite, on a low concrete wall, someone has spray-painted in bright red, "*La Storia Continua.*" A bumblebee black-and-yellow scooter shrieks by.

A quick-stepping Cinka rounds the corner dressed in a green skirt, her hair falling loosely around her white blouse. Antonio's heartbeat soars. She's an angel in full flight.

His legs wobble and turn into jello as he leaps up to embrace and kiss her long and hard. He's powerless to move. No explanation.

They drop to the bench, arms entwined around each other, unable to pull away from yet another passionate lip lock.

"I brought us lunch."

A breathless Antonio turns to show her the bag, but Cinka grabs his head in both hands and starts another interminable kiss that leaves them both love-struck and gasping.

Antonio has a momentarily silly, happy, slack-jawed look on his face, then remembers,

"Here!"

He hands her a fresh panini, a bottle of juice, and some napkins.

"You're so sweet! Thank you! You always think of me." Cinka kisses him on the cheek, then turns his face toward her and studies it.

"But Antonio, what's wrong?"

"Nothing . . . nothing's wrong."

"Come on. You're so easy to read. You can't hide it."

Antonio lets out a long sigh, and with one free arm tightens his grip around her shoulder. She snuggles closer into him.

"I don't know, Cinka. I'm angry. Fed up. Angry with this Fascist government, the imbeciles in power, the whole rotten system."

Cinka devours her sandwich as she listens, never taking her eyes off his.

"If I could, I'd walk in there and say, 'You're fired! All of you! Fuck off and don't ever come back!'"

Cinka laughs.

"If only it was that easy, my red-headed hero." She ruffles his hair. "Then you and Spartacus and your legions of freed gladiator slaves would chop off their heads, right?"

"Of course. But seriously. They have no right to treat you and other immigrants like this. It's a disgrace. I never thought I'd ever say this, but I'm ashamed to be an Italian. We let this happen. And people applaud and support them and believe all the bullshit lies."

Cinka shifts on the bench to face Antonio, both hands cupping his cheeks.

"But you're different. You don't believe the lies. And I know you're not alone. I've met your friends at the demonstrations. You speak out. You're setting an example. You're the 'other' Italy—the one I still care for. The one I still hope for. The one my people pray for."

She runs her hands through his hair, then leans her head on his shoulder. A young couple walk by. The man pushes a baby stroller.

"So what do your parents think?" she asks lazily as she gently massages Antonio's neck.

"About what?"

"You know, about us."

"What can they say?"

"I don't know. Are they happy for you? What do they say?"

"Uh, well, I haven't really told them yet."

"What? Why not?" Cinka sits upright.

"Because they wouldn't really be interested."

"Not interested about their son's new girlfriend who is a Romni refugee carrying his baby?" Her eyes flash.

"Not really."

"Why not?"

"Uh . . . because it's not a big deal."

"But you told me before that you're close to your parents. You said that. Why wouldn't they care?"

Antonio stands up, shoves his hands in his pockets, and shuffles a few feet away. He turns to face her.

"Because . . . to tell you the truth . . . they don't need to know yet."

"What do you mean 'not yet'? Why not?"

Now she's royally pissed, Antonio thinks. *I've fucked up.*

"I don't understand," Cinka digs in. "We spend all this time together and your parents still don't know? And now we're going through a difficult period, and we both love each other, but it's complicated, and there is a baby, and . . ."

Antonio crouches and places his finger on her lips whispering, "Shh. Look, if I told you, you wouldn't understand. They wouldn't understand. It's not a big deal."

Cinka knocks his finger away.

"Not a big deal? I'm not important to you? Is that what I won't understand?"

"No, honey, of course you are. You mean the world to me."

Antonio places his hands on her shoulders but Cinka pushes them off and stands up, arms folded, scowling at him.

"But not enough for you to tell your parents about? This is what it means? You can't tell them you will soon be a father?"

"It's not easy to tell my parents." Antonio drops his head and turns away.

"Why?"

"Because they're . . . they're . . . they're a bit racist."

"What? That's all? That's it? Look at me Antonio."

He knows the damage has already been done.

"It's enough, Cinka. I don't know what to say. I can't change them, make them see things differently. They . . . just don't understand."

"Antonio, it's not the first time. If you think it's better this way, I can accept this. Why didn't you say so earlier?"

"Because . . . I'm embarrassed? And I didn't want to upset you?"

"Antonio. I'm sure they're loving parents who raised you well and helped you become the man I love. If they can't accept me in the family, well . . . I will live with this. It's not that important. Maybe they'll change later. I don't need to be close to them."

Cinka turns away. Antonio feels a sharp pain in his stomach.

CINKA REFLECTS BESIDE THE FOUNTAIN

Postsunrise *Piazza di Spagna* finds itself hosting hungry pigeons, last night's leftover snoring drunks, and city workers patiently removing garbage.

Two men are already on their knees, tools in hand, repairing cracks in the sweeping Rococo stone stairway that leads to the square. A local artist once placed hundreds of thousands of brightly coloured plastic balls on these steps to protest the living conditions of artists in Italy. Politicians talked briefly about it, but nothing changed.

As Cinka hums a song and descends the two-hundred-year-old Spanish Steps—the widest in Europe, they say—a flower merchant sets out her wares under an umbrella on the landing in one corner; a fruit man in the other. Today, huge pots of dazzling pink azaleas adorn the staircase. Cinka stops every few metres to smell the blossoms.

The sun reflects off the ever-beautiful *Baraccia* fountain at the bottom of the stairs, turning its water into a giant mesmerizing aqua-blue jewel. It's one of Cinka's favourite spots to play.

At the fountain, she sits to listen to its soothing water, wishing she could shower. It's been so long. She usually bathes by hand wherever she can, including the washroom in Antonio's music studio. At least it's private, with a clean towel and soap that Antonio always provides.

My sweet Antonio, what would I do without you, she wonders. You're my lover, my friend, my fierce gladiator boy. You're my guardian angel, my lucky break, my red-headed Italian saviour knight in torn jeans. My boat anchored in calm water.

So what if your parents are racist? I don't need to meet them or have anything to do with them. I don't want more racists in my life anyway. There are too many already.

She studies the centrepiece of the fountain, a half-sunken stone ship in front of her. It overflows with water. Her stomach gurgles. She didn't eat last night, nor this morning and now feels light-headed. She'll have to wait until she earns enough money.

Antonio, she thinks, you're forever helping me, and I love you and appreciate everything you do for me. You give me food, money, support, and love. You have no idea what this means to my family and me. You make a difference.

You give me hope, respect, trust, peace. Everything I could ever ask for. But at the same time, you don't understand. You can't. You're a *gadjo.* This is the truth. Some things you will never understand.

Like right now. You have no idea how dangerous it is. My own people could turn on me simply for being with you and carrying your—our—baby. Worse, my family could be deported. We could be burned out of our home. Beaten. And you won't be there to protect us.

When I'm with you I know I'm safe. There are moments I can even forget everything else. Without you, I'm sometimes confused and don't know what I'm doing here.

As she starts to tune her violin, a police car pulls up. *Cazzo!* She freezes.

An officer walks toward her, shouting:

"Hey, Gypsy girl! You can't play here! Pack up and get lost!"

WE ROMA ARE A PATIENT PEOPLE

The shadow of a giant clay planter at the top of the Spanish Steps is hospitable enough to help hide Cinka. She squats on her haunches, and waits. Her blood is boiling. This is the third time in two days she had been ordered away from a popular busking site. She needs to start playing soon so that she can eat. She's feeling weaker.

As she watches Italians on their way to work, going about their business unchallenged by any authority, she recalls a campfire conversation in the refugee camp two nights ago.

A kind, soft-spoken, grey-bearded Romani elder, a former teacher, always with a smile for her and her family, overheard Cinka describing the increased police harassment. He told her:

"Remember, we Roma are a patient people. Do we have a choice? One hundred and fifty years ago we were slaves in Romania. Just like the blacks in America and in Canada. They were freed and so were we. That was in 1865. People who are black now have a better life over there—or so we hear. We do not know this.

"But we see black movie stars, singers, the rich ones treated like royalty on TV. Unthinkable for us. Here in Italy, like Romania, Hungary, Slovakia, the Balkans, the Czech Republic—for us Roma, it is different.

"We are no longer shackled like cattle. No longer kept under lock and key. We are free, yes? But now we live with indignity piled on top of indignity. Insults, beatings, refusals of entry, arrests, forced evictions, death threats. We have to beg for work or food. This is our daily life. This we know.

"But we Roma are a patient people. We wait. For the clouds to lift. For the 'civilized' people to return to their senses. For the hateful language to stop. For our children to be able to go to school without fear of violence. For the sun to shine and the gardens to grow. For the new day of peace and freedom, and a better life to come.

"Is this too much to ask? No, because we Roma are a patient people. Like the sun, we can wait all day for the stars to take our place. Like the moon, we can wait all night for the signal: it is time. Time to go and let the others take our place. To wait."

"But I'm tired. Tired of waiting," Cinka had said.

AGAIN, THE ROMA SLEEP OUTSIDE

Just like the stars winking above leave more questions and prayers unanswered night after night, Romani refugee families again sleep outside Rome's Tiburtina train station—on cardboard—on the sidewalk.

The lucky ones sleep under a bit of plastic. All try to keep out of view as much as possible. They have nowhere else to sleep. But this time, it is different.

Yesterday, a group of Italians brought fifty warm blankets for them. They awaken under them, warmer but still homeless, rub their eyes, stretch, and wonder.

Another day and they are still alive? Another day they must survive? Another day to pass before they can lie down again to rest. They look up. The same sun beats down on the skin of Roma and Romans alike. The same fluorescent moon shines for Roma and Romans. Perhaps today will be different.

Then the police arrive. They step out of their cars and smack their clubs into their plastic-gloved hands as they walk toward the Roma. The children aren't yet awake.

The police bark: "Give us those blankets! All of them! You don't need them! These are stolen blankets!"

They yank the blankets from still sleeping children and stuff them into garbage bags. The children scream and cry. Parents try to console them.

"Please! Don't take the blankets. Have mercy! The children! The nights are cold. What will we sleep on?"

"Sleep on cardboard!"

Every blanket now confiscated, the police roar off. It's 6 AM under a bright, glorious sun, the uncaring sun that shines on Roma and Roman alike.

THE MARCHING BAND DOCTOR

At one of the growing number of antiracist demonstrations they attend together, Cinka and Antonio fall in behind a radical marching band called TopoBando.

About twenty musicians—brass, percussion, woodwinds, and accordions—create an enormous wall of joyful, infectious sound that drives even the most dour protestors to move their hips and dance.

One of the four accordionists is Sylvia, a tall, robust woman in shocking pink leggings. Once a communist, now an anarchist, she works as a doctor in the emergency room of one of Rome's biggest hospitals.

"It's getting crazier and crazier," she tells Cinka and Antonio, resting between raucous songs. "At the hospital, I mean."

"Almost every day we treat people who have been assaulted by Fascists, cops or vigilantes in the street. Broken arms, hands, legs, burnings, stab wounds, head wounds, concussions, young people and old. All are immigrants, visible minorities. All are afraid to press charges, afraid of reporting the attacks to the police. Who can blame them? If the police assault you, who do you complain to?

"So many of your people are beaten while lying on their cardboard beds in the street. Attacked and kicked while just standing on a street corner. Soon, all the doctors will hold a press conference to denounce the assaults. We must speak out."

"I'll help you," Cinka offers. "People in my camp will support you."

"Me, too," says Antonio.

CINKA SPEAKS OUT ON TV

The antiracist demonstration in Rome's *Piazza dei Santissimi Apostoli* is several thousand strong and loud. People are incensed.

Another round of brutal refugee camp evictions across the country made the news. So did more beatings, more fire-bombings and more inflammatory public pronouncements from high government officials. Intolerance is the new order.

Cinka is pissed and vocal. She stands above the crowd on a street barricade outside a children's bookstore, one arm hooked around a street sign, the other sweeping the air. Antonio secures her from below.

TV journalists zero in on the agitated but highly photogenic and articulate young Romni speaking her mind. Reporters thrust microphones up at her. Cameras click. Pens fly.

"These racist politicians say we Roma are the problem. They blame us for everything, from bad food to the weather. But they are the real problem! They're like a virus. They will grow into a cancer and poison Italy from within. They will kill everything about Italy that is beautiful."

A journalist interrupts.

"Politicians say we must clear out your refugee camps and that will clean up our cities."

"Really? Clear out these lying, fear-mongering politicians. That will clean up the cities. Otherwise they will die a slow death as Italians fight Italians and fear everyone who is not born here."

"But your people steal children! Is this not a fact?" the journalist continues.

"That's a folk tale, not a fact!" Cinka glares at the TV reporter with the coiffed hair, stiletto heels, and designer sunglasses.

"But your people steal from tourists on the street!" another reporter yells.

"My people? What about your people who charge higher prices to tourists for everything? Is that not stealing too, but better organized? And permitted? No one complains about that. Shopkeepers say they're trying to make a living. My people, too. But sometimes we have no choice. It's steal or starve, and watch our children starve. Because no one else will give us jobs or a place to live."

"So how can we integrate you if you don't respect our laws?"

"Integrate us? First accept us as people. As humans. With the same needs as you. Respect us. Allow us to have the same rights as you. Treat us equally. Stop treating us like rats you want to kill. We respect your laws. Your racist, lying politicians don't respect your own laws. Like that senator, Roberto Fancazzista. He promotes hatred. He divides people. He wants to eliminate us. This is criminal."

Antonio is beaming. *She's amazing! She's on fire again, telling the truth. She's so good with the media. I'm so proud of her. I love her. But she shouldn't have named that guy. Fuck.*

One reporter is already on his phone to the Northern Patriot Party senator.

TODAY'S RESTYLED FORMER FASCISTS

Unable to sleep after the excitement of today's demonstration, Antonio lies awake in bed. He can't rid himself of a frightening image: Cinka and her family in the hands of neo-Fascist thugs, struggling to get away.

Everyone knows her face now, he realizes. They saw her on TV. She'll be in the papers tomorrow. Cops and fucking Fascists will be looking for her.

The so-called "restyled" former Fascists. They give themselves a new look—wolves in designer sheep clothing. They're still Fascists, restyled or not.

How can people be so stupid to think otherwise? What makes them different? Teeth whitener? They have the same objectives. The same twisted reasoning as the old Fascists. They try to present themselves as something less odious, less harmful, less violent. Fucking liars. If anything, they're even more dangerous than before.

A FOREIGN STUDENT AND THE POLICE

The ever-late Antonio said to wait for him on these stairs on *Via le Lollis* beside *La Sapienza* University. Cinka sits patiently reading the giant posters plastered on every wall in sight.

She notices a tall, thin, well-dressed black man nearby, probably a student from the university, leaning against one wall reading a book. His satchel is at his feet. Out of nowhere two policemen walk up to him and in loud voices demand to see his papers. One straight-arms the student against the wall. Cinka watches nervously, her heart in overdrive.

"But these are only copies! Where are your original documents! Where is your passport?"

"I never carry my original documents with me. I might get robbed," the student answers.

"Today is your lucky day then. Come with us."

"But what did I do?"

"You don't have your original documents."

They each take an arm and drag him, protesting, into a police car.

LEGALIZED VIGILANTES

"It's obvious. We want to protect Italy from the influx of criminals. From rising crime. From the drug dealers and prostitutes.

"We've been patrolling our cities ourselves without government support this past year. So now we propose that they legitimize our citizen protection patrols: ordinary Italians standing up to the foreign rabble. Everyone is agreed? Good. I'll speak to the minister tomorrow. It should be no problem."

Senator Roberto Fancazzista, the silver-haired, high-ranking member of the Northern Patriot Party, shakes hands with his four colleagues gathered around the table in the five-star restaurant. He grabs his attaché case and steps outside into the cool night. His driver pulls up, jumps out, and holds the passenger door open.

The senator pauses at the top of the stairs, adjusts his tie, looks up and down the quiet street, and smiles to himself.

It's a good night for Italy, he concludes. *We're on the road to cleaning it up. Soon our patrols will work hand-in-hand with the police, and we will win. We must win. Which reminds me.* He pulls out his cell.

"Remember that young Gypsy woman agitator I told you about? The one with her mug in all the papers? I didn't like what she said. Take care of it, all right?"

A distraught yellow moon watches him.

Two days later at breakfast with Cinka in a café, Antonio reads her the news:

"Parliament considers legalizing vigilante groups to help crack down on lawless immigrants. Citizen patrols to receive backing of local police."

"Jesus!" he exclaims. "This is exactly how Mussolini's Blackshirts operated. They're turning back the clock. It's exactly what the Northern Patriot Party wants, a free hand to terrorize people."

Cinka snatches the paper from his hands.

"What? More beatings by more thugs loose in the streets. Don't the police already do enough damage?"

Antonio answers. "Those crackpots have been advocating this for years. No one took them seriously before. Now the economy is in bad shape. Everyone is afraid of losing their jobs. It's perfect timing for more law and order measures."

"Law and order?" Cinka hisses. "Vigilante law. Racist order."

"Sure. Target immigrants. Scapegoat and criminalize them. Then eliminate them and pretend they've solved the problem."

"This is sick! Sick!" Cinka shakes her head. "Like Hitler! Like Mussolini!" She waves the paper in the air. "Why do Italians fall for this? Why do they support this?"

"Because people are afraid. And fear makes people vulnerable, easier to manipulate. No one thinks of the consequences, no one says 'no.' There is no opposition to the government, no one speaking out."

"So? What are we waiting for? What are *you* waiting for? You're Italian. Stand up! Speak out!" Cinka bangs her hand on the table. Antonio winces.

"Sweetheart, if it was just that easy. What can I do? I'm one skinny little Italian."

"And these guys are big overfed Italian bullies. Why not fight back?"

"It's not that easy."

"You want to see me and my family driven out of Italy? You'd stand by and watch that happen?" Cinka's eyes narrow disapprovingly. Antonio frowns and squirms.

"No, sweetheart! I'll never let that happen. Never. I swear." He grabs her hand and kisses it. "But how can I or anyone else influence the government to change their mind?"

"You mean you can't think of another way?"

HEADING TO PONTICELLI

The German 1970s experimental rock group Can is blaring from the car stereo. Antonio grips the wheel of the little beat-up Panda doing his usual 140 kilometres per hour heading south on the *Autostrada del Sole*. His passengers, Cinka and Chira, hold their breath.

Approaching Naples, he notices: everyone takes out the

garbage but no one picks it up. Growing piles line the highway on the outskirts of the city, morphing into mini-mountains of putrid, rotting, rat-infested, twenty-first-century detritus—a testimony to waste culture and an unresolved labour dispute with collectors.

"Christ! This city is one big garbage dump," he shouts to Chira, a friend and native Napolitana sitting behind him.

"No one's happy about it," Chira yells over the music, "but no one does anything about it except add to the piles. It's out of control. Guess where the rich citizens of Naples take their garbage? They jump in their Alphas, BMWs, and SUVs and dump their crap here. In poor Ponticelli. Look at the mess!"

Ponticelli is one of the many poor and decaying suburbs of Naples where half the residents are so-called "illegals"—unregistered immigrant workers—and the other half are underemployed or unemployed Italians.

"Who can they complain to and who would ever listen?" Chira says.

They exit the highway, edging around one particularly prominent mountain of refuse.

Cinka directs Antonio to turn into a large refugee camp behind a wire fence. Her distant cousin lives here. Established long before the garbage dispute started, the camp is home to several hundred Roma living amid the stench of garbage that doesn't belong to them.

Within minutes, a tall, beautiful woman wearing a headscarf, a long brown skirt and a white sweater, with a baby boy in one arm, spots the three visitors wandering the camp. She cries out Cinka's name and waves to her.

"Welcome, welcome!" Surana, her much older distant cousin, embraces Cinka and smothers her with kisses.

Cinka, glowing, pulls away and pushes her friends forward.

"Surana, these are my friends from Rome."

"Welcome! Please, sit. Have some tea. I'm sorry we don't have much to offer."

With her free arm, Surana pulls two wooden boxes out from under a small rickety plastic table. She places cushions on them and offers them to Antonio and Chira. They sit outside Surana's home, a small wooden structure with a sheet metal roof.

"Don't worry. Look, I brought you something." Cinka hands Surana two bags full of food.

"You are too generous, Cinka, just like your father. May he rest in peace."

Antonio notices a little shrine on a table under a stretched blue tarp. Flowers surround a photo of a handsome young man. There is an empty Peroni bottle on a lace doily, a glass, and a violin.

"That was my husband," Surana says. "He was attacked one night coming home three months ago. We don't know who did it. They stabbed him. He died in the hospital."

"I'm very sorry," Antonio says.

Cinka embraces Surana.

"Mother told me to tell you that you and your baby are welcome to come live with us. Anytime. Please think about it, Surana. We can take you back with us today in the car."

"That's very kind of you," Surana says, wiping away tears with her sleeve. "Let me think about it. But what do you mean, you're returning to Rome today? You must stay the night! There is a wedding celebration. When the neighbours heard you were coming, they asked if you could play. You can use my husband's violin. Please stay. The neighbours have a bigger place, and there is room for you and your two friends."

"I have to get back to work early tomorrow, but here's some bus fare, and you can stay, OK?" Antonio hands Cinka some cash. She kisses him on the cheek.

"I have a place in Naples, thank you," said Chira.

"No, you come to the wedding too!" Surana insists. "There will be food and drink and lots of music and dancing. Please stay. Cinka, you *must* stay."

Cinka beams. "OK. I'll stay, I'll play, I'll dance, too! And we can talk."

A ROMANI WEDDING

The wedding is all-night, nonstop singing, dancing, playing, clapping, whistling, drinking, eating, cheering, laughing, embracing, and toasting.

Cinka plays for hours. Chira dances with Surana and dozens of guests. Out of sight, young Italian men with gelled black hair ride by on scooters, circling the camp at a distance, watching.

Waiting.

AFTER THE PARTY, THE ITALIANS

It's a steel grey Napoli morning. Already, it has amassed an army of menacing low-lying clouds awaiting orders to unleash their fury. A plane drones below them. Two dogs fight. An unusually cool wind whips up a few dust devils, chases them, then rips them apart.

Cinka rubs her eyes awake and stretches as she strolls through the *Ponticelli* refugee camp. She buttons her sweater against the chilly breeze. It looks like every other camp she has ever known in Italy: chaotic, but organized. Ramshackle housing built from scrap, but clean inside. Shoes left outside. The dusty grounds, generally littered, but around each shack, swept neat.

Rumour has it that when the rain pounds the sheet metal roofs here, you can hear it in the centre of Napoli.

Cinka's arm is slightly sore from playing at last night's joyous wedding—people kept requesting favourite songs. Now she needs a coffee.

The camp bustles with early risers heading off to work, or to look for work. Apart from the overpowering stench emanating from the piles of rotting garbage outside the fence, this camp resembles hers. It stands on the site of a former and probably still toxic dump. A busy, noisy highway runs nearby.

She sits on a plastic chair outside her hosts' hut and studies the faces. People nod her way. Wedding guests from last night shake her hand and compliment her on her playing. Children on their way to school glance at her shyly and giggle.

There had been no violinist in the camp since the death of her cousin's husband, so her presence was appreciated.

Last night, she thinks, we were dancing, drinking and singing together. For a few hours, everyone forgot their worries. Today, it's back to survival mode. Earn some money, scrounge enough food, feed the family.

Cinka and her cousin are heading back to the camp after a little walk when they run into a group of Romani women with children talking excitedly just outside the gate.

"It was terrible!" Two older women are almost hysterical, throwing their hands in the air and wailing.

"We were shopping in the supermarket. We didn't bother anyone."

"These Italian women surrounded us. They called us names and said we had no right to be there."

"That Roma weren't welcome. That we were dogs."

"That we should leave or they would beat us! Can you imagine?"

"There must have been ten of them or more. It was frightening. They pushed and shoved us toward the door."

"What did we do to deserve this? What were they thinking? Women, just like us, with children, too!"

At that moment, two young Roma drive up on their scooter, shouting: "They're coming for us! Leave right away! Everyone get out! Now!"

"What's going on?" Cinka yells.

"We were outside the supermarket. People ganged up on a Romanian guy."

"A big crowd."

"They beat him and stabbed him."

"They saw us, chased us, and threw bottles at us."

"They said they were coming to finish us off. We have to leave! Right now!"

"But where?" Cinka asks.

Her cousin points. "Oh no! Look! They're coming! We have to grab our stuff and run!"

Beyond the wire mesh fence is an ugly sight. A few hundred screaming Italians led by a group of women are heading for the camp. They brandish clubs, brooms, shovels. There are children among them.

"Out, out, filthy Gypsies! Get out!" they chant.

Cinka and her cousin join the fleeing mass of terrified women with babies in arms and kids in tow. There are hardly any men left in the camp. Women and children run for their lives.

The enraged mob attacks the flimsy wire mesh fence with their weapons. Hundreds of them yank it down. They pour into the camp, shouting insults and throwing rocks and bottles at the Romani shacks and trailers and at stragglers still gathering their belongings.

Roma and their children are screaming and running out of their huts in every direction. There is no escape from the wrath of the Italians. As they run, the mob keeps throwing rocks and bottles at them, yelling insults.

"Run, you dogs! Run back to where you came from and don't ever return!"

A group of young men overturn cars and vans and set them on fire. The crowd cheers. In an instant, one of the shacks is on fire, the flames roaring higher. Again the Italians cheer and clap, watching the hut go up in smoke.

A man with a crowbar smashes windows in a trailer, pours gasoline inside, and flicks a match into it.

Terrified mothers abandon their baby carriages, grab their infants, and run. The few men still in the camp try to protect their shacks as their wives scream at them to leave.

"You filthy scum, get out of here!" A huge Italian man wielding a metal club leads the attack on the men, clubbing one after another to the ground. Other Italians use their clubs to drive the Roma away. The Roma are heavily outnumbered.

Left and right, shacks are engulfed in flames as the crowd erupts into cheers again. The strong wind fans the flames and drives the black smoke higher into the already darkened sky.

One of the women who set a hut on fire screams, "This will teach you! Italy is for Italians, not for scum like you!"

The crowd roars its approval. Other women slap her on the back, congratulating her.

Another woman yells, "You didn't go when we asked you to leave nicely! Learn your lesson!"

A few fire trucks and a string of police cars, sirens wailing, now pour into the camp. Black smoke billows everywhere. As the firemen try to douse the flames, Italians scream abuse and pelt them with rocks and bottles.

"Get out of here, you jerks! We didn't call you! Let it burn, you fucking idiots! Leave it!"

An Italian man severs a fireman's hose with an axe. The hose dances wildly as other firemen try to grab it. The crowd laughs.

Among them are children—the same children who the next day in school will draw pictures of the burning huts and print under them, *"Out, Gypsies, out. They are bad people."*

A phalanx of police escort the last remaining Roma out of the camp while the crowd jeers.

"We won! We won! Get out and stay out! Don't ever come back!"

As more huts and cars burn and the sky above blackens with swirling heavy smoke, Cinka and her cousin watch from a hilltop.

That day, in two separate camps, the enraged mob burned down four hundred huts. More than four hundred families— a few thousand people—fled for their lives. Part of the mob came back that night and the next day to burn whatever was left standing. The next morning the Pope denounced the action. The Italian government was silent. So was the international media.

> They watched and they clapped
> While the flames shot higher . . . Ponticelli!
> They watched and they clapped

While the homes went up in smoke . . . Ponticelli!
They watched and they clapped
While the ground was scorched black . . .
The Beast of Intolerance
bared its teeth
that fed the fear
that lit the fires in Ponticelli
And the whole world—
said nothing

SOON THEY WILL COME FOR US

On the bus back to Rome, Cinka's brain keeps replaying the hellish images of her cousin's camp disappearing in flames while the ugly mob cheered. Many Roma were injured in the attack, some seriously.

That night they hid in empty buildings and heard stories from other survivors about roving gangs who had followed the fleeing Roma and beat them on roadways and in the bush. Camps across Napoli were firebombed. Everyone spoke of leaving. Cinka and Surana didn't sleep, fearing more attacks.

Two days later they returned to the camp to retrieve any possessions from Surana's home. All they found was a heap of charred wood.

"My husband built this," Surana wailed. "First they took him from me. Now they took my home."

Despite Cinka's plea to come to Rome, Surana decided to stay with her husband's relatives outside Napoli.

She's a single mother with a baby and her husband's violin, Cinka thinks. And me? At least I can return to Antonio and my family. Thank goodness my violin is safe in his music studio. But soon they'll come for us.

We can leave now, or stay in the camp. Antonio can't stay with us. He dreams of finding an apartment to keep us all together with the baby, but how will this work? He's not practical. And it's a *gadjo*'s dream. He has three roommates now, because that's the only way he can pay the rent. How can he afford something else? I can't earn much more. Can he find another job? He's still a student. And who will rent to a Romani family? Where is the fortune-teller when I need her? *Cazzo*.

THEY THOUGHT THEY COULD BE SAFE

A fine light drizzle veils the city as most of Rome sleeps peacefully. Workers sweep the streets. Alley cats couple under balconies. Rats nose through the garbage. A few drunks crawl into bed trying not to waken their partners. The moon bides its time, blocked momentarily from peeping into the cracks and windows of the darkened metropolis.

On the northern edge of Rome in the *Tor di Quinto* refugee camp, Cinka dozes with a smile on her face. She's enjoying one of the four new sleeping bags and foam pads that Antonio bought for her family. Unlike the old rugs, the bags and pads help ward off the damp and cold. But like the rest of her family, out of habit, she still wears her coat over her sweater as she sleeps.

Their makeshift home bends and billows with the wind. Not even a shack, it's a scrap wood, metal, and plastic lean-to somehow held together with rope.

About three metres long by two metres wide, it stands a metre and a half high. Neighbours helped build it. On evil-weather days, it threatens to blow away. There is no room for furniture.

Cinka's dreams are rudely interrupted. It's the ominous rumble of bulldozers. She bolts upright.

"Get up! Hurry!" She shakes her family awake. "They're coming! Hurry! We have to leave!"

Within seconds they hear the telltale crunch of steel against wood. Neighbours yell and scream. Babies and children are crying.

Someone barks orders through a megaphone: "Get out! Everyone out! Now!"

Holding hands with her mother, sister, and younger brother, Cinka stumbles outside into the blinding glare of police flashlights.

In the chilly, damp, early morning blackness they shiver and hold one another tightly. They're not fully awake and unsure about where to go or what to do. Her brother and sister are sobbing. Frightened shadows run in all directions. The panic of the ambushed and the hunted. Sheer terror reigns.

Everywhere they look, police are yanking people out of their homes swearing at them, pushing them, jabbing them with clubs.

Bulldozers attack shacks with people still inside screaming, refusing to leave. It's a merciless iron fist of destruction and the camp inhabitants are helpless in its path.

"This way! Hurry! Let's go!"

Cinka leads her family into the blackness, slipping and sliding on the muddy ground as they pick their way through the wreckage, crouching, turning, trying desperately to avoid being snatched by the police.

Without warning, someone kicks her hard from behind. She stumbles and lands on her hands and knees in the mud. A sharp pain crosses her stomach. Before she can get up, a lone policeman clubs her on the shoulder. She screams in pain. He hisses,

"*Zingari del cazzo!* Fucking Gypsies! Filthy dogs! Get out!"

Cinka's mother shields her and pleads with the officer not to hurt them.

"Please! My daughter is pregnant!"

But he hits her first, then Cinka again. Now mother and daughter are both on the ground.

"*Zingari di merda!* Gypsies of shit! Go back to your own country!"

The young brother and sister swarm and beat the officer with their fists, but he clubs first one, then the other.

"You stink! You live like rats! I should kill all of you right now, you vermin!"

Cinka leaps up to grab the officer but he straight-arms her in the face. Her rage is boiling over. She ignores her throbbing shoulder, her bleeding nose. She is breathing hard, fighting back an urge to rip his face to pieces. Her family are all on the ground sobbing uncontrollably.

We must escape before it's too late, she tells herself. She glowers at the officer thinking, one day, *testa di cazzo*, one day.

But the police officer has other plans.

Cinka's mother is on her knees, holding onto his leg begging him to stop. He spits on her and growls, *"Sei un pezzo di merda!* You are a piece of shit! You won't cooperate? Try this!"* He raises his club to strike her again.

In a blind fury, Cinka reaches for a long piece of wood on the ground, spins around, and with a loud grunt, smashes it against the side of the officer's head.

There is an ugly thud. Dazed, he reels, clutching his head.

She pulls back and whacks him again even harder. This time he collapses to his knees and falls over.

She drops the piece of wood and grabs her mother, brother, and sister.

"Run! This way! Quickly!"

In the confusion and the dark they scramble madly on hands and knees up a steep rocky hill. Cinka tastes blood in her mouth. Her nose is bleeding, but she's oblivious to the pain searing through every pore of her body.

They fight their way through the tangled bushes and half walk, half run away from their home of the past two months.

At the top, they pause, doubled-over, to catch their breath. Cinka looks down at the long line of police vans with lights flashing, blocking the road to the refugee camp.

Here in this gully, out of sight of anyone, they once thought they could be safe. Just yesterday, thirty families lived here peacefully in thirty shacks bothering no one.

We planted flowers and gardens, she thinks, and tried to clean up this former dump. Now we flee with the clothes on our backs.

From here, she can see police checking people's papers and loading them into the vans. The new law! Certain deportation!

"Mama! We have to get away fast!" They hold hands and run.

The same routine, she thinks. Since they arrived in Rome a year ago, she had lost track of how many times they were forced to move from temporary camps like this one.

Find a neglected, hidden piece of land on the edge of a dump. Somewhere Italians wouldn't normally go. Scrounge the garbage for scrap material. Build a small shelter. Add a plastic or tin sheet for a roof. Call this "home." They never had electricity, heating, plumbing, or even toilets. They used plastic bags.

Exhausted, bruised, aching, and hungry, she is unsure where they should now go. Anywhere but back. They have to get away. The police will be looking for them.

Did she kill the officer? She doesn't think so. But the police will be angry—very angry.

Her brother and sister are injured and cry softly. Her mother clutches her own shoulder and tries to console the children. Her brother has been running a fever for three days now. Her sister lost a shoe and is limping. Cinka puts her arm around her.

"Where do we go now?" her sister sobs.

"I don't know," Cinka says. "Don't worry. Just keep walking. Keep walking."

Secretly, she hopes for shelter somewhere in the darkness ahead. She remembers telling Antonio about a similar experience a few months previously; and again, a few months before that. He helped them through the last one. Add Napoli to the list, and now tonight.

"My people," she told him, "call these walks 'death marches.' Our elders say the Germans used gas chambers and ovens. Today Italians use the cold, starvation, and disease. I call it 'ethnic cleansing.'"

CINKA'S FAMILY ON THE HIGHWAY

There is no moon to guide us, but my mother, brother, sister, and I finally reach a busy highway far from the camp. My brother helps my mother. My sister leans on me. I ignore the sharp pains in my stomach and pray that the baby is OK.

We walk on the gravel shoulder and hope no one will notice us: a group of exhausted, wet, cold, and hungry fugitives running from the police, looking for yet another new place to hide our faces and live in peace.

We were only trying to defend ourselves, but who will believe us? Who will support us?

Romans whiz by in their cars on their way to work, oblivious to us and the devastation we left behind. A strong wind blows from the east. The rain stops and a hint of sunrise teases the horizon.

It was my father's dream to bring our family to Italy and start a new life.

"They will treat us better. You'll see. They are a civilized people."

Dear father, your dream became our nightmare. Tens of thousands of us Roma from Romania now live here with no help from anyone because we're Gypsies. It's the curse, the blessing, and the colour of my skin that can never change, that no one will ever ignore or take away from me.

Are we destined to live generation after generation a despised people, always the outcasts? A people no one wants near? A people no one will accept because they refuse to see beyond our skin, to try to understand us and see us as equals? This I will never understand.

Yes, certainly Italy is a lovely country; Rome a beautiful city—if you're a tourist snapping pictures of fountains and statues, or if you're not a poor Italian and you have rights.

But this government, the journalists and the police, deny my people the right to be human, to have housing, food, work, or medical care.

The mayor—a neo-Fascist—promises to purge us from the city. The prime minister calls us "the army of evil." Why? We mean no harm. We are a peaceful people. They are the ones promoting hatred and violence. Not us.

So we walk. Yet again. Not because we are stereotypical "romantic Gypsies" or "nomads" who like to wander because we cannot stand still. Not at all. We walk because like every other Romani refugee in this country and across Europe we are despised as "an inferior race" and we have been chased out.

We are forced to walk. We walk to seek a safe place to rest. We walk like our grandfathers and grandmothers walked onto trains to concentration camps where half a million were murdered. We walk like our ancestors before who were whipped into the chains of slavery. Or the ones before that who were forced to stumble into arenas to be eaten by lions.

We walk because we are not allowed to live like others do, like these Romans whizzing by with no clue.

Once, a gang of Fascists torched a refugee hut in our camp, killing four children. We had proof of who did it and their names. But the police blamed the parents, charged them with negligence, and jailed them.

Ahead, I see a gas station. It's boarded up and closed for repairs. I tell my mother,

"We can stop here to rest. It should be safe. I see a fast food restaurant over there. I'll find something to eat."

I tell my brother and sister,

"Stay with her. Don't go anywhere else. Stay out of sight and wait for me. I'll be right back."

I hunt in the garbage bins behind the restaurant for anything to eat. I don't notice the four men sitting inside a parked van nearby, watching me.

PART X

CIAO BELLA

CINKA SPEAKS

In her own way, Cinka was speaking to no one and to everyone.

She spoke to her people huddled in a circle under the overpass, sitting on rocks with no food in their bellies.

She spoke to the tourists who asked a Romani mother begging with her child if they could take her picture.

She spoke to the senators lounging in their chamber, bored, whiskies and cigars in hand.

She spoke to the Italian woman and children who brought blankets and food to the family of four sleeping in a cave in the cliff behind the luxurious Rome hotel.

She spoke to the policeman who said he disagreed with his colleagues about almost everything; to the pleasant Danish family eating their lunch on the beach; to a Ukrainian cleaning woman who kept mopping; to the punk rocker trying to explain his concept of beauty to his drunken friends; to the student who asked her teacher why she talked disparagingly about the Roma; to her brother, sister, mother, father, and all the ancestors who she could only dream about before. She spoke to the thin trees, naked and cold, bowing side to side in unison with the wind.

Who else would listen?

As she spoke, the moon nudged the darkness, and the darkness asked a pebble on the edge of the highway, "She is with us?"

The pebble replied, "She is."

CORNO GRANDE, THE HIGHEST PEAK

In Abruzzo, the centre of Italy, you'll find the highest peak in the Apennine Mountains: the rocky and barren *Corno Grande*—the Large Horn—part of the *Gran Sasso d'Italia*—the Great Stone of Italy massif.

A forbidding 2,912-metre-high rock, its jagged snow-covered peak pierces the sky and snags wayward clouds. Below its northern face, an amphitheatre-like valley holds Europe's southernmost but disappearing glacier. Southwest is the breathtaking but earthquake-ravaged city of L'Aquila, built in the thirteenth century. An hour further west is Rome.

On one of the lower sunny grassy slopes, under a brilliant, cloudless blue sky, a flock of sheep graze, guarded by a tired old shepherd and his seven white *Abruzzese* sheepdogs. The shepherd is dozing on a flat rock while his guard-dogs work the meadow.

Out of nowhere, a man's clear robust voice breaks the mountain silence and echoes down the valley, across a rushing river and back up the side of the mountain:

"Antonio Discordia . . . born in a village in Abruzzo . . . a blue-eyed musician and philosophy student now living in Rome . . . he loves her . . ."

The sheepdogs bark. The shepherd cracks open his eyes. He scans the mountain and valley left and right, but sees no one except for a pair of golden eagles circling above. He closes his eyes again. A second equally strong and clear voice, but female, from the opposite side of the valley, now responds to the first:

"Cinka Dinicu . . . born in Romania . . . a violinist . . . immigrated to Italy in search of a better life . . . she loves him . . ."

Again, the voice bounces across meadow, bushes, and rocks, and trails off into the distance. The dogs bark a warning. With the help of his walking stick, the shepherd now sits up, shields his eyes with one large, bronzed hand and squints into the mountain vastness. He sees no one.

"It's only the wind playing tricks on me. One moment a man, one moment a woman. What's next?"

To be safe, he crosses himself, whistles for his dogs, then goes back to sleep.

CAZZAROLA! THANK-YOUS

I would like to thank the following friends, colleagues, and others who helped make this book possible with editing suggestions, fact-checking, research material, translations, interviews, general inspiration, and more:

Agnese Riso, Alan Zisman, Ambra Gallina, Andrew Winchur, Antonio Riso, A/Rivista, Augusto, the entire Benvenuti family (including Enrico Monier, Francesco, and Simone), Bruno Massé, Chiarastella Campanelli, Chiarastella the singer, Chiarastella from Napoli, David Lester, Davide Turcato, Deanna Radford, Don Stewart, Editrice il Sirente and their wonderful extended family, EveryOne Group with Roberto Malini and Dario Picciau, Fabio and Rita, Federica Rigliani, Francesco Campanelli, Giampiero Cordisco, Gino Lucetti, Gregory Nipper, Jacqueline Bui, Judy Perry, Julia Lovell, Katie Kellogg, Leidia, Lorenzo Consoli, Maria Antonietta Fontana, Massimo Colella, Megan Ellis, Michele Teonesto, Modena anarchists, Peter Gelderloos, PM Press, Podere Carpinaro, Ramsey Kanaan, Ron Sakolsky, Ronald Lee, Sandy Plage, Sebastian Yeung, Stephanie Pasvankias, Sylvana Gorgevic, Terry Bisson, Tommeso Mele, Vivian Nawrocki, and countless, nameless others, including dozens of Roma refugees.

FOR FURTHER RESEARCH:
European Roma Rights Centre is an international public interest law organisation that monitors the human rights situ-

ation of Roma and provides legal defence in cases of human rights abuse. For more information about the European Roma Rights Centre, visit the ERRC on the web at: http://www.errc. org.

Roma Community Centre (RCC) works to strengthen and unify Roma peoples across Canada in striving for self-determination, social justice, and human rights. We celebrate Roma cultural diversity, history, and achievements. The RCC also works with the general public in combating anti-Roma racism and negative "Gypsy" stereotypes and strengthening community partnerships in Canada and abroad.

http://www.romatoronto.org/

EveryOne Group is an organization of people operating on an international level outside any political wing or faction in defence of human and civil rights. Its main priority is to save human lives and to prevent violations of the fundamental rights of the individual or peoples.

EveryOne Group for International Cooperation on Human Rights Culture

www.everyonegroup.com

BIOGRAPHY

Norman Nawrocki is the author of several books of poetry and short stories. He's also an internationally acclaimed cabaret artist, sex educator, actor, and musician, and has released over fifty albums. He teaches at Concordia University about how to use the arts for community organizing and radical social change, gives workshops about "creative resistance," and tours the world, performing theatre, music, and cabaret. *Cazzarola!* is his first novel. He has written and performed a theatre piece based on the book and released an album-length soundtrack—both with the same title—to accompany it.

ABOUT PM PRESS

PM Press was founded at the end of 2007 by a small collection of folks with decades of publishing, media, and organizing experience. PM Press co-conspirators have published and distributed hundreds of books, pamphlets, CDs, and DVDs. Members of PM have founded enduring book fairs, spearheaded victorious tenant organizing campaigns, and worked closely with bookstores, academic conferences, and even rock bands to deliver political and challenging ideas to all walks of life. We're old enough to know what we're doing and young enough to know what's at stake.

We seek to create radical and stimulating fiction and non-fiction books, pamphlets, T-shirts, visual and audio materials to entertain, educate and inspire you. We aim to distribute these through every available channel with every available technology — whether that means you are seeing anarchist classics at our bookfair stalls; reading our latest vegan cookbook at the café; downloading geeky fiction e-books; or digging new music and timely videos from our website.

PM Press is always on the lookout for talented and skilled volunteers, artists, activists and writers to work with. If you have a great idea for a project or can contribute in some way, please get in touch.

PM Press
PO Box 23912
Oakland, CA 94623
www.pmpress.org

FRIENDS OF PM PRESS

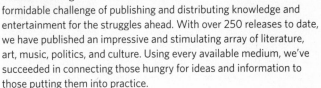

These are indisputably momentous times—the financial system is melting down globally and the Empire is stumbling. Now more than ever there is a vital need for radical ideas.

In the six years since its founding—and on a mere shoestring—PM Press has risen to the formidable challenge of publishing and distributing knowledge and entertainment for the struggles ahead. With over 250 releases to date, we have published an impressive and stimulating array of literature, art, music, politics, and culture. Using every available medium, we've succeeded in connecting those hungry for ideas and information to those putting them into practice.

Friends of PM allows you to directly help impact, amplify, and revitalize the discourse and actions of radical writers, filmmakers, and artists. It provides us with a stable foundation from which we can build upon our early successes and provides a much-needed subsidy for the materials that can't necessarily pay their own way. You can help make that happen—and receive every new title automatically delivered to your door once a month—by joining as a Friend of PM Press. And, we'll throw in a free T-shirt when you sign up.

Here are your options:

- **$30 a month** Get all books and pamphlets plus 50% discount on all webstore purchases

- **$40 a month** Get all PM Press releases (including CDs and DVDs) plus 50% discount on all webstore purchases

- **$100 a month** Superstar—Everything plus PM merchandise, free downloads, and 50% discount on all webstore purchases

For those who can't afford $30 or more a month, we're introducing **Sustainer Rates** at $15, $10 and $5. Sustainers get a free PM Press T-shirt and a 50% discount on all purchases from our website.

Your Visa or Mastercard will be billed once a month, until you tell us to stop. Or until our efforts succeed in bringing the revolution around. Or the financial meltdown of Capital makes plastic redundant. Whichever comes first.

Fire on the Mountain

Terry Bisson
with an introduction
by Mumia Abu-Jamal

ISBN: 978-1-60486-087-0
$15.95   208 pages

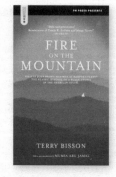

It's 1959 in socialist Virginia. The Deep South is an independent Black nation called Nova Africa. The second Mars expedition is about to touch down on the red planet. And a pregnant scientist is climbing the Blue Ridge in search of her great-great grandfather, a teenage slave who fought with John Brown and Harriet Tubman's guerrilla army.

Long unavailable in the US, published in France as *Nova Africa*, *Fire on the Mountain* is the story of what might have happened if John Brown's raid on Harper's Ferry had succeeded—and the Civil War had been started not by the slave owners but the abolitionists.

"History revisioned, turned inside out... Bisson's wild and wonderful imagination has taken some strange turns to arrive at such a destination."
— Madison Smartt Bell, Anisfield-Wolf Award winner and author of *Devil's Dream*

"You don't forget Bisson's characters, even well after you've finished his books. His Fire on the Mountain *does for the Civil War what Philip K. Dick's* The Man in the High Castle *did for World War Two."*
— George Alec Effinger, winner of the Hugo and Nebula awards for *Shrödinger's Kitten*, and author of the Marîd Audran trilogy.

"A talent for evoking the joyful, vertiginous experiences of a world at fundamental turning points."
— Publishers Weekly

"Few works have moved me as deeply, as thoroughly, as Terry Bisson's Fire on the Mountain... *With this single poignant story, Bisson molds a world as sweet as banana cream pies, and as briny as hot tears."*
— Mumia Abu-Jamal, prisoner and author of *Live From Death Row*, from the Introduction.

Calling All Heroes: A Manual for Taking Power

Paco Ignacio Taibo II

ISBN: 978-1-60486-205-8
$12.00   128 pages

The euphoric idealism of grassroots reform and the tragic reality of revolutionary failure are at the center of this speculative novel that opens with a real historical event. On October 2, 1968, 10 days before the Summer Olympics in Mexico, the Mexican government responds to a student demonstration in Tlatelolco by firing into the crowd, killing more than 200 students and civilians and wounding hundreds more. The Tlatelolco massacre was erased from the official record as easily as authorities washing the blood from the streets, and no one was ever held accountable.

It is two years later and Nestor, a journalist and participant in the fateful events, lies recovering in the hospital from a knife wound. His fevered imagination leads him in the collection of facts and memories of the movement and its assassination in the company of figures from his childhood. Nestor calls on the heroes of his youth—Sherlock Holmes, Doc Holliday, Wyatt Earp, and D'Artagnan among them—to join him in launching a new reform movement conceived by his intensely active imagination.

"Taibo's writing is witty, provocative, finely nuanced and well worth the challenge."
— Publishers Weekly

"I am his number one fan. . . I can always lose myself in one of his novels because of their intelligence and humor. My secret wish is to become one of the characters in his fiction, all of them drawn from the wit and wisdom of popular imagination. Yet make no mistake, Paco Taibo—sociologist and historian—is recovering the political history of Mexico to offer a vital, compelling vision of our reality."
— Laura Esquivel, author of *Like Water for Chocolate*

"The real enchantment of Mr. Taibo's storytelling lies in the wild and melancholy tangle of life he sees everywhere."
— New York Times Book Review

Vida

Marge Piercy
ISBN: 978-1-60486-487-8
$20.00   416 pages

Originally published in 1979, *Vida* is Marge
Piercy's classic bookend to the Sixties.
Vida is full of the pleasures and pains, the
experiments, disasters, and victories of an
extraordinary band of people. At the center
of the novel stands Vida Asch. She has
lived underground for almost a decade. Back in the '60s she was a
political star of the exuberant antiwar movement—a red-haired beauty
photographed for the pages of *Life* magazine—charismatic, passionate,
and totally sure she would prevail. Now, a decade later, Vida is on the
run, her star-quality replaced by stubborn courage. She comes briefly to
rest in a safe house on Cape Cod. To her surprise and annoyance, she
finds another person in the house, a fugitive, Joel, ten years younger
than she, a kid who dropped into the underground out of the army. As
they spend the next days together, Vida finds herself warming toward a
man for the first time in years, knowing all too well the dangers.

As counterpoint to the underground '70s, Marge Piercy tells the
extraordinary tale of the optimistic '60s, the thousands of people
who were members of SAW (Students Against the War) and of the
handful who formed a fierce group called the Little Red Wagon. Piercy's
characters make vivid and comprehensible the desperation, the
courage, and the blind rage of a time when "action" could appear to
some to be a more rational choice than the vote.

A new introduction by Marge Piercy situates the book, and the author,
in the times from which they emerged.

*"Real people inhabit its pages and real suspense carries the story along…
'Vida' of course means life and she personifies it."*
— Chicago Tribune

*"A fully controlled, tightly structured dramatic narrative of such artful
intensity that it leads the reader on at almost every page."*
— New York Times Book Review

*"Marge Piercy tells us exactly how it was in the lofts of the Left as the 1960s
turned into the '70s. This is the way everybody sounded. This is the way
everybody behaved.* Vida *bears witness."*
— New York Times

"Very exciting. Marge Piercy's characters are complex and very human."
— Margaret Atwood

The Wild Girls

Ursula K. Le Guin

ISBN: 978-1-60486-403-8
$12.00   112 pages

Ursula K. Le Guin is the one modern science fiction author who truly needs no introduction. In the forty years since *The Left Hand of Darkness*, her works have changed not only the face but the tone and the agenda of SF, introducing themes of gender, race, socialism, and anarchism, all the while thrilling readers with trips to strange (and strangely familiar) new worlds. She is our exemplar of what fantastic literature can and should be about.

Her Nebula winner *The Wild Girls*, newly revised and presented here in book form for the first time, tells of two captive "dirt children" in a society of sword and silk, whose determination to enter "that possible even when unattainable space in which there is room for justice" leads to a violent and loving end.

Plus: Le Guin's scandalous and scorching *Harper's* essay, "Staying Awake While We Read," (also collected here for the first time) which demolishes the pretensions of corporate publishing and the basic assumptions of capitalism as well. And of course our Outspoken Interview which promises to reveal the hidden dimensions of America's best-known SF author. And delivers.

"Idiosyncratic and convincing, Le Guin's characters have a long afterlife."
— *Publishers Weekly*

"Her worlds are haunting psychological visions molded with firm artistry."
— *The Library Journal*

"If you want excess and risk and intelligence, try Le Guin."
— *The San Francisco Chronicle*

"Her characters are complex and haunting, and her writing is remarkable for its sinewy grace."
— *Time*

"She wields her pen with a moral and psychological sophistication rarely seen. What she really does is write fables: splendidly intricate and hugely imaginative tales about such mundane concerns as life, death, love, and sex."
— *Newsweek*

Send My Love and a Molotov Cocktail: Stories of Crime, Love and Rebellion

Edited by Gary Phillips
and Andrea Gibbons

ISBN: 978-1-60486-096-2
$19.95   368 pages

An incendiary mixture of genres and voices, this collection of short stories compiles a unique set of work that revolves around riots, revolts, and revolution. From the turbulent days of unionism in the streets of New York City during the Great Depression to a group of old women who meet at their local café to plan a radical act that will change the world forever, these original and once out-of-print stories capture the various ways people rise up to challenge the status quo and change up the relationships of power. Ideal for any fan of noir, science fiction, and revolution and mayhem, this collection includes works from Sara Paretsky, Paco Ignacio Taibo II, Cory Doctorow, Kim Stanley Robinson, and Summer Brenner.

Full list of contributors:

Summer Brenner	Cory Doctorow
Rick Dakan	Andrea Gibbons
Barry Graham	John A. Imani
Penny Mickelbury	Sara Paretsky
Gary Phillips	Kim Stanley Robinson
Luis Rodriguez	Paco Ignacio Taibo II
Benjamin Whitmer	Ken Wishnia
Michael Moorcock	Michael Skeet
Larry Fondation	Tim Wohlforth